"Everyone has the right to freedom of opinion and expression; this right includes freedom to hold opinions without interference and to seek, receive and impart information and ideas through any media and regardless of frontiers."

United Nations, Universal Declaration of Human Rights (Article 19)

"If Liberty means anything at all, it means the right to tell people what they do not want to hear."

George Orwell

"The moment you say that any idea system is sacred, whether it's a religious belief system or a secular ideology, the moment you declare a set of ideas to be immune from criticism, satire, derision, or contempt, freedom of thought becomes impossible."

Salman Rushdie

"You have enemies? Good. That means you've stood up for something, sometime in your life."

Winston Churchill

By the Same Author:

Crump (2010)
A Cat Called Dog (2013)
A Cat Called Dog (illustrated shorter version, 2015)
Rasmus – a Television Tale (2016)
A Cat Called Dog 2 – The One with the Kittens (illustrated, 2017)
Santa Goes on Strike (illustrated, 2018)

Author's Note

When I published my first campus novel in 2010, I promised myself I would never write a sequel. This is it. Having said that, I would emphasise that this book can be read as a stand-alone novel, for those readers unfamiliar with my first novel, *Crump* (2010).

About the Author

P J Vanston (who also writes as Jem Vanston) was born and brought up in Dartford, Kent, to a Welsh mother and a Flemish-Belgian father. He now lives in Swansea, South Wales.

As well as being an author, he is a published song writer, a sometime journalist and English teacher, an occasional film producer, was a part-time carer for ten years, and now runs his own education, training, editing and proof reading companies.

Through his mother's family, he is related to the father-and-son team who wrote the Welsh national anthem in 1856, and, more distantly, to Vice-Admiral Horatio Nelson, though he has no immediate plans to join the navy.

He does, however, very much enjoy watching boats bobbing around on the bay from his window when writing – that is, when he is not being distracted by his demanding diva rescue cats, Honey and Bumble.

The author created this campus novel a literal stone's throw from the house where Kingsley Amis wrote his 1954 campus novel *Lucky Jim* and a short walk from the family home where Dylan Thomas grew up and wrote his early poetry.

Author website: www.vanston.co.uk

'Happy to be Home this Christmas', words/music by Jem PJ Vanston, lyrics used with
kind permission of the publishers. Listen to the song here:
https://soundcloud.com/user-217675148/happy-to-be-home-this-christmas-by-jem-
vanston-2015.

Matador
9 Priory Business Park,
Wistow Road, Kibworth Beauchamp,
Leicestershire. LE8 0RX
Tel: 0116 279 2299
Email: books@troubador.co.uk
Web: www.troubador.co.uk/matador
Twitter: @matadorbooks

ISBN 978 183859 308 7

British Library Cataloguing in Publication Data.
A catalogue record for this book is available from the British Library.

Printed and bound by CPI Group (UK) Ltd, Croydon, CR0 4YY
Typeset in 11pt Sabon by Troubador Publishing Ltd, Leicester, UK

Matador is an imprint of Troubador Publishing Ltd

MIX
Paper from
responsible sources
FSC® C013604

To the late, great comedy writer David Nobbs, who was kind enough to read and critique my early novels and offer invaluable advice.
He was a mentor to both me and many other aspiring authors, and encouraged me to continue writing my satirical novels. Without that, this book would not have been written.

Somewhere in Europe

A 'CRUMP' CAMPUS NOVEL

P J Vanston

CHAPTER ONE

Starting Over

Kevin Crump was not happy.

He was not happy that he was driving through the relentless rain towards The Town – a small provincial city in South Wales which he would now be calling home.

He was not happy that he had been 'rationalised' from his Foreign Office training job in London as part of its 'diversity and inclusion' drive, despite over seven years of exemplary service, and sent on secondment to teach at the local university for goodness knew how long.

But mostly, he was not happy that he was now over forty, balding and increasingly paunchy, as he hurtled haplessly into encroaching middle age and the inevitable decrepitude that came with it.

And he knew he could do nothing whatsoever to stop any of these three things happening.

The last time he'd taught in higher education had been a decade before, at Thames Metropolitan University, an ex-polytechnic in thrall to the looniest forms of 'political correctness', where grade inflation and dumbing down were standard. Now he was being forced back onto that academic career path, against his wishes and better instincts, and all so his training job at the Foreign Office could be taken by someone more 'diverse' – in other words, someone who was not a white man like him.

'Positive action' was what they called this 'rationalisation' that had lost him his job in the city he called home. Needless to say, it didn't feel very positive to Kevin Crump.

It wasn't all bad, though. For one thing, he'd get to see his old mum again, and at regular intervals too, more than the one Saturday afternoon every three months visits from London he had been doing. She was in a care home in The Town following a small stroke two years previously.

Her end-of-terrace home had been empty since then, waiting for the day her savings ran out and the council made a land grab for it to pay the care home fees – his mother's reward for working hard as a nurse for almost forty years and obeying the rules society had laid down. That was where Crump would now live – which would give him a chance to sort through everything, clear stuff out, declutter.

Then there was the location. The Town was situated near one of the most beautiful coastlines in Britain, which Crump knew well having holidayed there from the age of eight, on account of his Welsh mum's family living in the area. So he would take full advantage of the coastal walks and beach culture to try to get a bit fitter. That was the plan, anyway. Maybe it would do him good to get out of London too, even though he did consider it home – albeit a dirty, annoying, extortionately expensive, crime-ridden one in which he'd never be able to afford to buy a house, or even rent more than a basic flat in a tolerable area.

And, if he was honest with himself, he knew he'd been getting a bit stale in the same middle-management position at the Foreign Office training department. But it was a job with a secure contract, rather than any 'zero hours' exploitation – which was called 'associate lecturer' in the education and training sector. And anyway, it seemed that most people sleep-walked through their jobs and their lives with a sense of hollow misery about them.

It was very telling that people's jobs or careers were rarely mentioned on their gravestones in cemeteries. Work was important, but only to a certain degree. It was always best to keep things in proportion.

It happened to most of us – the 'settling' for a steady job and regular income, the time-serving plodding along, staying in the same unsatisfying career 'because it was there' – like Everest, but much *much* flatter. Just like people settle for mediocre marriage partners they can just about bear to breed with, so they won't grow old alone. People always *settle*, in the end, much like the ash from their incinerated hopes and dreams. It was just what most people did and had always done, no doubt.

"How on earth did I get so old?" mumbled Crump to himself as the motorway traffic braked to a halt. It was a fitting metaphor for his life.

The last thing he knew he was young – a fresh-faced student at university with his life before him. Then he got his first proper professional job in further education before moving into university teaching, with results so disastrous he spent the next three years teaching English abroad to recover. After his return to the UK and job applications galore, he finally found his feet in the Foreign Office training role he thought he'd quite possibly occupy for the rest of his life.

Until recently, he'd had a job he could tolerate, a girlfriend and a flat – and now all three were gone. The girlfriend went as soon as he told her about his job situation, and with her went the pleasant-enough flat, on which they shared the rent: not even a moderately well-paid civil servant like Crump could afford to buy or rent a nice place alone in London – not these days.

And so that evening, he found himself driving his old rusting car through the wet Welsh rain to his mother's hometown, in a situation which felt no further forward than when he was twenty years of age. The big difference was that now most of his life was behind him and he knew it. It was back to the future past with next to nothing to show for all the effort, the work, the struggle of the previous two decades. No wonder he felt sick – though that might have been the effects of a distinctly unhappy burger meal at the Severn Bridge motorway services earlier.

At that precise moment, the tragic tone of John Lennon singing *(Just Like) Starting Over* came on the radio. No doubt the ex-Beatle thought he was to do just that when he recorded the song in 1980. How was he to know that several dum-dum bullets fired from a deranged fan's handgun would explode his heart beyond repair later that year and leave him dead at the age of forty – younger than Crump was now?

'We never know when the axe will fall or how,' was all Crump could think. 'So always best to live each day as your last, because it may well turn out to be.'

That day certainly felt like his last anyway, because he didn't want to be there. He wanted to be back in his London job, in his London flat with his London girlfriend, all London-y, and vibrant and diverse, and feeling alive.

But it could have been worse, he knew. At least he had a job. *Worse things happen at sea*, as his mum used to say, and she was right. *Life is real, life is earnest* was her stoical Welsh Chapel mantra.

Where there's life, there's hope. What can't be cured, must be endured. A stitch in time saves nine. Many a mickle makes a muckle. Blah blah blah.

That twisted knot of anxiety, that old companion from childhood, was writhing like an eel inside him, gnawing at his innards, eating him from the inside out. It was his curse to be a worrier, he knew, to let things affect him like that and cause him so much stress. But his life had changed and he had no choice in the matter, so he took

4

three deep breaths, as his old mum had taught him when he was a boy, and carried on regardless – because what else was there?

And all the time, the lighthouse at the edge of the bay, blinking and winking and wishing him back to the ugly, lovely town by the sea.

Crump peered through the watery swish of the windscreen wipers, gawping blankly at the back of a foreign lorry stuck in the static traffic in front of him. He thought back to the 'rationalisation' meeting that had led him here.

"So, it's an exciting opportunity, Kevin."

Opportunities were always 'exciting' in management-speak, even when they meant you were, in effect, getting sacked.

"But… teaching…" said Crump, "at a university… again—"

"A *world-class* university."

"Not in London though, sir."

"Call me Clive," said Crump's ultimate big boss, with a charm-dripping smile.

"Clive," said Crump, blankly.

"Your mother lives in South Wales, I think?"

"Yes," said Crump, "I know, but—"

"Kevin," sighed his boss, "we at the Foreign and Commonwealth Office take diversity and inclusion very seriously."

Crump nodded seriously, right on cue.

"It is thus imperative that the Civil Service reflects and celebrates the diverse, multicultural face of modern Britain, as part of our diversity learning journey, going forward. You know how it is. That's why we're rolling out this key initiative, our exciting rationalisation programme. It's a real no-brainer game-changer we're running up the flagpole now."

"So, I'm being… *'rationalised'*?"

Crump groaned inwardly. He knew he was getting culled for sexist and racist reasons because he, as a white man, was part of the only racial and gendered group it was acceptable – no, recommended – to mock, demean, hate and discriminate against in modern Britain, and all in the name of equality too. He was now branded undesirably 'male, pale and stale' as surely as if some member of the pc gestapo had tattooed it on his arm. He was being laid off, given the push, fired, sacked, 'let go'. No matter what pretty new term they used to describe it.

And it was all done absolutely legally too, in the name of promoting equality and diversity. Crump always thought it worth remembering that Hitler never actually did anything illegal – but then, that was the law: slippery, expensive and easily manipulated by those who knew how.

"You'd still be employed by us here, Kevin, paid by us, full Civil Service pension etcetera, but on secondment to a world class educational institution – the most improved university in South Wales, actually."

'Oh yippy-do,' thought Crump, understandably taking umbrage.

He knew he could count the universities located in South Wales on the fingers of one hand – maybe one and a half.

"Sometimes we have to 'punch a puppy' as part of our mission. Do you see?"

No, he didn't see. What did a puppy have to do with anything? Was he the puppy? Was he being punched? Why couldn't these senior people speak proper *English*, for goodness' sake? Management training courses had a lot to answer for.

"Of course," smarmed Clive, "if you were to reject this offer, then you would be seen to be *not* abiding by our diversity and inclusion policy, which would be a serious breach of your contract of employment, which we would have to take very seriously indeed, going forward."

"Of course," said Crump, seriouser and seriouser.

"It is our duty, Kevin, as privileged white men, to accept that we have had it far too good for far too long—"

"Have we?"

"Well, yes, though we may not realise the fact of our white male privilege," said white, male, privileged Sir Clive Silverback (educated at Winchester and Oxbridge, grandson of a regional governor for the Raj in India, silver-spooned son of a diplomat and a socialite mother allegedly related to royalty) to white, male, non-privileged Kevin Crump (son of a nurse mum and a railway union official dad, and grandson of a Welsh miner who grew up in poverty unimagined by the likes of Sir Clive Silverback).

"Are *you* being *rationalised*, too, sir?" asked Crump, provoked into boldness.

The little laugh that followed soon swallowed itself and died inside the efficient folds of Sir Clive's wilting smile.

"Just accept the offer, Kevin – it's for the best, really," said Sir Clive, quietly yet firmly, ignoring the question from his inferior, a man he knew would never rise higher than that always-disposably mediocre layer of middle management.

Kevin Crump nodded and sighed his stoicism into the elite elegance of his superior's office.

"Who knows," lied Sir Clive, his slick smile restored, "one day... in a year... or two... after an exciting learning journey at a world-class university, you could be right back here, maybe with a promotion, maybe one day even doing my job."

'Yeah, right,' thought Crump.

"Thank you, sir," he said.

"So it's all good, going forward. Just sign here, and here," said Sir Clive Silverback, placing a form on his elegant desk, and handing his underling an equally elegant and expensive fountain pen, which no doubt cost as much as Crump earned in a month.

And so, with a couple of scrawled signatures, Crump's future was sealed.

'It's off to Wales we go,' he whistled in his mind's ear as he left fluent business bullshitter Sir Clive's puppy-punching learning-journey game-changing no-brainer culling room. 'Hi bloody ho.'

*

"I'm Dylan," said Dylan. "Dylan Powell – I'm your buddy."

"Crump. Kevin…" said Kevin Crump. "But everyone always calls me Crump."

"Yeah, whatever. It's cool."

Like many institutions, Cambrian University had a buddy system for new members of staff, and appointed someone to show them the ropes – although Crump was a bit perturbed by Dylan's youth. He was a fresh-faced mixed-race kid, surely no older than twenty-one or, two, though old enough to be a postgrad student. Crump knew Dylan owed this paid gig to his mum who worked in the university Diversity Department.

But he supposed Dylan knew the place as well as anyone else, so made a mental note not to be ageist about it. After all, wasn't Crump himself always annoyed when people made assumptions because of his age or gender or ethnicity or anything else? Merit is all – and he would give Dylan the benefit of the doubt.

Later that day, there was to be a meeting in the Richard Burton Theatre for all new lecturers and established ones too, if they wanted to be there – one which all members of the university's senior management would attend.

But there was plenty of time before that for Dylan to show Crump around the campus of Cambrian University.

"They call it *The Learning Tower of Pizza,*" sniggered Dylan. "Coz like it's The Learning Tower... and the refectory on the ground floor does a wicked slice of pepperoni."

Crump forced a smile but not quite a laugh as he gazed up at the fourteen floors of The Learning Tower. It was the sort of predictably glib name educational institutions used a lot these days – like calling a library a 'learning zone' or a medical centre a 'happiness hub'.

In the forecourt, on either side of The Learning Tower, a pair of blue starry EU flags flew, and a notice attached to the building proudly stated that EU funding had enabled the building's creation. These flags and notices were all over the campus and The Town too – though Crump always thought it worth remembering that the EU was only giving back to us some of the money the UK paid to it. Whose money was it anyway? Not free money, that's for sure: money never is.

The EU notices weren't the only ones on campus. Crump had clocked immediately the large number of A4-size posters about lost pets that had been stuck to many walls, fences and noticeboards. Crump leant forward to read a trio of posters sellotaped to a glass door nearby.

There were pictures of three cats – whose names apparently were NELSON, CHARLEMAGNE and NAPOLEON.

"I know that cat," said Crump to Dylan, pointing to a feline face.

Indeed, a handsome ginger and white cat bearing a striking resemblance to the pictured Nelson had miaowed and yowled at him in the car park earlier. Crump made a note of the number given – of a Mrs Trichobezoar. He'd give her a call later.

Dylan then walked Crump to the School of Arts and Culture, home to the Dylan Thomas Department of English Studies where he would be based – though he'd also be working with the Department of Politics and Governance in his teaching of international students keen to learn about the British political establishment from an insider who'd actually worked within it, at the Foreign and Commonwealth Office.

Suddenly, the sound of wailing and crying – sobbing, even – filled the air. Crump looked quizzically at his buddy.

"Oh, don't worry, that's just the Creative Writing Department – they're always like that," said Dylan, leading Crump away.

They walked past the Rowan Williams Department of Theology and Philosophy, the Donald Davies IT Department, the Bonnie Tyler Beauty Therapy Studies Department, the Ann Dillwyn Gender Studies Department, the Frances Ridley Havergal Music Department, the Hywel Dda Law Department and the Owain Glyndŵr Department of Celtic, Welsh and Diaspora Studies.

By this time, Crump was getting tired and not a little bored of staring at all the concrete and brick and EU flags and notices everywhere.

The university was in a lovely location though – a stone's throw from the wide sandy bay which defined The Town. Crump knew he'd find himself down there sitting on the sand and reading, or marking essays, come the better weather of spring. At least it wasn't raining today, though the dark clouds above threatened it.

Crump looked out to sea from the hill where Cambrian University perched like a castle of learning. Three derelict and swayingly drunk old men dressed in overcoats were arguing on the grass verge in front of the university entrance down towards the beach. Crump thought it sad to see so many homeless and hopeless people on our streets, or even our grass verges next to gloriously sandy beaches. What had gone so wrong in these people's lives that they had fallen so low?

"Used to work here, kindathing," said Dylan, nodding in their direction.

"No, really?" mouthed Crump. "In what capacity exactly?"

"Well, the oldest guy is Mr Scumble, former head of university maintenance, and the younger one's his assistant, Dean Guttery. They were… let go… couple of years back."

"And the other bloke?"

As Crump said the words, the third man, ginger-bearded and wild-eyed like a late Van Gogh self-portrait, seemed to turn and look straight at him, as if he'd heard them, though that was impossible – they were too far away and speaking quietly.

"Jim Slingsby," said Dylan with a sad sigh. "Tragic case. Random."

"Why?"

"Used to be a law lecturer here, like, until… someone… accused him of rape, or sexual assault, anyway."

"Really? So what happened?"

"Pleaded his innocence and found not guilty at trial, so comes back to teach in the law department, but…"

"But?"

"No smoke without fire, kindathing… people never treated him the same after that, he was always under suspicion, all the dirty looks and stuff…"

"And?"

"He cracked, innit? Lost the plot. Turned to drink. The end. Most def."

Crump sighed sadly.

"Who accused him?" he asked, at last.

Silence. Dylan gazed into the distance.

"We lose two or three every year, walking into the sea – top themselves kindathing…"

"That's… just… so tragic. All that potential and talent gone to waste. They've got so much to live for, their futures all ahead of them. Why do students do it, eh?"

"Nah, not students – lecturers."

There was nothing Crump could say to that, so he didn't.

"A few students top themselves every year too, of course – usually overdose on pills or hang *theirselves*. Lecturers prefer to walk into the sea. Dunno why. Maybe more poetic, eh?"

"Maybe…"

"Same difference though, in the end, right?"

Crump had experienced stark and overwhelming sadness before – that numb eternity of nothingness, that stale stasis of existence. But he would never, as far as he could tell, get to a point where he'd walk into the sea to end it all, no matter how poetic.

He looked at the three tramps who were now arguing over something that looked like a can of lager. Cambrian University didn't mention any of this in its glossy prospectus – but why should it? Crump knew from his time at Thames Met University the lengths institutions would go to in order to bury bad news.

"Wanna see something *different*?" asked Dylan with a grin.

"Why not?" Crump shrugged.

Dylan led Crump past the Catherine Zeta-Jones Counselling Hub and the Shirley Bassey Diversity and Inclusion Re-education Centre, to outside the university grounds and past the local hospital where, Crump noticed, a large sign proudly gave directions to the Tom Jones Department of Genito-Urinary Medicine.

Soon they were in a pretty park where, Dylan explained, the university ran a small zoo for the benefit of academics, students and local people. This sounded great – it was just the sort of inclusive community-involving activity universities should be involved in, if only to off-set the many issues with noise and behaviour that a doubling of student numbers in the last two decades had caused long-term residents of The Town.

There were ducks and swans on the pond, and various breeds of chickens in cages in the zoo: some really beautiful birds, and some funny-looking with fluffy feet!

They walked past a couple of goats and sheep in a compound and on to an enclosure at the far side of the zoo.

"And this is Sandra the pig," announced Dylan.

As if on cue, Sandra oinked and snuffled, looking up at Crump from her enclosure.

"Wow!" said Crump, admiring the massive size of the pretty pig.

It was enormous – a true pig of pigs.

The animal was an attractive chestnut brown colour and had an open face which seemed friendly and welcoming.

"We give the kids rides on her back in summer," said Dylan, patting Sandra on her big round head, before offering her a couple of peanuts he'd taken out of his pocket on the open palm of his hand.

The enormous brown sow looked so sweet, so friendly, so – well, almost – human, that Crump had no fear in reaching forward to pat her head too.

But before he knew what was happening, the big pig ducked then sprang up and bit his hand.

"Arrrrrgggggghhhhh!" yelped Crump. "The porker bit me!"

Dylan looked at Crump's outstretched palm.

"Ahhh it's only a little nip – bit of anti-septic cream'll sort it," said Dylan, and as if by magic, he pulled a tube of it out of his coat pocket.

A small bead of blood oozed through the wound at the base of Crump's thumb.

Dylan applied the cream to Crump's hand. Sandra looked on, her round brown face now a portrait of porcine smugness.

"I thought you said she gave kids rides in summer?"

"She does – she likes children. Most def. Not so much strange men – she can be funny like that, with strangers, kindathing."

"Well thanks for telling me!" said Crump, closely examining his thumb wound.

Dogs look up to us, cats look down on us, but pigs treat us as equals – supposedly. But not this pig. She clearly did not see Crump as an equal. As he gave Sandra a last wary look before leaving, he was sure she was looking down her snout at him and seemed, in a way that surely should not have been possible for pigs, to be gloating.

The tour was over. Crump thanked Dylan, who gave him his mobile number in case he needed any help at any time.

He had been in a such a rush the day before he had simply parked at his mum's house, and gone inside with his overnight bag to sleep. His belongings, those boxes of junk that laughably represented his life, were still crammed into his old rusting Ford, now parked in university grounds. Plenty of time to unpack later.

Crump headed to the library to do a recce and familiarise himself with the location of relevant books and journals in his subject areas, and also take out a couple of favourite novels as bedtime reading to help him sleep. He had a good ninety minutes before the university introductory meeting at the Richard Burton Theatre, and the darkening sky signalled rain – so what better way to spend that time than with books, the 'children of the brain'?

And so, he walked into the modern concrete and glass library – which Crump was delighted was called a 'library', unlike the 'learning zone' at Thames Met – and located the shelves of 20th century novels.

He was looking for *The Great Gatsby* – that classic compact *Jazz Age* novel by brilliant but hopeless drunk F. Scott Fitzgerald – but he couldn't find a copy on the shelves.

It must be out – well, it was a popular novel. Crump had read it the first time for A-level and several times since. It was that sort of book. And short, which helped.

The lighting was bad in the library – with two or three aisles in total darkness and the strip lights flickering annoyingly in others. 'Can't they get the maintenance department to fix them, or change the bulbs or tubes?' thought Crump with a tut.

He considered making a complaint – filling in a feedback form to highlight the issue – but then ruled it out: it was the first week of term, after all, and there were bound to be glitches. Besides, no doubt the maintenance department was very busy with other things, and no doubt fixing the library lighting was on their 'to do' list. Crump didn't want to get a reputation as a whinger and trouble-maker in his first week of a new job too, so against his better instincts, he decided not to mention it.

He sat down by a computer and typed in the title and author.

NO RECORD FOUND blinked the computer screen at him, with definite and defiant digital certainty.

Crump approached the library information desk. There he found a friendly-looking young woman whose name badge introduced her as one *Arwen Redmore*.

"Errr I wonder if you could help me," said Crump.

Arwen said something in Welsh which Crump didn't understand, not being able to speak more than a handful of words in the language.

"I said, *'it's what we're here for'*," translated Arwen, with a bilingual smirk.

"Ummm, yes, I was looking for a copy of *The Great Gatsby*, but—"

"Trigger warning!" snapped the young woman.

"Sorry?" said Crump, confused.

"Trigger warning," she repeated, louder this time, as though he was deaf and/or stupid.

Crump was just about to ask what that meant when the librarian explained.

"It means the book is on the banned list because it contains offensive, racist, sexist, disablist, homophobic, Islamophobic, transphobic or other material which goes against the university's diversity and inclusion policy, and which may trigger students in a negative way."

"But... it's a classic novel. I did it for A-level," wailed Crump.

"Recently?" said Arwen, looking at the old man before her.

"Well, no – over twenty years ago, but—"

"Times have changed – and for the better too. We now respect OC students..."

The fact that Crump hadn't a clue what that meant was obvious to the wondrously 'woke' and correct Arwen.

"People *of colour*," she explained, eye-rollingly, as if educating a backward child about the basics of potty training.

"Oh..." said Crump.

"Microaggressions, too, must be challenged and exposed."

Crump knew that 'microaggressions' were those everyday slights which supposedly communicated hostility towards so-called 'marginalised' groups – anyone except straight white men, basically.

"We have progressive policies at universities now," insisted Arwen Redmore.

'Oh what, like the "progressive" policy of banning books,' thought Crump, but he said nothing.

He knew how slights were never forgotten by those in higher education. If he got on the wrong side of this librarian, he could expect to be relegated to last in the queue for any request he may make in future. Though he realised, too, that perhaps he was already in that lowly position merely by dint of making a request for a book considered so racist, sexist, *whatever-ist-y* downright dangerous that it was incarcerated in the incendiary trigger section of the library, hidden away in a secret stash like the worst pederast and bestial porn of Ancient Greece and Rome at the British Museum – just in case it could have such a dangerous effect on students that they may actually start thinking for themselves. Well, one or two anyway.

"A full list of banned books is available on request," stated Arwen, more robot than human.

"So," pondered Crump, "can I make a request – for the full list?"

Arwen sighed histrionically in annoyance and rooted around in a drawer of her information desk, before handing Crump a piece of paper.

"Fill in this form," she droned, "but we don't get many requests for the banned books list, or for banned books..."

'Hardly a surprise,' thought Crump, 'because... if they're banned, students can't find them on the shelves, or even know those books exist, especially if they're not on any syllabus or reading list.'

"... and it may take some time to process."

Crump had heard about the new 'snowflake' culture at universities, the constant demand of such students for safe spaces, and the discouragement or outright banning of controversial opinions which may 'trigger' those over-sensitive souls who now bore the collective name 'snowflakes'. This was a possibly derogatory or maybe tongue-in-cheek name created to describe their inflated sense of uniqueness, their unwarranted sense of entitlement, their over-emotional fragility and inability to deal with opposing opinions, and their woeful lack of resilience too.

But he had no idea that it had led to the actual banning of books. Surely, a good education meant being exposed to a whole range of views – a diversity of opinion – and if any novels or other books were somehow 'offensive' to people now, perhaps because they reflected the prejudices of the age in which they were written as present-day literature usually does the same, then surely they shouldn't be banned, but studied and discussed in an atmosphere of free and open debate?

Crump always thought of Mark Twain, whose books were banned from libraries in the USA over a century ago for showing black and white people getting along just fine together, yet which were now often banned in our day and age by the same libraries for promoting some sort of unacceptable 'Uncle Tom' blackness. Bigotry was very *bendy*, it seemed, and as immortal as lack of thought.

Tolerance was good, but it seemed the signs were not. Students – and others – may not want to hear anything 'upsetting' or 'offensive' for fear of being triggered, but surely being challenged was 'a good thing'? It was the basis of the Socratic Method of teaching, after all. Questioning, challenging, upsetting: disagreement and dissent were essential in any mature, decent, civilised and intelligent democratic and open society, surely? Maybe that's not what we were any more, then? Maybe the infantilisation of everything and everyone was the new normal? Maybe there could be no diversity of opinion any more, in our brave New Puritan Age?

This banning of books was snowflakery at its finest – or, perhaps, its most terrifying and misguided.

There's not much difference between the UK and China, or any other undemocratic failed state or thuggish dictatorship, if the self-appointed thought police continue to ban books they dislike or cleanse the airwaves of anything they find 'offensive' – and who are *they* to judge anyway, even though *they* assume they occupy the moral high ground on a permanent basis?

On his way out, Crump noticed a notice pinned to the information noticeboard:

Witnessed an act of bias?
Then call this number and report hate thought if you think a lecturer has said something offensive during class.

'Bloody hell,' thought Crump. '1984 is here and now – though possibly that book will not be available in the library either if some sensitive snowflake soul has complained and claimed it has upset or triggered them in some way or other?'

The Socratic Method of education was as dead as the old philosopher himself – that playing devil's advocate intelligent provocation by great teachers to make students really think. Maybe no-one working in education could risk it any more, just in case a student complained. Crump had heard of lecturers who no longer told jokes in class, just in case someone took offence – though judging by the typically trite and unfunny quality of most educators' attempts at comedy, perhaps that was no bad thing...

But fear of speaking out and debating surely harmed the educational experience for students too? Was this the silent surrender of hard-fought civilised values like free speech? Was 'offending' someone's feelings now the worst crime in this diverse world of 'political correctness' and safe spaces – a world where seeking offence, craving victimhood and demanding action/apologies/compo were the new national sports in a victim Olympics?

Offending people was a *good thing*. 'If students at university were never offended,' thought Crump, 'maybe they should ask for their money back?'

Crump ordered a slice of pepperoni and a cup of something claiming to be coffee in *The Learning Tower of Pizza,* and sat down at one of the brightly coloured plastic tables to fill in his form.

He glanced outside at the university forecourt. The starry blue of an EU flag fluttered defiantly at him as it started to pelt down with rain. He watched students scuttling into university buildings out of the downpour.

They were old enough – or young enough – to be his own children, though he hadn't regretted not having kids. He was always broke enough as it was, and kids were money-munching machines, as he knew from friends who had them. Anyway, he was only just over forty, so plenty of time left yet: his own parents had been over forty when he was born.

That made him think of his mother in the care home. He'd make time to visit her tomorrow, after all the usual university guff and bumf was done and dusted. She wasn't going anywhere, after all.

Crump took a bite of his cheesily spicy pizza and started to fill in the library form.

*

"Abstainando Jones, yes, indeed, absolutely," trumpeted the sing-song Welsh-accented tones of Cambrian University's Vice-Chancellor Angharad Ap Merrick to the audience of new and established lecturers at the Richard Burton Theatre.

"Our great and illustrious founder, whose devout Welsh chapel adherence to abstinence of alcohol, idleness and, errr, marriage, meant he died without issue, so his substantial fortune, earned from the blood, sweat and toil of our forebears at the iron and copper works owned by his family, was used ultimately for the public good, to found and build this very university, over a century ago now – yes, no, indeed, absolutely…"

Crump could tell immediately that the Vice-Chancellor was basically a man in a dress, which was rather unsurprising due to a stubborn refusal to shave off the beard beloved of so many academics, not all of them male. Beards were all part of that affected academic pose, an attempt to fit the image of the stereotypical intellectual, and highly popular, especially amongst the more mediocre men of academe. Some universities had almost no male staff who lacked a beard, and not a few of the women too.

The VC had started life as Aneurin not Angharad – as Dylan had happily informed him earlier – so it didn't come as a shock. In these genderfluid days, it was no more than Crump had come to expect.

Like everyone else, Crump had taken a badge on entering the theatre, which stated he was a hetero-man with appropriately male arrow-on-circle image, and *PRONOUN = HE* written on it.

He could have chosen any badge from the array on offer, to state his pronoun was SHE, or IT, or one of the new transgender ones such as ZE, or XE, XYR or VE, or ZHE, or YO, or E, or AE, or EY, or HU, or PEH, or PER, if he wanted to show that he was genderfluid, transgender or non-binary.

Crump hated this labelling culture – he remembered the days when people could just be people, other than obviously male/female sex differences. Now anyone who was gay was expected to wear a badge stating as much, and everyone was encouraged to choose a gender from the fifty-seven genders available to them, which was how many Facebook offered anyway (though that had recently been upped to seventy-one for some reason) which always reminded Crump of Heinz 57 varieties, for some reason, and baked beans. Gender studies departments had a lot to answer for.

This transgenderism had become common over the last five or so years, and Crump knew of it from the Foreign Office which, too, was in thrall to whatever was 'on trend' this month in diversity-world.

Whether Crump actually believed anyone could just choose a gender – any gender – from the scores on offer was not so certain. Having studied biology at school and read a great deal about Darwinism, he knew there could logically only be two biological sexes, male and female, although deformities, mutations and hermaphrodites had always existed. Gender, however, was not sex – it was a construct, a concept, a hairdo of an identity which, at least as we are told, was something we could choose off the rack like a favourite shirt. People had the right in our self-aware age to choose any identity – they could even say they were black when they appeared white, according to the theory of self-definition.

The real concern for Crump was children. The way a bullying, aggressive, influential transgender tribe was apparently encouraging kids online to self-identify as a sex they were not born to was disturbing, as was adults pandering to their demands and putting these kids on medication from infant school age to stunt puberty and control hormones – something arguably tantamount to child abuse. After all, if your young child turned to you and said they felt like a dog today, because a website said so, would you strip them naked, put them on a lead and walk them down to the local park for a poo, and a wee up a tree, and an afternoon of chasing squirrels, before dragging them back home to snaffle a big helping of Pedigree Chum out of a bowl on the floor?

He knew a lot of this new transgender stuff was done to meet legal criteria anyway and avoid getting sued – the reason why schools may well stop even using the words 'boy' and 'girl', or 'men' and 'women' in the near future, and even have unisex toilets and changing rooms. *What could possibly go wrong?*

But Crump was never one for bullying or prejudice, no matter how much such things baffled him. 'Live and let live', was his motto, an ethos taught to him in childhood by both his parents. He remembered his father – a man born in poverty who left school aged twelve and worked his way up on the railways to be a union official, though over-work had probably led to his dropping dead from a heart attack in front of his fifteen-year-old son. One day when Crump was around ten or eleven, they'd witnessed – on holiday in South Wales – a group of yobbish local lads shouting names at a black family who were obviously on a day out to the seaside. The yobs soon got bored and moved on, swaggering down the beach, off to cause grief to others.

"The thing about hating people for no reason, mind," his father had said, "is that those you hate for being different are quite likely to end up in your own family one day – and then what'll you do?"

He was right. Just ask Prince Harry.

Suddenly, a shout of 'Fuck!' came from the stage. Then 'Wank!'. Then 'Cunt!'. The Vice-Chancellor seemed not to hear it, or at least carried on as though he hadn't.

Crump could see that the shouts were coming from Mike Mumpsimus, Dean and Quality Control Director, who was seated to the VC's right.

"He has Tourette's," whispered an attractive young woman seated next to Crump who, he could see from her badge, was called Fatima and was cisgender, i.e. identified as the gender AKA sex she was born as, in other words, female (*cis-* being the opposite prefix to *trans-* in Latin).

Crump smiled at the young woman – a dark, perhaps North-African-heritage individual – whose accent he could identify as French, even from three words.

The Vice-Chancellor continued:

"When my own illustrious ancestor, Richard Ap Merrick, a name then anglicised to *Americke*, funded Welsh king Henry VII's first expedition to the New World in 1497, thus giving his name to the new continent America, as many scholars believe, he did not fear risk or the perils of adventure, oh no, yes, indeed."

"Fuck!"

"And that is why we, both the staff and students of Cambrian University, shall pursue our own journey and adventure, into the unknown—"

"Wank!"

"—through the squalls and storms on the oceans of pioneering academic research and the quest for a new nation of knowledge, no matter what the future—"

"Cunt!"

"—challenges may be, especially in this dark age of Brexit. Oh no, yes—"

"FUCK WANK CUNT!"

"Indeed—"

Mike Mumpsimus, the Tourette's-suffering Dean, was undergoing a sweary episode, so decided it better if he left the stage.

Crump knew how people these days craved a label to help with advancement via 'positive action', and how spurious those identified disorders and conditions could often be in this age of medicalising ordinary human behaviour. But the Dean certainly had an unfortunate verbal affliction, and such a severe one that Crump wondered how he could possibly do his job effectively. Maybe people just learnt to make allowances? Or wore ear-plugs?

The Vice-Chancellor Angharad Ap Merrick's very male baritone continued:

"Thank you, Mike, and thank you all for coming this afternoon – no, yes, indeed – and may I wish all present here today a successful and fruitful academic year."

Crump started to applaud – clap in the usual manner he had being doing since infant school or perhaps even younger, as taught to him by teachers, in an age before the world went mad. But he was the only one clapping...

Everyone turned round to stare at Crump, who blushed at the attention. He then noticed that everyone in

24

the audience was doing 'Jazz Hands' – waving the palms of their hands in the air, as if they'd come to the end of an amateur dramatic stage musical, or perhaps a rendition of Al Jolson's *Mammy*.

"No clapping, in case it is triggering autistic persons," whispered Fatima to him. "It is written, in here…"

She handed Crump a programme for the afternoon introductory meeting.

"Thanks, Fatima," he mouthed.

It was the first time he had seen it. Why didn't he have one? Perhaps, he thought, because he hadn't yet got round to opening the pile of post waiting for him at his mum's house…

Crump started doing his Jazz Hands like everyone else. He could see the Vice-Chancellor nodding at that – though whether in a good way or a bad way he couldn't tell. He really didn't want to draw attention to himself on his first day in his new university job but, by committing the triggering crime of politely clapping after a typically tedious speech by a senior academic, that is precisely what had happened.

The next speaker stood up.

"Maybe we could start a conversation," said Ms Parminder Zugswang in a timid, fragile voice, peering shyly at the audience, "about conversations on diversity and inclusion, widening participation, and the increased need for positive action and full representation of women and people of colour? Thank you."

More Jazz Hands. And so sat down Ms Parminder Zugswang, woman of colour who quite possibly had those box-ticking diverse features to thank for her meteoric rise through the university ranks to become Pro-Vice Chancellor, Head of Strategy and number three in the university's power pyramid – as, perhaps, her direct superiors had their own diverse features to thank for their lofty positions.

There were a few more speakers, as everyone sat on stage behind a long table, rather resembling Leonardo's *Last Supper*. Jazz Hands after every speech, so much so that Crump was on the verge of singing *Mammy* more than once, but he would certainly draw the line at blacking up, if anyone asked (you never knew how post-modern ironic universities could be these days).

Crump cricked his neck. It was going to be a long afternoon.

He surveyed the audience around him and noticed only then that it was about two-thirds female.

'Of course,' he thought, remembering the university prospectus and information sheets for staff he had hurriedly read the night before.

The university now had a policy that *at least* 50% of all lecturers and tutors at all levels of all departments would be female. Moreover, great efforts were being made to recruit more BAME (Black and Minority Ethnic) staff, and Crump could see he was one of very few white men in the audience – no more than 20%, maybe less. He wondered how many qualified, educated and talented white men had been deliberately rejected at the application stage to achieve this – but no doubt those responsible would call any such racist and sexist discrimination against them to achieve the present situation 'true diversity in action'. Whether the large number of BAME lecturers reflected the local area was a moot point, as he knew Wales as a whole had a population that was over 95% white.

As if on cue, Kwasi Wakanda, joint Head of Diversity and Inclusion, took to the stage. He held something up in the air. What was it? Crump was too far away to see.

"This *Oreo* biscuit, wiv a white creamy centre surrounded by black, well, biscuit stuff… is a powerful symbol – of racial harmony, inclusion, *diversiteeeee* for you and *meeeee!*"

Crump sighed. He hated those damn biscuits – bafflingly the most popular in the USA – which taste as sickly as most American chocolate. He also knew they'd been massively promoted here since the government stupidly allowed a US food giant to take over the great and historic British firm Cadbury, supposedly after a promise was made not to close any UK factories. The US firm then proceeded, within months, to move production to Eastern Europe to cut costs.

"D'ya get me, yeah?" yelled Kwasi with a very London-y street accent, which had not a trace of African in it, before snaffling the Oreo biscuit in a single bite.

After Kwasi, it was the turn of the two middle-aged men, who were obviously identical twins, to speak – though as Gruffyd and Morgan Tewdwr were the Principal Lecturers in Welsh Studies, they spoke only in *Cymraeg*, so Crump hardly understood a word. But just watching the twins co-ordinate a joint speech so smoothly was, well, a little creepy. It reminded Crump of those two twin girls in that movie *The Shining* – even though the two identical twins mirroring each other's actions and words on the stage were two middle-aged-spreading, rather angry-looking men who also, Crump noticed as he peered through his glasses, were distinctly cross-eyed – or maybe swivel-eyed? Who knew?

Yet more silent Jazz Hands. *Mammy... Mammy...*

Then more speakers and more trite, turgid words spoken by the usual self-adoring bore-fest bloviator academic managers, until finally, the last speaker took centre stage. He was, he said, the Head of Celtic, Welsh and Diaspora Studies, and not a character anyone could possibly ignore, being a very fat ginger-haired Scot wearing a kilt with an enormous furry sporran and tartan everywhere. On his head he wore a wee Scottish cap which perched precariously there within the nest of curly, unkempt ginger hair like a tiny, terrified tartan baby bird.

"The rabidly reactionary Little Englander Anglo-Saxon hordes may try to Brexit our Celtic homelands into dire and dreick disaster, och aye, and I cannae tolerate it, or I'm not Donald Dougal Angus Hamish McGinty McDonald McClounie!"

Inevitably enthusiastic Jazz Hands from fellow nationalists, and also anti-Brexit Remainers on the stage and in the audience, which meant most staff present.

"Aye, the English colonisers cannae be trusted – ever – and especially not in the here and noo! I cannae wait until independence for all Celtic nations, but until that great day, I shall resist the Anglo-Saxon scourge of Brexit with every fibre of my strong Scottish brawn and brain, och aye the noo!"

More Jazz Hands. Yet Crump, a language specialist with a good ear, couldn't help noticing how very strange Donald McClounie's accent was – and would any real Scot ever say *och aye the noo* anyway? It was unlike any Scottish accent he'd ever heard – except, that is, when people not from Scotland try to do a Scottish accent. When non-Welsh people tried to do a Welsh accent, they often inadvertently sounded Pakistani; but when non-Scots tried a Scottish twang they sounded, well – they sounded just like Donald McClounie.

"They say he learnt how to speak Scottish from telly, kindathing," said Dylan, who'd reappeared for coffee and tea and biscuits in the Ruth Madoc and Windsor Davies Rehearsal Rooms. "I think he's from Cumbria, wherever that is — "

"Dylan, it's not hard to look at a map. It's up north somewhere – past Liverpool, I think. Lake District-*ish* — "

"Whatever," said Dylan, "but he's a TV historian, presented *A History of the British Celts* on telly — "

"I *thought* I recognised him," said Crump – who recalled the TV series from a few years back, and remembered thinking at the time they could rename it

A History of Why the English Are Such Complete and Utter Bastards, such was its victimhood-craving, Anglo-phobic, mythical/fabricated Celtic Scots nationalism.

"So I'll tell you something about Kwasi Wakanda, joint Head of Diversity…"

Crump waited.

"Well, what?"

"My mum works in that department, so I know his real name ain't Wakanda – he got that off that *Black Panther* movie…"

Crump hadn't seen that particular box-office smash – he hated superhero movies with a super-passion actually.

"And," continued Dylan, "his real name's not Kwasi either. It's Keith Cheese. He's from Brixton, I think."

"Keith Cheese?" chortled Crump. "Well, if that were my name, I'd change it too."

"YOLO," said Dylan, and he slunk off to snaffle some more biscuits.

Even a non-digital native like Crump knew that meant 'You Only Live Once' – and he supposed everyone had a right to change their name if they wanted. But it was, if one thought about it, rather fake just to choose an African name at random and reject your given name, just because you're black. Because *nobody* chooses their name, first or last. If Crump did one of those DNA tests and discovered he was mostly Viking or Russian, should he then change his name to Sven Bloodaxe or Vladimir Trotsky, just because he was white and wanted a cool and pure ethnic identity? No, far better to stay the mongrels we were all born to be, Crump always thought.

Crump glanced around the room at his fellow new lecturers. At least three were women (or he assumed they were women, at least) in burqas. He hoped they wouldn't be teaching in his departments and that there were no students with burqas in his classes.

Crump wondered how communication could take place when one person was, in effect, wearing a mask? He wondered how could one talk to a piece of fabric? If you could see no facial expression, no feelings, no humanity, he pondered, how could effective and normal communication take place? It couldn't. Full stop. Crump thought that the way British schools allowed pupils and teachers to wear that imprisoning, impractical garb was another example of pandering to extreme demands from minority ethnic and faith groups and was just plain wrong.

Wearing the burqa or even the headscarf was not required in Islam, Crump knew. Even if one played the flawed literalist game of looking up what it said in the Koran (which also had verses recommending slavery, murder, polygamy, wife-beating, child marriage and more), one could see that all that 7th-century tome advised, like most other old religious books, was that women should dress *modestly*.

Anyway, forcing women into burqas was originally a practice of Byzantine Christians in the 11th century, one which invading Arab Muslims stole and made their own, in what could perhaps be called a shameless act of cultural appropriation. The headscarf was solely cultural, and was worn by women of many cultures in the past as a practical aid to stop their hair falling into their face as they toiled away on menial tasks, due to the biological fact that women had smaller foreheads than men and tended to grow their hair longer. But at least a headscarf didn't hinder communication like a full-face veil.

Crump wondered what the reaction of pc university managers would be to his demand to express his own culture by permanently wearing a Halloween mask, for example – for that ancient British festival was part of his heritage, and predated Islam by at least three thousand years.

The French had happily banned such garb from educational institutions ages ago. But the British plodded on pandering to any minority group's demands, especially if they had a dark skin and a minority faith. Maybe these women in burqas were Saudi – Crump knew that this university and many others had links with the regime. And they brought in big wads of dosh, like the Chinese, so all UK universities were always extremely reluctant to challenge the values and traditions of such cash cow students.

"That is making me so angry," said a voice behind him.

It was Fatima, who had been sitting next to him in the theatre. In the brightly lit Rehearsal Rooms, he could see now how stunningly beautiful she was – with gorgeous green eyes, long luscious dark hair, an attractive olive complexion and a smile so sexy and kind that Crump felt like taking a photo on his smartphone – though he was far too shy and polite to do such a thing.

"Why you British allow this?" asked Fatima.

"Well, if it were up to me—"

"They say this is empowering and is making Muslim women strong and independent. Empowering? *C'est de la folie!* This is the madness!"

Crump nodded in agreement – he doubted he'd feel empowered if he wore a full body covering too.

"I am Muslim woman – I refuse to wear burqa or headscarf, like many modern Muslim women in all the world. Why you people think all Muslims must be like the village peasants from Pakistan or damn Wahabi Saudi slaves, eh?"

"Well, not me, actually, I—"

"Oh sorry," said Fatima, visibly willing herself to calm down, "it is just making me so angry. It is so wrong, this hypocrisy, *non*? I am member of *Ni Putes Ni Soumises* in France – it means something like *Neither Whore nor Doormat*, or *Nor Submissives...* something like this."

"It's a shame we seem to have no organisation like that in the UK," said Crump.

31

"It is organisation founded by the Muslim women, yes, but it is now for all women – against violence, oppression... I am lecturing *low* – "

"*Low?*"

"Yes, *low* – you know this, the *low* is an asshole."

"Oh, the *law* – is an ass. Yes, I dare say it is..."

Crump looked at his fellow lecturers in the Ruth Madoc and Windsor Davies Rehearsal Rooms. He was one of the few white men there and also clearly one of the oldest new lecturers. He had decided not to tell anyone he was sort of on secondment from the Foreign Office – some people could be funny about things like that, perhaps thinking he was spying on them, especially Muslims or other minority groups.

He looked over to a young man in a wheelchair who had no legs. He was laughing and joking with a black man who was probably his carer. There were a couple of other youngish men with them – one attractive doe-eyed man who looked oddly familiar somehow, and another who looked half-Chinese.

"He is Pete Parzival, the one who look like Chinese, and he is with Johnny Blue – he is former famous child actor..." said Fatima.

"Oh yes, I thought I knew that face," said Crump.

He had watched the spooky *Children of the Twilight* when he was doing teacher training in his first year after graduation. It was kids' TV, but that was often better than anything on for adults – back then, anyway. He could argue – just – that he was doing research watching kids' TV to prepare for teaching teenagers. But it was an enjoyable series for all ages anyway, all ghostly and mysterious, about ancient stones in a circle who used to be people. He hadn't seen Johnny Blue in anything on TV after that.

Crump would have loved to be introduced to Johnny Blue, but at that moment, everyone was called back into the auditorium as the Chancellor of Cambrian University was about to begin speaking.

As at all UK universities, and for reasons best known to no-one Crump knew, a Chancellor was merely a titular and ceremonial role in higher education, demanding nothing more than a bit of media PR which helped recruit students, especially international cash cow ones, and appearances at degree ceremonies, when they got to dress up in robes and mortar boards and act all regal. The real power lay with the Vice-Chancellor, who usually issued the Chancellor with an honorary degree, whether they had a real degree of their own or not.

And so, the Chancellor, local legend and old-school comedian Boyo Bellylaughs MBE, was going to entertain them all.

"Aye aye!" Boyo Bellylaughs announced to his new lecturer audience with his well-known catchphrase.

"Aye aye!" replied those members of the audience familiar with the routine.

"Don't worry, I's not gonna tell any rugby jokes. On the other hand, I might *try*."

Laughs and groans.

"Anyone here married?" asked Boyo.

Some hands went up.

"Marriage is a wonderful thing, wonderful. I recently watched my wedding video backwards. I love the bit where I take the ring off her finger, leave the church and go drinking with the boys!"

Loud laughs, from Crump too.

"I haven't spoken to my wife in eighteen months – I don't like to interrupt her!"

Laughs.

"Anyone here teach maths?"

A few hands went up.

"Maths made simple, right. If you have thirty quid and your wife has twenty quid, then she has fifty quid –

remember that and you'll never get divorced, boys, eh? Aye aye!"

"Aye aye!"

Crump was enjoying the old-school stand-up routine now, from a man who was such a local comedy legend and charity fundraiser that even the achingly 'politically correct' university authorities could tolerate him, despite his music hall borderline sexist jokes – though his shows were boycotted by some of the more humourless feminists.

"My wife said she'd go on top tonight. I love our bunk beds. Eh?"

Laughs.

"I spent some time digging my wife's grave yesterday. Bless her. She thinks it's a pond!"

Some groans amongst the guffaws. Crump saw some university managers who had spoken on stage earlier walk out at that one.

"Only joking, only joking. Have he got it yet?" said Boyo Bellylaughs MBE, using another of his famous catchphrases, pointing directly at Fatima and Crump.

"Yes," laughed Fatima, turning to smile at Crump.

This feminist was obviously not humourless and seemed to be thoroughly enjoying the show.

"Where you from, love?" asked Boyo MBE.

"France," called out Fatima.

"Beautiful country, oh aye. Full of French people, of course…"

Fatima mock-pushed him away with her hand.

"Only joking, only joking. The Bayeux Tapestry – made in Wales, oh yes. It was so named because when they asked the Welsh women who made it where they wanted the delivery boys to put it… Down *by yer*, they said and that's why it's called the *By-yer* Tapestry! Aye aye!"

"Aye aye!"

"Have he got it yet? You's gotta be Welsh to get that one, boys."

Crump got it – he'd been hearing a Welsh accent from birth thanks to his mother, and visits to South Wales in boyhood meant he got a lot of local linguistic idiosyncrasies.

"Oh, we gets a lot of rain here in Wales, don't we? Why our hills are so green, of course. But since it's been raining, all my wife has done is look sadly through the window. So sad she looks…"

"Awww," sympathised the audience.

"If it gets any worse, I'll have to let her in."

Huge laughs at that, and a couple more walk-outs.

"Wales is just like the South of France sometimes, oh yes. We's got some topless beaches here too – there's no sand on 'em!"

Crump heard Fatima laugh loudly.

"And we's got caravan parks, down on the coast. How does a caravan feel when it goes on holiday? *Ecstatic.* Geddit? *Ex-static!* Eh? Aye aye!"

"Aye aye!"

"Anyone here from London?"

"Yes!" yelled Fatima, pointing at Crump. He wished she hadn't, but forced a frozen smile.

"The house prices in London, eh? Just crazy… bonkers, boy, eh?"

Crump nodded. At half a million quid for a studio flat in a bog standard area, he knew how true that was.

"A mate of mine in London finally got on the property ladder, oh yes. He's a window cleaner…"

Crump laughed, perhaps more loudly than anyone else in the room.

"Another mate of mine told me his grandmother's a touch typist. That's nothing, I says – my grandfather's a touch racist! Aye aye!"

"Aye aye!"

"In this town, we usually calls our grandfathers 'bampi' – just to *heducate* you in the ways of South Wales, like – so anyway, my bampi races pigeons. He does – he races 'em. I don't know why – he never catches 'em. Eh? Have he got it yet?"

And so it went on, quickfire old-school musical hall humour that actually made people laugh – and really laugh too, unlike so much alleged comedy on TV these days.

For the first time since he'd been told he was being 'rationalised', Crump felt good – or vaguely positive and optimistic about his future, at least.

Though, if Crump were honest with himself, he knew that that probably has more to do with the warm tingle within him inspired by the beautiful, intelligent, lovely young French Muslim woman called Fatima sitting right beside him than any of the old jokes being told by local hero university Chancellor and tireless charity fundraiser, Boyo Bellylaughs MBE.

CHAPTER TWO

Settling In

"Oh are you Jewish?" said Tanya Snuggs, the joint Head of the English Studies Department.

It was the first thing she'd asked him when he'd entered her office that morning, after she'd given him a clinging hug of welcome, that is, which made Crump cringe inwardly – and outwardly too, probably.

"Errr, no…" said Crump, baffled. "Does it matter?"

"Course not! We're diverse and inclusive here."

Crump nodded obedient approval.

"I ain't never been *anti-semantic* but the university boycotts all Israeli academics and products, coz it's like a really bad racist Apartheid state."

With her ample bosom and gap-toothed cheeky smile, Tanya Snuggs resembled nothing less than an African-Caribbean version of Barbara Windsor from the *Carry On* films. She was dressed head to foot in pink: pink bouffant dress, shiny pink high-heel shoes and even a pink girly ribbon in her big hair – which was curly black, not pink. Predictably, her wrist-watch was pink, as was her mobile phone, as was almost everything else in her office. It was like having a meeting with a big black Barbie.

"Well, I've never been to Israel," said Crump, "and I don't think I've ever bought anything Israeli either – maybe some nuts once, but —"

"Great!" grinned Tanya Snuggs. "Yay! Though I'm not an *anti-septic*. I love Jews – there's Stephen Spielberg, innit? Awww, I loved ET... bless... he was an *extra-terrestrian*... Have you seen him?"

"Well, the film, yes... not... in... person..."

"*The truth is out there*, eh? And aliens. Do you believe? I believe. Yay! And that Barbra *Stryland*, she's got a lovely voice..."

"But... errr... I don't really agree with banning everything from Israel – it is a democracy, after all, unlike the countries that surround it."

Tanya's flummoxed face flashed a fixed smile at him. She reminded him of the dimmer girls he'd known as a teenager. But then, dressed all in pink with a pink ribbon in her big hair, she seemingly *was* a teenager, or perhaps even a tweenager, in a near-middle-aged woman's body.

"Maybe we can start a conversation?" she said.

Crump waited – for a conversation to start.

Tanya Snuggs blinked blankly – but she did not converse.

"Errr... you mentioned... a... conversation?" queried Crump.

"Yes, a conversation!" giggled Tanya Snuggs, bouncing in her chair with her ample breasts.

Silence. Of conversation, there was none.

"You ain't from here, is you?" said Tanya Snuggs.

"Errr, no, but my mother's Welsh. I was born and brought up in Kent, on the borders of Greater London."

"Oh, great! I'm from *Sarf* London, innit – "

"Snap!" said Crump, unable to stop himself smiling at Tanya Snuggs giggling.

On first impressions, she was probably the most pleasant manager he'd ever known in his educational career, though possibly the dizziest, and quite probably also the dimmest – and that was against some rather stiff competition...

"I was headhunted for this position," continued Tanya Snuggs, "coz in London I was discriminated."

Crump waited for the 'against' to go with the transitive verb, but none was forthcoming.

"I was discriminated *against*," he said, as politely as possible.

"Oh, was you discriminated too? Terrible, ain't it? All this *discriminatory-ness* goin' on..."

Crump didn't know what to say. But again, he couldn't help smiling at Tanya Snuggs' girly giggly gap-toothed smile. She just had that effect on him. Like bubbles.

"Happy Diversity Day, by the way!" chirped Tanya Snuggs.

"Oh, is it? Well, yes... Happy... Diversity Day..." said Crump, who had no idea that very day was 'Diversity Day' or indeed, what it was supposed to be for.

"Yay!" squealed Tanya Snuggs.

"Yay," echoed Crump, limply.

"I love diversity, don't you?"

"Yes, well, it's... very diverse..."

"Yay! Oh and remember, don't forget the consent training today – y'know, the anti-rape course."

"The *what*?"

"An email *was* sent to all new staff, Kevin..."

"Oh yes, sorry – I haven't got a connection yet where I'm staying, so can only go online when I'm here, and I just haven't had a chance yet to check through emails."

"Well, you better get a wiggle on," giggled Tanya Snuggs.

"OK," he said, "I'll... get... a wiggle on..."

Crump wondered what other emails he'd missed – the ones aimed to train him not to murder any students or throttle any irritating university managers, maybe?

"It's really very very *very* important training..."

'Oh yeah,' thought Kevin, 'no doubt it's *seminal* too, and without anti-rape training I'd just be raping rapingly away all over the raping place, just like all men, who are basically rapists who need to be trained out of their rapingly rapist instincts and intentions.'

"If I could just add a *caviar*," grinned Tanya Snuggs, "all lecturers who identify as male must attend anti-rape training, coz it's like very important, what with #MeToo and #WhatsUp—"

"Isn't it #TimesUp?" questioned Crump.

"Oh yeah, time's up now – time flies, innit? Any probs, contact me or Karen Crisp, Joint Head of Department. She's on period leave."

"Period leave?" asked Crump – he'd never heard of that before.

"Yeah, coz like women are special with our... time of the month, y'know, an' stuff, so we get up to five days, leave a month if we want it. It's great to be working at such a progressive university, ain't it?"

'Bloody hell,' thought Crump. 'Talk about period drama!'

Women lecturers got up to five days off a month – paid, no doubt – because they may have a few aches and pains. Crump thought back to the massive brain-splitting skull-smashing hangovers he'd taught through in his teaching career, especially overseas and at summer schools – he doubted any PMS could be worse than that. But he just carried on regardless, no matter what.

Moreover, how could women, and the feminists who purport to represent them (though they never asked!), claim women were equal to men if they were so disabled by their bloody periodical affliction that they needed five extra days off a month? He doubted many women would agree with such policies, if asked. His own mother certainly wouldn't – she worked as a nurse night and day for forty years with hardly a break. She just got on with it, without complaint.

"Just follow all guidance in the emails – you were sent a department handbook too – and, the world's your *lobster*, as they say, innit?"

'Yay!' thought Crump, wondering whether the linguistically-challenged Tanya Snuggs possibly thought that lobsters were *'crushed Asians'*.

*

"All men are rapists," said the goatee-bearded Chris Cockpea, trans-man trainer in the university's Shirley Bassey Diversity and Inclusion Re-education Centre, "potentially, at least."

'Phew!' thought Crump. It felt so unrapingly good only to be a potential rapist!

"This consent, or anti-rape, training today is to help you – men – to live better and more empathetic non-misogynistic lives by negotiating and making the right non-sexist choices in a patriarchal world of rape culture and toxic masculinity —"

"Not toxic femininity then?" said Andy Stone from his wheelchair.

"There is no such thing. Women cannot rape men – and women do *not* lie either. That is just yet more *mansplaining* by the patriarchal misogynistic media, created by men, for men."

"Seriously?" said Johnny Blue. "The TV industry is dominated by women in my experience, and publishing too."

"Oh, I am being very serious indeed," said Chris Cockpea, seriously and scowling like the girls' school PE teacher she once was. "Could you all put on your pronoun badges, please!"

Crump dug around in his bag for his badge which yet again informed everybody that he self-identified as male and his chosen pronoun was 'HE'.

'What a relief!' he thought. 'If I don't put this on, people may think I'm a woman or want to be called "it".'

"Why do you assume we all need anti-rape or 'consent' training anyway?" said Johnny Blue. "I've never raped anyone and never would."

"Yes, well, you men all say that, don't you?"

"Aren't you a man?" asked Crump, but his question was drowned out by a collective:

"WHAT?!"

"OMG," gasped Pete Parzival.

"The statistics speak for themselves," continued Chris Cockpea. "Only 15% of rapes are reported to the police — "

"Alleged rapes," muttered Khalid, a fellow lecturer.

"Women who accuse men of rape are *never* liars!" yelled Helen Huffle, fellow anti-rape trainer, from where she was sitting at the front of the class. "The victim must always be believed!"

'Alleged victim,' thought Crump, in silence.

No man present dared say anything to that, possibly on account of the presence of the very masculine-looking and musclebound, man-woman-mountain called Helen Huffle who looked dangerously like a *roider* rugby player who could quite easily kick the shit out of anyone, or everything there, all at once.

Chris Cockpea continued:

"The research shows 20% of all women have been raped or sexually assaulted, and only 5.7% of rape cases end in a conviction for the perpetrator."

"Excuse me, I am a lecturer in law," said Khalid, "and I know that's misleading. Of rape cases that go to court, around 24% result in a conviction which is roughly comparable with burglary cases, though rape and sexual assault cases are often one person's word against another's, and alcohol is usually involved and perceptions differ, hence the current conviction rate. The law must be based on evidence and evidence alone."

"Get out!" screamed Helen Huffle with a piercing screech that made Crump jump. "GET OUT NOW!"

"Fine," said Khalid, leaving the classroom. "I was merely stating facts."

"And *that* is what a rapist looks like," said Chris Cockpea when he had left the room.

Pete Perzival went to put his hand up, but thought better of it.

Andy Stone bit his lip and shook his head wearily.

"Rape culture, misogyny, mansplaining – it's everywhere, like a virus we must eradicate!"

"You can't spell *man*ure without man!" added Helen Huffle.

'No,' thought Crump, 'and you can't spell *men*struation without men either, or S*cunt*horpe without c – '

"Can you *men* please get it through your sexist heads," continued Chris Cockpea, "that you are all part of rape culture in this misogynistic, patriarchal society, so you need to be re-educated and trained out of the toxic masculinity you have learned."

Crump the rapist closed his eyes.

It was going to be a very long morning indeed.

*

Happily, the anti-rape training only took ninety minutes, and so Crump and his fellow rape-y male lecturers were now unrapingly ready for lunch in the EATZ refectory in The Learning Tower.

Crump had so much to do, what with ploughing through the hundreds of emails waiting for him, plus setting up an online connection at home. But he was tired and hungry, and was happy for the company of fellow 'newbie' lecturers too.

"Chicken curry, please," Crump said as he slid his plastic tray along the metal rack at the counter.

A large, 'big-boned' woman, whose nametag identified her as *Pam Fadge*, pointed to a notice on the side wall –

where no customer could see it, naturally, unless they bothered to turn around 180 degrees while on the EATZ conveyor belt.

Crump looked round. Under a sign proudly declaring that no pork or ham was available and all meat products sold were 'Halal' – something Crump did not agree with at all, for the sake of animal welfare, though he would have respected a choice and clear labelling – there was a sign which stated NEW CULTURALLY CLEANSED MENU.

"Curry is cultural appropriation, so it is," drawled Pam Fadge in her *tick* Irish burr.

The notice went on to say that certain dishes were now banned as they were offensive examples of 'cultural appropriation'.

"But typical takeaway curries were basically first created in post-war Britain," said Crump, with a slight whimper in his voice.

"I only work here, so I do," said Pam Fadge.

"Any Coronation Chicken then?" asked Crump.

"No, coz it's racist, so it is."

'Racist?' thought Crump, knowing the dish had been created for the Queen's coronation in 1953 – in London, he presumed, and definitely in the UK.

This was bonkers. And more importantly, Crump was starving hungry!

"Got some lovely stew and dumplings for yers," smiled Pam Fadge with a wink.

Crump nodded. He had to admit he did love British-style dumplings – way more than the Chinese or East European versions he'd tried. British dumplings were the only ones made with suet, apparently, so maybe that was why. He loved the way they were crispy on top but soft and fluffy and meat-juicy underneath. He remembered his mum used to make it when he was a kid. He hadn't had stew and dumplings for years and years.

"And have yourself a diversity doughnut – only a pound, so it is – all goes to help the poor starving babies in Africa."

"Diversity doughnut?" asked Crump. "Oh, OK, why not… do you have any with the white icing on top?"

"No, that's racist – we have black icing, brown, pink, yellow, red, blue, purple, and green for the old country, so it is, so it is, so it is!"

"Green then, thanks."

"And you have yourself a happy Diversity Day, son," boomed the big butcher-y frame of Pam Fadge.

"Happy Diversity Day!" said Crump with a stoical smile as he paid.

"OMG. Don't they realise that if the food here is cultural appropriation, then so is most world cuisine? After all, they had no chillies in Asia until Europeans brought them here from Central America – so does that mean Indian curries or Chinese dishes made with chillies, or tomatoes or potatoes, are all 'cultural appropriation'? That's nuts! Rant over…"

The half-Chinese Pete Parzival said just what Crump had been thinking.

They were all sitting at a long table by the window at EATZ, enjoying their non-racist non-culturally-appropriated lunches together.

Crump stared out at the university forecourt where the rainbow flags of diversely diverse groups were fluttering diversely to celebrate Diversity Day.

All religions and ethnicities were represented, and lots of banners and flags with the usual blue starry EU standards were all around the campus. Others stated **BOLLOCKS TO BREXIT** or had **#StopBrexit**, **#PeoplesVote** or **#FBPE** (Follow Back Pro-EU) Twitter hashtags. The black flag of ISIS was also there, he noticed, from the more radical faction of the Islamic Society, as well as flags of various African national groups and other nations, the usual Palestinian flag and a BDS banner (Boycott, Divestment, Sanctions against Israel), flags of various racial and cultural groups, LGBTQIA banners, which Crump knew stood for lesbian gay bisexual transgender queer intersex and asexual, though one banner read LGBTQIAGNC and another stated LGBTTQQIAAP, which stood for who knew what? When Crump was at university there was just an LGB society handing out photocopied leaflets. How many more letters could the activists add to that? Was there any limit?

Then there were the feminist activists, including the traditionalist TERF element. They were basically at war with the transgender and non-binary activists who believed that anyone and everyone was free choose a sex/gender other than the one they were born to, at any time of life too. TERFs were having none of it. They believed a 'trans-woman' was merely a 'mutilated man', not a woman in any way, shape or form, and never could be, and they refused to accept such people should be referred to as 'women' and claim access to female spaces (including toilets and changing rooms).

There were colourful rainbow banners stating:

HAPPY DIVERSITY DAY

and:

HAPPY TRANSPHOBIA AWARENESS WEEK

Crump hadn't realised that glorious week of trans-jollification was here too, what with all the attention being on DIVERSITY DAY, but now he knew...

And that was the reason for a noisy protest by the TERF activists. The *TERF* war continued...

TERF stood for *Trans-Exclusionary* (or for the more extreme feminists, 'eliminationist' or even 'exterminationist') *Radical Feminists*. These were the sort of angry, sometimes man-hating and always loud feminist groups, often dominated by lesbians, that Crump remembered from his university days, but which certainly didn't really represent any women he knew then or now.

Though these days, these feminists found themselves hoist by their own petards really, challenged by a 'political correctness' they once promoted, as now anyone was free to choose a gender from the pick-and-mix array on display. So any man could suddenly claim he was female and demand to be treated as such and use female facilities including toilets and changing rooms even if he was in possession of a fully functional and loaded penis. *That* was what irked the sisterhood so – that and the fact that any men could claim to be women and, just by stating that self-definition, be accepted as such – though, of course the reverse was true too. More than a few feminist groups existed specifically to exclude men, not to welcome them if they claimed suddenly to be women!

It was all the natural conclusion of the wacky world of gender identity politics, with all its rampant, strident narcissism and certainty in its own unrelenting and absolute 'correctness' in all things, so it was really quite amazing they hadn't seen it coming. After all, wasn't it these feminists who'd demanded unisex clothes, gender-neutral toy departments in stores, and no social conditioning based on gender, or treating boys and girls in any way differently, or assuming any innate difference between the sexes? We're all pansexual now...

The local Cambrian police were there, too, to keep an eye on things. A few were wearing rainbow-flag costumes, one of which made the female officer inside look like a giant gay rainbow egg, and two male plods wore shocking pink helmets on their heads as they stood by a police car painted with a rainbow flag design. Apparently, all this was sponsored by one of the major banks, keen to link their corporate name to a lucrative gay-friendly pink-pound cause. This particular bank was one of those responsible for wrecking the economy in the crash of 2008, forcing thousands into homelessness and poverty, creaming off huge profits from the whole corrupt fiscally illiterate fiasco, and totally getting away with it too. Hoorah!

Yet more placards of varying levels of professionalism and lack of irony-awareness stated:

END WHITE MALE PRIVILEGE!
NO MORE MALE, PALE AND STALE!
GAMMON – GO NOW!
STAY IN YOUR LANE!
ZIO-FASCISTS OUT!
SHOW RACISM THE RED CARD
INTERSECTIONALITY NOW!
DOWN WITH HETERO-NORMATIVE
ORTHODOXY!

and, predictably:

#MeToo
#TimesUp
#BlackLivesMatter
END RAPE CULTURE
SMASH TOXIC MASCULINITY!
WOMYN
WIMMIN
WOMXN
FOREVER!

There were also banners stating:

EQUALITY FOR ALL
DIVERSITY FOR ALL
SAFE SPACES FOR ALL

This latter demand was something Crump simply did not understand.

Cambrian University supported a 'safe space' policy which, in recent years, had led to the creation of special, segregated, 'safe spaces' for a multifarious montage of ethnic, religious and identity groups, from Muslims (separate safe space rooms for Muslim men and women in a supposedly non-sexist university), the neuro-diverse, the transgender community including QTPOC (queer-trans people of colour), women in general (though there was no dedicated safe space for men), those of African-Caribbean heritage, Chinese students, various Asian groups, vegans and numerous others. The 'Resisting Whiteness Group' had a safe space where no white people were allowed. Rooms had been requisitioned from all departments, as well as the usual conversion from smoking spaces into prayer rooms. That was maybe why Crump and other newbie lecturers didn't have the luxury of an office of their own and had to 'hot desk' it through the day as best they could.

There were also the neuro-diversity activists out on campus that day, fighting for rights of the neuro-diverse, and all who self-identified as such, though some seemed rather distracted and wandered off, and yet others were waving their arms in the air crying and wailing, no doubt triggered by the stress of the diverse occasion.

Vegan extremists (sometimes called *Veganazis*) held banners demanding an animal-free menu on campus and for the English language to be changed thus, supposedly so as to not encourage people to abuse animals:

FEED TWO BIRDS WITH ONE SCONE
FEED A FED HORSE
BRING HOME THE BAGELS
TAKE THE FLOWER BY THE THORNS

Which, Crump supposed, were meant as cruelty-free substitutes for the followings: kill two birds with one stone, flog a dead horse, bring home the bacon, and take the bull by the horns. He could not, off the top of his head, think of any occasion when he'd been tempted to kill birds with a single stone, flog dead horses, or take a bull by the horns literally after hearing those idioms, and had never swung a cat in a space in which there was no room to do so either. The passion of these vegans was perhaps admirable, though their targets were rather absurd: the English language does not take orders, as linguistic history made perfectly clear. Crump slyly wondered whether iron and vitamin B deficiency was causing impaired brain function in any vegan who believed that.

Then there were the anti-Brexit campaigners and tub-thumpers, plus the anti-Israel and anti-Zionist groups with their banners which intertwined the Star of David with a swastika, and the FAM (Fat Acceptance Movement) activists, mostly obese females in tightly fitting brightly coloured skin-tight leggings and leotards.

And the comrades from the Socialist Workers Party had at last shown up, bright and early at half past twelve after their usual lie-in, though the absence of many such students from lectures suggested they were more Socialist than worker.

Crump was enjoying meeting up with his fellow newbie lecturers in EATZ.

"Happy Diversity Day!" announced Andy Stone from his wheelchair, waving his black-icing-ed doughnut at Crump. His carer Casper held up and waved his pink-icing-ed doughnut too. Then they kissed.

Crump hadn't realised. Not that it mattered. He thought that Andy Stone hadn't 'seemed gay', before chastising himself in his head for making such shallow assumptions – as if all gay men mince around with limp wrists and speak like drag queens. But anyway, Andy

Stone wouldn't be mincing anywhere even if he could, what with having no legs…

"Before you ask," he said, "I lost my pins in Afghanistan – IED. Can't get used to the falsies. Maybe one day. And yes, we are together."

"I am from Zimbabwe – that beast Mugabe want to kill all gays. He kill so many."

"Casper claimed asylum – and has been my carer for, what, nearly two years now?"

Casper nodded. They kissed again.

"I'm a new lecturer in Peace Studies – or War Studies, as I calls it," Andy laughed.

Crump knew the Head of Peace Studies (who was also the university's 'Professor of Race') was another African man who went by the name of Hitler Mazimba, which was probably perfect for the courses on Hitler Studies they taught there, as well as all the courses portraying the British – or, rather, English – Empire (for that is what universities called it now, despite the Scots and Welsh and, indeed, Irish being an integral part of it, good or bad) as the most evil empire ever in the existence of humanity. Crump had always thought that weird. The British Empire was of its time, yes, but it was by far the most benevolent empire in history – which a quick glimpse at the German, Russian, Japanese, and ancient Asian and African empires would confirm.

The British Empire spread the rule of man-made law around the world, and human rights, and forced a slavery ban on the Spanish and Americans – and African slave traders – who did not want it. The British 'West Africa Task Force' freed 150,000 slaves from ships off Africa bound for the Americas after 1807, and one third of the British navy died in such exploits – though Crump knew that was never ever taught at schools or colleges, as it did not fit the 'nasty white British Empire = all bad' agenda.

Khalid looked at his phone, flicked through text messages and tutted.

"Looks like I'm for the high jump," he sighed. "That's where a good legal education gets you…"

"It just wasn't fair, what he… she… said to you," said Crump.

"That trainer was so crazy, an imbecile," agreed Fatima. "You have just stated the facts, Khalid."

"Oh, I know, but…"

Crump doubted they'd get rid of a highly talented law lecturer for something like that – especially one from an ethnic minority with a Muslim name – though he may well get a first warning and have to repeat the awful anti-rape training.

"I'm all rape-y now obviously, as I didn't complete the consent training," grinned Khalid. "So be *very* careful, guys…"

They all laughed, all except Johnny Blue – who never ever seemed to even smile, Crump suddenly realised.

"It's so ridiculous, and offensive," said Johnny. "There's so many real problems in the world – over-population, especially, which causes pollution, climate change, wars for resources, species extinctions… ."

Johnny Blue was a lecturer in Environmental Studies, and clearly passionate about his subject. He was an older version of the teenage TV actor Crump remembered, and still prettily attractive in the same doe-eyed androgynous way.

"Yes, and so much real oppression of the women, and men, in many countries," said Fatima. "Real oppression. Not these self-obsessed #MeToo American women who hate the men, and want the witch hunt, like McCarthy, *non*? And for what? Because a man, he is flirting! They think women are all like the vulnerable children, need to have the protection, yes? *Bof!*"

"At least you didn't have to do anti-rape training," said Crump.

"Forcing all men to do that is just *so* offensive," said Johnny Blue, clearly angry now. "As if all men are natural-born rapists who need to be trained out of it."

Crump agreed totally, but he was used to the mad bonkers pc fashions in the education system, after his previous experience teaching at Thames Met – though he had to admit that the mad bonkers level had gone up a couple of gears in the decade he'd been away.

"And Diversity Day – what the hell is that?" snapped Johnny Blue. "The earth is dying, so many species are endangered, habitats are being depleted at an unsustainable rate, the oceans are polluted with plastic and over-fished, the climate's changing with global warming, and we human cockroaches are scuttling across the surface of the over-populated Earth in our over-breeding droves, with two thirds of populations of Africa and Asia under thirty and consuming ever more as they destroy the planet – and all people can worry about is silly fucking gimmicks!"

"Happy Diversity Day!" said Crump with obvious irony, holding up his second doughnut of the day – this time, with purple icing.

"Happy Diversity Day!" parroted everyone back at him, including diners at adjacent tables, holding up their own diversely coloured doughnuts too, though one brandished a gingerbread neutral person.

"Oh, I'm not hungry," muttered Johnny Blue, standing up and leaving after saying: "If you're not worried, you haven't understood the problem…"

"He seems really upset," whispered Fatima to Crump.

"May I?" said a confident female voice.

"Sure," said Khalid, and a smartly dressed young woman sat down in the place vacated by Johnny Blue.

"I'm Esther Isaacs," the voice announced, brightly. "I'm a Jew, a Scouser and a Tory – oh, and I campaigned for Brexit."

"Eh up!" said Khalid. "I'm from Yorkshire – we non-nonsense northerners should stick together."

"Exactly!" grinned Esther Isaacs, "though I have no time for professional northerners."

"I hear unprofessional ones are much more fun," smiled Khalid.

Crump knew exactly what Esther meant by 'professional northerner' – the sort of northern English person who sneered at anyone from the south for being 'middle class' just for speaking Standard English, assumed everyone north of Birmingham was 'salt-of-the-earth' working class and consequently continually oppressed, and who could moan and whinge for England about it too. He'd known a few like that at university, often loyal Labour voters, now no doubt on large five- or sometimes even six-figure salaries, yet who still claimed to be 'working class' – always with a short 'a' vowel – and were determined to deny access to their victimhood-craving class-obsessed club to anyone with a southern accent.

"OMG," said Pete Parzival, his Brummie accent showing, "I'm surprised you haven't been lynched!"

"Oh, believe me, they've tried," Esther replied, with a wry smile, "but I'm a tough cookie – you develop a thick skin if you're a Tory in Liverpool and a Jew in the university sector. We're rare as hen's teeth!"

Sniggers around the table, because it was true. It was common knowledge that at least 90% of academics were what could be called 'left wing', supporting Labour or the Green Party, or Welsh or Scottish nationalists. A similar or larger proportion had rooted for Remain in the 2016 referendum, though this was possibly inspired mostly by self-interest, and a desire to retain funding from EU academic bodies, so it was hardly surprising.

What was unspoken, but generally known, was that any academic of any political persuasion who supported

Brexit, and who 'came out' as such, could expect to be denied promotion, to be ostracised by 'right-thinking' Remainer colleagues, and may well lose out on funding or other opportunities, despite the much-touted devotion to diversity and equal opportunity expressed by every single higher educational institution in the UK. That devotion did not celebrate diversity of opinion, for sure. So most in education who supported Brexit kept it very quiet indeed, as did anyone who voted Tory, or for anyone other than left-leaning parties. And all with Jewish heritage were advised to keep that quiet too, unless they hated the state of Israel, in which case they were encouraged to shout their anti-Zionist leanings from the rooftops – or maybe, the minarets.

Esther Isaacs busied herself like a mother hen, tidying up the mess on the table, collecting the empties and taking them to the recycling bins. She was clearly a *do-er*, a hard-working, ultra-efficient, no-nonsense woman not to be messed with. But she seemed cheerful and pleasant with it, and Crump instantly liked her.

His own political leanings were liberal with a small 'l', though he had no party loyalty or affiliation, and he was still undecided on Brexit. Crump had abstained in the 2016 referendum by putting a cross in both boxes, as he simply could not decide between them – he could see the pros and cons of Britain being both in, and out of, the EU. Only time would tell, he thought, then and now, if the British voters had made the right decision – a decision all political parties had declared they would abide by at the time, he recalled.

Just then, a group of burqa-clad women entered EATZ. Fatima tutted and spat out words Crump had never learnt in his French lessons at school, that's for sure.

This babble of burqas was followed by three massively obese women, in tight brightly-coloured leggings and leotards – fat acceptance activists from FAM.

"Yeuk!" shuddered Esther Isaacs. "Why do people let themselves go and get so disgustingly obese!"

"Maybe they cannot be helping it?" proffered Fatima.

"Oh, nonsense. They eat too much, that's why they're so flabby and fat!"

The males round the table kept very quiet. It was bad enough being branded as rapists who needed to be trained out of their rape-y instincts. They all knew commenting on women's appearance, however ugly, would always rebound on them.

"Well..." started Fatima, but Esther kept on going.

"I volunteer at a local food bank and the number of mothers who come in who are *so* obese – *and* they smoke. They have children, for goodness' sake – and kids should always come first. Most of them are obese too, of course. And so it goes on, like a flabby family tree—"

"But these mothers have no husbands to support them, no?"

Esther Isaacs chortled a sniffy laugh.

"Not in broken Britain, Fatima. You're French, I think?"

Fatima nodded.

"You see, you French still have a belief in the family, as do most nations and regions of the world," said Esther. "But here in Britain, half of marriages end in divorce and we have an epidemic of single-mother families – which all research shows to be bad for children in every way, not to mention the increased risk of child abuse if Mummy has multiple boyfriends! Not that we're allowed to ever condemn anything like that these days."

"But there have always been single-parent families – during wars, for example, or after them," said Khalid.

"Of course, but we had extended family networks back then so children would have had other male, and female, family members as role models."

"I don't think you can generalise—" started Crump, but Esther interrupted.

"Course you can – what do you think the feminists do?"

She had a point there.

"You won't hear any of this in the so-called 'liberal elite' media but children brought up in families with step-parents are four to five times more likely to suffer sexual abuse. Think Cinderella. That is the truth, no matter what the 'right-on' opinions of today say. I am not a believer in the nonsense of 'political correctness'."

"Never?" said Crump with a grin, and they all smiled.

Esther took it all in good humour.

Crump liked the way Esther Isaacs didn't take herself too seriously and could laugh at herself. It was pleasantly refreshing in the constantly pompous world of academia which always took itself ever so seriously, especially when it was being utterly ridiculous.

"I'm just thinking of the children – they always come first in my book. Always. Not what Mummy wants, or Daddy come to that, though so many kids these days have no father – so they look to gangs of older boys on the street, as the research clearly shows."

Nobody could argue with that. Crump remembered an old retired teacher he once knew who, when asked which one thing he would change to make the school system better for all children, replied that he would try to ensure as many as possible grew up in stable, and if possible two-parent, families.

"Gosh, those three women are so disgustingly fat – like a lardy version of the three graces! Yeuk!"

Crump was only hoping that the three fat activists didn't hear what Esther was saying, as she was speaking in her trademark no-nonsense loud and certain voice.

"Maybe... we should have some empathy, *non*?" said Fatima.

Esther Isaacs laughed, probably at herself.

"Sorry if I offend anyone, but that's what I think. WYSIWYG, I think they call it – *what you see is what you get!* This is me just being honest."

"Good for you, mate!" said Andy Stone.

"Happy Diversity Day!" said Khalid.

"Happy Diversity Day!" chanted everyone back.

"Give me strength," said Esther Isaacs, probably the most diverse person there.

Were it not for her commitment to being totally and out-spoken-ly honest, Crump wouldn't have been surprised if Esther Isaacs ended up as Prime Minister one day – the first Jewish Tory PM since Disraeli, perhaps? But he also knew honesty was never the best policy for ambitious politicians, and mavericks like Esther Isaacs could only rise to the top of institutions or the political system in exceptional circumstances. However, recent times had been the most politically exceptional that Crump had ever lived through, so who knew? Prime Minister Isaacs was a distinct future possibility.

Crump peered out of the window. He now saw that a largeish, Labrador-type black dog was with the Diversity Day banner-wavers. He was dressed in a rainbow-flag costume and sat under a sign which stated:

SPONSOR DIVERSITY DOG TODAY!

Crump thought back to all the posters of missing dogs and cats plastered on walls around the campus.

He wished 'Diversity Dog' a happy Diversity Day, as he took another bite of his second non-racist diversity doughnut of the day with a smile.

*

That afternoon, Crump took advantage of a tour of the library made available to newbie lecturers.

"This tour of the *lib-wa-wee* and IT *wee-source* centre will take *wuff-wee* half an hour," said Dr Tomos Splodge, Head of the IT department and Manager of Knowledge Exchange and Connectivity, whatever that meant. He was a short man in thick pebble spectacles, whose eyes seemed to be stuck in a permanent squint.

Crump had so much to do, but he needed to get his head round the IT system at the uni, especially as he would have no office or computer of his own on campus – it was all hot-desking now, like it or not.

First of all, however, both he and the group of newbie lecturers with him had to get their heads around Dr Tomos Splodge's appearance – for his face bore what was probably the cruellest birthmark Crump had ever seen.

Crump could see several fellow lecturers biting their lips so as not to burst out laughing – after all, Dr Splodge could not help having a speech impediment or a massive birthmark on the left side of his face which looked like an anatomically accurate image of a big red cock about to be thrust inside his open mouth. There was even a pair of red testicles at the other end, one either side of the penis base, up towards his ear.

'How he must have suffered at school,' thought Crump as Dr Splodge started the tour. Maybe that was why he had retreated into the digital world of computing, a place where everything was beautifully binary and logical, and nobody called him names. No 1 or 0 would or could ever take the piss or belittle him, or make him feel like an outcast or a freak, and maybe that had made him a successful geek in the end – so good luck to him!

They walked past the often-flickering or completely non-functioning lights of the library aisles, before their guide reached forward to open a door. The handle came off in his hand.

"Oh *wee-ally!*" tutted Dr Splodge, who had had to cope with the shoddy maintenance lately at the university. He put the handle in his pocket and carried on.

They all took the lift up to the fourth floor of The Learning Tower, where the IT suite was situated. Dr Splodge continued to explain in digital detail the intricacies of the university intranet. Crump took notes – he always found it hard to remember processes on computers, so found it useful to write it all down for future reference. Younger lecturers had no need to do so, being 'digital natives' who'd grown up with computers and had seemingly been attached to their smartphones with a virtual umbilical cord since birth.

Crump would make time to check all his emails at the IT suite and/or on his smartphone before leaving the campus that afternoon. He simply had to catch up. He'd also give his broadband supplier a call – he needed an internet connection at home, and quick.

"Good afternoon," came a voice, interrupting Dr Tomos Splodge who, if Crump were honest, had delved rather deeper into system design than he had ever wanted to go: that always tended to be the way of 'experts' in any field, whose total lack of self-awareness when not amongst other specialists in their subject areas, was typically solipsistic.

"Ah *w-ighty-ho*," announced Dr Tomos Splodge. "This is Professor Pip Pooman, from the Medical School – anatomy – and also the University Manager of Managing Fairness Fairly…"

"Splendid!" grinned Professor Pip Pooman.

"Any *pwob-lems* with student cheating, then Professor Pooman's the *wight* man to *wee-port* any *plagia-wism* to, isn't that *wight*, Pip."

"Oh yes, as Manager of Managing Fairness Fairly, we take fairness fairly seriously at this university. Feel free to come up and see me anytime in my lovely lab on the seventh floor, to report wrongdoers."

"Always *wee-port wong-doers*. It's w-eally *w-eally* serious, guys," said Tomos Splodge, like a right-on schoolteacher any class knew it could ignore and mock at will, without fear of consequences or punishment. "It's never all *wight* to copy and cheat."

'Except for foreign students,' thought Crump, who had seen an academic blind eye turned to cheating on an industrial scale by some Chinese students many times before, 'and for senior academics who get junior staff to do their research for them then give them no credit when the paper is published... '

Professor Pooman had cold blue eyes and a long pointy nose which made him look like a ferret. He also bore a distinct smell which, after Crump has discreetly sniffed the air as close as he could get to the professor, was, if he wasn't mistaken, the chemical whiff of formaldehyde, all mixed in with the sweet scent of sweat, or maybe something else...

'Occupational hazard, like someone who works in a fish and chip shop stinking of cooking oil,' thought Crump, remembering a fellow student from his own university days.

After the tour, Crump got on with going through his avalanche of unread emails. After an hour of plodding, and deleting hundreds of spam messages, he had finally waded through the backlog and had now received, and read – or at least skimmed through – the copious emails sent from various university departments. He would read them in detail later, and print them off at home once he had everything set up. You couldn't beat hard copy for important things.

Crump wistfully remembered the days before emails. *Remember them?* Everything worked just fine without them really, and far less time was wasted back in the day when people actually talked to each other and wrote messages on paper. Something about technology meant people always feel they had to use it *because it was there*, hence the daily deluge of emails sent to every working person in the land for little or no purpose. No wonder some big businesses banned emails: they were productivity-plummeting soul-sapping naggy little nuggets of nothingness, mostly, and best banished to the bloated bureaucratic faff-factory whence they came. Never happen though. Far too sensible an idea, as Crump well knew.

He now had an appointment with Mx Kim Vyshinsky, Head of the Department of Politics and Governance.

Due to his Foreign Office experience, Crump would be doing some politics teaching on top of his English Studies classes. He was happy to be flexible, and the variety of teaching would stave off boredom: that was the theory, at least.

Crump didn't know if Mx Vyshinsky was a man or a woman, on account of the 'Mx' neologistic honorific which was developed specifically so as not to indicate gender, and the fact that Kim could be a name used by both sexes. The department website photo didn't help either, as Mx Vyshinsky had one of those faces that could have been either male or female, and the smart suit dress in the website head and shoulders photo was unisex too.

He entered Mx Vyshinsky's office when instructed to do so by the efficient-looking secretary Miss Nip.

The besuited Head of Department was standing still by the window with her (or his?) back to Crump.

Crump did a little brittle cough, just so Mx Vyshinsky would know he'd arrived.

"Errr, it's Kevin Crump here for the appointment."

Silence.

The office was spartan, very Art Deco in design with one or two ornaments of the period on shelves, together with a great many books. Crump could read the titles on the spines from where he stood – lots of heavy volumes about the Soviet Union, and its threesome of heroes: Lenin, Engels and Karl Marx. Bronze busts of all three, as well as other comrades Crump did not recognise, sat on the bookshelves.

"Good afternoon, Mr Crump," said a deep female (or was it male?) voice. "Sit, please."

Crump did so. The man/woman standing by the window still had his/her back to him.

There was a slight scent in the air – something flowery – though behind it there was a heavy tinge of tobacco, more cigar then cigarette, Crump could tell. His eyes wandered to an open packet of cigarillos on the desk. How on earth did she/he get away with smoking in a university office? Smoking was banned inside all buildings and discouraged even outside on campus (vaping preferred). A miserable little pagoda was available by the bins for the nicotine-addicted to huddle under when it was raining. And yet, Mx Vyshinsky smoked – and in this very office, if Crump's nostrils were telling the truth.

Just then, Mx Kim Vyshinsky turned round to face – or, rather, look down on – Kevin Crump. She was dressed in a grey collarless suit, almost in the manner of Joseph Stalin, or maybe Kim Jong-un? Crump still wasn't sure if a man or a woman stood before him.

"Have you ever heard of the Democratic Republic of Moronia?"

Crump scrunched his eyes up in thought. Geography was not his strong point.

"Errr... yes..." he lied.

"Do you know, per chance, where it is situated?"

"Somewhere in Europe?" he proffered. "East-ish...?"

"Correct!" said Mx Vyshinsky, "Bravo! Most people haven't got a clue. Moronia is indeed 'to the east'. More specifically it borders Ukraine and Romania, was a bloody massacre sandwich between the Nazis and Soviets in

World War Two, and is home to many ethnic groups who generally hate each other. It is, moreover, the poorest country in Europe."

"Oh," said Crump, who thought that was Albania. Times change, obviously.

Kim Vyshinsky was standing statue-still, staring unblinkingly at him, in a way that felt a little 'Hannibal-Lecter-y'. Crump felt his blood pressure rise.

"We have a contract," she/he announced, "with the government of the Democratic Republic of Moronia."

Crump didn't know what to say, so just said:

"Yay!"

He immediately regretted it. Mx Vyshinsky was no Tanya Snuggs.

She sat down on the hard, wooden chair by the desk, pulled a brown cardboard file out of a drawer and handed it to Crump.

"This is for you, Mr Crump," she/he said.

Crump took the file. He half-expected it to be labelled 'TOP SECRET', and to be told this was his mission, if he chose to accept it.

He opened the file. There was a fact sheet about Moronia, a booklet about the place, and then a register of names.

"They are your new students here at the Department of Politics and Governance. It's perfectly logical. You've worked at the heart of government, in the Foreign Office — "

"Oh well, I wouldn't say that really, I was just a — "

"You know how capitalist government works. Therefore, logically, you are the perfect candidate to teach a class from the Democratic Republic of Moronia about our political system, and improve their English at the same time, of course – which is your academic specialism, I believe?"

"Yes, that's right. My degree is in English, but…"

"They're waiting for you now, in classroom 34G."

"Oh, but I haven't prepared anything or—"

"Share your knowledge, Mr Crump, of the Western capitalist system."

Crump stared into the steely eyes of Mx Kim Vyshinsky, still unsure of his or her or its gender. Maybe it was an 'it' – a sexless robot – an academic android, all efficient and logical and immortal, forged in some top-secret lab from the best Soviet steel, sometime during the Cold War?

Mx Vyshinsky stood up and turned round to stare out of the window at the logical clouds floating by in the rational sky.

"I think we understand each other, Mr Crump. Do not let me down."

Crump left without a word and made his way to classroom 34G.

*

"Moronia is land of contrasts," said a tall, athletically built man who introduced himself as Marek. "We have mountain, we have river and lake, we have forest and farming land—"

"Oh well, thank you for educating me about Moronia—"

"*Democratic Republic* of Moronia," said Marek with what Crump could only call an enchanting smile.

"Oh, of course, I didn't mean to—"

"Since many years before, Communist Russians fuck off. Before, was Soviet Union…"

Several students mimed spitting at the floor, which caused a couple of others to mutter darkly to themselves.

"Yes, well…"

Another student raised his voice at Marek – speaking, Crump recognised, Russian – and Marek argued back

65

in Russian too. He heard the name 'Vladimir' in the otherwise-unintelligible dialogue.

"You can sit down now, Marek, thank you."

He sat down and some fellow students applauded, though others in the class of twenty-five sat with arms tightly folded and scowls on their faces.

"So, what is the biggest export of... the Democratic Republic of Moronia?" asked Crump.

"Prostitutes," piped up a woman who introduced herself as Oksana.

"No, seriously," smiled Crump at the joke.

It wasn't a joke.

"Is true," said Oksana and all members of the class nodded, shrugged and muttered in agreement.

"Oh," said Crump, embarrassed – he was aware he was beginning to blush.

"Moronia is farming country, not modern like UK," said another student called Svetlana. "People is very poor."

"Is tragedy," said a stern-looking bearded student called Zoltan, pronouncing the word with a hard 'g', as in Russian. "In my village, many young woman going in Germany and other place to prostitute..."

"Errr... OK..." said Crump, thinking perhaps this was not the best time to inform Zoltan and the others that even though one could 'prostitute oneself', as perhaps he himself was doing teaching in this university when he should have been back in his Foreign Office job in London, one could not really say that prostitutes 'prostitute' for a living – though goodness knows why not. It would have been a perfectly logical and no doubt useful English usage.

"They must to sending money back to home village," said a thin young man who introduced himself as Tomek Glusky.

"I see, yes, lots people have to move to other countries to work. Many come to the UK from all over Europe and the world, and many British people go abroad to live, too, of course. A few years ago, I myself went abroad to work."

"As prostitute?" grinned Marek, and Crump couldn't help himself laughing along with the class. "I only joking."

Crump looked deep into the Moronian's dark, friendly, intelligent eyes and was aware he was blushing more now.

Marek was, without doubt, just about the most handsome man Crump had ever met – but not in any kind of 'gay' way. No, Marek was more like a masculine ideal, an impressively built man, a superman of sorts, supremely confident and relaxed in his manhood, sure of his proper place in the world, and utterly comfortable in his own skin. Crump wanted to love him and be him, all at the same time. In the Stone Age and the imagined lands of pre-history, he would have been the tribal leader, the Alpha Male, the top dog, the ancestor of us all. Or, in the relatively modern political age, he could have been history's first known ruler Sargon of Akkad in the third millennium BC, or one of the great kings or emperors or caesars of history. One of the born leaders in life, inspiring others to do their best, as if by magic, through the pure lure of charisma.

"I don't think I would have earned very much as a… well… 'escort', but then again, I certainly wasn't earning very much as an English teacher."

Oksana interrupted:

"My cousin is prostitute in Germania, and she is earn with one fuck what she can to make in factory in my country in two week… maybe three."

Crump was taken aback by the open admission an extended family member was in the 'oldest profession', but chose to focus on the linguistic issue instead.

"Yes, err, if I can just say the… 'F word'…"

"Fuck!"

"Yes, that one… Well, it's a—"

"Is international word, yes?"

"Yes, everybody knows the... errr... 'F-word'... all over the world, but please... it's a swear word so not polite to use in general conversation – in class, for example."

"But why?" asked Tomek.

"Just... because..." said Crump, to audible muttering and whispers – it was clear some more able students were translating for others.

"OK," said Marek with his wide smile again. "Continue, please, teacher."

"OK, student..." said Crump, as he always did when anyone addressed him as 'teacher'.

"I sorry, *Kev-een*," said Marek, smiling.

It didn't matter how many times he asked everyone to call him Crump, these students persisted in calling him Kevin, or the Moronian-accented version of it anyway.

"So, there are many different peoples in your country, I think," said Crump.

"But why peoples?" asked Svetlana. "My English teacher say we must to say 'people' not 'peoples'..."

"Ah, yes, usually, that's true, in most everyday usage, but I refer to different ethnic groups, as in 'the peoples of the world'..."

Svetlana frowned, looked in her dictionary and muttered something under her breath.

Marek stood up again:

"In my country, we have many ethnic group. We have Moronian Cyrillic, Romanian, Ukrainian, Hungarian, Russian—"

At this point a couple of students boo-ed, only for a couple of others to shout back rudely at them.

"Fuck Russian pigs!" growled a dark, thick-set student called Taras.

'Probably a Cossack', thought Crump, with his extensive knowledge of Cossack names gained from watching epic early 1960s movie *Taras Bulba* starring Yul

Brynner on telly one rainy Sunday afternoon when he was about eleven years old.

"Please!" asked Crump, holding a hand up. "Let Marek speak."

"Bulgarian, Czech, Slovak, Polish, Belarussian, Kazak, Tatar, Cossack, German—"

More boos.

"Many gypsy but not many Jew – they all are killed by German Nazi pig and also Russian Communist pig—"

More shouting and yelling across the class.

Crump waited for silence. It'd take him a while to learn all the names – Taras, Tomek, Artur, Magda, Martina, Olga and the rest – but, apart from the many ancient ethnic and tribal hatreds between them, the students seemed to rub along rather well together, all things considered.

"Thank you all for introducing me to your country – I shall do my best to learn more as we proceed with lessons every week. I think we'll stop there for today."

Marek started clapping and indicated for others to join in. It was quite possibly the best round of applause Crump had ever received from a class. In fact, it was the only round of applause he'd ever received from a class – but the best, too. He was aware that he was blushing again.

As he was packing his bag and preparing to leave, Marek approached him and put a hand on his shoulder.

"You good teacher, Kev-een. I am like you," he said.

"Well, thank you, Marek. But maybe you mean 'I like you' not 'I *am* like you'?"

"Maybe," said Marek through his wide confident smile.

*

"Where's your car to?" asked Dylan, rushing up to Crump as he made his way to the university car park.

"Highlands, where I live."

"Oh, bummer," said Dylan. "I was off surfing."

"You go surfing? Really?"

"Nah, I just watch, and smoke – I got some surfer mates, kindathing, into it big time."

Crump wasn't at all surprised.

"Well, happy surfing," he smiled.

"YOLO," shrugged Dylan. "Laters."

Crump pulled his car keys out of his pocket, and with them the scrap of paper on which he'd written down Mrs Trichobezoar's number. He called her on his smartphone before setting off.

"Oh I am so *heppy*!" said Mrs Trichobezoar, her accent perhaps Germanic or something more exotic, Crump thought – Hungarian maybe, or something else Eastern Europe-y exotic and unusual.

"I recently saw a cat that looked like Nelson, on the poster, but not the other two."

"Awww, poor Napoleon and Charlemagne," said the old lady's voice, weakly. "Is my Nelson here?"

"No, sorry, I just saw him – I didn't actually catch him."

"Please, if you see again, you take him and bring to me, yes?"

"Errr… well, I could try," said Crump, adding: "He looked perfectly healthy though, just so you know – he ran off very quickly — "

"I pay you reward!"

"Oh, no need for that, Mrs Tricho… If I see him again, I'll try and keep him here, somehow, then call you – how's that?"

"Yes, you call me. I pay you," said Mrs Trichobezoar, ringing off.

After a quick shower at home, Crump was out again, this time to the care home where his mum now lived.

He'd have to get some food on the way back from there – his cupboard was literally bare and the fridge too, though at least it was working when Crump plugged it in. No-one had been living in his mum's house for many months, and the whole place smelt stale and dank. The kettle had so much fur in it that it resembled an inside-out cat. Time for a good spring clean at the weekend when he had more time – open some windows, let the cold autumn air in, bring the place back to life.

He'd unpacked some of his own stuff earlier, books especially, and also some of the ornaments and things that had been boxed up before his mum had gone into care. There were so many cardboard boxes stacked in every room that the place looked like a warehouse.

The ceramic ornaments, mostly figurines of animals, made the house more homely somehow, sitting on various windowsills and shelves and surfaces, even though they weren't really to his taste.

"Mum," said Crump, quietly.

He was in the day room of the large care home in the east of The Town, sitting at a table with his elderly mother, who seemed to be staring into space.

She looked frailer than he remembered – smaller too, as if she'd shrunk since their last meeting.

Being an English language specialist, Crump couldn't help remembering that the verb 'to shrink' was ultimately derived from the Old Norse/Icelandic word '*skrukka*' meaning something like 'wrinkled old woman'. But he cursed his brain for forcing that etymology into his thoughts at that particular time and place. It was not welcome, so Crump shooed the linguistic intellectual intrusion away.

"Mum?" said Kevin again, then once more, much louder – he knew her ears weren't what they used to be, even with a hearing aid:

"*Mum?*"

His mum looked up at him weakly, squinting through her failing eyesight at her son.

"Kevin!" she said, in her stroke-slurred speech.

Her quiet eyes smiled as she recognised him. She kissed his hand.

Crump leant over and kissed his mum on the cheek. It felt cold and dry as rice paper, and looked almost translucent too, as if the old woman was fading away into a transparent nothingness. Maybe that's what happened when you got old? He reminded himself that it was the lucky ones who got to reach this over-eighty stage of life.

The care home staff were clearing the plates away, as the residents had just finished dinner. Crump noticed a lot of food left on his mum's plate.

"Did you enjoy your tea?" he asked.

His mum nodded and squeezed his hand.

"No, thank you, not really," she said.

"D'you want a pud, Margaret?" asked a staff member, loudly, and then to Crump: "I'm Claire, by the way."

His mum shook her head weakly.

"Maybe later, is it, sweetheart?" said Claire, loudly.

His mum shrugged.

Crump told his mum about how he was now teaching at the local Cambrian University. He had told her before – in a phone message passed via care home staff, and also by letter. But she seemed surprised, as if this was the first time he'd mentioned it. The stroke must have affected short-term memory, he supposed.

"That's nice," his mum said in a small, fragile voice. "Your dad would be so proud."

She squeezed his hand in her own little child-like hand, and kissed it.

"I'm in your old house now, tidying up…"

His mum nodded and smiled another weak smile. He could tell she'd rather be at home than in that care home, even though it was a good one, with private rooms for each resident, and regular activities. The food didn't look half bad either.

"Tea or coffee, sweetheart?" asked Claire and she trundled the trolley into the day room. "You have one too, Kev. Milk and sugar?"

"No sugar, just milk, thanks," said Crump, deciding not to make an issue of her using the detested diminutive of his Christian name.

"Just like Mam, eh?" said Claire, and his mum smiled at that.

It was strange, but Crump did not know what to talk about with his mum. He couldn't exactly talk more about his boring job or the university, and he didn't want to moan about how he'd lost his Foreign Office job really, or his ex-girlfriend, whom his mum had never even met anyway. Was his life really so empty and boring that he was stuck for words, talking to perhaps the only person who really knew him, the mother who had given him life and brought him up?

It was like a story he heard about John Lennon and Paul McCartney meeting up, with Yoko and Linda in tow, in the late seventies in New York. After an hour or two of reminiscences and nostalgia, they quite literally had nothing to say to each other. How insane was that? And oh, how sad…

His mum was, he realised with a twinge of sadness, the only person he knew now who really remembered him as a boy from early childhood, and who also remembered his father. They'd had no extended family where he'd been brought up, and the couple of cousins he had in Wales had only known him as an adult. The older ones who'd known him as a kid had all died off.

"Oh, I had a lovely dream last night," his mum said, at last.

"Did you?" asked Crump. "What was it about?"

"We were having a birthday party in the back garden for you…"

Crump remembered the way his mum had organised birthday parties for him – the last when he was around nine, he thought.

No expensive tents or marquees or hired clowns and entertainers in those days for kids' birthday parties, thank goodness, and no expensive show-offy parents trying to outdo each other with pricey gift bags for every child. No parental paranoia either or helicopter mums hanging around to protect their 'cotton wool kids' from the multiple dangers that the scaremongering media told them were waiting in an unsafe world to hurt and abuse their precious darlings.

Just sitting on the lawn playing party games in the sunshine – that was what Crump remembered. Musical chairs, on cushions outdoors, with his mum tuning the transistor radio to a music station and turning it on and off. And pass the parcel, but not the *all must have prizes* version they do these days where no child is ever allowed to fail or lose – no, only one winner in the old days.

"I used to love those parties," said Crump, and his mum squeezed his hand tightly, as if she hoped that by doing so, she may be able to melt into the past somehow, go back to the way things were, decades ago, and get better.

After tea and biscuits, Crump helped his mum with her stick, back to her room. He told her he loved her and kissed her goodnight.

Claire the carer said his mum slept a lot these days – up to twelve hours a night. How different from the way she used to be, never going to sleep until midnight or 1am yet up for 7am the next morning always: that was what Crump remembered from his school days when his mum acted as his alarm clock, in the days when he always wanted to lie in. These days, apparently, his mum rarely got up before nine.

Crump knew there was nothing he could do. It was just age and the effects of the stroke. At least the care home was pleasant, and his mum could still see and hear and walk, though did all three with difficulty. She was making the best of her senescence.

But the body fails, no matter what we do. And the brain too eventually. It gets us all in the end, if we are lucky to live long enough. Though Crump thanked goodness his mum was not suffering the ravages of dementia as so many of her age do, as they outlive their lives in their final, long, unremembering days. That was a blessing, at least.

He left his mum reading the obituary page of the local paper, with a lighted magnifier, no doubt keen to see how many of her old friends had departed the world that week.

As Crump exited the building and walked to his car, he felt like crying. He swallowed down the sadness, and carried on, just as his mum had done during every difficulty – just as she had taught him to do. That stiff-upper-lip stoicism was rare in this always-emoting, feelings-obsessed snowflake-y age, but Crump knew it was the right thing – the best way to live.

He remembered his mum always getting cross when people started crying on TV programmes. "Bah!" she used to say. "Feeble!" Or, "They're just showing off!" In these psychobabble days, that approach tended to be seen as lacking empathy or somehow being unsympathetic. But the real older generation had lived through war and poverty and hardship that today's sixty- and seventy-something baby-boomer blubbers, wokeling snowflakes and millennials, all the Generation X, Y and Zedders – Genzennials – could not imagine, so Crump was with his mum on this. It was a shame stoicism was not a national trend really.

He parked near the parade of shops in Highlands and got some fish and chips, after a quick supermarket shop for essentials. He really couldn't be bothered to cook that night, though he had promised himself he wouldn't eat takeaways much any more – he did need to lose some weight and get fitter. But fish and chips now and again was fine – and it was always a great meal, though hardly cheap these days.

Lovely crunchy chips with a centre like a cloud – that's what he loved – and cod cooked to perfection in crisp golden batter. Yum! Just, YUM! The chips were the thing, though. No wonder the British built the biggest empire the world had ever seen. With a national cuisine like that, how could you possibly fail? How could any foreign power, all those potential enemies who envied you, not submit? *Give in to the chip!* You know you want to.

It was as he was driving the short distance home past the parade of shops in Highlands that he saw it. A young-ish man came out of a local café and threw a bucket of water over a homeless person sitting on the pavement, begging.

Crump could hardly stop in the middle of traffic and remonstrate, but he did stare at the man who'd done it. He caught Crump's eye and grinned nastily.

The homeless man, meanwhile, struggled to his feet and shuffled off, carrying a plastic bag which no doubt contained all his worldly belongings. Crump noted that he was a white man too, as were the vast majority of homeless people. So much for 'white male privilege'…

At home, Crump put the wrapped cod and chips in the oven to keep warm, then had a long relaxing bath. He needed it.

Just as he was getting out, there was a loud knock at the front door.

"Oh bugger!" said Crump to himself, rubbing a towel over his wet hair and donning his dressing gown. "Coming!" he shouted downstairs.

He opened the front door to see two police officers standing before him – though as he wasn't wearing his glasses, the world was something of a blur.

"Yes?" he said.

"Can we come in?" said the female officer, in a monotone voice.

"I suppose," said Crump, opening the door wider. "What's this about? I've just had a bath—"

"We can see that," snapped the male officer, curtly.

Crump closed the front door then led them into the living room.

"I'm PC Christopher Cockwomble and this is WPC Jade Tugswell, of the Cambrian Police," said the officer, in what Crump recognised as a strong Valleys accent.

"Oh and I'm Crump, Kevin Crump."

"Yes, we know," said the WPC, rudely.

"Errr… is there a problem?" continued Crump, baffled.

He was dripping onto the carpet and water was trickling down from his hair onto his face and neck. He gave his hair a good rub with the towel, only just managing to stop his dressing gown flapping open to display his nakedness to the local constabulary. He didn't want to risk a charge of indecent exposure, though he was sure no local plods would be that petty. *Or would they?*

"Pigs," said PC Cockwomble, stone-faced. "You like pigs, do you, Mr Crump?"

Crump wasn't sure what to say.

"Well, errr, they're alright… bit of a nasty one in the university zoo, mind, but—"

"Are you aware of the Public Order Act 1986, sir?" said WPC Tugswell.

"Errr… well—"

"Section 4 of the aforementioned act states that it is an offence for a person to use threatening, abusive or insulting words or behaviour that causes, or is likely to cause, another person harassment and distress."

Crump nodded and frowned at the same time, wracking his brains to try and think when he had ever said anything threatening or abusive to anyone, though his academic brain immediately flagged up the fact that whether words or behaviour were 'insulting' was as much in the subjective eye and ear of the beholder as whether words or actions were 'offensive'.

"Hate crime is a very serious matter," continued the thick-necked PC Christopher Cockwomble.

"*Hate crime?*" squinted Crump, even more baffled now.

"The Racial and Religious Hatred act 2006 made it an offence to incite hatred against a person or persons on the grounds of their religion, sir."

"Sorry," said Crump, getting annoyed now, "but what has all this got to do with me?"

He was getting cold and was still dripping bath water onto the carpet. And he wanted his fish and chips. *Now!*

"Pigs," said PC Cockwomble, "on the windowsill."

Crump followed the officer's gaze to his mother's ceramic animal ornaments that he had arranged on the windowsill the previous evening. Some were of pigs, though there were horses, sheep, owls, foxes, dogs and cats too. But pigs predominated, it was true.

"Oh, they're my mum's ornaments," said Crump, matter-of-fact.

"They could cause offence to certain faith communities, sir," snapped WPC Tugswell.

Crump chortled a laugh. The police officers did not laugh. Crump rubbed his hair with the towel.

"They're ceramic pigs – so what?"

"*So what*, sir?" said WPC Tugswell, narrowing her eyes at him.

"They can be seen from the street —"

"Well, the front window does look onto the street – amazingly – what with the house having been built on a street."

"Put them away – the pig ones anyway," ordered PC Christopher Cockwomble.

"Is this a joke?" said Crump, raising his voice slightly. "They're ornaments! Harmless ceramic—"

"We'll decide if they're harmless, or if they are inciting hatred against a religious group, and thus constitute a hate crime, for which you could be prosecuted, sir."

"Ceramic pig ornaments on a windowsill are a hate crime? Oh *purlease!*"

"You need to check your thinking," ordered WPC Tugswell.

"I could make your life very difficult," said PC Cockwomble in a dark whisper.

Then, leaning in close to Crump and staring him hard in the eye, he said:

"Take. Them. Down."

"OK," said Crump, feeling suddenly very vulnerable where he stood cold and naked under the dressing gown in his own home before two law-enforcers in uniform who could, he knew, arrest him for being in possession of ceramic pigs on a whim and make him spend a night in the cells, even if he would, he was sure, be released without charge.

"We'll check back late, sir," stated the WPC as the officers left. "I'm recording this as a non-crime hate incident."

Crump closed the door behind them and leant against it.

"Bloody hell," he mouthed to himself, wondering what on earth had happened to the country he had grown up in.

What made it worse was the fact he knew that, if he needed the police, because of a burglary or theft, they'd take hours to come round, if they bothered at all – usually they just gave people a crime number for the insurance these days.

'We're now living in a land where a pizza will arrive at your home before the police when you really need them,' he thought, as he picked up his mum's much-loved ceramic pig ornaments, one by one, from the windowsill. Then he began wrapping them carefully in newspaper before placing back in the cardboard box he'd liberated them from less than twenty-four hours earlier.

"Sorry," said Crump as he stored the ornaments away, "poor little pigs…"

Poor pigs indeed.

CHAPTER THREE

Coming Out

"I don't want to pee on your sugar sandwich," said a Danish student called Mads.

"Don't want to *what*?" smiled Crump. He was in the middle of teaching his first English class to foreign students at Cambrian University.

"Oh, it's what we are saying in Denmark, it means something like, 'I don't want to spoil or... ruin... your fun.'"

Another Scandinavian student nodded in agreement.

"Well, thank you, Mads – I shall add that brilliant idiom to my burgeoning collection."

Crump was about to continue the discussion on food when a student called out:

"British food is shit!"

It was Jordi from Spain – though he identified as Catalan and was happy to express hatred of España at any given opportunity.

"Really shit!" said Heiner from Germany (or was it Austria?).

"Total shit!" said Valentina from Russia, and she mimed puking under the desk complete with *Exorcist*-style vomit-y sound effects.

Crump was used to this blatant anti-British racism from foreign students as he had heard it so many times before, so he knew these students would never even have tried most traditional British dishes, or even basic things such as the vast variety of UK cheeses on offer. People from most countries really were conservative with cuisine and just stuck with what they knew, like the worst of Brits abroad.

He politely chose *not* to point out that the world hardly seemed full of German (Austrian?), Russian or even Spanish restaurants – most in Britain were Italian, French, Indian, Chinese, and American/British.

"And what British dishes have you tried then – anyone?"

"Fish and chips," said a short-statured Italian boy called Massimo.

That was it.

"I must admit," said Crump, "that because British people are so open-minded, a lot of the food we eat these days is very international – which does not mean Brits don't like their own wonderful, traditional dishes, such as Lancashire hotpot, shepherd's pie, toad in the hole—"

"Toad is like frog, yes?" asked Valentina, in a low whisper.

"*Mein Gott in Himmel*," said Heiner.

"*Crapaud? Mon dieu*," gasped a French girl called Julie.

"*Ella malaka!*" said a Greek boy called Costas who, like the others, did not seem to realise that Crump, and many other Brits, had a smattering of foreign languages so could understand every single word, especially the sweary and dirty ones – and especially as Crump had lived and taught English in Greece...

"Not *real* toads – it's traditional British sausages, baked in sort of Yorkshire pudding batter – lovely served with onion gravy. You should try it before judging."

The class stared at him suspiciously, as though he were pushing drugs.

"Of course, British sausages are the best in the world…" said Crump with a smile, awaiting the predictable outrage.

"No, German!"

"Russian!"

"Spanish chorizo!"

"Italian salami!"

"French is best!"

If teaching a class of foreign students English did one thing, it showed you in stark living colour how people's loyalty was always to their countries, and if not to nations first, then to regions, and that was the foundation on which they built their identity. No matter what anyone claimed, nobody was really loyal to the EU as an entity, as people had been loyal to the British Empire, the Roman Empire, and even the Soviet Union. The EU was an empire in theory, and maybe even in practice, but certainly not on an emotional level. Nobody's chest heaved or heart fluttered at the sight of the blue and starry EU flag, not unless they had angina, or needed a stent fitted in a cardiac artery. Just watch World Cup football to witness how loyalty to the nation state is still what thumped proudly in the hearts of humanity.

"Then there's steak and kidney pudding, lots of different kinds of pies, pasties and puddings, savoury and sweet," continued Crump. "Good hearty winter food is British cuisine."

"And fish? Why you not eat fish here?" said Jordi.

"*H-yes! H-why?*" demanded Jesus, another Spanish student. "*In-errr E-Spain*, we eating too many errr-fishes."

"Also in Catalonia," insisted Jordi.

The two students exchanged something that sounded like snide insults so Crump raised his voice to quell the Iberian civil war:

"Well we do eat fish, but not as much as our island status might suggest, and nowhere near as much as in Shakespeare's day, when a quarter of calories people consumed apparently came from it. More industrial societies prefer meat, traditionally, so maybe that's why. Less industrial or pre-industrial societies eat less meat so, I suppose, more fish. The French call us *rosbif* because back then, beef-eating Brits were eating at least twice the amount of meat as Napoleon's troops, who had to make do with bread and cheese, which is a meat substitute, I suppose."

"If I am see food, I eat it," said Nikos, a baby-faced Greek boy who must have weighed at least twenty stone.

Everybody laughed – nicely – at, or with, him for being such a good sport about his obesity, though Crump always felt uncomfortable if students had to mock themselves in that manner. It was a defence response really – those who were different getting the attacks first, before anybody else could. It was defusing a bomb before it was hurled in their direction, making the bully laugh to disarm him or her. He could never be really sure if the smiling students who did that were smiling or crying inside. It was the fat equivalent of camp humour, perhaps…

"And fish in shells," said Jordi.

"Shellfish, well yes, this area is in fact famous for cockles – lovely in a traditional Welsh breakfast with oatmeal, bacon and laverbread, which is seaweed, and the same type as they use in the Far East…"

The shy Japanese and South Korean students smiled proudly.

"… though there it's dried in sheets and here it's boiled for hours, which is typical Welsh. You can buy it in the covered market. Even my mum likes them in a Welsh breakfast and she usually hates seafood. Locally caught fish are sold at the market too – like *sewin*, which is sea trout, and hake and coley and…"

Crump realised he was waffling on and veering off his lesson plan, but then this was only an introductory class so they could all get to know each other. He had already done what he always did in first lessons and gone through the university's regulations and its eternally expanding universe of equal opportunities and diversity policies.

"I stay with family and all they are eating is frozen pizza and 'ready meal'," said an Italian girl called Giulia.

"Well, yes, and that's a shame."

"Italians eat Italian food," she continued. "It is *autentico*, how you say?"

"Authentic," said Mads, "but where are Italian tomatoes coming from?

"*Italia*," said Giulia, falling right into the trap.

"Originally?" continued Mads.

"*Italia*." repeated Giulia, confused. "Eh?"

"They from South America," smiled Ahmed, an Arabic-speaking student.

"Indeed, they are, Ahmed," said Crump, "and chillies are from Central America originally too, so any Indian or Chinese food with chillies is not *really* authentic either then, is it?"

"And potatoes," said Valentina.

"So yes, basically, there is no such thing as authentic, is there? Everything's a mash-up, as the kids say these days."

"In England, you are always eat mash potato —"

"Maybe, but we're not in England, we're in Wales —"

"In Wales, people is eating kebab, every day," said Rashid. "I working in takeaway."

"Now, you see, that is what's known as 'confirmation bias'," said Crump. "Maybe the people who tend to go to kebab shops eat more kebabs?"

"And people is always drunk, every day," said Rashid, shaking his head.

"Is true!" said Ahmed, laughing. "I am also working in take-away."

"In my country, no alcohol," continued Rashid.

"No alcohol in Muslim country – official story," said a bearded Arab student called Mohammed through a wry smile, and all the Muslim men shared a conspiratorial snigger.

"Well in northern Europe, people do tend to go out to get drunk, yes, though the British aren't any worse than anyone else. I think the French consume more alcohol than us actually, but mostly at home and with meals."

A hand went up.

"Yes, go on," Crump smiled at Fanny, a girl from South Korea, delighted one of the usually mute Southeast Asian class members was volunteering to speak.

"Why women in your country cannot to cook?"

"Is true!" said a student with a headscarf called Aisha.

The whole class seemed in agreement – many of them lived with host families or had had the experience before, when at summer schools in the UK.

"It's probably true that in the UK, girls don't learn to cook from their mothers and grandmothers as in many more traditional countries," Crump explained. "But Britain was the first industrial country – in fact Wales was the first nation in the world where more people worked in industry than on the land. The world's first-ever train journey happened right here in South Wales too."

"Was it delayed?" said a Flemish-Belgian student called Koen.

"No, it was cancelled!" said Nygren, a tall blond Swede.

"Leaf on the line!" shouted someone, mimicking an announcer.

The class fell about laughing.

"British women, if they are not cooking, why they are so fat!" said Pakey, a young South Asian student.

"Because they always drunk and eating kebab!" laughed Rashid.

"Maybe they'd be less overweight if they are learning how to cook," suggested Birgitte, another Dane.

"I like to cook," said Mads.

"I like cooking too!" said Crump, insisting on using the more traditional gerund rather than the more American infinitive which now seemed to have successfully mounted a linguistic invasion of Britain. "Nothing fancy, though, and only when I have time."

The Scandinavians and north Europeans in the class nodded and smiled.

Those from southern climes, or from outside Europe, however, giggled and shook their heads, the women included.

"In my country," said Aisha, "only women are cooking and looking after childrens..."

"If man work, then woman care for house and cooking, this is fair," said Pakey.

"In my country, if a man he is cooking, we say he is... like this... *fi-fi shi-shi*..." said Mohammed, swaying and waving around his limp wrist in a theatrically camp manner.

"I don't know why," said Crump, primed for a wind-up, "men don't cook with their penises, do they?"

The Japanese girl Yuki giggled and covered her mouth with her hand. But most of the other female students were giggling too, and a few of the more enlightened males.

"Maybe in his country," said Koen, which led to angry shouts in various languages which were probably better left untranslated.

"And now is *trans-sexiness* week at university, yes?" asked Ahmed.

"Transphobia Awareness Week," corrected Crump.

The Muslim students looked at each other with nasty smiles and shook their heads incredulously.

"So what is man, and what is woman?" asked Ahmed.

Rashid, Mohammed, Aisha and Pakey all nodded and shrugged.

"Well, I suppose, women don't have penises," said Crump, embarrassed but determined to deal with the question, "and if it's got a penis and testicles, which are the *test* – the proof – of being male, which is where the word ultimately comes from, then it's a man."

"It is like this, yes!" grinned Ahmed.

"But then some believe you can choose your gender, and it is of course wrong to bully, insult or abuse anyone, or discriminate against them, even if we happen to disagree —"

"In your country," interrupted Mohammed, "you get girlfriend, you having sex, you having childrens, and then after maybe you getting married, and then after, you getting divorce. What is point?"

"Yes, is crazy – what is point?" repeated Rashid.

"No idea," said Crump. "I've never been married and don't have any children, so I'm probably not the best person to ask."

"You are a gay, yes?" said Valentina. "Like all Englishman – I see on TV."

"No – no, I'm not gay," said Crump, "but would it matter, if I were?"

"Maybe for your wife…"

Crump didn't know what to say to that or the giggles from some students.

"But you have been having sex, yes?" asked Bjorn.

Crump couldn't stop himself from blushing.

"Ummm, well, yes, but it's a rather personal question and not one we'd usually ask strangers in English."

"But you is so old…" said Pakey.

"Erm, thanks for that —"

"So old, and with no childrens," said Aisha.

"Empty branch!" called out Chang, a Hong Kong Chinese student – it was the first words he had ever heard spoken in class.

Koen put his hand up.

"Yes," said Crump, pointing at the Belgian.

"Can we learn some English now, please?"

*

"Happy One-ness Day! Yay!" said Tanya Snuggs at the English Studies Department meeting.

"Yay!" everyone said, though Crump only mouthed it – he was sick of 'yays'.

"Different but the same, the same but different, all together as one, differently, to all *intensive purposes*."

"We're all individuals," mumbled Crump.

"Actually, I'm a real team player – ask anyone, Kevin – I ain't never been *ego-testicle*."

"There's no 'I' in 'team'," parroted Crump.

Tanya grinned her big gap-toothed grin.

'No,' Crump thought whenever he heard that oft-repeated team-building mantra, 'but there is sometimes a "u" in "c—'

"Come on, people!" bubbled an ebullient Tanya Snuggs, all at one with One-ness. "Always best to be part of the team, innit? Yay!"

"Yay!" responded everyone, though as Crump repeated the meaningless word, he wondered whether that included Hitler's team, or Stalin's. Pol Pott's, perhaps? Chairman Mao's? Kim Jong-un's?

"We can all be the same in many ways, yet unique and different too," proffered Hilary Squonk, department dialect expert, "just like snowflakes."

"Snowflakes?"

"The cold and wintery sort, not the, y'know, human variety according to the derogatory insult recently coined by rabid reactionaries to describe tolerant and empathetic young persons."

"Do you want to *interjaculate* something, Kevin?" asked Tanya Snuggs.

"Oh… no," said Crump, shaking his head.

"Because I don't want to go off *on a tandem*, not now, what with the new inclusive *diversificated* syllabus for

English literature which is out today. Yay!"

The roomful of lecturers yay-ed, though Crump remained yay-less.

He was fed up enough what with having no proper desk or place to sit, and having to hot desk it from here to there depending on whichever senior academic entered the team room. He saw nothing to celebrate in his present situation.

"So, the new list has been designed specifically to cleanse the syllabus of racist imperialist bias and white male privilege —"

"To redress the balance of a patriarchal misogynistic society," added Melanie Spunch. "Dead white men have been clogging up reading lists and dominating the syllabus with their Eurocentric toxic masculinity for decades."

"Totally," said Tanya Snuggs, "we gotta get rid of anything that could be, like, potentially offensive, innit?"

"Not to mention the unconscious bias that women and people of colour have to suffer day in day out from privileged white males, the offensive stereotypes, the microaggressions —"

"It's all about equality, diversity and inclusion, and fair representation," added Hilary Squonk.

'So not about exposing students to the greatest literature in existence, if it happens to have been written by nasty-wasty white men?' thought Crump, but he said nothing – it just wasn't worth the aggro.

Crump knew what this was all about. This utterly anti-literary tosh was now mainstream, and practised in every higher education institution in the land, a result of pc tutors' obsession with 'decolonising' the curriculum. He thought the argument that every text on a syllabus had to be 'relevant' was total tosh too – and racist and sexist. Anyone of any race or gender or nationality could surely appreciate great work of literature. The idea that a black student, say, could only appreciate or 'get' a novel or play or poem if it featured people who looked exactly like them was: one, spuriously simplistic; two, insultingly racist to those readers in its assumptions; and three, just plain wrong. And yet this idea was now mainstream in all schools, colleges and universities. If Crump didn't realise it before, now he did: he was part of an academy that was rotting from within.

He'd heard about the censoring taking place to avoid ever causing offence or trauma or 'triggering' to the delicate cotton-wool kids of Generation Snowflake, to create 'a culture of safety' in this New Puritan Age. Upsetting the hyper-sensitive members of Generation Blub had to be avoided at all times – a culture of safety had to protect these vulnerable cry-babies from hurt and harm, just in case they were 'triggered' by being exposed to the real world, with all its messy violence and complex problems and pain.

Exam boards had removed 'upsetting' things from syllabuses to avoid causing students 'undue distress', such as studies on suicide from Psychology A-level curricula; books branded as being 'offensive' had been removed from libraries (though Crump was still awaiting a full list to be emailed to him) or, at the very least, came flagged with a 'trigger warning'.

Even famous films and songs had been banned if the pc politburo decided they were racist, sexist, misogynistic, transphobia, Islamophobic or able to offend or trigger an audience in any way. Songs such as *Delilah* by local Welsh hero Tom Jones were banned on account of the alleged promotion of domestic violence; *Baby It's Cold Outside* was cited as a pretty little ditty about date rape that thus had to be silenced forever; *When a Man Loves a Woman* was disgustingly transphobic and hetero-centric. Moreover, *Snow White and the Seven Dwarfs* was banned for the obvious offence it could cause amongst various assorted homunculi and midgets of the vertically challenged community, and even *Schindler's List* was banned on some campuses for promoting Zionism.

Somewhat absurdly, all works by the Bauhaus architect Gropius had been banned and removed from shelves, just in case his name triggered anyone who had ever been 'groped'.

It was a tyranny of 'wokeness', the silent surrender of hard-fought values like free speech, and one Crump could never agree with, though he said nothing. Fascism does tend to have a silencing effect on people, especially when they are made aware of the unfortunate consequences of honest and free debate.

The first sentence students should hear at a university, in Crump's view, should be as follows: 'Welcome to a liberal education where you will be exposed to many things which will anger, upset, offend, distress and infuriate you.'

But the dull thud of conformity drowned out any criticism, so censorship of books and topics because 'they might cause some people offence' was now rooted so deeply in universities, like some giant poisonous weed, that it overshadowed everything else that tried to breathe or live.

Crump could not get a copy of *The Great Gatsby* from the library, and now, it seemed, most dead white men had been culled from the curriculum too, all in the cause of 'equality' and 'gender balance'.

So, it was out with Shakespeare – though Crump had taught with some female lecturers who insisted he was, in fact, a woman, or even intersex – and out with the other nasty DWM (dead white men) too: Chaucer, Keats, Shelley, Wordsworth, Coleridge, Byron, Blake, Dickens et al. And it was *in* with literature by female and BAME authors instead.

But even Agatha Christie and PG Wodehouse were banned on account of the glut of upper-class men and subservient women in the woke-less, pre-progressive pages of their *class*-ceiling-ed classics.

Everyone belonged to the great club of suffering these days, except white men, who were always and forever seen as *the enemy* according to the 'new normal', and responsible for all that was, is and will ever be bad in this wicked willy-waggling world.

"Isn't that a bit limiting?" said Crump, quietly, as he read through the diverse new curriculum booklist, bulging with novels and poetry by women, and the Asian, African and Caribbean diaspora. He couldn't help it: the truth forced itself out like a fart.

Shabs, the resident departmental rap lecturer, and official 'Creative Diversity Champion', sucked the air through his teeth and shook his dreadlocked head.

"Limiting?" said Tanya Snuggs, unusually unsmilingly. "I think that must be a *pigment* of your imagination, Kevin. How can diversity be limiting? It's *diversity*! Yay!"

'Oh, not again,' groaned Crump, inwardly.

The notion that diversity – by which they always meant racial, skin colour and gender diversity only, never diversity of opinion or experience, or even social class and background – was intrinsically good, and so any diverse team of candidate chosen by committee for their diverse surface features would, in itself, be effective and successful simply because of that race/sex diversity. This was a myth now rooted so deep in modern media and political culture that it was never ever even challenged. As if a diverse multi-racial multi-gender team of aeroplane pilots would automatically be better, because of their diversity, than an all-white and all-male better-qualified and more experienced crew. What mattered, surely, was selection based on merit, irrespective of an individual's skin colour or gender? Sadly, any university staff member brave enough to state a 'common sense' view like that ran the risk of getting themselves suspended, or even sacked, for not abiding by the university diversity and inclusion policy. The phrase '*common sense*' was also frowned upon, as being dangerously patriarchal and imperialistic.

The same applied to all levels of all jobs and careers, thought Crump, and he could see the evidence all around him in the over-promoted mediocrities who climbed to the top of academia, using their 'diversity' to leapfrog over arguably perhaps more able candidates, constantly defining themselves via their race, disability or gender to get ahead. After all, the three top people at Cambrian University were a transwoman (i.e. a man in a dress), an Asian woman who had leapfrogged over many more qualified and experienced people to occupy her role, and a man with such a bad case of Tourette's he rarely appeared in public, though he'd had a massive sweary hand in boosting the disability representation in senior management.

"The older traditional curriculum promoted the white male supremacist establishment and the phallocentric Western paradigm whose aim is, and always has been, to marginalise invisible minorities and promote inequality based on race, gender and sexuality," lectured Melanie Spunch, on message and ticking more boxes than Tesco's.

"Research shows that *real-world harms* are caused by gender stereotyping," added Hilary Squonk, though Crump wondered about how much confirmation bias there had been in that supposed research and who had done it.

'*Real-world harms*' – what a ridiculous, not to mention illiterate, phrase, Crump thought. And since when was the word 'harm' a countable noun? It was an unnecessary new phrase and one that stank of the think tank.

These days, a giant leap had been made from certain books, films, online content or adverts being considered potentially offensive and hurtful to certain people, especially those from minority groups, for racist or sexist reasons, to a matter-of-fact statement that such things could actually *harm* people, mentally, emotionally, morally, maybe even physically – like real-world abuse. It was a hell of a leap, and one used to justify the banning of anything anyone claimed may cause 'harm' to anyone – ever. It was a kind of cultural health and safety gone stark raving mad.

Being upset or offended by something may cause hurt, but it cannot and will not cause permanent *harm* – as real mental, emotional, physical or sexual abuse can. The claim that it could was beyond offensive – although massively offensive to human intelligence. And yet this nonsense was now generally accepted as fact by those in charge of education as well as governmental policy-makers, and even prime ministers talked darkly of 'online harms' and how to prevent them. It was a world turned infantile and self-pitying, exaggerating personal hurt for effect and to ban and silence anything anyone happened to find unpleasant. It was a deeply sinister development.

"People of colour and women and the differently abled need to see themselves in literature, to make it relevant, innit?" said Tanya Snuggs. "So let's get a hustle on! Happy One-ness Day everyone! Yay!"

Crump did get a hustle on – he hustled himself out of the English Studies team room in search of a working toilet, which was easier said than done on the campus of Cambrian University.

He knew the men's toilets in the English Studies block were out of order, so set off in search of relief in departments hitherto unexplored.

Crump wandered down corridors of the main building first. He saw several toilets for women, but none for men. He was just about to try looking on various floors in The Learning Tower when something caught his eye: a mural which stretched several metres down a corridor of the History Department.

It was a mural of the First World War and showed soldiers following each other back from the front line –

reminiscent of the famous painting '*Gassed*' by John Singer Sargent which Crump had seen on a visit to the Imperial War Museum in London some years earlier.

However, this scene was different. Gone was the all-male all-white parade of soldiers, their eyes blinded by mustard gas and bandaged, each with an arm on the man in front as they shuffled along, surrounded on all sides by other injured soldiers.

No, this mural was a spurious 'woked' 'alternative history' showing a line of injured soldiers, more than half of whom were female, with black and Asian troops amongst them too. Of course, soldiers of the British Empire fought in World War I and II, but they would be in separate battalions of, say the West Indian or various Indian regiments, often reflecting religious affiliation. They would not make up 20% of the Welsh Guards, for sure, and it was an incontrovertible fact that WWI troops were 100% male, with no female soldiers amongst them – though these days 3% of soldiers were women. The mural he was looking at, open-mouthed, was a specious gender and colour-blind version of history cleansed of its truth, however un-diverse-ly male-dominated and white-skinned that reality actually was. It was a long egregious lie in paint, rather badly done too, and Crump wondered if students – and even staff – would now believe this is what a First World War battlefield actually looked like.

History history history.

History keeps repeating itself.

This time it was perhaps Stalin's doctoring of photos to 'vanish' people who had fallen out of favour, simply 'disappear' them from recorded history, which was the precursor to the 'woke' tragi-comic lie of this WWI image on the wall. The instinct was certainly the same, as was perhaps the intention – to mislead, to deceive, to hide the truth, and inculcate instead a 'correct', factually incorrect version of history in the populace.

The mural had been commissioned after a visit to the university a couple of years previously by the TV historian Dr Winnie Sheard CBE, who had condemned the 'hideously white male' artworks and statues to be seen around The Town. As a consequence, the mural was commissioned and several statues of 'Dead White Men', such as those who had founded the many industrial works locally, making copper, iron, zinc and much else besides for the whole country and, indeed, the world, had been taken down and relegated to out-of-the-way positions in the less salubrious local parks, or else put into storage at the museum.

Moreover, the council had announced jointly with the university and museum authorities, that only statues of women and ethnic minorities would ever be erected in future, and that strenuous efforts would be made to remove as many paintings by and of white males from display as possible, and replace them with artwork by and of women and 'people of colour' (but not the Teletubbies, presumably). *This was true equality in action!*

The claim had no doubt been made by the usual campaigners that to have a mural of white males only in the First World War would be offensively non-diverse and may well trigger some students to be upset, traumatised and psychologically harmed by such a realistic depiction, which may well threaten their well-being and mean the university was failing in its duty of care to students and staff.

How ironic, thought Crump. 'Shell shock' – now known as PTSD (Post-Traumatic Stress Disorder) – was first documented in the First World War, where soldiers (all male) developed the neurological, mental condition as a result of genuinely harrowing traumatic experiences in the trenches. Soldiers returning home may later be 'triggered' by a car backfiring or other sudden loud noises, getting flashbacks to the hell of Flanders fields, reliving traumatic events. How obscene that the word 'triggering' had now been appropriated by the present generation, and university management, in order to describe the reaction that any trivial and non-life-threatening artefact or material deemed 'offensive' may have on any student, if they claimed as much. It was nothing less than an insult to the dead and the genuinely traumatised and damaged people of the past, but typical of the new Snowflake Century where craving offence was a competitive sport in a Victim Olympics that had no closing ceremony yet scheduled.

It was all rather like the campaign to remove statues of 'dead white men' such as Cecil Rhodes because of the Oxford donor's supposed links with the slave trade. The 'hideously white' statue remains, but with an apologist plaque now on display beneath it.

Crump also wondered what pc expressions and beliefs of now would be seen as 'offensive' and morally wrong in fifty or a hundred years, if humanity survived that long. The thought never seemed to occur to the noisy activists getting het up about statues of those whose beliefs of almost two centuries ago did not mirror the morally acceptable values of now.

Interestingly, too, many protestors against the Rhodes statue were from families from the often-corrupt South African elite and at one of the world's most elite universities, with their studies paid for by the ill-gotten gains of their wealthy well-connected parents. South Africa is the most unequal country in the world, with 1% of the population owning 70% of the wealth. Those 'woke' students wanting to topple the Cecil Rhodes statue were usually from that 1% – the black South African ANC elite. Or else, from the privately educated white and minority ethnic native British virtue-signalling Social Justice Warrior (SJW) elite.

A plaque below the Great War mural stated that it was unveiled by the Equalities Minister in the Welsh Assembly

Government in 2015, the centenary of the founding of the Welsh Guards, though one imagines the dead from World War One may well be spinning in their graves at the historical absurdity on display.

Maybe that was the humming sound Crump kept hearing everywhere in the university buildings? More likely, though, it was caused by the calamitous electrics and lack of maintenance thereof, which seemed to be at crisis level. But why? Surely the university could afford a competent maintenance crew?

Crump eventually found a functioning men's toilet in The Learning Tower, though he had to climb up to the Theology and Philosophy Department on the eighth floor to find one. The lifts were 'out of order' – again – and though usually Crump wouldn't have minded climbing the stairs for the extra exercise, doing so when he was busting for a wee was not a comfortable experience.

When he finally found the eighth-floor men's toilet, he stood at the urinal relieving himself with an exquisitely eye-rolling and toe-curling sigh of relief which almost made the prelude of pain and desperation worthwhile.

Of course, he could have risked it and gone into one of the many female toilets he passed on his toilet-searching travels. But could he really risk it, at that university? All it would take would be an allegation from a 'triggered' woman (staff or student) who objected to his using a cubicle reserved for 'those identifying as females', and he'd have a lot of explaining to do. Of course, if he donned a frock and claimed to be a woman like the Vice-Chancellor, he'd have been able to use the women's toilet without problem, and probably get offered a promotion too…

"Damn it!" shouted Crump as the water squirted from the tap onto his groin area as he washed his hands.

All he had done was turn the tap gently and the water had spurted out like champagne from a shaken bottle.

Now it looked like he had wet himself, no matter how much he tried to dry his groin area with paper towels – which then, predictably, ran out.

It seemed that today Crump had finally met his *watery-loo*...

Just as he was leaving the eighth floor to make his way down the stairs, he heard something that sounded like a speech coming from one of the offices. He edged along the corridor towards the voice, and was soon standing by the half-open door of the one where the sound was coming from.

"God does not want everybody to be rich and successful, of course, or a talented award-winning writer such as I. That would be absurd, wouldn't it? We need people to be cleaners, waiters and waitresses, shop assistants, carers, bus drivers, labourers, call centre operatives, and to do all the lowly dirty jobs out there. There is honour and glory in work, even on minimum wage. But just because God has given you no discernible talent, it does *not* mean you are worthless and not loved. Remember that God loves you, even if you are poor and talentless. That is the true diversity of creation. Acceptance is all – there is a reason for every life, however poor and apparently pointless, even if we cannot clearly see it. That is the true mystery of His will. God loves you, so praise Him and be thankful. Amen."

Crump looked up to see Pete Parzival at his shoulder.

"OMG. That's Ridley Crick, the author," he whispered, "recording his *Thinking Today* broadcast for BBC Radio 4. A nice little earner, no doubt."

Crump had heard it once or twice, but it was usually on too early for him, and so unbearably smug and sanctimonious he turned the radio off, or over to a music station, as soon as he realised what he was listening too.

Ridley Crick was a Senior Lecturer in Theology at Cambrian University, though was seemingly often off in Africa 'spreading the word', and plugging his own books, of course. They didn't question things there as they did here – which was probably why the continent was so popular with white privileged Christians, no doubt, tired and weary of the relentless scepticism of post-Enlightenment Europe, especially irreligious Britain.

Just then, a door opened and two men proceeded to march down the corridor arguing loudly.

"Androo Spoon, Humanist lecturer, and Saladin Malik, resident imam and Islamic scholar," whispered Pete Parzival, pretending to read a noticeboard as they passed by.

The door to Ridley Crick's office slammed shut, no doubt to silence the sound of theological argument.

They made their way to the stairwell.

On the next floor down, Pete paused.

"This is Professor Pip Pooman's domain," he whispered.

Crump remembered that from the tour of the library with the cock-faced Dr Tomos Splodge.

Pete Parzival lifted a finger to his lips.

"Shhh!" he shooshed.

They entered the seventh-floor corridor. The lights were flickering badly, as in many university buildings, making the whole place seem eerie. It was like a set from a horror movie.

The stench of chemicals hit Crump first. Formaldehyde and other things.

The two walked as quietly as they could down the corridor.

A door was ajar.

And Crump could definitely hear sounds – of *animals*? At least it sounded like that…

"There there," came a voice. "Won't be long now… Splendid!"

Then a definite whimpering bark which had to be a dog, and then some cat sounds – pathetic weak miaows, more like yowls really.

Suddenly, Pip Pooman appeared on the corridor. He stared suspiciously at the two eavesdroppers.

"We were just trying to find the... lifts," said Pete.

"We're... a bit lost," said Crump, but he could tell the Manager of Managing Fairness Fairly knew he was lying.

"Lost, are we?"

The two men nodded and shuffled on their feet like guilty schoolboys.

"The lifts..."

"Out of order," boomed Professor Pooman, "as per usual. Use the stairs! Young men like you should be fit enough."

"OMG. Good idea," said Pete Parzival.

Crump nodded and smiled weakly.

"Splendid!" snapped Pip Pooman, before retreating into his laboratory and slamming the door with a scowl.

*

"Happy One-ness Day, kindathing," yawned Dylan.

"Yay," groaned Crump, wearily, sitting next to him on some steps.

"Most def," said Dylan.

"Is that even English?"

"Whatever – it's *my* English, yeah?"

"Most *definitely* it is, young man," said Crump, sending himself up as the traditionalist schoolmaster.

At least the weather was fine – with sunshine occasionally blinking through the clouds of a mild day in early autumn.

"Had an accident?" asked Dylan, looking at the wet patch on his groin.

"I had to walk miles to find a functioning men's toilet. The plumbing in this place is as bad as the electrics. Why can't maintenance sort it out?"

"Doubt it. The new maintenance department is all-female."

"What?

"Yeah, Mr Scumble and Dean Guttery would've got it well sorted," said Dylan. "Now look at 'em."

The two drunks were swigging cans on the grass verge by the university entrance in the distance.

"Where's the other one – Jim…?"

"Jim Slingsby," said Dylan. "Up in the hospital, like – walked in front of a minibus, 'pparently smashed up bad – loadsa broken bones, kindathing."

Crump sighed sadly. "I understand the good intentions behind the university quota for 50% of academic staff to be women, at all levels, but—"

"A hundred per cent of the maintenance crew must be female now, they said. Couldn't find enough qualified ones, so they're training beginners up…"

In that very instant, it all became clear, like muddy clouds clearing to leave a limpid pool of perception. The flickering lights, the naff plumbing, the broken doors with handles that came off in your hand, the inexplicable and ubiquitous electric hum – it all stood logically explained. It was all because people had not been appointed on *merit* in the maintenance department, but instead because of some absurd gender *quota* which neither reflected reality, career choices or, arguably, innate and unchangeable aptitudes typical of males and females.

Just then, a celebrity walked into view. Crump recognised her from a TV show – and, to be frank, you couldn't really miss her.

Because Kylie Kalamazoo looked just like a golliwog. She had very black skin, and big hair which stuck up as though she'd had an electric shock.

Crump remembered that this was some mad German model woman who had been giving herself melanin injections to make her skin permanently black, because that is how she self-identified. He thought at the time that this was but a logical conclusion of the absurdity of the principle of self-definition, whereby if someone says they're black, then they are – the ideology now accepted by many race and equality campaigners. The same self-definition had now stepped sideways to the wonderful world of gender too. So, if he so wished, Crump could claim to be a black woman and could demand that he was respected as such, despite looking physically like a white ginger-haired bloke. Such was the surreal absurdity when one overdosed on diversity doughnuts…

Apparently, Kylie Kalamazoo was a special guest of the Shirley Bassey Diversity and Inclusion Re-education Centre for that year's One-ness Day.

Students were clamouring to take selfies with this fake black woman.

It used to be *'I am what I am'* with Shirley Bassey; now it was *'You're not who we want you to be'* – or, maybe, *'I'm not who I want to be, so I'll choose a race and gender from the pc diversity menu and start again'*. Though that didn't really have the same poppy ring to it.

"Did you know that more people are killed every year taking selfies than in shark attacks, kindathing," drawled Dylan through a yawn.

It didn't surprise Crump at all.

Suddenly, a squeal of tyres pierced the tired silence as a minibus, and one with a bad dent on its front bumper, skidded and swayed round the corner and screeched to a sudden halt, right next to the sign that said TAXI, and above it, TACSI, just in case native Welsh speakers didn't understand the English.

"Lucy Skidmore, in charge of university drivers and vehicles," sighed Dylan.

An obese, very masculine-looking woman with a shaven head got out of the minibus – though on the passenger side. Crump heard a little tinkle. Was she holding *a handbell*?

Then a man got out of the right-hand driver's side of the vehicle – he was wearing dark glasses and holding a white stick.

"For heaven's sake, no!" gasped Crump, open-mouthed. "I mean... a blind driver is *totally* insane!"

Dylan shrugged. "It's uni inclusion policy – no job or role should be denied to anyone with any disability."

"But... how?"

"The navigator in the passenger seat rings the little bell, kindathing, once for go, twice for stop, three times for left, four times for right..."

"And five times for OH MY GOD *WE'RE GOING TO CRASH AND DIE?*" said Crump.

Dylan giggled.

"YOLO," he smiled. "BOOM!"

Crump shook his head in disbelief. He had seen and heard of all sorts of nonsense done in the name of diversity. He had even almost had a car crash once because of a driver wearing a burqa, who obviously had a restricted view, so pulled out into the right-hand lane of a dual carriageway without warning, forcing Crump to brake hard so the van behind almost ploughed into him. But this – this was special, and especially nuts.

Needless to say, anyone – student or staff – who dared go against the university's diversity and inclusion policy, for example, by saying the process of halal meat preparation was disgusting and an example of animal cruelty, or that burqas should be banned, or that perhaps it was not such a great idea to employ blind people to drive minibuses, could be suspended from the university for 'failing to abide by our diversity policy' or 'bringing the university into disrepute' and forced to successfully complete diversity training and to sign a 'conduct agreement' silencing freedom of speech and expression – which, in itself, went against the EU and UN Conventions on Human Rights.

Thus, everyone kept their mouths shut and went along with the absurdity for purely selfish reasons of self-preservation. All it needs is for people to be silent…

"Dylan?" asked Crump.

"Yep," said Dylan, looking younger than ever.

"You've been here a while, as a student and now postgrad and working for the uni too…"

"My bad," said Dylan.

"How do you… deal with it? All the pc lunacy and diversity quotas and the rest… You're always so… relaxed…"

Dylan smiled dopily.

"It's all about acceptance – *Zen*, innit – realising life is but a dream within a dream, so you just have to go with the flow…"

Crump nodded and smiled a smile of fake equanimity.

"That, and smoking huge quantities of cannabis resin."

In front of them, across the university concourse, the celebrations of One-ness Day continued, with flags of all aspects of identity politics fluttering merrily in the autumn breeze, including lots of blue starry EU flags. The university buildings also had these on flagpoles, as well the obligatory signs celebrating 'European Union Funding' for various projects. There was a Union Jack, and a few Welsh Dragon flags too.

All the usual identities were represented – all BAME ethnicities, faith groups, every sexuality group you could think of, plus of course the non-binary ones and the transmen and transwomen on the pansexual spectrum.

Crump also saw a banner for BMER. He had to ask someone what that was: 'Black and Minority Ethnic and Refugee'. Would this acronym replace BAME? As BAME and 'people of colour' had replaced 'ethnic minority', and 'coloured'? As 'mixed-race' had replaced 'half-caste' but which was now being replaced by 'dual heritage'? How people fussed so much about the nomenclature of race and identity! How ready they were to condemn those in the past who used words now considered offensive and insulting! And how ignorant they all were to think that the presently accepted terms would always remain so and not, as surely would happen, become the focus of disdain and condemnation themselves in future as the decades dragged self-righteously by.

As per usual, the TERF protesters were out and proud as well, holding a huge banner which read:

A PENIS IS NEVER A FEMALE ORGAN

Crump could only agree with that really. It was just common sense, surely? Though there was precious little of that in these genderfluid days.

Several police were there again too, in rainbow flags and pink helmets, enjoying dancing with the pretty student girls and boys, and smiling a lot. It was really great that so few crimes, such as theft or burglary or violent attacks, were being committed in The Town these days, which left the police with plenty of time on their hands to party with the local diverse community. *Hoorah!*

The Student Union was out in force, as usual, its three elected university representatives giving speeches on a podium, all of which seemed to start with the word 'so'.

"So, we've got to be different but the same, individuals as one, yeah?" pleaded Olivia Octothorp, the very posh-sounding pretty blonde English student who was SU President (elected, or rather, selected from an all-female shortlist).

"So, let's hear you, people, celebrating transgender students, all faiths, especially Muslims who have to fight Islamophobia, yeah? *Diolch yn fawr!*" yelled spotty Welsh student and joint Deputy SU President Aled Rantallion with a whoop. "And big it up for the innocent Palestinians who suffer under the Jew Nazi regime in the illegal Apartheid State of Israel..."

Boos and jeers from the young GenZennial crowd.

"So, yeah, equality for everyone, coz we're, like, the same, differently... diversity in unity, yeah, coz it's, like, so cool..." mumbled Londoner and joint Deputy SU President, access and liberation officer, and anti-oppresion educator, Shelley Shunk.

Into this throng of youth and one-ness marched a woman who had more facial piercings than Crump had ever seen on anyone, wearing some sort of punk garb made of black plastic and maybe leather, and with an electric blue Mohican haircut, with the rest of her head shaved. She seemed somehow to be buzzing with anger – her facial expression certainly seemed to be perpetually screaming pure fury at the world for reasons best known to herself.

"Abi Rainbow, University Women's Officer," said Dylan. "She's the one who accused Jim Slingsby."

"Seriously?" Crump interrupted.

"Best not to get on the wrong side of her, kindathing," warned Dylan. "She's accused loads of men of sexual assaults and rape and stuff. It's, like, her hobby —"

"Her *hobby?*" said Crump. "Whatever happened to stamp collecting?"

Suddenly, the intimidating, angry-looking intersectionalist feminist Abi Rainbow climbed onto the podium and grabbed the microphone from the Student Union Officer speaking.

Somebody made the mistake of booing.

"You!" screamed Abi Rainbow at the offender – a young male student. "Mind rapist Nazi of the misogynistic patriarchy of rape culture, toxic masculinity and phallocentric hegemony!"

As slogans went, it didn't really have the same ring to it as, well, any famous slogans – it was pure gender studies jargon, the sort which may well get you extra marks in sociology essays, but nothing more than extra yawns at demonstrations.

"I've been putting up with rapist abuser men like you all my life!" screeched Abi Rainbow, her face contorted into a pierced mask of sheer hate, topped by that blue Mohican haircut that made her resemble nothing so much as an angry parrot.

"We don't want you in our beautiful area, or at our diverse and inclusive tolerant university – you *rapist!*"

The young man was stunned by the attack on him, and was soon seen to slink off and leave, to a chorus of jeers and boos from more enlightened, tolerant students.

"One-ness Day means we must become one, by excluding anyone – any *man* – who refuses to accept the new feminist gender dialectic," she continued.

Crump always mistrusted anyone who used the word 'dialectic' with a straight face…

"No more *mansplaining*! No more *manspreading!*" ranted on Abi Rainbow. "No more patriarchal males pushing their vile white supremacist agenda, a form of oppression which intersects with all gender and ethnicity identities, and aims to marginalise minorities and promote inequalities based on gender, race and sexuality!"

Cheers from some; bafflement from others; indifference from most there who chatted quietly while licking ice-creams in the intermittent sunshine or snacked on crisps or sipped from canned drinks of various kinds.

Suddenly, Crump sensed Dylan tense up. He turned round to look at him. His eyes were fixed on a thin female figure walking slowly and methodically across the concourse.

As she drew closer, Crump could see her face, which had a cold, blank, emotionless expression fixed on it. The long black hair and sharp features made her look rather witch-y, as did her long black dress.

Crump recognised her from the Cambrian University Prospectus – this was Lesley Snyde, in charge of PR and marketing. Why would the usually half-comatose Dylan be so anxious and fearful at the sight of her?

He turned back towards Dylan to ask him as much, but he was gone.

There was no sign of him when Crump scanned the faces of the crowd. But he did see Fatima, who was just leaving a university building.

He'd had more than enough of listening to semi-literate students playing politics and a screeching, shrieking mad middle-aged woman with a ridiculous blue Mohican haircut and enough metal pierced and studded into her scowling face to make her a serious risk to innocent magnets.

"Fancy a coffee?" he asked Fatima.

"Why not?" she smiled – and it was a warm, friendly smile. Or maybe it was something more? "I hate these modern Western feminists – they're the worst role models, for sure."

Crump was surprised. He knew Fatima was a feminist, so assumed there'd be some sort of solidarity between various sisterhood groups.

"The focus of feminism used to be equality – equal opportunity for women and men, not claiming women and men were the same, that they couldn't be different in talents, or that they couldn't flirt – this is normal, *non*? This is the natural human life of love and sex…"

Crump felt himself blush like a bashful schoolboy at the mention of the word 'sex', so he just nodded and said nothing, for fear of making his embarrassment worse. Thankfully, Fatima had not seen the massive damp patch on his groin either.

"No, these feminists shifted focus from equality – because in the West, they have it, mostly, and sometimes it is men who are treated less equally, as in family law…"

She still pronounced 'law' as *'low'*. Crump loved Fatima for her wonderful sultry French accent, her wit, her intelligence, her courage, her looks – the lot.

"So these feminists, they have cultivated the victimhood only, always playing victim and saying men are to blame, and this it has made the movement toxic. And…"

Crump was happy to let Fatima speak. He loved the soft, smooth tones of her exotic voice curling their vowels deep into his open ears.

"… and they always turn blind eyes to what Muslim men are doing, and to Muslim women who are suffering much oppression and not just in the Muslim countries, in the UK too, and Europe. I hate this! This is hypocrisy, and not equality!"

Crump nodded – he loved Fatima's passion, her commitment to justice, her courage to mention such unmentionables…

"But these feminists who want to be victims are only attacking white men from the West – who are the most tolerant men of all, mostly – and in USA and here they are claiming, if a man looks at you or touches your knee, then he is rapist and guilty of the sexual assault! *Zut alors!*"

Crump imagined himself saying the same. Though if he was overheard at the university and reported, by any student or staff member who took offence, he'd no doubt be hauled before the equality enforcers and forced to endure diversity training to 'correct' his Islamophobic views. But what Fatima was saying was true – he knew it was true, and if other people were honest with themselves, they knew it too.

Sure, it was probably a cultural and social class thing as much as religious, but many Muslims in the UK did force their daughters into marriage at a very young age, often to an older first cousin, and then did expect them to perform the role of baby-making machine in between cooking duties in the kitchen all day long.

Yet how many times had Crump heard feminists even mildly criticise those responsible for these things? Never. And there was barely a squeak from any feminist organisations over the decade or more that Muslim Asian gangs in English cities had groomed and gang-raped young white girls as young as eleven either. Though, in their defence, it seemed a blind eye was turned by councils, the local media, the police and teachers too. It was wilful blindness of shocking proportions. And maybe it was still going on.

"I have to go," said Fatima, "lecture…"

Crump stood. Fatima grinned. She'd seen the damp patch on his groin.

"Oh, what has happened? You are wet!"

Crump blushed as he bade farewell to Fatima, more awkwardly than he would have liked. It was way too early for even an attempted kiss of friendship, he thought, though he knew that she, unlike British females trained to see rape-y shapes in the clouds, would not be offended or scream 'sexual assault' if he had leant forward to give her a peck on the cheek.

*

Crump did some work hot-desking it in the English Studies department and got some much-needed photocopying done for lessons later in the week.

'Ah, the photocopy – the comfort blanket of every teacher. How I've missed you!' thought Crump as the machine whirred and clunked its copies into the tray.

It was slow, but at least it worked. If it packed up, it would probably never get mended, knowing the present non-maintaining state of the university's maintenance department. But then, he could always go back to chalk and talk, in a way so many university teachers, who'd never really taught at the coalface, as Crump had done overseas, would be able to cope with.

Crump left his car in the university car park and set off on the half a mile or so walk to the town centre from the campus. The weather was fine and he could do with the exercise.

He strolled through the park where the university farm was situated, past the quacking ducks on the pond and the exotic caged chickens of multiple colours. He peered into Sandra the pig's enclosure. The damn animal was there, smugly turning her surly sow face to him, as near to smiling as porcine anatomy would allow. Crump's hand was still sore where she'd bit it, but no more than that – the antiseptic cream had done its job. How could they let that malicious and monstrous piggy thing give kiddies rides in the Summer? It was an accident waiting to happen.

"Pork chops!" declared Crump to Sandra the pig, just because he felt like it. "With English mustard – in Wales. Or apple sauce. Yum yum yum!"

An observing mother quickly hurried her worried-looking children away from the weirdo insulting a pig.

"Pervert!" she squealed.

The pig oinked loudly in what Crump heard as a laughing tone.

"Sausages!" he taunted, though Sandra kept on laughing. "And bacon!"

He was relieved to leave the park and the big pig it contained.

Walking through The Town, he realised that the last time he'd been to the shopping centre or round the shops was at least two or three years before, on a visit to see his mum.

He'd remembered coming here as a kid on holiday. In those far-off summer days of the 1980s, he remembered more shops open. Now lots were boarded up and/or empty or charity shops or pound shops or the inevitable barber shops that had bafflingly appeared in town and city centres in recent years, ever since it became fashionable for young men to have their hair styled weekly into a look that always reminded Crump of photos he'd seen of 'mental defectives' in the 1950s: shaved back and sides and pudding bowl tops – though now of course many had hipster beards to trim and style too.

When he visited as a kid, so many Welsh men had moustaches that you could be mistaken for thinking that you'd wandered into a Freddie Mercury convention if you walked through the centre of town. This was just the way the local area was slow to change, as boys copied their dads' shaving habits – a moustache proved you were a man back then in macho Welsh culture. It usually took fashions around fifteen years to travel up the M4 from London to South Wales, and so when they did, the moustaches were 'out', and now the hipster beards and 'mental defective' haircuts were 'in', a full decade or more after the fashion started in Shoreditch and Hoxton.

Crump also noticed how very *fat* people had become. That was never ever shown in artists' impressions of proposed new developments, of course – many which bore the placards boasting 'EU funding' with prominent blue starry flags – where the stick figures standing handsomely on spanking new concrete piazzas were all slim and pretty. The reality was the opposite – obesity seemed pretty standard in most of the population now. With two-thirds of Brits classed as officially obese, the UK was the fattest nation in Europe and third in the world behind the USA and Tonga in the international chubby charts. Bronze medal. Brown gold! Champions!

And you saw *seriously* obese people these days – Crump never remembered seeing anyone like that in his childhood. Some people were so massively fat they must have weighed thirty stone or more; people unable to walk because of their weight so who were using mobility vehicles; people weighing over fifty stone for whom specially converted ambulances were now being ordered by the NHS. They never showed them in artists' impressions for pretty new shopping centre developments, did they? That imagined world was always completely and defiantly slimline.

Crump wandered through The Town to the High Street. This run-down, ugsome, litter-strewn street, all boarded-up shops and closed-down pubs, was where his own grandparents had met while working in a shop as teenagers. The High Street was swanky back then, *the* place to go shopping, especially for clothes and fancy goods. Now look at it. It was merely an artery connecting the train station to The Town centre's main shopping areas, nothing more, and clogged with the accumulated failure of decades of neglect – though there were some pubs, restaurants and shops bravely trying to buck the trend. But why should people go there to shop, especially when they have online shopping and, in previous decades before the internet, shopping centres and out-of-town malls? It was the same in Crump's hometown of Durnford in north-west Kent, and in all high streets throughout Britain.

Some units were being converted into accommodation, mainly for students but also locals, especially childless singles and couples. Maybe that was the way forward – the future of these numerous town and city centres which all now had far too many shop units to fill, though for reasons best known to themselves, they were always building yet more retail developments.

Suddenly, a man fell out of an alleyway and puked at Crump's feet. Some of the watery yellow vomit splashed onto his shoes.

"Arghhhhhh… ." groaned the man, now prostrate on the broken and cracked High Street pavement. "Sorry, boy…"

The derelict man looked sounded younger than Crump, maybe in his thirties, but looked far older. Drugs or alcohol? It was usually one or the other or both, and often mental illness too, which led to such a destitute life of homelessness and despair.

And this man wasn't alone. As Crump approached the station, he noticed dozens of other street people – the vast majority white and male, with the occasional woman – huddling in doorways, sleeping in alleyways, or begging in front of boarded-up shops.

Crump walked to the station, pausing outside the building where his grandparents had met – or, rather, its replacement. The original handsome building had been replaced by an ugly, grey monstrosity in the 1950s. What damage the Luftwaffe did to the town centres of Britain, the town planners of the second half of the 20th century finished. And yet, these architects never seemed to live or work in the depressing, cheap and nasty concrete blocks that they actually designed and built. No, they were for the workers – the proletariat that they idealised and romanticised as much as any Soviet politburo member of the commissariat – who should be grateful for their gloriously grey and functional future, even as the privately educated millionaire architects who had erected this fresh hell of identikit tower blocks and faceless shopping centres spent their smug days in modernist mansions in Surrey and Islington.

As Crump walked back from the station towards the long-ruined castle and the city centre, he looked back. He imagined the High Street in its hay day, as he had never ever known it – back in the Edwardian era, or the 1920s and 1930s. He saw the ladies in their finery off to buy the latest fashions from the drapers or department stores or new elegant hats from the milliner, or the men in their suits and spats, off to work or accompanying their womenfolk, or the grafters fresh from the docks or industrial works in the pubs. Now all Crump heard was the ranting and yelling of homeless folk. He wondered what had happened in their lives to lead them there and why no-one seemed to be helping them, addressing their addictions or mental health issues. This state of affairs all seemed tolerated as 'the new normal'. That was wrong, somehow. Crump never ever remembered it being like this when he was younger. *We can do better than this, surely?*

Then he saw it. A police officer kicked a homeless man on the ground and spat at him. He was too far off for Crump to hear what he was saying to the collapsed figure on the ground, but he doubted he was enquiring about his welfare or health. A woman police officer helped her colleague drag the homeless man back off the street, and throw him into an alleyway, like a human bin bag full of rubbish.

Crump considered doing something – saying something. But soon the police were off, plodding back to their headquarters, laughing and joking with each other. And anyway, what if they turned on him? He'd heard stories about the Cambrian Police. And he also couldn't forget that they'd called round to his house to demand the removal of 'offensive' hateful ceramic pig ornaments from his windowsill in what could only be called a very brusque manner. He'd rather not get known by them, or risk arrest, not now he was teaching at the university – though he had done absolutely nothing wrong. He hated himself for turning a blind eye to it all – but he also knew that was what everyone did. Crump wondered if they hated themselves for it too.

He checked his emails on his smartphone – after noticing a sign, with an inevitable EU Funding blue starry flag on it, which boasted FREE WIFI. A quote from the 'Director of Futures and Clouds' declared that the council aimed to create 'an urban canopy of connectivity' in The Town. Handy for him, sure – but utterly irrelevant to those destitute homeless people who didn't know where they would spend the night or get their next meal.

It all reminded Crump of what he'd read about places like India, where the desperate poverty of 300 million people – a full quarter of the ever-increasing population, and ironically what the entire population was under the British Raj – existed side by side with millionaires and even billionaires who funded high-tech firms, IT company call centres, and the sending of satellites into space, not to forget nuclear technology. Had his country really become as divided as that? Or was it perhaps on the way to being so?

"Oi Crumpet!" shouted a voice as he made his way down the pedestrianised main shopping thoroughfare.

Crump knew an Estuary English accent when he heard one – the slow tonal twang of his youth, back in north-west Kent.

"I thought it was you!" grinned an overweight, besuited man with a friendly laugh.

"Tyler?" said Crump.

He recognised that cheeky smile from school – back in the days when teachers called grammar school boys by their surnames only, and so, often, did the pupils themselves.

"Rob Tyler?"

"The very same!" said Rob, giving Crump a manly pat on the back.

"Must be, what… twenty years?"

"More like twenty-five! You ain't changed a bit, Kev," chuckled Rob.

"Well…"

"Nah, only kidding – you've changed loads. But then, haven't we all? I'm a fat-arsed middle-aged bastard now, not a thrusting young whippersnapper, ha-ha!"

"*Tempus fugit*," said Crump.

Rob laughed.

"Bloody Latin, remember that?"

Crump did.

"You always was the clever one – intellectual – what with your book-learnin' an' all. S'pose we all had enough brains to get into the grammar school in the first place, but I was never like that..."

Crump smiled at the memories. Rob Tyler was always good fun at school, ever-cheerful and always joking – probably because he had simple tastes and never seemed to think too deeply. He hadn't changed.

"I'd bet my right bollock you work at the local uni. Am I right?"

"For my sins," sighed Crump, "though before that I was at the Foreign Office – "

"Bet you was a spy, eh? *'The name's Crump, Kevin Crump'*... Ha-ha!"

"Oh no, just training."

"Training spies, eh? Like M, or is it Q?"

"No, not really. So, what're you doing now, Rob?"

"After school, I got a job in the City, made meself a packet. Currencies. Derivatives. Futures. Usual bollocks. Financial crisis 2008, boo-hoo-hoo. Went my own way, blah blah. Now own properties all round London and in this backwater too – the ex-wife was from here, the mad Welsh bitch. Divorced. Two kids, grown-up. You got any?"

"Me? No – "

"Always knew you was a bender!"

"Oh, I'm not gay or – "

"Only kidding! Never saw you get a stiffie in the showers, eh? Ha-ha! Drink? On me."

"Yes, why not?"

Something about Rob's uncomplicated honest cheerfulness was just what he needed right now.

Also, he had a free morning the next day, which he had intended to spend reading the university handbook and all the email guff he'd been sent, as well as preparing future lessons. But he was more than prepared to exchange all that tedium for nursing his expected hangover instead. He remembered from teenage days that Rob was never one to have just the *one* can of Special Brew...

They went to a pub called The Coal Hole, which Crump had last been to a decade or so before.

As Rob was at the bar, Crump looked around the saloon. It hadn't changed, except for one noticeable thing. He always remembered old black-and-white photos on the wall here – of Welsh miners, with helmets on their heads, exhaustion in their eyes and coal dust blackening their faces as they emerged from their anthracite burrows underground, blinking alive in the wide daylight for the photographer's lens.

But now, they were gone. There were some replacements which showed industrial buildings, but there were more empty spaces on the walls, rectangles framed by the otherwise nicotine-discoloured wallpaper – memories of a time when smoking was allowed and almost compulsory in pubs.

Where were all the old photos of miners with faces blackened by coal dust, fresh from a shift at the pit?

Then, when Crump was on his way to the toilet, he saw a sign which explained all.

It stated that all photos of #blackface miners had been removed and destroyed throughout all public and private buildings in The Town, by order of the council, after a successful campaign by a 'woke' American #blacklivesmatter campaigner and Master's degree student at Cambrian University called *Rasheesh X+Y* – or, at least, that was the name he'd given himself after ditching his 'slave name'.

'How utterly ridiculous,' thought Crump as he watched his wee splash and gurgle into the urinal, though these days he was never really surprised at any absurd nonsense the diversity and equality industries could cobble together in their endless quest to see offence in everything. The world had gone mad.

Another sign, with a happy rainbow flag design, and a cartoon image of happy multicoloured faces, stated UNITY IN DIVERSITY and EVERYONE IS WELCOME.

'Not long-dead Welsh coal miners, though,' thought Crump as he zipped himself up.

He returned to the table to see Rob flicking through the notebook he'd left on the table.

"Do you mind?" said Crump, annoyed.

"Sorry, Kev, couldn't resist 'avin' a butcher's," and then Rob laughed a hearty laugh so loudly that a couple of other drinkers looked over.

"Something funny?" said Crump, taking a long satisfying glug from his cold pint of lager.

"Ching, Chung, Chong, Chang, Ying-Ying, Yo-Yo, and Yang-Yang?" Rob chortled. "What're you teaching – pandas?"

Crump rolled his eyes at the casual racism. He knew the Chinese students, who these days were all massive nationalists, were probably a lot more racist about him and white Westerners in general in their own language every day.

"Rob, please – they're my Chinese students –"

"*Ah so!*" Rob mimicked with a Chinese takeaway accent. "*Me love you long time!*"

Crump frowned and gave him a very hard look.

"Don't worry, Crumpet, I ain't no racist. Me, I love the Oriental girls. Japanese, Chinese, Thai 'specially – all better than British bints... Fanks but no fanks. I tells you, when you've tasted real quality Kobu steak you won't go back to economy beef burgers, thass for sure..."

"So, sexist as well as racist now then, are we, Rob?"

Rob sniggered like a schoolboy.

121

"Jeez, Kev, I hope you ain't turned into one of the dreaded wokie pc brigade thought police – can't say this, can't say that, this joke's offensive, so is that one, blah blah…"

"Hardly," said Crump.

"Listen, I live my life just the way I want. I'm stinking rich, own over thirty-five properties, divorced and over forty, so why shouldn't I have some fun, eh? Cheers!"

"Cheers!" said Crump, and they drank.

"Now if I was a woman and said the exact same *fing,* then the feminazis would all be praising me for being a strong, independent woman, eh? Getting what I want out of life – livin' it large on my own terms. But oh no, just coz I'm a man, living like that makes me a male chauvinist pig. Ha ha! Such femi-hypocrisy, innit?"

Crump couldn't really disagree with the observation. There did seem to be a great many such double standards in the gender debate.

"Listen, the vast majority of homeless people are men, most murder and violent crime victims, most suicides, and women get way more NHS funding than men, *and* men usually don't get any custody of their kids even if they want it shared, and loads get no access at all – but it's always pity party self-obsessed women moaning and whingeing saying #MeToo boo-hoo-hoo life's not fair? What a joke!"

"Bad divorce?" asked Crump.

"Could've been worse. Like any man of means I made sure I kept some of my plum assets tucked away from prying eyes, so when my bone idle ex, who's never worked a day in her entire bleedin' life by the way, got awarded enough money to keep her in luxury for the foreseeable, I made sure I had more. Natural justice, if you like. So then the bitch tries to turn the kids against me—"

"What happened?"

"Well, I asked myself this: do you want to be a daddy or a saddy?"

"A *saddy*?" Crump groaned. "That's not even English."

"Well, we are in Wales, *yucky da*! That means 'cheers' in the local lingo – the one what most locals can't speak. I nicked the *saddy* line from some crappy Hollywood movie or other… Cheers!"

"Cheers!"

They supped on their pints.

"Nah, I decided to be a responsible dad and pay for me kids' education, good schools and top universities eventually, and to establish and maintain contact with them. Thing is, they both liked me – David and Meghan, yeah, y'know, just like Harry's princess – and knew what a piece of work their mother was – and is. They got the other side of the story from me, not the Rob-hating version their twisted shithead mother tried to brainwash them with—"

"It's always a shame when splits aren't amicable," said Crump, not really wanting to get involved with somebody else's marital disharmony.

"When are they ever? Nah, my wife was very temperamental – half temper, half mental, ha-ha – and the kids knew that. David's working in finance in Singapore now – chip off the old. Meghan's in New York, fashion industry… doing brilliant."

"You must be very proud–"

"Oh yeah. It's kids, innit?"

Crump shrugged and nodded. Funny to think that his school-mate now had grown-up kids.

How on earth did I get so bloody old?

"I always think slugs are like snails who've been through a divorce, ha-ha!" laughed Rob. "But yours truly stayed a snail… You know I still feel like I'm thirteen or fourteen years old…"

"Really?"

"A *teeny* bit, anyway, Geddit? Ha-ha! There's a twenty, get the beers in – and vodka or tequila or sambucca, I call the shots!"

If Crump had spent the afternoon at the university, and not in the pub getting sloshed with Rob, he would no doubt have seen the urgent memo which informed him of an extraordinary meeting which was to take place in the Richard Burton Theatre that afternoon, at which the Vice-Chancellor was to make an extraordinary announcement:

"Yes, no, indeed, absolutely," said Angharad Ap Merrick through his/her beard, "Cambrian University's illustrious founder, Abstainando Jones, was keen to ensure that the independence of the institution he established lived on long after he himself had left us."

Pause.

Hush.

Complete and total silence in the auditorium.

"That is why, we are proud to announce, in these dark and dismal days of Brexit, yes, indeed, that we at Cambrian University are hereby asserting and declaring our full independence from the United Kingdom, and our continued membership of the European Union, as permitted by law with royal assent in our founding treaty, and the rights thereby afforded by that binding contract to those who are responsible for the continuing success of this great place of learning, our own beloved Cambrian University, for evermore – yes, no, indeed, absolutely. *Cymru am byth!*"

Huge cheering from the audience and wild celebrations. Those who had been campaigning for the UK to Remain in the EU and to block Brexit were ecstatic, and literally dancing in the aisles. Britain may well be transitioning with Brexit, but Cambrian University would stay intact and unchanged, an outlying Euro-enclave, loyal to the European Union and all it stood for.

"So let us go forward, building a new united European future in unity, like the crystal symbol of a new faith. Wales forever! *Cymru am byth! Cymru am byth! Cymru am byth!*"

If Crump had been at home, then he would have seen the announcement featured on both local and national TV news, as well as the cheers and celebrations locally and nationally that had greeted the shock announcement. He would have seen it too if he'd perused the newsfeed on his smartphone – but that was happily off. Crump did not want to be contacted or to think any more about his new job that day.

As it was, his only source of news as he got increasingly pissed in the pub was a creased copy of the local rag, the *Cambrian Daily News*, which had splashed on its front page a story about a bloke who'd found 'a thing' in a tin of beef curry, which 'looked like an alien' but which was obviously gristle from a cow's innards. Such was the nature of local news – and yesterday's news at that.

On the inside pages, there were the usual moans of locals about parking, potholes, student noise and anti-social behaviour, as well as Highlands resident Paddy Muldoon, whose face regularly featured in the local paper thanks to his mate being a senior reporter, whose dog had apparently been on a Slovakian TV travel show about Wales. And another piece on veteran local author, creator of the hit Welsh comedy theatre play *Another Corned Beef Pastie for Bampi, Mam*, whose solo campaign to install public toilets throughout The Town continued irrespective of a complete lack of local support or anyone's willingness to cough up yet more council tax (at a rate of sixty to eighty grand per bog) to provide them.

Later, much later, Rob helped his old classmate into a taxi home.

Crump drunkenly asked the driver to stop at the local Highlands shops – he always got hungry after beer. He staggered into the local kebab shop.

"Hello, teacher!" said a kebab shop worker.

"You see, we are right, yes? People is always drunk here!" said another.

It was Ahmed and Rashid from his class.

Crump was too hammered to care, though he'd rather not bump into any students when out and about the worse for wear – or stone cold sober, for that matter.

And so, full of beer and dubiously sourced kebab, to bed.

Hush, the babies are sleeping, the call centre operatives, the zero hours delivery drivers, the unemployed and unemployable, the old and sick and the OAPs, the lecturers junior and senior, the drunk, the devout, the divorced and the desperate.

And if you listen carefully, you can hear their dreams scream, hear them breaking with their disappointed hearts in the sly silence of the noiseless night, as the cats nap in their careful corners, aloof to it all. They dream darkly of diced mice, murdered birds, splashing happy in puddles of blood, and of taking over the wicked, whiskerless world.

If they can ever be bothered, that is.

CHAPTER FOUR

Getting Stuck In

"Happy Vagina Day!" said Dylan in an indifferent drawl.

"Whatever," said Crump, wearily.

As if Vagina Day wasn't horrific enough, it was also Halloween, though Cambrian University had banned all costumes and masks because of the offensive 'cultural appropriation' they supposedly represented.

It was more than a fortnight since the bombshell announcement that Cambrian University would resist Brexit and declare unilateral loyalty to the EU, but the campus was still crawling with media people, and from all over the world. You could tell they were media folk, no matter where they were from, by their shaved heads, spectacles with red, blue or other brightly coloured plastic frames, and the smart-casual look – never ever with anything so uncreative as a tie. This was wannabe cool TV producer uniform the world over.

There were many EU representatives and negotiators knocking around too, and various officials from Westminster and Cardiff (you could spot them by their own uncool grey-suited uniforms) desperate to restore order, though they had all committed to considering any historic claims submitted.

Crump didn't really understand how the university could unilaterally claim loyalty to, and continued membership of the EU. But, considering how bonkers politics had been in the UK of late, he was not really surprised at anything any more, so let it all wash over him like some surreal EU tsunami – a sort of '*EUnami*' maybe?

The blue starry flags of the European Union fluttered everywhere, on every university building, often draped outside windows too, in the manner of national flags when a football tournament was on. It seemed the university's decision was unanimously supported by all students and academics – or, at least, that was the impression. Anyone who disagreed and supported Brexit was keeping very quiet indeed, so as not to attract attention and the accompanying abuse and career annihilation it might well bring. *This was true democracy in action!*

The Head of the Department of Media, Film and TV Studies, the ex-BBC managers Penelope Plunch and Della Beach-Spode, couldn't believe their luck. Their various fruitless attempts to attract media stars to speak at their middling university were but a bad memory. Such people always tended to gravitate to the top universities and Oxbridge for their speeches. But now, they wanted to come and give speeches here, at Cambrian University, and all thanks to its brave pro-Remain pro-EU stance.

Even Stevie Tweezer and Caroline Crinoline-Dopez, world-famous feminist role models and authors of the supposedly 'seminal' tome, *Why All Men Are Bastards,* had offered to speak. TERF activists were delighted because of their comments that transwomen were merely 'mutilated men' and not 'real women' at all. Anti-TERFS wanted to no-platform them both.

University PR guru Lesley Snyde slyly coiled amongst them like a snake, ever aware of a great marketing opportunity.

The Media Department sent students out to interview these TV people, though they often found themselves interviewed instead. Most students who expressed a preference were big EU supporters (though it was noticeable that most young people couldn't be arsed to vote in the 2016 referendum), and were excited to be interviewed on TV. Crump had seen the hypnotic effect of TV cameras before – they always seemed to turn people into children really, all malleable and obedient, as they clamoured to be on camera.

Most students were also delighted, if a little bit baffled, by the university's unilateral declaration of independence. Britain could Brexit if it wanted to – but they wanted to 'stay with nurse for fear of something worse', as the old saying goes. Of course, membership of an EU dedicated to further European integration and borne of the Maastricht Treaty in February 1992 was all they had ever known. Their elders remembered the EEC that preceded it and maybe even the Common Market, the trading club Britain joined in 1973 and then voted with a three-to-one majority in the 1975 referendum to remain in, but no-one under fifty did.

Crump was very wary. He knew from experience that TV people had the morality of rats – which was probably rather unfair to rats. You just couldn't trust them – ever. Every interview was constructed in the edit, and everything was biased, despite the many claims of the media, especially the BBC, of impartiality.

Their star reporter Jason Hussein was there too. He was a man whose ethnic and minority faith status had enabled him to truly soar on the wings of the diversity bird to the very top rung of the BBC perch. But this diversity-quota privilege was never ever mentioned. The last person who had even slightly suggested that Jason Hussein had gained promotion or presenting gigs due to diversity quotas and 'positive action' had left the BBC the same day and was never heard of again. He was feared lost somewhere in Channel 5, or possibly exiled to local radio for life.

The massive irony, of course, was that the 'Beeb' was stuffed with privileged, privately educated women and ethnic minorities who had all enjoyed unfair advantage thanks to their ethnicity or gender, and yet was almost completely devoid of those from the state-educated white working class or even lower-middle class, especially if they'd had the misfortune to be born male.

Crump remembered watching the BBC1 news and weather a few days previously, and not seeing *one* white male face amongst all the vibrant and diverse presenters and correspondents. Fifteen faces on screen: twelve female, three male – and all three of them from an ethnic minority. Maybe the BBC should rename itself the '*BB-She*', Crump pondered with a wry smile smeared on his irredeemably and hideously white, male face.

No doubt the BBC, with its constant obsession to mould the entire country in its own 'liberal' pc image, would argue this was real diversity in action, and all 100% legal, and would deny in the strongest possible terms any suggestion that it was blatant sexual and racial discrimination against white men. But then they would, wouldn't they? No wonder social mobility in Britain happened at a glacial pace.

Dylan and Crump sat on a wall watching the Vagina Day celebrations. The usual campaigners were there, holding up banners as well as several big hairy latex vaginas – the Student Union representatives, various women's groups, the TERF activists who hated the transwomen, the transgender groups protesting that the word 'vagina' was discriminatory so demanded the use of the preferred trans term 'front hole', the 'freebleeders' campaigning against the use of tampons and sanitary pads (for what appeared to be bloody-minded reasons), the Socialist Workers (late again, after their usual lie-in), the Welsh nationalists, the various 'people of colour' race campaign groups, though the Muslim groups were absent together with other religious groups – they tended to avoid any campaigns which were diametrically opposed to their very conservative scriptural teachings.

The police were present too, with the usual rainbow car and other gay-friendly and pink costumes left over from Diversity and One-ness Days.

But they had new costumes too to add to the usual rainbow egg woman and the rest. Several police officers, female and male, were wearing on their heads balaclava-type headgear, which could only be described as sex organ snoods. They reminded Crump of the daffodil headgear Wales fans wore to international rugby matches. The vaginal slit opened length-wise on their faces and, like the plastic models some protestors were holding aloft, some rather woolly-looking 'pubic hair' flanked each side of the 'front hole' through which they peeked.

"I've always said the police are a bunch of cunts, kindathing," quipped Dylan with a grin.

Oh, how they laughed… but then stopped instantly as a fanny-faced copper plodded by with a suspicious look on his labial face.

Vagina Day was more of a celebration really, rather than a protest. Why vaginas should be celebrated, and why penises were not, was something never stated – ever – by anyone. It was diverse. It was feminist. It was all about #MeToo and equality and women, ergo it was intrinsically good and had a purpose, even though no-one could work out what it was yet, off the top of their vaginal heads.

As if to make the occasion a fun day out, some enterprising soul had installed a huge inflatable vagina on campus. Students were encouraged to squeeze themselves through it, to 'give birth' to their new vagina-empathetic selves, supposedly to raise awareness of childbirth issues – though they needed no encouragement to behave like children.

"Well, I suppose it's one way of widening participation," sighed Crump as he watched another young tattooed body squeeze and wriggle itself through the large, inflatable vaginal orifice.

A week before, there had been a 'Feel at Home' day for students, many of whom apparently suffered terrible homesickness.

How things had changed. When Crump had gone off to university, he and his contemporaries couldn't wait to get away from home, and the accompanying control of their parents – which was nothing back then compared to the paranoid parents, helicopter mums and lawnmower dads these days. Their constant monitoring of their children's lives ensured they reached late adolescence with teenage bodies which houses unresilient toddler brains, stuffed so full of self-esteem and a sense of entitlement, yet so utterly unresistant to the trials and tribulations life may throw at them. Most had never been allowed outside to play alone until they reached secondary school age, unlike Crump's 'benign neglect' generation which had played outside whenever it wasn't raining from early primary school or even infant school age, only coming home when it got dark. Too much internet and not enough 'outernet' these days.

This stunting of development, all done by loving parents in the name of 'keeping children safe' – an utterly spurious belief that the world outside posed a perpetually major threat to their well-being, as promoted by a scaremongering rating-chasing media – was literally disabling young people and sometimes even, in effect, killing them through an overdose of fear. It was certainly sapping what little resilience they were allowed to develop growing up, and leaving them totally lacking in defences against the vicissitudes of life. And this at a time when children were safer than ever before in human history – in the West, at least. People – even otherwise intelligent and educated people – were utterly useless at assessing risk, so believed the media myth of a dangerous world 'out there', despite the home being the most dangerous place a child can be, and its parents and family the ones most likely to cause children hurt and abuse and pain.

These cotton-wool kids thus often suffered severe anxiety at the slightest setback in life, and struggled to cope, once their safe-guarding parents were no longer around. But they were still there, of course, all day every day 24/7, on the phone and on social media. There was now no escape from the apron string ties that bind, and which strangle and stifle the life out of the young.

In common with other UK universities, and mindful of possible legal action from parents if any students attempted suicide, successfully or not, Cambrian University had created a Happiness Hub where students could go for advice and guidance, as well as introducing 'Happiness Lessons' for all first years – which would now count for a full 20% of that year's assessment marks.

How young people had changed – and all in the space of a generation! It seemed good intentions and bad ideas were setting up a generation for failure. The kids themselves now demanded 'protection' from a harmful threatening world via 'safe spaces', 'trigger warnings', and 'no-platforming' where any speaker who may say something any student may find offensive or which may upset them could now get banned from university debates. As the Student Union said: 'The right to freedom of expression must not take precedence over freedom from oppression.'

In modern Britain, hypersensitivity was rampant like some paralysing viral epidemic, which in turn led to massive self-censorship in order to avoid confrontation and attack, especially on social media, where everyone claims to want open, honest and genuine dialogue, but only when they agree with you!

Universities were now branding themselves as an extension of students' homes, and not a first step – badly-needed amongst Generation Snowflake – to independence. Some psychologists had argued that young people today only reached the level Crump's generation reached in late teenage by their mid-to-late twenties, and he saw the evidence all around him. Yes, students had always been prone to childishness – but not like this.

His generation's immaturity revolved around risky behaviours and general non-specific stupidity involving alcohol, or occasionally drugs for some, or sexual behaviour, possibly with dropping out, or at least not attending many lectures.

This new generation was different – it seemed they didn't want to grow up or take risks. They wanted to stay 'safe' and protected in the bosom of their controlling parental prison, and largely live their lives online too, via a computer screen. Universities had now recognised the fact – and had no doubt listened to legal advice too – so were happy to oblige in becoming surrogate parents for the toddler-brained 'kidults' of Generation Z.

It was the wholescale infantalisation of a generation, leaving them stranded like a teenage tribe of hairy toddlers, helpless in a world they had no tools or strategies to survive in, with no immunity or resistance to its diseases and no resilience to any hardship or stress in the adult world which would have been considered simply part of growing up a generation ago.

But now they had the safe spaces they'd demanded to protect them from hurt feelings and upset and possible offence, though they didn't seem to realise that all they were really doing was simply parroting and ventriloquising the hysterical fears about safety and the paranoid parent catastrophising that they had been brainwashed with since infancy.

"I don't suppose there's a Penis Day?" Crump happened to mention back in the English Studies Department.

Melanie Spunch confirmed as much:

"Of course not. That would be a clear case of phallocentric hegemony and misogynistic patriarchal oppression."

"Thought so," Crump mumbled.

He badly needed to write some lesson plans and notes but, having forgotten his own notepad, looked around the team room for some plain white A4 paper for the purpose. He even looked in the photocopier. But there was no white paper anywhere.

It was now all coloured in various shades, ranging from the usual light blue, pink, yellow, cream, to darker shades, including brown and even near-black. Why?

He asked Shabs, the Creative Diversity Champion.

"It's a new diversity drive – anti-racism, coz, like, why should da paper always be white, innit, d'ya get me, bruv?"

Indeed, #papersowhite had been a Twitter tag for a campaign aimed at making the colour of paper more diverse across all educational institutions, and this year, Cambrian University was happy to roll out a multi-coloured paper drive across all departments to mark Black History Month.

"How can paper possibly be racist?" said Crump.

But answer there came none, because at that moment, the ever-ebullient and pink-suited figure of Tanya Snuggs bounced into the room. It seemed she was still alone as Head of Department, as the alleged joint head, Karen Crisp, who had no doubt recovered from her period leave, was at a conference somewhere foreign and far away and sunny, which was no doubt so massively academically important that she just had to be there. All at the university's expense, of course.

"Hiya!" Tanya trilled. "Happy Vagina Day! Yay!"

"Yay!" all the English Studies staff echoed back – except Kevin Crump, who groaned.

"It's so exciting, isn't it? We're remaining in the EU now! I'm on *clown* nine! Yay!"

"Yay!" cheered the others, but not Crump.

Tanya Snuggs noticed his silence.

"We all voted Remain in this department, Kevin," she said, ominously.

The other members of staff all nodded as one. They stared at him, suspiciously.

"Well, I didn't," he confessed.

Gasps and open mouths from his fellow lecturers.

"Though voting in a democracy is meant to be secret, so nobody has to reveal how they voted really – ever."

Could they have a traitor in their midst? Could their department have within it someone 'not like them', a member of the #Brexit enemy?

"But I didn't vote Leave either…" he said.

Sighs of relief breathed and heaved before him.

"So…" said Tanya Snuggs, befuddled. "Were you ill, Kevin?"

"No, not at all. The truth is, I just couldn't decide," continued Crump. "I could see both sides. I listened to all arguments and… well…"

"You didn't vote?" said Tanya Snuggs.

"I abstained, I suppose – I put my cross in both boxes."

"So… you vote Leave and Remain, like?" said Shabs, sucking the air through his teeth. "Dat is well messed-up, d'ya get me, blud?"

His fellow lecturers were still regarding Crump suspiciously in the team room.

"It's democracy," he said, at last. "You can always abstain, spoil your ballot, as I did. It's a human right."

Silence.

Crump had always thought it funny how people prefer deceit to honesty. Funny, but not funny at all, when you think about it. Now, if he'd lied and said he'd voted Remain, his new departmental colleagues would all be beaming a welcome at him, for thinking, and being, and doing just like them. Because he had been honest, he would now be permanently under suspicion. Imagine if he'd voted Leave and admitted it? But surely honesty was better than lies? *Discuss.*

"Melissa Jenks wants to see you, Kevin. In ten minutes..." said Tanya Snuggs.

"Really? I didn't get any..."

"I *did* ping you an email earlier this morning –"

Damn it! He hadn't had time to check his emails. Crump remembered with a nostalgic sigh the days before emails, when people actually talked to each other, or wrote letters or memos well in advance, and didn't expect instant replies in an always-on world.

"You better get a wriggle on, innit?" said Tanya Snuggs.

And so, Crump wriggled quickly out of the team room, off to see the Head of the Faculty of Humanities, Melissa Jenks. About what, he had no idea.

That knot of anxiety in his stomach, that worm of worry, that old familiar friend from childhood, accompanied him on his journey squirming and writhing inside his rumbling guts.

'Be polite, look interested, and don't – whatever you do – tell them what you really think,' pondered Crump as he sat in Melissa Jenks's office on the third floor of The Learning Tower of Pizza, thinking back to Shakespeare:

Have more than you show,
Speak less than you know.

King Lear, that – but then look what happened to him.

Melissa Jenks was an imposingly obese woman, at least twenty stone, maybe twenty-five. She wore bright red lipstick which contrasted with a pale white face that was framed by a bob of jet-black hair. If she'd removed her thick, red-rimmed glasses she would have resembled a huge, life-sized china doll, or perhaps a creepy ventriloquist dummy from a vintage lost episode of *Dr Who*. She looked like a woman not to be messed with.

On her wall, together with the usual certificates and diplomas, were photos of her with notable academics, politicians, speakers – and also snapshots of her at Gay Pride and Fat Pride. It seemed Melissa Jenks was a leading light in FAM, the Fat Acceptance Movement, battling 'fatphobia' and campaigning to promote plus-size models in all media and advertising. A banner held aloft by fat activist women in a large framed photo on the wall said *EVERY BODY IS BEAUTIFUL*.

'Seriously?' thought Crump. 'What, even when naked?' He was thankful the adipose activists in the photo were clothed, at least – though some leggings were so tight they left little to the imagination. It is a truth universally acknowledged that most people look a hell of a lot better with their clothes on than without...

Crump wondered if she and the FAM campaigners were also promoting type 2 diabetes, heart disease and strokes. He'd read recently that almost one in three UK adults was obese and at least one in three children when they leave primary school. Was that really something to be proud of, especially in the fattest nation in Europe?

He wondered if the identity politics of her sexuality or size-ist pride – or both – had also helped Melissa Jenks in the general Victim Olympics box-ticking recruitment and promotion race.

Crump stared at the name plate on the Head of School's desk. It had so many initialisms and degrees and memberships and awards listed after it, that he realised he was in the presence of a woman with more letters after her name than in it.

Melissa Jenks put down the documents she was reading, sighed heavily – or, perhaps, wheezed – took a deep breath that made her ample bosom swell like two great balloons, and spoke:

"It is our aim at this university to embed equal opportunity and inclusion in all that we do, and to celebrate diversity in all its forms. We expect all our staff to do the same."

Crump nodded and maintained Melissa's gaze. 'So far, so good', he thought. No wild or false accusations against him – yet…

"The thing is, is that we have a duty of care, Kevin, to all our wonderfully diverse students and staff from all over the world and of a great many nationalities, ethnicities, sexualities, genders and identities generally, to ensure their experience at Cambrian University is happy and safe, and free from all offence, prejudice, discrimination, negativity and hurt, especially when international students are so important to the financial health of this institution."

Crump hated when people said the word 'is' twice and next to each other in the same sentence, as in "*the thing is, is that…*". Just delete an 'is' before you open your mouth, instead of launching yet another mangled sentence into a world of human communication already strangled by them!

"There have been complaints," said Melissa Jenks sternly, flicking through a document in front of her.

Crump watched her several chins wobble. He wondered if she was proud of them. Maybe she had given them names?

"Oh?" he said, non-committal.

What complaints could there have been? He'd been plodding along in his often mind-numbingly uninspiring job, just like all the many mediocre academics around him. He was not aware of anything that had made him stand out, or go against the university's beloved diversity-worshipping policies.

"Do you recall events of our Transphobia Awareness Week?"

Crump thought back. Was that the week with the inflatable vagina? Oh no, that was earlier today, but it just seemed so long ago... Maybe that was the Diversity Day week which also had One-ness Day in it?

Yes, that's right! Rainbow flags and multicoloured police cars, angry TERF lesbians, transmaniacs, diversity doughnuts and all. Hoorah!

And who could forget Diversity Dog?

"Yes," said Crump, innocent eyebrows raised.

"And, do you remember saying anything to students in your classes, about women and men?"

Crump thought.

"Could you be more... specific?"

"Oh yes, Kevin, I can be very specific indeed."

It didn't sound good. Something about the tone of voice meant the accusations would soon be a-flying.

"You said, and I quote, 'Women don't have penises. If it's got a penis and testicles, then it's a man.' Is that correct?"

Crump thought back to his biology exams at school, specifically the first year, where the class of eleven and twelve-year-olds all learnt about the difference between male and female, in humans, plants and animals – bizarrely, by using a textbook which showed rhinos mating. That showed his age. Rhinos were almost extinct now due to Chinese demand for their horns to crush into powder to supposedly 'cure' cancer, or perhaps as an aphrodisiac (or was that another species being hunted to extinction to satisfy Far Eastern demand?). He wondered what animals they used now in sex education in schools. Non-binary budgerigars perhaps? Hermaphrodite hamsters? Transgender terrapins?

"Yes," he said, "I did. It's… biology—"

"It's transphobic abuse!" shrieked Melissa Jenks. "Possibly the worst and most ignorant instance of transphobia I have heard in a very long time."

"Errr… is it?" said Crump, quietly.

"Yes, it is! A man can have a penis, yes, but so can a woman!" Melissa Jenks asserted, thrusting the words through the wide space between her and the penis-possessor before her.

"Really?" said Crump.

"We take such things very seriously at this university, Kevin."

"But… I mean… it's biology."

"Gender is not fixed – we are not all born in the right bodies."

"So a person with a penis… and testicles… can be female?"

"Of course! You are clearly in serious need of seriously reviewing your rather ignorant cis-male understanding of gender."

'And she is seriously in need of a good dose of common sense,' thought Crump, 'or maybe just a year seven grammar school biology class.'

"Sorry, but I was always taught that a male mammal had male reproductive organs, such as a penis, and—"

"Testicles!" snapped Melissa Jenks, like a vice.

"Yes, and that a female mammal had, well, female reproductive organs, like, well, those… bits…"

"I *could* agree with you," tutted the Head of Faculty, "but then we'd both be wrong."

Crump wondered how many times this adipose academic had used that in tedious academic debates, which were never of anything but, well, academic importance.

"Words such as man and woman, boy and girl, are merely social constructs and seriously outdated..." she continued.

'So what are we all then – things?'

'If not "he", or "she", then what?'

'Are we all 'it' now?'

"Transgender, non-binary, pansexual, genderfluid exist too, and in growing numbers, and we have a legal duty under the Equalities Act 2010 to take measures to promote inclusion and equality with regards such matters. Do I make myself clear?"

Crump could seriously feel a diversity course coming on...

"That is why we are referring you to the Shirley Bassey Diversity and Inclusion Re-education Centre."

'Oh goodie!' thought Crump. 'Showtime!'

"But that is not all that is of concern to us here today."

"No?" said Crump, pondering the diverse doom that awaited him.

"No. We have had complaints from students that you used both the P-word and the N-word and even the C-word..."

Crump was baffled and shrugged.

"I honestly have no idea what that is about," said Crump, honestly.

Melissa held up a document.

"One student reported a ginger-haired staff member – i.e. you – shouting out the words 'Paki' and 'Coon' and... the 'N' word..."

Crump thought back. Then he thought again. And again, once more, this time with his eyes shut. Until, quite suddenly, a memory bubbled up into his conscious brain like a fart in the bath.

"Oh, I see what's happened!" said Crump, his intelligent eyes lighting up as he remembered. "There's a perfectly simple explanation. You see, I had to give coursework back to some of my EFL students, Pakey and Koen – he's Flemish, from Belgium, y'know, it's a name there – and Nygren, a Swede, I think, or…"

Crump considered ending the sentence with 'a turnip', but thought better of it.

Melissa Jenks took off her thick glasses, rubbed her eyes, replaced them on her round china-doll face, then shook her wobbling chins and sighed.

"Kevin, you are lucky that we here at this diverse, award-winning university were prepared to give you a position at all, what with you being a racist."

"I'm not a racist," said Crump, getting annoyed now.

"But you did admit to being a racist at London's Thames Metropolitan University?"

"Only to avoid a suspension. And anyway, that was a decade ago!"

"Once a racist, always a racist," smiled Melissa Jenks, as judgemental as a nun.

"What, like Prince Harry?" shrugged Crump.

Melissa's face fell like a lump of lard melting into itself.

"Look, back at Thames Met, I used the word 'niggardly', which is a perfectly good word, and a student – "

"Complained? Like the students here have complained about your racism and transphobia? Perception of racism proves racism. Perception of prejudice of all forms proves it too. That is the law."

Crump sighed deeply. He knew she was right, legally speaking. He also knew he'd never win this fight, not these days, not in the mad bonkers clownworld of the British university system.

"I have contacted Sir Clive Silverback at the Foreign Office, who'll soon be in touch…"

'Oh yippee-doo,' thought Crump.

143

"I have also contacted Cambrian University's Principal Diversity Officer, Mustafa Fouk, to ask for... guidance. Something funny, Kevin?"

'Don't laugh don't laugh don't laugh,' thought Crump, biting his lip and closing his eyes and trying as hard as he could to thrust the name Mustafa Fouk as far from his memory as he could shove it. But it stayed and grew tumescent inside him, until his chest was heaving with humour and his whole body shook with mirth.

"Laughing at the names of students or staff members from our diverse inclusive community is taken very seriously at this university," warned an unsmiling Melissa Jenks. "We take *not* taking things seriously *very* seriously indeed. I'm serious, Kevin!"

But he couldn't help himself. To be called Mustafa Fouk was on a par with being called Ben Dover or Norma Stitz or Ivor Biggun. It was a comedy name, and so Crump laughed and laughed and laughed.

Just then, there was scream from outside in the university forecourt, which was followed almost instantly by a loud metallic crash, then the boom of an explosion. Both Melissa Jenks and Crump got up and went to the window.

Outside, a university minibus was on fire – it had obviously been driven straight into a tree, and its front half was a crumpled mass of burning steel. However, that did not explain the scream. That had been emitted by a young woman lying prostrate and still on the lawn nearby. On the first floor above, several studiously concerned faces were poking out of an opened window, looking down at her unresponsive body.

Melissa Jenks tutted.

"Damn Creative Writing Department," she swore under her breath. "It's always defenestration with them... I seriously..."

She started, but Crump didn't get to hear what she was taking seriously this time, due to the fire alarm – a piercingly loud siren – screeching in his ears. Intermittently, a recorded female voice issued orders to immediately evacuate the building – first in Welsh, and then English. 'The language' always had to be respected, even if you were burning to death.

Melissa Jenks and Crump left together, walking – or waddling, in her case – down several flights of stairs to the exit.

Crump watched the ambulances arrive, all sirens and flashing blue lights, as everyone else was evacuated from the various university buildings. No fatalities, apparently. No life-threatening injuries – except for the tree, whose trunk had been split by the minibus crashing into it. He heard someone say the driver had been distracted by a woman falling from a window. More likely, the blind driver's bell-ringing navigator had overdone the tinkles at the sight.

The ever-present TV people were filming everything, of course, and the entire scene was being live-streamed online by students who were taking footage on their smartphones. This was the new *visuate* reality – all life was lived through a lens. No-one could ever do anything these days without taking a photo of it, or a video. No TV news feature was without the requisite 'optics', however banal. No-one could just look at a view or an artwork and just simply enjoy it, without that craving for a camera to capture a snap of the moment, which would and could only ever be an arranged display of pixels which never succeeded in capturing 'the moment' at all, not really. Two billion photos uploaded online every day – and for what?

"Englishman!" boomed a voice behind him.

Crump turned around. It was the professional Scotsman, Head of the Department of Celtic, Welsh and Diaspora Studies, Donald McClounie, complete with kilt, bagpipes and pet sporran.

"Actually, my mother's Welsh, as is all that side of my family, going back centuries."

"Aye, wee laddie, if ye say so. But we all know, you're nae Celt," he continued in his weird comedy Scottish accent.

"Do we? And what's a Celt then?"

The huge and heavy-set frame of Donald McClounie held one of his enormous arms out towards the three young men beside him, all dressed in kilts too, but Welsh versions. Crump could read their names on the large plastic tag pendants which hung from the lanyards around their necks: Huw Pugh, Richard Pritchard, and Hywel Harlech.

Crump nodded a 'hello' at the three students whose adolescent, acne-erupting, and no doubt Cymraeg Celtic, faces seemed to scream 'EASILY LED'.

"The Celtic colonies of the perfidious English Empire will be free again, or I'm not Donald Dougal Angus Hamish McGinty McDonald McClounie!"

"Wales was a land of warring princedoms only united by a common language before English rule, I believe?" Crump countered. "And then the Tudors were a Welsh dynasty – Elizabeth I even spoke Welsh!"

"Aye tis true, and now we're staying in the European Union, as a *univarsity*, and soon as a nation, when the people of Wales and Owain Glendŵr arise again! Och aye! Freedom!"

The three young kilted Welshmen raised their fists in the air and roared. Crump rolled his eyes. It was like some predictable panto performance, though worse – much worse. And that was saying something. Crump had always hated panto.

"I think the Welsh nationalists got just 3% of the votes in the last general election, didn't they?" smiled Crump – he always liked to have the facts at hand to back up his arguments.

Donald the fake Scot frowned his red angry face into a scowl.

"You rich thieving English come here to our Celtic lands – you're the invader, the coloniser, the enemy of all true Welshmen and all Scots!"

More cheering from the racist nationalist bigots.

"Well, I'm no thief and not rich either, and only half English, and —"

"You're nae working class like me, laddie," sneered Donald. "Yar a wee reactionary southern Sassenach, so y'are!"

For 'working class', he used the short vowel, as in 'ass' rather than 'arse', though he was probably both. Crump knew that as Head of Department, Donald the alleged Celt would also be on at least £80k a year, and probably more with benefits, and a nice fat pension too, courtesy of the taxpayer. He was also, in effect, unsackable – like most established tenured academics, no matter how mediocre, incompetent, ineffectual, time-serving and bone idle they were – and also lots of freebie holidays every year as he was invited to give his hate-spewing nationalistic anti-English racist hypocritical Celtic-cowboy long-haul lectures around the world, all expenses paid.

"Och, I dare say you're nae a Remainer, just another reactionary Brextremist."

"And how do you know how I voted in the referendum?" said Crump.

"Can yer nae see it's obvious, laddie! As plain as yer wee English ginger heed!"

"A majority in Wales voted for Brexit, as indeed did most Scots outside the inner cities, and a clear majority of Brits voted to leave the EU, in fact more than have voted for anything else in British history – ever."

"Ach that cannae be allowed to stand – the Leave campaign was nae honest, t'was full o' lies – the people dinnae know what they were voting for!"

"The lies were from both sides. I think maybe you should trust the people more – it's called democracy."

The beady English-hating cod-Celtic eyes of Donald Dougal etc McClounie burned with raging Caledonian pride:

"Brexiteers are nae welcome at this *varisty*, son—"

"Firstly, I'm not your son, thank goodness. Secondly, if you must know, I abstained and didn't vote for either Leave or Remain. And thirdly, I don't know exactly how the university is trying to convince everyone it's got the right to remain in the EU, but it all seems well dodgy to me. Democracy matters."

And with that, Crump went back inside, off to teach his classes. He didn't need to pander to such a cod-Caledonian clod. Donald the fake Scot was as bad as all the 'plastic Paddies', wearing green on St Patrick's Day (and that saint was a Welsh slave, as it happens) especially in the USA where one Irish great-great-great-grandparent made you claim loyalty to the 'old country'. It was all fake, all affected and all complete and utter bollocks. Crump's experience with Melissa that morning and the knowledge he'd soon have to suffer the enforced boredom of some dull diversity course had not put him in a good mood.

But the points he had made were sound. Britain had voted decisively to leave the European Union. That was the free and fair decision of the British people.

He knew the exact result of that referendum on 23rd June 2016:

REMAIN = 16,141,241 votes.

LEAVE = 17,410,742.

Total number of voters was 33,577,342, a 72.2% turnout – massive compared to the usual, especially the under 30% who vote in local and European elections.

The result was 51.9% to leave, 48.1% to remain; a majority of well over a million.

53.4% to leave in England, which represents over 80% of British voters.

52.6% in Wales to leave too, much to the shock of many in the Labour political establishment of the principality.

44.2% leave in Northern Ireland.

And 38% leave in Scotland, over a million voters, with 62% to remain, mostly in the cities, by traditional Labour and SNP voters.

That may seem close; however, 406 UK political constituencies had a majority to leave; just 242 to remain. Also, nine of twelve UK regions voted to leave.

And yet, a large majority of MPs in the House of Commons voted to Remain and have since then seemingly attempted to block Brexit in one way or other. That, whichever way you see it, is a crisis for British democracy.

Crump could see the pros and cons of EU membership. He also knew that Britain joined the Common Market in 1973 (after France had blocked Britain from joining their *'grand projet'* for fifteen years previously), which was supposedly solely an economic entity. That then became the EEC (European Economic Community), then the EC (European Community) and then, only with the Maastricht Treaty in 1992 did this become the European Union which aimed for ever-closer union and political, not just economic, integration. The promised referendum on Maastricht at the time never took place, in Britain, at least.

That treaty also created the Euro, though some commented at the time how there could be not fiscal union without political union, i.e. creating a federal Europe which, in effect, ended the concept of the nation state, to replace them with a 'country called Europe'. The referendum to ratify that in Denmark was lost, so the EU reran it to get the required result of 'YES'; in France, there was a tiny 'YES' majority, with 50.8% in favour, known at the time as the *'petite oui'*. That referendum was not rerun. The turmoil in currency markets, together with speculators after a quick buck, led to the UK leaving the Exchange Rate Mechanism in September 1992.

Crump wanted Britain to be part of Europe and the world, to trade with all and be friends with all, however unrealistic that sounded. But he did not want to be part of a country called Europe, and neither did the vast majority of Brits, from what he saw and heard.

He could see the advantages of membership of the EU. Free trade in the single market, for example, though that could also block or limit trade from outside the EU. Funding from the EU for many projects in Britain, in the most deprived 'Objective One' regions, including South Wales. And the closer harmony and, hopefully, peace between European states with their multiple languages, cultures and traditions, and of course their blood-soaked histories.

But he could see the disadvantages too. The cost of membership was £50 million a day, with £200 billion, in today's money, being paid into the EU's coffers since 1973. So, the EU funding to UK projects was no gift – it was our money being returned to us, minus a 50% deduction to pay for EU projects elsewhere. The UK got 50p back for every pound it put into the EU. Fact. Other countries had profited substantially from EU subsidy – Ireland, Spain, Portugal, Greece in the past, and now newer Eastern European members all got multiples of many times the membership sums they paid – so no wonder they wanted to be in the EU and to remain in it. France broke even, because its heavily subsidised farmers gobbled up a full half of the CAP (Common Agricultural Policy). No surprise then that France had always vetoed any attempt to reform it. People were still loyal to their nation states and regions, no matter what it said on paper.

Immigration mattered too, and why shouldn't it? Being concerned about it did not automatically make you a bigot, a racist or in any way right-wing either – which was an insult bandied about constantly by the Remainer side. The UK had had at least five million incomers since the early 1990s, three million from the EU whose citizens had a right to come to the UK and claim any benefit available to native Brits – compared to just two million immigrants between 1945 and the 1990s. That mattered. It had huge effects on housing – and sky-high property prices in the UK have caused a housing crisis while enriching some with unearned wealth – and put massive pressure on services such as healthcare, schools, the benefits system. Yes, many immigrants do jobs native Britons seemingly will not do. But then, surely the welfare system in the UK, not to mention the training and education system, needed urgent reform to address that? Immigrants themselves use services, and then grow old and get ill, so need carers and benefits – so what to do then? Invite in yet more millions? Up to what limit? Or is there no maximum limit? So where were all these people going to live in our small island? South-East England was already the most densely populated part of Europe. And that's not even considering the effects on quality of life or social cohesion…

Add to this the labyrinthine bureaucracy and actually very Gallic way of doing things in the EU – the top-down centralised approach, with an unelected, unsackable, self-serving, out-of-touch, often corrupt, and very well-paid (plus expenses) Eurocrat elite running everything. The way, for example, the entire EU Parliament spends countless millions of Euros going to Strasburg in France for four days every month, to a purpose-built parliament building there, for reasons no-one can quite comprehend, though no doubt it keeps thousands of pen-pushing bureaucrats in their cushy jobs.

And doesn't the EU export twice as much to the UK as the UK exports in goods and services to the EU? So, the single market seemed to benefit them more than us really. Worth remembering too that the EU represents only 15% of world trade and falling, and even though now 40% of

Britain's trade is with Europe, that was down from 55% three decades ago, representing a general decline and stagnation of European economies.

Peace in Europe was wonderful, of course, although war raged on in the former Yugoslavia, Ukraine and yes, Northern Ireland. However, to claim sole credit for the EU or the organisations that preceded it was arguably spurious in the extreme. And perhaps it was doubly ironic, as many argued that the original European Coal and Steel Community, established by six countries in 1951, was a natural successor to the co-operation, or collaboration, between Vichy France and Nazi Germany in the war – certainly many politicians in the original organisation had gained experience from that. Its founder, French foreign minister Robert Schuman, had argued the ECSC was to make war unthinkable and 'materially impossible'. Some might argue it was a Franco-German pact, with France as the senior member over the defeated Germany (West, initially), and a sly means of keeping alive the idea of a French Empire which, elsewhere in the world – in places such as Algeria and Viet Nam – was soon to be fought for and lost.

Crump knew his history. There were two opposing sides, as per Manichaean method. Two choices, each with advantages and disadvantages. It was an agonising decision because, in short, no-one could predict the future – whether the referendum result was Remain or Leave.

And so, Crump spoiled his ballot and abstained on that rainy day in June 2016. He had no regrets. He was as undecided now as he was then – and he wasn't the only one…

We like to think our political opinions are an intelligent response to the world around us, but, in reality, they're a personal collection of hunches and prejudices cobbled together through our little lives as we perch on the shifting tectonic plates of fickle emotion and experience.

Would the Euro crash and the EU collapse, what with most southern European economies now unable to control their own financial affairs and, in effect, subsidised by a generous guilt-riddled Germany?

Remainers always portrayed leaving the EU as the risky option, and staying in as a guarantee of perpetual prosperity and peace. The truth was that staying in was just as risky as leaving. With so many EU countries with huge debts, stagnant economies – some in recession – and huge and growing unemployment at least double Britain's, it was hardly an economic Utopia.

What if Germany pulled the subsidy plug? That could easily happen if a coalition opposed to the EU took power there. What if other countries voted to leave too – Denmark, Sweden, the Netherlands were favourites to go next – Dexit, Swexit and Nexit. What if other net contributors left the EU? Where would the money come from then to prop up the Euro? Would that currency crash and bring the entire EU edifice crashing down with it? Nobody knew. Just as nobody really knew what Britain would be like post-Brexit, and anyone who claimed they did was indulging in spouting opinions masquerading as fact. It was all an unknown, just as the future always is. We all just have to wait and see.

Crump also remembered the dire warnings of disaster from the Bank of England, and others, if the UK didn't sign up to the single currency – something Tony Blair wanted but which, apparently, Gordon Brown blocked on economic grounds. The Bank also predicted an economic crash immediately if Britons voted to Leave in 2016 – and that didn't happen, did it? And neither did the 'millennium bug' panic which saw authorities squander over a billion pounds, a lot of it public money, on seemingly pointless payments to savvy IT consultants to tackle an apparently non-existent threat.

Would a Britain outside the EU lose trade and economic advantage long-term?

Who knew? A spin of a coin was likely to be a more accurate predictor than any political pundit, most of whom, let us not forget, predicted a clear victory in the referendum for Remain.

But democracy was democracy. The referendum was agreed on by all major UK political parties and the result, they vowed, would be binding in a one-off vote. That was what troubled Crump about the demand for the UK to Remain in the EU, or for a second vote (or third, or maybe best of seven? Or seventy-seven?) and Cambrian University declaring unilateral independence from Brexit and continued membership of the EU. That was quite apart from the fact that Crump didn't really understand how they could even do that, just on the basis of some old treaty – and the media was split too, with much mockery of the decision from some, yet huge praise from others. How would it all end?

He knew it was wrong to portray all Leave voters as ignorant, racist, right-wing bigots who supposedly didn't know what they were voting for. Just as he knew Remain voters were not all anti-British traitors kowtowing to a foreign power.

Labour leader Hugh Gaitskell was against joining the Common Market in the 1950s, and many on the moderate as well as the hard left had always been ambiguous, at best, about the European 'project', if not downright hostile – MPs such as Dennis Skinner and Frank Field, for example. It was, indeed, the traditional Labour voters in safe seats in northern England who finally clinched victory for Leave in the 2016 referendum, not 'right-wing' voters at all. Indeed, a great many traditional Tory voters in southern England voted Remain. There was no 'left' or 'right' any more, as used to be generally understood, though many commentators seem not to have noticed. We're living in non-binary times indeed.

The diehard hard-left Labour Party minister Tony Benn once said: "I saw how the European Union was developing and it was very clear that what they had in mind was undemocratic." His fears were shared by many union leaders on the left, who had been opposed even to joining the Common Market in 1973, and campaigned for a LEAVE vote in 1975, when REMAIN won a 75% majority of votes.

Benn may well have been thinking of the words attributed to Jean Monnet, founding father of what later became the EU, who is alleged to have said: "Europe's nations should be guided towards the superstate without their people understanding what is happening."

Trying to grapple with arguments for and against Europe was indeed like trying to juggle jellyfish and herd cats all at the same time, when blindfolded.

In 2016, the Tory government and the leadership of all political parties (except the relatively small UKIP) told the British people to vote to remain in the European Union. But the British people will *not* be told what to do. Any politician, native or foreign, who thinks they can be has fundamentally failed to understand the British character, as much as any wannabe invader, Napoleon and Hitler included, who has ever ordered Brits to submit. Even Remainers would have to admit that Britain was never a good fit with the European project, not really. Not for us rule by the collective committee. Britain was, and is, a nation of individualists. We always go our own way.

One thing was true: the Leave campaign in 2016 won by appealing to people's hearts – emphasising the cost and control of the EU. The rather elitist and out-of-touch Remain campaign tried to appeal to people's heads. The referendum was about the soul of this country, not its spreadsheets. Hearts beat heads every time.

Lies, truth, what does it matter? It's the best *story* that wins, always.

In his mum's house earlier, Crump had come across the brochure sent to every UK household in 2016 from HM Government – in both Welsh and English, as all official documents and signage were in Wales – recommending that people voted Remain in the referendum. And there it was, stated in black and white, from David Cameron, the Eton-educated PR consultant millionaire Tory Prime Minister, stating the 2016 referendum was:

'A once in a generation decision.'

And then, below it:

'This is your decision. The Government will implement what you decide.'

Crump was later discussing the issue of the EU, Brexit and the university's declaration of unilateral independence with his classes.

The all-Chinese classes he had didn't have much to say, as usual, and Crump suspected that was not only because they didn't really *get* democracy, but also because a great many students lacked adequate English to join in discussions. A few could speak, but in general, the level of English was laughably low, something confirmed when these students submitted the homework he had set. Crump had seen it all before, and knew he was not allowed to ever fail such lucrative students, no matter how bad their level of English.

The classes he taught in the Department of Politics and Governance were more animated, as would be expected, though most of the students from EU countries stated quite clearly that the main benefit of membership was getting money, the funding taken from richer countries and send to poorer regions such as theirs. The Scandinavians bristled at this, though some, but by no means all, still grudgingly supported the EU project.

One even dared to mention mass immigration from Asia and Africa, and how that has transformed some cities in Sweden. But most avoided touching on a subject that could get them branded a racist – or worse, suspended from the university and facing possible expulsion. Diversity of opinion was certainly not celebrated in the pc echo chamber at British universities these days. Crump had often thought an alarm may go off if anyone ever expressed an original or controversial thought, such was the oppressive, overbearing imposition of 'correct thinking' on debate, which must not veer away from oh-so-inclusive and inoffensive 'politically correct' parameters – or else.

Crump's 'snowflake' classes, the ones populated with undergraduate Brits he taught English language and literature to, were predictably pro-Remain and largely delighted that their university had unilaterally declared that it would maintain its membership of the EU.

There was no real surprise there: any youngster who dared express a preference for Brexit would find themselves ostracised at the very least, and possibly hounded and bullied day in day out for their beliefs.

Most of these homegrown students were fine. True, some of them seemed mostly bone from the neck up, and needed things explained to them in words of one letter. They also almost all seemed to indulge in 'upspeak', lifting the last word or syllable in a sentence, no doubt as copied from Australian soap operas. Crump found this as irritating as the Americanisms that had crept into the language, but knew there was no point making an issue of it – that was just how these *digital native* kids spoke.

But what on earth were girls these days doing with their eyebrows? For some reason, the last decade had seen young women's eyebrows plucked and painted on to such an extent that most seemed to have stuck two black caterpillars above their peepers. Was that meant to be attractive? Did they have any idea how awful they looked? What was wrong with eyebrows as they were before the black caterpillar fashion started? Crump had to admit he just didn't get it at all. He was too old – thank God.

Then there were the clothes. Some girls seemed to like wearing jeans cut so low they were practically skimming their pubes – if they had any left after a session at the stylist and a full Brazilian, or Hollywood, or whatever 'shave haven' was on trend this week. The feminists always argued that it was every woman's right to wear whatever she wanted, of course, which is how – bizarrely – they defended and supported the wearing of burqas. 'Yes, but… ' thought Crump.

Yes, but…

What if a man wore a tent to work, or maybe a *'mankini'*, Would anyone really want their kids taught by a man dressed like that? Would any feminist mum?

And then there was the young couple who always came to class dressed in what they referred to as 'Steam Punk' gear. It was an odd mix of Victoriana and fake-technology, supposedly inspired by the late-eighties film *Brazil*. It was the sort of thing Crump might have enjoyed when he was about eight years old, when he loved watching *Dr Who*, in the days before it went full-on pc preachy madness 'woke'. But for adults to dress like that? It seemed a sort of sad S&M without the sex for anyone who hadn't spent enough time rooting around in the dressing-up box as a kid.

As for tattoos and piercings – they all had them, his native students, or a good nine out of ten of them. Crump always pondered how that would have looked radical when he was a kid, but now it was like a uniform worn by the young. If you really wanted to stand out as a rebel these days, have no tattoos or piercings! That was what he would tell his own kids, if he ever had any.

It was when Crump was teaching academic English to one of these classes of mostly British youngsters that he noticed something worrying. Of all twenty class members, amongst all the Olivers and Harrys, Emilys and Charlottes, Archies and Alfies, no more than one or two knew how to use an apostrophe properly.

Yes, they had all been through many years of education – nurseries no doubt, then infant school, primary from Year 3, then secondary from Year 7, on to SATS, GCSEs, A-levels, then here at a middling UK university. How many hours of education was that in total? Thousands. And yet they had managed to get through it, usually with stunning grades, mostly As and A*s, without really knowing how to use an apostrophe, in effect the genitive case in their native language. Ironically, foreign students were often better at this, and grammar and spelling too, than native Brits.

But then, how many of the teachers who had taught these kids could spell and use an apostrophe properly? Crump had no idea, but seeing as many of them had graduated from the same education system which put little emphasis on the importance of such things, and deducted very few, if any, marks from exams for poor spelling and use of English, it was perhaps unsurprising. Crump's mum had once told him when she was at primary school in the 1940s, they'd done a spelling test every single morning first thing. Do that, and you learn how to spell. Don't, and you won't. Shrug and say it doesn't really matter, and you get the present semi-literacy of the mass of the population. It's not *rocket surgery*, after all, as some of his students would no doubt say.

So, Crump did what he often did, though he knew his managers and any observers or inspectors would frown at such maverick behaviour – he metaphorically tore up his lesson plan, which was on subordinate clauses and complex aspects of academic English, and taught on the hoof what he had been taught aged twelve in his old grammar school in a rather non-descript part of north-west Kent: a lesson on apostrophes and how to use them.

Crump remembered that he had, throughout his school career, referred to the back page of an exercise book from his first year. His rather old-fashioned traditionalist English teacher, a former Major in the army with Monty in the North African desert according to his stories, had made all the boys in his class write down all the rules of apostrophe usage, with examples.

As a twelve-year-old, Crump had thought that lesson boring, a waste of time. What he had not realised at that ignorant age, was that he was being provided with a foundation on which he would later be able to build – the boring and inevitably grey concrete base which had to be there, in order for a well-punctuated palace of words and sentences in good, well-written English, to be constructed in the future. You needed that knowledge to be able to use the English language well; you had to have that solid epistemical foundation on which to build.

Same with numeracy, though Crump was certainly no mathematician or abacist. Same with all education and general knowledge. Those unlucky enough not to have such a foundation were building their houses on sand. It really was a scandal that so many left our school system without enough basic literacy and numeracy skills to successfully function. Supposedly, 20% of the population were functionally illiterate and a full 40% innumerate, with many more having a low primary school ability with both. That was a scandal.

Crump utterly rejected the present trendy view of some *soi-disant* 'experts' that 'what you know doesn't matter' because you can find all information online these days. 'Only if you want to be a slave to others', he always thought. And anyone who believed everything they read on the internet was an idiot indeed, in need of a good, traditional education, which taught them 'stuff' – knowledge to remember – not just which button to press or link to click to find made-up misinformation online.

"Unbelievable!" said Esther Isaacs. "They just screamed 'safe space, safe space' and so it was cancelled."

She was referring to a debate, with speakers for both sides, with the title *'Israel Has a Right to Exist'* which had been held the previous week at a London university. The protestors who'd disrupted it were somewhat unsurprisingly from their Islamic Society. However, these hard-line Muslims were also joined by hard-line feminists, who also shrieked their demand for 'safe spaces' and stood in solidarity with their Islamic brothers (not sisters, as Muslim women were not allowed to join the protest) claiming that allowing such a debate to go ahead would 'be a violation of the university's safe space policy'.

Crump sipped his coffee. It tasted more bitter and insipid than usual.

"It was a debate, there was a whole bunch of guys there representing all sides," said a young man with a goatee beard who Esther introduced as Larry Wolfstein, visiting from New York State.

"They said having the debate was offensive and Islamophobic," scoffed Esther.

"OMG," said Pete Parzival.

"I'm from Yorkshire, and nothing shocks me," said Khalid, "but—"

"Nothing is offensive *per se*," continued Pete, the philosophy lecturer. "People choose to be offended. If I decide to, I can be offended by a piece of cheese, as some vegans no doubt are. That does not make cheese offensive, *per se*."

"I bloody hate cheese," said Khalid.

"Replace 'cheese' with anything else—"

161

"I usually do…"

"Not in my name, *c'est* ça," said Fatima. "Neither whore nor doormat!"

Khalid, the only other Muslim present, agreed.

There were, however, more conservative and illiberal Muslims at the university – Crump could see some queueing up at the counter of the EATZ cafeteria. And nearby were some TV people, of indeterminate nationality. The campus was still crawling with them.

"Weren't you at Thames Metropolitan?" asked Fatima.

That was the university Esther and Larry had visited for the Israel debate.

"Oh, a long time ago," winced Crump. "Not… the happiest experience…"

"They've got a big Islamic Studies Department there, right?" asked Larry.

Crump nodded.

He remembered…

"Oh yes, they've got a lot of everything there," he said, mysteriously, before changing the subject: "There's a new New York diner opened – anyone fancy going there later? Say, 5-ish?"

"I'm in!" said Andy Stone, and Casper agreed.

"Me too!" said Pete and Khalid together.

"Not me – I wouldn't eat that processed crap if you paid me," said Johnny Blue.

"I don't expect New York diners cater much for vegetarians," said Crump.

"You got it!" said Larry. "New Yorkers like their crisp American bacon, and pastrami on rye!"

"Oh, bugger it, I can't!" tutted Esther. "Got another bloody meeting."

"*Moi aussi*. Sorry," said Fatima.

"Will you be OK?" asked Esther of her guest.

"Sure, I will – don't worry, Mom," Larry laughed. "I'll come back to the campus after, meet you here, yep?"

"Sure thing!" said Esther Isaacs in about the worst American accent ever.

"Great," said Crump. "It's a plan!"

And so, it was decided.

"Forty-two million of them just thrown away, every single day," said Johnny Blue, looking at Fatima's plastic water bottle on the table. "Water is 800 times more expensive than tap water when they sell it in plastic bottles too."

"I know, I must... errr... buy one of those environmentally friendly, not-disposable bottles... or —"

"A million animal species now under threat of extinction. A hundred million hectares of tropical forest lost in the last twenty years, just to make farmland to raise cattle to provide beef for... New York diners —"

"Maybe not just New York diners..." said Larry. "And they grow soya there too, right?"

But there was no stopping Johnny Blue, lecturer in Environmental Studies who, it had to be said, knew his stuff:

"Half the natural world lost and the human population doubled in the last fifty years. Climate change, refugees, epidemics, wars over resources, extinctions. Who'd want to bring a child into this world?"

"People have always imagined the end of the world," said Crump.

"People are the worst pollution of all," said Johnny.

"Savonarola in Florence, he has said end of the world would be in 1500," added Fatima.

"And the Mayans," said Larry.

"Human sacrifice. OMG. *Apocalypto*. Great film – dickhead director," added Pete Parzival.

"Countless self-declared doom-monger prophets in British history too," said Crump.

"But this time it's different," said Johnny Blue, his eyes clear and determined and true. "This time it will happen. The population is just too big, and getting bigger. Humanity will kill itself. Nature will cull us."

No-one said a thing, until Crump offered:

"Maybe hope and despair need each other? No despair means no hope either. So we need to..."

But Johnny Blue had already left.

Just then, a plastic water bottle – no, more than one of them – smashed down on the table, scattering half-drunk cups of coffee over all those seated.

Yells and shouts. Male voices.

Then Fatima was yelling back in Arabic. Khalid too.

And then it was over.

The men in robes were gone.

"Goddammit!" yelled Larry, wiping the spilt coffee off his clothes.

"What the hell was that about?" asked Crump.

"Mad Muslims, what else?" said Andy Stone. "The bad bigoted ones."

"They are saying I must wear headscarf because I am Muslim woman, like usual."

"Won't the university do anything?" asked Crump.

Fatima laughed, cynically.

"They say I must wear headscarf because if I do not then I am provoking to the Muslim men, so it all is my fault. *Bof! Je m'en fous...*"

Crump knew that meant '*I don't care*', but he cared – he cared very much. For Fatima. And, in fact, for all his friends round the table who were in the same 'newbie' boat.

"Casper gets abuse too," started Andy Stone from his wheelchair, "and me an' all, course, being ex-army, a former Crusader in Muslim lands –"

"Oh no, please, Andy," said Casper – the shy Zimbabwean rarely spoke.

Andy touched his hand, lovingly.

"It's OK," said Andy to Casper, and then: "The Mugabe regime had its spies everywhere, loads of students at UK unis an' all."

"I had no idea," said Crump.

"Even now that monster Mugabe's gone, his deformed children still rule," added Casper.

"They hate gay people in Africa – want to kill us all," said Andy. "Bless…"

Crump just had time to go home, have a shower and get changed before meeting up at The New York Diner.

His industrious new cleaning lady, sixty-year-old Eva from Poland, was there when he got home.

"You not worry, I cleaning bathroom, now I will must to cleaning kitchen!" she said, like a house-proud mum.

He'd first hired a local girl to do some cleaning for him, but she refused even to clean the hob of the cooker, or really scrub the kitchen floor – she just wanted to waft around dusting. Then he'd seen an ad put up by Eva in a local newsagent and was delighted he had. Her English grammar may have been up the spout, but she cleaned quickly and thoroughly, and Crump instinctively trusted and liked her.

There was a ring at the door. Marek. With several large bags and packing cases. On his doorstep.

"You forget, yes?" asked Marek.

Crump had completely forgotten he'd agreed for him to store some stuff in his loft during a move.

He helped him in with his bags – though they were massively more heavy than they looked.

"Books weigh a tonne, eh?" said Crump, huffing and puffing.

"Yes, books," said Marek. "Is OK, I can to carry all."

Eva then entered speaking Polish on her mobile to someone and Marek smiled widely.

"*Polski, tak?*" he said.

Eva smiled and ended the call.

The two then proceeded to chat away in Polish. She seemed as enamoured with the Moronian as Crump was.

Marek seemed to speak practically every European language – in class, he flitted between languages like a bee between flowers. Yet another aspect of the handsome Moronian to envy...

Crump looked at his watch.

"Marek, I don't want to interrupt, but..."

"I sorry I sorry," he said. "You show me to –"

"Loft."

"Yes, loft. I put in. I strong," smiled Marek, and indeed he was.

He looked the way Crump would have wanted to look, if, well he hadn't been him. Or something...

"Hi, can I get a regular fries and a quarter pounder?" said Dylan, who had joined them all at The New York Diner.

The unsmiling, tired-looking waitress wrote the order down.

"*'Can I get...?'*" scoffed Crump. "'Are you American now, Dylan? What's wrong with '*May I have...?'*'"

"S'the way I speak, kindathing," he said, blankly.

Crump raised his eyebrows and sighed. Was that really how kids spoke these days?

"Americanese," said Pete Parzival.

"Sure thing!" laughed Larry, the sole American there.

The New York Diner was furnished like an American diner, certainly, with pictures of the famous US landmarks hung on the walls, all Empire State and Chrysler Building and Statue of Liberty vistas, and the same fixed-down wooden tables and chairs and stools as at many diners in their native land. But there the similarity ended. For The New York Diner was about as American as McDonald's was Scottish, or ex-President *O'bama* was Irish, or Waterloo Station was Belgian. In other words, it wasn't. Not in any way, shape or form.

Crump could see Larry squinting suspiciously at neighbouring tables, baffled at the meals people were eating – they were things you would never find in any *real* New York diner.

"There's a whole bunch of guys here eating 'The Monster', so I guess I'll have that too," said Larry, at last.

"Same here," said Crump.

'The Monster' was a massive budget meal served all day, with so many fried eggs, rashers of bacon, hash brownies, chips, and beans that most people could not finish it, so a great deal always got binned.

Crump was thankful Johnny Blue hadn't joined them – he'd been going on the day before about how on average UK eateries throw away 40% of their food. At this fake American joint, it must have been 60% or more. And what did the 'pile it high, sell it cheap' mentality say about the quality of the food. Just where did it come from? No doubt it was the cheapest factory-farmed meat and eggs they could buy, which did not bode well…

Apart from Dylan, the only person there not to order 'The Monster' was Khalid, who as a Muslim didn't eat pork, though he didn't insist on halal for other meats. He stuck to poached eggs on toast with beans – something Crump could have knocked up better at home in ten minutes for much less money.

Crump could see a scruffy ginger-haired thirty-ish man hovering outside by the door.

Inside, next to the door, was a sign which declared the owners to be gay married couple COLIN AND KARL KUNTI.

'Probably an Italian surname,' thought Crump – lots of Italians had emigrated to South Wales, especially in the first decades of the 20th century, and many had opened cafés at the time.

He was looking at Karl, the queeny younger partner, dressed in a flamboyant Hawaiian-style shirt, who seemingly had a snide sneer permanently smeared on his smug face – and recognised him as the person he'd seen before, when driving by in his car, chucking a bucket of water over a homeless person begging outside. Not nice.

Eventually, the food arrived, 'The Monster' on enormous oval-shaped white plates.

"Good job!" said Larry.

"OMG. It's well mega," said Pete.

"It's *yuge!* A whole bunch of heart attacks on a plate…"

There must have been well over 3,000 calories-worth there – four eggs, too many rashers of bacon to count, four cheap-looking sausages, toast, beans, hash browns. More calories than an average man needed in a whole day. It was all just too much. Crump looked enviously at Dylan's burger and fries, and Khalid's poached eggs on toast.

They all started eating. Crump chewed. First some fried egg, then a rasher of bacon – which tasted cheap – then some of a sausage, which tasted very odd indeed.

'You should never ask how two things in the world are made: the law, and sausages.' Isn't that what they say?

Judging by the taste of these alleged sausages, no quality meat went into them – no doubt just all the bits of gristle left over, and scraped off the factory floor at the end of another bloody day at the abattoir. They were, without doubt, the most disgusting sausages Crump had ever tasted – and that was against some quite stiff competition…

Just then, the snide-eyed Karl Kunti minced by carrying a bucket of water.

Crump knew what it was for. He had to act.

He jumped up from the table and ran outside.

Kunti swung the bucket of water back, to get greater momentum to chuck it over the homeless man outside – but Crump caught him just in time. Somehow, he managed to deflect the bucket away from the beggar, so all water splashed over the entrance to The New York Diner as well as over Karl himself who was now drenched.

"Show some fucking respect!" yelled Crump.

Kunti said nothing. But Crump could see the rage glowing on his over-moisturised face, and the anger seething in the beady queeny eyes under his over-groomed eyebrows.

By now Khalid, Larry and Pete were outside too, together with the fifty-something obese owner Colin, who gazed adoringly at his soggy husband, dripping onto the pavement.

Crump hadn't finished his meal though. So he went inside, collected as many rashers of bacon and pieces of toast as he could from his and other plates, and wrapped them in paper napkins. Then he went outside and gave the food parcel to the young homeless man outside. He wouldn't wish the vile gristle-sausages on anyone, so left those on the plates ready to be binned with most of the greasy caf crap this joint served up.

"Don't come here again," sneered Karl Kunti, and minced off down the street.

"Don't worry, we won't!" shouted Khalid after him.

"You got it, asshole!" yelled Larry, and then to Crump: "How can they claim it's American anyhoo? Aren't there laws?"

"Trade Descriptions Act doesn't cover this," said Khalid. "But just think, if you guys were Muslim, you could have avoided the pig gristle sausages and ordered the factory-farmed eggs on cheap plastic bread instead..."

Andy Stone and Casper joined them outside. It was now dark, and various students and party-goers were dancing past in their Halloween masks and outfits. But the alleged food they had all eaten was horror enough...

"Cor blimey, what a dump," said Andy.

Casper agreed:

"Too greasy, even for an African! And we really like our cooking oil..."

Dylan shrugged:

"So… the chips were sort of alright, kindathing, but burger was well gross, like, proper horrible."

Everyone said their goodbyes and left. Crump had promised Dylan a lift home, so set off walking up the hill, back to his house in Highlands where his car was parked.

Just then, there was a voice behind him. It called his name:

"Excuse me, sir."

Crump turned round to see two police officers before him, standing beside a smug-looking Karl Kunti, his over-whitened, vindictive teeth shining bright through the descending darkness.

"Could we have a word?"

PC Barry Bent and WPC Dawn Goodhead introduced themselves and informed Crump that, in 'throwing' the bucket of water over Mr Kunti, he *may* have committed an assault.

"Lucky for you, Mr Crump, that Mr Kunti does not want to press charges," said PC Bent, after taking his name and address.

"But… I did not assault anyone. I was protecting… him…"

"Who?" asked WPC Dawn Goodhead.

The young man had vanished. Crump didn't blame him, what with the way the local police treated the homeless.

"Do you mean a vagrant? Who was breaking the law by begging?" she continued.

"He's homeless – how else is he supposed to get enough money for food, eh?"

PC Barry Bent leant in towards him.

"I could make your life very difficult," he whispered close in a low growl, before leaning back and booming: "Now, don't do it again."

'Great,' thought Crump. Almost arrested for assault, and for what? For preventing some evil *Kunti* from chucking a bucket of water over a vulnerable and homeless human being.

The disgusting slimy gristle sausages churned with the worry in his stomach. He couldn't hold it in any longer. In one giant retch, Crump bent over and vomited 'The Monster' fry-up he had just eaten onto the pavement. He could see the undigested chunks of sausage sitting in the worryingly-puce puddle of puke. Well, it made a change from diced carrots...

"Y'alright?" asked Dylan.

Crump spat out the sick taste and washed his mouth out with water from the bottle the kid offered him.

"Can't somebody *do* something about the homelessness problem round here?" he said, as they were slowly walking up the steep hill to Crump's house.

"Peter Might may," said Dylan, "but then Peter Might may not, kindathing."

"Who?"

"Local councillor, innit? Always around..."

After giving Dylan a lift back to his mum's house – a large detached place in one of the prime locations in The Town – Crump parked his car back outside his house.

But he didn't go inside – he felt like a long walk, after all the stress of The New York Diner incident and yet another encounter with the local police, especially as it was Halloween.

They didn't make nearly so much fuss about it when he was a kid, or even a student. These days, every calendar date was an excuse to sell yet more stuff to people and make money. All Crump remembered from his boyhood was a hollowed-out turnip with a candle in it, maybe a cheap horror mask or two, and that was it. Now Halloween was an American consumerist festival of orange and black. But Crump liked the masks and costumes, and the history of this ancient British festival.

171

What he hated was the Americanised consumerist version of it. Because, in its modern incarnation, Halloween came from the USA – like drive-by shootings, crack cocaine and enormously fat people. And he sometimes wished they'd send it back. This version of it, anyway. After all, Britain already had Guy Fawkes night on 5th November, which was once the bigger festival (and the only time you ever used to see fireworks) before the awful orange of Halloween had smudged itself across it.

He remembered a joke he'd heard that morning on the radio – *'What did one ghost say to the other ghost? Do you believe in people?'* – and allowed himself a wry smile at the absurdity of it all.

Crump wandered around the streets, smiling fondly at the kids in their costumes and masks. 'Like British burqas,' he thought, as he saw a gaggle of girls giggling along wearing witchy costumes. 'But only one day a year and you aren't allowed to wear them to work or school!'

The obsessive focus on 'cultural appropriation' was thankfully only enforced on university grounds – and that, in itself, was a wholescale import from the United States too where the ignorant and victimhood-craving stupidly thought Halloween originally came from Mexico!

There was no tradition in the UK of dressing up as Mexicans or even Red Indians for Halloween, though, just ghouls, ghosts, witches, werewolves, vampires, Frankenstein's monster and the rest. Supposedly, some Mexicans claimed 'cultural appropriation' of Halloween from their *Day of the Dead*, but that was certainly not where it started. It was an ancient British festival at least 5,000 years old when it was appropriated by the church as the eve of All Saints' or All Hallows' Day. Crump really couldn't really see how anyone could claim to be offended by supposed 'cultural appropriation' – except maybe Hollywood, whose 1920s/30s Universal Horror Movies created the image of these ghouls and monsters in the popular imagination and led directly to the tradition of wearing Halloween costumes and masks. And it was the maimed and deformed bomb blast victims of the First World War, whose survival with horrendous facial injuries had been the inspiration for many of those horror movies in the first place.

Crump thought how absurd the concept of 'cultural appropriation' was, as he meandered through the lamplit streets of The Town. After all, we all take from other countries and cultures – look how people all over the world wore Western-style clothes and listened to British pop music and watched Hollywood films.

Even the burqa, that assertive badge of literalist and devout Muslim identity, had been stolen from the Byzantine Christians in the 11th century AD – so it was not the Muslims who had first draped their women in that uncompromising garb. Now that was real cultural appropriation in action!

He remembered an unfortunate former Cambrian University student that Dylan had mentioned earlier. Apparently, this young man had been to a local tapas restaurant and won a free sombrero – but then had made the mistake of wearing it on campus. Someone had complained, as someone always does, and so the unlucky kid was suspended awaiting a disciplinary hearing for his insensitive, offensive and possibly even racist 'cultural appropriation' of a hat. The young man's rotting, crab-ravaged body, or what was left of it, was washed up a month later at a beauty spot a few miles down the coast. He was nineteen years old.

If you're not worried, you don't understand the problem.

Crump continued on his walk, through the back alleys and down past the park.

From the hills he walked down, he could see the lighthouse winking and blinking its light at him in the distance from where it stood on its rocky outcrop by the pier. It was like an old friend, constant and unchanging, waving a welcome at him, just checking he was still there.

And then he saw – he was sure he saw, through the iron park railings – Nelson the ginger and white cat, being chased by a big black beast.

Was it the Hound of the Baskervilles perhaps? The Beast of Bodmin Moor on holiday here in The Town? The Wolf of Wall Street maybe?

No – it was Diversity Dog! He was sure of it.

And he was outrun by Nelson, who scrambled up a large tree. The crafty cat was now sitting smug on a branch and gazing down at the barking dog, winding him up something rotten.

As Crump walked past the park, he heard the squeals and yelps and chatterings of animals. He saw foxes fighting in the moonlight, hedgehogs hiding from the fight.

"Happy Halloween," he smiled at them, and also to the beautiful moon, massive and still, shining bright as an eye above him.

CHAPTER FIVE

Kicking Off

"You have many *bitch* in your country," said Marek.

"Sorry?" said Crump.

Other Moronian students in the class agreed.

"Big *bitch*," said Oksana.

"Nice *bitch*," said Svetlana.

"I was on real good *bitch* in weekend," said Vladimir, with a thin grin.

"Plenty *bitch*," agreed Tomek, "with the sand and the stone also."

"Oh, you mean *beach* – plenty of *beaches*!" said Crump, relieved.

"Is what I say," said Marek. "*Bitch*."

"Plenty *ship* too," said Zoltan.

"*Ships* everywhere in the Wales!" said Oksana. "In my country, I am making the good goulash with *ships*."

"Yes, we eating all *ship* – head, heart, stomach..." agreed Svetlana.

"Ball of eye is best," said Taras, kissing his fingers with his Cossack lips to signify how tasty sheep eyeballs were.

Crump could see that some pronunciation practice was called for.

A few minutes later, every student in the class was chanting '*sheee-eeep*' and '*beee-eeach*' as if they were two-syllable words. That was a trick Crump had learnt – he knew this was the best way to extend that long vowel for foreign learners.

Standard English had twenty vowel sounds, more than any other language – some European ones had as few as five – so differentiating between the short and the long vowels in English pronunciation had to be learnt and practised.

Crump had picked up a lot of tricks in his teaching career – such as encouraging students to pronounce the tricky English word *'clothes'* as *'cloze'*, which sounded almost the same anyway and avoided any pointless tongue-twisting gymnastics with the 'th' sounds, always tricky for many non-native speakers.

However, he was unable to teach Fatima how to pronounce the word *'law'* as anything but *'low'*. He had no idea why, but this affliction was typical of the French, and some other nationalities.

Despite his knowledge of all these tricks and long experience of teaching in a variety of contexts and countries, he remembered how at Thames Met he had insultingly been referred to as a 'beginning teacher', despite his many years' experience. Unfortunately, teachers sometimes had a tendency be so rude and snooty to each other, which was no doubt all about asserting superior status.

That was perhaps partly, but not only, because the teaching profession was so female-dominated these days – in Crump's experience, girls were always the worst (best?) bullies, and their bullying often manifested itself in exclusion or spreading false rumours and other psychological attacks. These were very hard for teachers to spot, amongst students and, perhaps, when teachers themselves bullied colleagues: teaching had the highest rate of bullying of any profession, apparently.

Boys were easier – if they didn't like each other, they either had a fight or just avoided each other totally. It was like that when Crump was at school. But girls...

Women beware women, perhaps, was good advice for any new female teachers.

Most teachers were deeply conservative – with a small 'c' – and resistant to change, not to mention rather institutionalised, so it was doubtful if this would ever change. They may have abhorred the British class system – especially the more left-wing amongst them – but they clung on to their own nominal badges of status with vehement pride. Call a *senior* lecturer a mere lecturer at your own risk. Such was the hypocritical vanity of it all.

The students were right about the great beaches in the area though. There was the wide bay itself, sandy and shallow, right opposite the university campus. But a few miles away, there were the numerous bays and beaches of Gower, some more accessible than others, but all connected by coastal paths, and home to many varieties of wildlife, both plant and animal. He had walked this coast in the past, on holiday, and had seen so many colourful varieties of bird, as well as the occasional baby adder basking in the sun on the paths, and seals bobbing off the rocks at low tide, taking an occasional dive as the mood suited them.

Crump liked driving out to these beaches of a weekend, or if he had an afternoon off – that was probably the only real reason he liked owning a car. It got dark early now as November nudged on, but he expected that, when the evenings grew longer in the Spring and the clocks sprang forward an hour, he'd be down by the sea daily.

He suddenly realised on one of these walks that, much to his amazement, he was not really missing London at all. Of course, The Town was provincial, and the local mentality too. But if he ever wanted to visit the capital, it was less than three hours' away by train.

There was always such a buzz to London, yes, and so many theatres and museums and the rest. But there were undoubtedly many downsides too – the expense, of accommodation and travel, and the time that took as well; the constant hovering threat of crime, especially mugging, which was a scourge, and now much more often with knives than in the past; plus the general stress of everyday life which seemed to put everything and everyone on edge – he had certainly felt that when living there, mentally and physically.

And anyway, so many people who lived in or near the capital never really took advantage of what it had to offer, often staying in zones 3 or 4 or further out, for years sometimes, without ever visiting the West End or any of the many free museums. They could be living anywhere, in fact, and were every bit as provincial as most of the people in The Town, including many of Crump's neighbours in the Highlands district.

Crump knew that he was one of a small minority of those who were not provincial, whose dream was not a job for life with the council or at a degree factory university, who could see beyond the near horizon and didn't live under a tub, as his mum used to say.

It was all like Brexit really – there were arguments for and against. But the negative expectation of change, of moving out of London, had not materialised at all. In fact, he was glad he had left now. The downsides of the place just seemed to outnumber the positives, for him anyway – though he could understand why people, especially in certain careers and industries, gravitated to the capital, as did a great many multilingual international criminals and *gangstas* too, no doubt 'celebrating die-versity' with knives and guns, and all the Russian oligarchs and Arab princes and the Chinese super-rich, whose wealth dwarfed the struggling ordinary people whose home city they now largely owned. Was London even England any more, or Britain? It seems many had their doubts, so alien was the look and feel of the place.

It was now late November, so well on the way to Christmas – which the university insisted on referring to as 'Winterval' – and with it, a much-needed holiday.

There was a 'Seasonal Tree' decorated in the campus grounds – in reality a pine tree that was always there anyway, but with some lights stuck on it, and various decorations including, bizarrely, baubles featuring the faces of Palestinians killed by Israeli attacks on Gaza and some cardboard cut-outs of them too, which were now all looking rather sad and soggy in the rain.

November was 'Israel Apartheid Month' at Cambrian University, where awareness was raised to pro-Palestinian anti-Zionist heights as high as the Golan ones which were, as much promotional material declared, stolen by Israel together with the rest of its territory.

No mention was made, of course, of the over 800,000 Jews expelled from Arab lands who found a secure home in Israel after its creation. And no criticism was ever made of the many undemocratic and brutal Muslim dictatorships around the Jewish State whose expressed aim was to destroy both it and all its inhabitants, and who usually did not treat their own citizens much better if they dared oppose the present regime, or follow a faith other than the version of Islam demanded by the state and its imams, or if they happened to be women who refused to obey tradition, or gay, or atheist, or Christian, or ex-Muslim, or 'the wrong kind of Muslim', or *different* in any other way.

According to the promoters of Apartheid Week, Israel, the only democracy in the Middle East which had rule of man-made law and human rights, was a state as bad as South Africa or even Nazi Germany in the past. The Star of David merged with a swastika was displayed on flags and banners everywhere on campus, and on leaflets being handed out by BDS volunteers. Some more direct slogans were scrawled on banners which intermittently appeared on campus and also around The Town. These included:

ZIONISTS DIE
EVERY JEW IS A ZIO-FASCIST
ISRAEL HAS NO RIGHT TO EXIST
JEWS CREATED CAPITALISM
JEWS FINANCED THE SLAVE TRADE
FIGHT APARTHEID FOR PALESTINE
BOYCOTT, DIVEST, SANCTIONS AGAINST
ISRAEL NOW!
ISRAEL = THE NAZIS OF NOW

These 'anti-Zionist' banners and Palestinian flags flew alongside the many blue starry EU flags which fluttered – or, rather, sagged soggy in the wet Welsh weather – all over the campus. The Town was the rainiest in Britain, apparently, so downpours were hardly unusual in winter – or summer, come to that, and spring and autumn. It did put off a lot of protestors, of course, though a few determined Palestinian fans and even some un-shirking Socialist workers huddled together under umbrellas, the comrades occasionally braving the rain to hand out leaflets to passing students.

Mx Abi Rainbow, the much-pierced blue-Mohican-ed University Women's Officer, had demanded the phallocentric symbol of patriarchal oppression – otherwise known as a Christmas tree – was chopped down and shredded into sawdust, and that no such phallus would ever be erected again on the diverse and inclusive safe space of the campus. Her demand was rejected – mainly, it seems, because it was a nice old pine tree which the management rather liked.

They also rejected her demand that 'eye rape' become a new offence under the university's diversity code, because banning people from looking at other people on threat of expulsion from academia was seen by some as a tad extreme even for the radical feminists, and possibly even a teeny-weeny bit unfair for any heterosexual young men on campus with their healthy Darwinian urges. Radical feminists had arguably always been po-faced puritans, as much as any dictatorship in history, keen to crush individual freedoms and demand submission to whatever dogma they deemed 'correct' at any given time.

However, some demands were met – mistletoe was now banned on campus for being a historically anti-women symbol of male oppression, for promoting 'rape culture' and not creating 'an inclusive environment', although the Pagan society protested, saying the church had banned the ancient fertility symbol for centuries too. However, all varieties of holly, which also has ancient fertility symbolism, were allowed on campus, possibly partly because there were several mature bushes and trees planted in the grounds and the university wanted to keep them, if only to avoid the cost of replacement. It was, of course, always good to know which plants were sexist or racist, in order that they could be rooted out immediately!

That particular week was also '*Shwmae Su'mae*' or 'Speak Welsh' Week at Cambrian University, though the language activists were annoyed that over 90% of native British/Welsh staff lacked the ability to speak *Cymraeg*, and no foreign lecturer did either. The radical nationalists had demanded that only Welsh be spoken or used in lectures, something the university management was apparently sympathetic to achieving at some unspecified point in the future (ironically at a time when many universities overseas, especially in European countries, such as the Netherlands, Germany, Switzerland and the Czech Republic, had begun to teach courses entirely in English) though even the Plaid members in management realised that the demand might be a tad impractical. It was agreed instead that this would be a 'stated aim', which calmed down the more hot-blooded angry swivel-eyed nationalists a little – for a short while, anyway. A few native Welsh speakers on the staff persisted in giving lectures and tutorials in 'the language', even though it was one that a very few of their students understood.

Outside on the campus forecourt, the nationalist language activists competed with the Israel Apartheid Week protestors in the rain, keen to catch passing students and dispense of leaflets and advice about learning Welsh. The problem from their point of view was that they mostly insisted on only speaking in Welsh, which only a small minority of passing students could understand. Consequently, they had huge piles of left-over, untaken leaflets dripping from their damp hands, which were, like they themselves, getting damper and soggier by the minute.

Before the end of term, Crump had been told, in an email, that due to his behaviour in classes, he had to attend a training course at the Shirley Bassey Diversity and Inclusion Re-education Centre. His first session was due that afternoon.

In a break between showers, Crump was standing outside in the forecourt with Dylan, getting some fresh air. He sipped from a cup of alleged coffee and winced at the weird plasticky taste.

Everywhere, students were milling about as usual, on their way to or from classes, staring zombie-like at smartphone screens, often with over-sized headphones on their heads or ridiculous-looking white plastic Wi-Fi tags stuck in their ears – and, of course, carrying around the obligatory plastic bottles of water, as if they all faced the imminent threat of finding themselves lost in the middle of the Sahara Desert and dehydrating to death.

How very ridiculous! When Crump was at school twenty-five or thirty years earlier, did everyone carry around a bottle of water? No. And did they ever lose anyone who died of thirst during double maths on a Wednesday afternoon? Not as far as Crump knew, though the subject lost him frequently. There were no bleached bones by the roadside of poor unfortunates who had forgotten to carry a water bottle on the walk to the bus-stop in the suburban deserts of north-west Kent. There was never a barefoot trek of hundreds of miles to refill plastic bottles at the nearest watering hole either. And yet, these days, everyone behaved as though lack of a water bottle would mean imminent dehydration and death.

And, for that matter, were there in those days constant queues of people outside phone boxes (remember them!) desperate to call everyone they knew continually to check they were still there, safe and alive, as everyone did now on mobile phones? Of course not. They had something called 'common sense' back then, instead of constant over-hyped paedo-hysteria in the media.

But these were the times Crump was living in, however ridiculous, hysterical and facile. He would just have to adapt and survive, be Darwinian and pragmatic, accept change even if he hated it and thought it pointless and daft. It was the same feeling most teachers probably got on the regular occasions when the Department of Education changed policy on the National Curriculum.

'How did I get so bloody old?' thought Crump as he gazed amazed at a changing, youthful world that he found he liked less and less as the years rained by. These youngsters were almost a different species to him, and he knew it. It was ridiculous, but he yearned sometimes to '*turn back the clock*', as smooth 1980s synth duo Johnny Hates Jazz once sang – not that any kids now would have heard of them or that decade's melodic pop songs, so used were they to the factory-farmed electronic bleeps of EDM or the immodest facile rants of cacophonous crappy, yacky grime rap.

Suddenly, Dylan tensed up, and hurried inside The Learning Tower. Crump turned his head to see the robotic and witchy Lesley Snyde walking past. What was it with her? Why was Dylan so nervous and scared whenever she appeared?

A chemical stench twitched in his nostrils. He turned to see Professor Pip Pooman heading in the other direction, no doubt back to his lab on Floor Seven of The Learning Tower. And with him, bizarrely, was Colin Kunti from The New York Diner. Why? Crump couldn't work it out.

It was when Crump approached the Shirley Bassey Diversity and Inclusion Re-education Centre that he saw Abi Rainbow skulking out of the Catherine Zeta-Jones Counselling Hub. He had to admit to himself that he wasn't surprised, as the blue-haired harridan seemed permanently angry and set to explode, usually at men, who, as far as Crump could make out, she blamed for all that was or is or ever will be bad in the world. He felt a sudden pang of sympathy for whichever counsellor was seeing her – whether Ms Crackmore, Miss Quirk or Mr Petrichor would be the one unfortunate enough to have to dive into the mind within the troubled, man-hating, raging brain of Abi Rainbow. Poor bugger, whoever it was.

Crump was just thankful he hadn't been sent to see any counsellor there, not after his last experience at Thames Met, though he appreciated the benefit of such support for some on certain occasions. He did wonder, though, whether the anti-resilience training all children seemed to get these days in our risk-averse, safety-fixated, cotton wool culture was actually harming them, stunting them from developing normally into adolescents and adults, and encourage them to think even the slightest failure or set-back in life – which Crump's generation just dealt with – were a reason for a serious mental health crisis and the stated need for counselling. Learned behaviour?

Crump remembered a friend of a friend in London who was a school counsellor, and the tales she told of the utter trivia that caused students to knock on her door – which included: not being asked to the cinema with others in a girl's class (which made her sob uncontrollably), or not getting A* in every single exam, or not winning at sports day, or just not feeling absolutely ecstatically happy all of the time. A shame they didn't teach Stoicism at schools more, Crump thought. Accepting that life has both good and bad bits in the round, and that happiness, like sadness, is part of life but not a permanent state of being, not unless you're brain-damaged or deluded or maybe a loonie-toon religious zealot, that is – or, quite possibly, all three.

Unhappiness is more common than happiness. So why assume you should always be happy? Life is a cocktail of both – of all.

"Pronoun badges on, please, guys," said Noman Ghosh, the Indian-accented senior trans-awareness trainer of uncertain gender who was also, apparently, a well-respected 'transformation coach', whatever that even meant.

Crump put on his HE/HIM/HIS badge, though he could have chosen SHE, or IT, or one of the new transgender ones such as ZE, or XE, or VE, or ZHE, or YO, or E, or AE, or EY, or HU, or PEH, or PER, if he wanted to show that he was genderfluid, transgender, pansexual or non-binary.

He noticed Noman Ghosh was wearing a badge that said AE – and which gave the object pronoun as 'AER' and the possessive as 'AER'. How the heck did you pronounce them?

But he also looked at Noman with a sort of awe, after what Dylan had told him earlier:

"He ain't *no man*, but he ain't no *woman* either…"

"So…"

"So he chopped his bollocks off back in India, and his knob, the works…"

"Bloody hell! He castrated himself? No way!" Crump said, stunned.

"Yes way. He says some men do that in India. Must be the heat, innit?"

"What, so he's like... Action Man?" was all Crump could think to say.

"No idea what that is," said Dylan, "but, he's a blank, basically... between his legs, like. I s'pose he must have a pee-hole, kindathing..."

Crump winced. But he had to admire any man with a pain threshold high enough to withstand self-castration. It reminded him of the 19th-century explorer, scholar and brilliant linguist Richard Burton's self-circumcision, done so he could 'pass' as a Muslim and enter Mecca in disguise. Talk about bloody dedication!

Crump focused away from the memory, back onto the training session.

Other diversity trainers there wore various pronoun badges: Polly Zog wore a 'SHE/HER/HER' badge, though seemed rather masculine; Manon Brattle was already wearing several badges, one which proudly declared 'it' to be 'non-binary intersex', but also had a XE/XEM/XYR' badge (again, how to pronounce that? As a 'Z' or as a Greek X, so more 'Chr'?); and transphobia trainer Gareth Gaybars preferred 'HU/HUM/HUS'.

The only trainer not sporting a pronoun marker went by the improbable name of Bambi Blip. She was wearing her own unique bright badge which said one word: 'TRANSPECIES'.

'No doubt if she'd felt like a tree, she'd have identified as a "TRANSPLANT",' he thought, 'or maybe if she'd put on weight lately, she'd be "TRANSFAT"...'

Crump closed his eyes and took a deep breath. It was going to be a very long day.

He looked around at his fellow transgressors, all of whom had been sent to be 're-educated' in the wonders of transgenderism – though most were clearly students, so perhaps needed an education first, before any re-education.

The one thing they all had in common was that someone had reported them to one of the university's many 'harassment advisers', perhaps using the free helpline number or email address on signs displayed at various locations on campus. Precisely who had reported them, and why, was kept confidential. 'How very Stasi,' thought Crump, but he said nothing.

Maybe he should have been annoyed that he, a lecturer and staff member over the age of forty, should be 're-educated' in the wonders of transgenderism in a class where most others were less than half his age – and at least one was one of his own students too!

In reality, however, he found it refreshing. Crump had rarely got hassle from any students in his teaching career, and often got on well with them. Fellow teachers, however, were another matter – what with all the office politics, career ambitions, passive bullying and asserting of status in the educational class system. He had always hated that.

One thing he noticed immediately was that most in the class were white British. This was odd really, because from Crump's long teaching experience both in the UK and overseas, he knew that both men and women in the vast majority of the world, especially the developing world, tended to believe in rather rigid gender stereotypes and, in the main, did not accept homosexuality as a lifestyle. He'd lost count of the number of times international students had told him that women should cook for their husbands and look after the children, not the man. And yet, if such students expressed that, or any perceived homophobic or transphobic opinions on campus, and even if they were reported to 'harassment advisers', no action was seemingly taken. Was there perhaps one rule for white British students and another for ethnic minorities, such as UK Muslims (who were rarely accepting of modern gender freedom or homosexuality), or African Christians, or other minority ethnic faith groups, who shared the same prejudices?

Crump glanced around at his fellow students. Their names were British and/or Welsh: Chris, Darren, Rhys, Kyle, Caleb, Geraint, Claire, Courtney, Hannah, Cat, Megan, Bethan, Lauren, James, Dale, Dean, Ashley, Connor, Noah, Kellie, Anwen, George... Not a single Mohammed amongst them, nor anyone with an 'ethnic' name. All very strange really as Crump knew as a fact that well over half of UK Muslims and the black community too (both African and West Indian) stated in polls they wanted to recriminalize homosexuality, and even a belief in executing such people was not uncommon. So he really doubted these ethnic and faith groups would be very tolerant about transgenderism really. He could be wrong, but...

"Right, guys," said Noman Ghosh. "It is now high time to learn about transgenderism and the multiplicity of gender, isn't it?"

A few nods and 'yeahs' from the student body.

"It is the right of all persons to be choosing their gender identity. Transphobia is discrimination, harassment, bullying, hate crime, or unconscious bias based on gender identity and expression, isn't it?"

'Errr, yes?' thought Crump, but he stayed silent.

In no way did he ever believe in bullying anyone for anything, or persecuting or discriminating against anyone on grounds of race, gender, sexuality, belief or opinion. In that, he out-liberal-ed the majority of self-identifying 'liberal-minded' progressive persons, he knew, who were often all for silencing those with the 'wrong' opinions and hounding them out of careers, for example, in the name of tolerance and equality.

They then had a 'thought shower' which was what pc universities called 'brainstorms' these days, the latter word now banned in case it offended people with epilepsy – though Crump wondered how many epileptics had actually been asked for an opinion.

There was soon listed on the whiteboard everything that could be considered transphobic, including making derogatory remarks, unacceptable behaviour, ignoring someone's chosen pronoun preference or failing to use *'they'* when asked to by someone who is non-binary, speculating if someone is a man or a woman (which Crump couldn't help himself doing with the trainer Noman Ghosh), and talking about someone's gender history. Using the wrong pronoun was, apparently, a hate crime…

"It's a human right to live as the gender you want to be," said Polly Zog, in a very deep voice.

"The Equality Act protects trans people from hate crime and abuse in law," added Manon Brattle.

"Yeah and so it's trans-misogyny to discriminate against transwomen…" added Gary Gaybars.

"Such as enforcing gender rules by telling a transwoman that they cannot use a female toilet," added trans-species trainer Bambi Blip, whose eyes looked rather odd, Crump now saw. Perhaps, even, a tad 'deer-like'? Was that possible? Were people having cosmetic surgery to change species now?

Crump knew of a lot of feminists – the TERFS and the cis-gender females – who aggressively opposed the idea that transwomen, who were often still in possession of a penis and testicles too, though dressed as females and maybe on medication, should be able to use female toilets. There had been instances of rape in female toilets by such transwomen, and in places such as changing rooms and prisons too.

After various rather tedious 'fun' activities, Noman Ghosh continued:

"Transphobia is intolerance of gender diversity and is being based around the wrong idea that there are two sexes only, male and female, isn't it?"

"But there *are* only two sexes," said Crump, unable to hold it in any longer, "male and female – that is science, biology, evolution. It's just the way it is!"

"No, it isn't, isn't it?" said Noman Ghosh.

"Is it?" said Crump.

"It is, isn't it, but it isn't, is it?" said (or, perhaps, asked) Noman Ghosh – neither he/she/it or anyone present, student or teacher, was really sure.

"But… it is… I think…" mumbled Crump, totally confused.

He was thinking of a saying that he always used to counter Creationists and others whose dearly held beliefs and theories were not backed up by any evidence: 'You have a right to your opinions, but you do not have a right to your facts.'

"To illustrate what I am meaning, imagine two islands —"

"Oh, I loves Barry Island, I does, it's lush, it is," said a student called Dean, who seemed perhaps still a little drunk or stoned from the night before.

"Caldey Island's gorgeous in summer with all the seabirds," added a hippy-chick student called Bethan, "it's so spiritual… I'm a very spiritual person…"

Noman Ghosh stared at each of these students like a Hindu demon god. They hung their heads in shame and mumbled 'sorry' to the class.

"As I am saying, there are two islands, and no-one is permitted to swim between them. This is like the male and female gender stereotypes in the society. And anyone who is trying to leave an island and to swim in gender spectrum sea, is often penalised and discriminated against and that is transphobia, which is a form of sexism, isn't it?"

'Yes but, yes but, yes but… ' thought Crump. 'Please let's not do any daft diversity activities where we have to pretend to be living on a fucking island… '

"Isn't it?" grinned Noman Ghosh, glaring at him, seemingly reading his thoughts as if his head had been made of glass.

"Well..."

"Transphobia is intolerance of gender diversity, and based on the lie that there are only two sexes, male and female, which you stay in from birth," boomed Polly Zog.

"But there are, scientifically speaking, only two sexes in nature," said Crump.

He may have been an English specialist but he also knew his science – he had always liked biology at school too. There were two sexes, based on chromosomes, and that was it – though, as always in nature, there was variation, mutation and deformities. Indeed, certain Renaissance dramatists such as Christopher Marlowe, Ben Jonson and Shakespeare, too, were rather fixated on the idea of gender-bending and hermaphrodites, which was the 'transgender' of then, more or less.

"Stop your trans-bashing!" screamed the intersex Manon Brattle.

An entire classful of eyes stared at Crump, thankful it wasn't them being singled out.

"Look, there is a difference between sex and gender, surely? Gender, these days, can be anything you choose, but your sex can't, surely? It's all about chromosomes... the way you're born—"

"No, actually, it is not! Nothing is fixed, including gender. We are all born blank slates!'" shouted Gary Gaybars.

'Aye, there's the rub,' thought Crump – that, right there, is the conflict. The sex you were born to, versus the gender you choose from the smorgasbord made available by various sociological, women's and gender studies departments since the 1960s.

"Suicide rates amongst trans people are massively high because of haters like you!" screamed Manon Brattle.

Crump had suffered such diversity training sessions before, and knew how to survive them: his skin had become as thick and scaly as a trans-dragon's over the years.

"In no way at all do I ever – and I mean *ever* – support the bullying or harassment of anyone for anything, not their race or gender or anything else."

"*Vell*, I am quite pleased to hear it, isn't it?" said Noman Ghosh.

"Of course, the reported rate of suicide attempts is awful. However, could this not be because those who want to identify as transgender may well be suffering mental illness in the first place – which has made them confused and so yearn to change their lives by adopting a brand-new gender identity? It's 'grass-is-greener-on-the-other-side' stuff, surely, in lots of cases? Don't many who transition later do 'de-transitioning' to revert to their birth gender or sex?"

"So, I so disagree with letting children go transgender, yeah," said a very young student called Lauren.

"S'like putting the poor little tots on medication," agreed another, called Anwen, "like they's mentalists or whatever, innit, though?"

"But we *must* be letting children swim between the two gender islands, isn't it?" said Noman Ghosh.

"What about sharks?" said one student.

"Or drowning, innit?" said another.

"Some boy at my school died like that on the Gower, he did – rip-tide, they said," added a third.

And so, they all played pirates on the high seas between gender stereotype islands until the sun crossed the main sail...

Eventually, by the end of the gender re-education session, everyone was thinking 'correctly' and diversely, obediently parroting the transgender mantra of inclusion drilled into them by the various assorted trainers present.

Crump didn't want to fail the diversity training, so stayed silent – just like so many academics in the face of massive threats to free speech.

There was, apparently, an organisation dedicated to Academic Freedom which campaigns for freedom of speech and expression on UK university campuses. It has a mere 700 members. So just 700 brave named academic souls were prepared to stand up and be counted as supporting Enlightenment values, free debate and speech, on all matters and subjects, with one proviso: no inciting of violence. That was 700 from well over 100,000, possibly nearer 200,000 academics employed by over 130 UK universities – a fraction of one per cent. *For shame!*

Whatever happened to '*I disapprove of what you say, but I will defend to the death your right to say it*' – the soundbite created by Voltaire's biographer Evelyn Beatrice Hall to encapsulate his staunch belief in freedom of speech and expression? At UK universities today, saying as much could make you a heretic, an enemy of the hyper-sensitive, flake state of intolerant 'political correctness' we're living in. Sad, that – and worrying.

All that is needed for bad things to happen is for people to stay silent – and that, sadly, is what most UK academics chose to do, for reasons of stark self-interest, cowardice and wilful blindness.

Crump was ashamed of his silence too, but he knew from experience that he had to go along with whatever the present higher education regime demanded – or else. Was it really any different from people parroting the party line under Nazism or Communism or in any barbaric tinpot dictatorship, like China or Islamic states today? Conform or pay the price. Everyone working at universities knew that, and the vast majority stayed quiet, despite seeing the wrong wrought before them.

At long last, the diversity training ended. To round it all off there was a talk by Dr Paracelsus, a senior and highly popular psychologist at the university medical practice, who was known to be exceedingly liberal with his prescribing of medication, such as opioids, Xanax or Ritalin, and whose flaccid face, it seemed, was curved into a peaceful, almost beatific, and possibly permanently stoned smile of perfect equanimity.

After the transphobia gender diversity training session, which Crump was extremely glad not to have been kicked out of for his adherence to scientific fact, he went for a walk to clear his head. The rain had stopped now, though the sky was darkening, and it actually felt much colder than earlier in the day, with a real Arctic wind too. He badly needed some fresh air, and to be away from the university, so bought a bacon sandwich from an off-campus bakery nearby and wandered into the park to eat it.

Sandra the pig was there, as ever, in her compound, big and porky, and gazing up at him smug and plump as a sausage.

"This could be you," he said, taking a big bite of the bacon sandwich and remembering the nasty needless bite the sow had given his innocent hand.

She oinked loudly at him. This, no doubt, was pork talk for 'GO FUCK YOURSELF, LONGPIG!'

Crump laughed – at Sandra, and at himself, standing there in the park, talking to a pig.

Then something moved – in the corner of his eye. He turned and looked up to see – Nelson the cat, sat watching the world from a low branch of a tree.

The feline was staring at him with a look of complete and utter condescension and probably would, if it could, have shook its little ginger-furred head wearily and rolled its fixed yellow eyes.

"You should go home, pussy cat," Crump called out – but then, Nelson was gone.

A mother with two young children hurried quickly past Crump, glimpsing nervously up at the face of a man she was no doubt now convinced was the local nutter-cum-paedophile. All men, especially lone men, were under suspicion of that these days – always. One of the kiddies was transfixed by the screen of a smartphone, instead of looking around at the trees and nature on display in the park – a depressing image of present and future misery, if there ever was one.

Crump finished the last of his sandwich.

"Fucking animals," he mumbled to himself, wondering how a pig and a cat had now managed to get him flagged as the local pervert.

It was as he was ambling back to the university campus that he noticed a tiny snowflake dancing in the air in front of his eyes, then another, then more. Hardly a blizzard, but definitely snow, which was unusual for The Town, thanks to its mild damp weather courtesy of the Gulf Stream, direct from Mexico. More rural and hilly parts of South Wales sometimes got snow, but it was rare on the coast.

'Winter's coming,' thought Crump, with a little shiver.

Crump was due to visit his mum that evening at the care home. He did what he had to do quickly in the English Studies Department, staying for as short a time as he could, just saying a quick 'hello' to the ever-smiling pink bundle of ebullient bouncy joy that was Tanya Snuggs. There was still no sign of Karen Crisp who was apparently on sick leave now and no doubt enjoying her illness immensely.

It was as he was going home that Crump saw a new notice pinned to the department wall informing staff and students that the building of 'snowmen' was forbidden, and that anyway, the correct word to use for these seasonal transphobic statues was now 'snowpersons'.

'*Snow joke*,' smiled Crump at the gender-neutral command from above.

It was just so reassuring that the university knew how to prioritise the crucial aspects of higher education, especially in the run-up to the ancient festival of 'Winterval'.

No doubt university managers were concerned in case a transgender person saw a snowman and was triggered into ironic meltdown?

His mum looked very frail on his visit to her that evening, frailer than even a week before.

They shared some ready-salted Pringles, the usual cup of tea. Any calories his mum could eat were good, even high-fat processed carbs, as she had lost weight since her stroke, and now seemed thinner than ever. How different from the solid Welsh mother he remembered as a child, always worrying about her weight, tutting at the scales in the bathroom as the dial swung to double digits. She'd lost at least two stone since those long-ago healthy days, but now she never seemed to have much of an appetite, or to finish a meal.

"I love you so much, Kevin," said his mum in her stroke-slurred speech, holding her son's hand tightly in her small wrinkled fingers. "Your father would be so proud of you."

Crump's parents had married late, at forty, and he was their only child. Now he himself was over forty, of course. Lucky still to have a parent alive too. The curse of those born to older parents was to lose them at a younger age than many, and also not to have grandparents around, which was the case with Crump.

His mum then said something Crump couldn't understand clearly, despite being able to comprehend much of her speech. It was so frustrating when those who'd had strokes couldn't be understood – both for the speakers themselves and their loved ones. Just one little blip in the brain, and so much could go.

The brains of younger stroke victims could, remarkably, make up for the loss of any part damaged by a blood clot by using other areas of the brain to take over that function – a neat trick known as neuroplasticity. Not so easy for older people though, and his mum was over eighty.

His mum's old eyes grew moist and she looked emotional, which was not like her at all. She was never a blubberer.

"What is it, Mum?" said Kevin.

She pulled his hand to her face and kissed it, attempting a smile, though the facial paralysis of the stroke had robbed her of the beautiful beaming smile he remembered.

Crump stayed with her for almost an hour, but then could sense she was getting tired. He told his mum he loved her and kissed her goodnight. That were nothing more he could do or say.

Driving back home that evening, Crump felt blank. It was almost as though he didn't exist, or at least was some piece of driftwood floating around the world, or one of those plastic bags you see flying through the air on windy days, rootless, aimless and adrift.

The local radio news said schools would be closed because of the snow. But it wasn't snowing any more, and the feeble flurry of snow earlier that day had hardly settled anyway.

'Typical,' thought Crump. 'Three snowflakes fall in Lower Cymtwrch and every school within a radius of 200 miles closes down.'

That never happened when Crump was a kid, not once – and he grew up in north-west Kent which got more snow than The Town, what with South Wales being warm and wet by comparison. He remembered at least three winters, usually in January, where there was heavy snowfall and ice, and yet he never missed one day of school and none shut their doors either.

Was this yet another example of 'elf n safety' culture? More likely inspired by the fear of litigation raising its compo-chasing head. Parents would probably sue within seconds if their little darlings slipped on a snowflake, after all.

But this was not a healthy way to live, surely? Being so hysterically risk-averse actually damaged society and children too, who were trained by their paranoid parents to be incessantly scared and to see everything as a threat. That was why Crump saw kids on bicycles down the park, dressed up in so many protective pads and the obligatory crash helmet, and Mummy or Daddy worrying along a few feet behind them, in case they had the tiniest of mishaps or accidents.

How different from when Crump was a boy. He was outside having adventures on his bike with no padding or helmet from aged six or so, falling off it, grazing his knees, sure, but brushing himself off, dusting himself down and carrying on regardless, and learning how to deal with, and assess, risk. Life was certainly healthier back then, especially for children. Modern society was toxic for kids in Britain, ruled by hysteria about 'keeping safe' and fabricated myths that bogeymen paedo-monsters were hiding everywhere behind every lamp post ready to pounce on them and gobble them all up. No wonder those overprotected children grew up to be the enfeebled and unresilient toddler-brained teenagers of Generation Snowflake.

The local radio news started talking about Cambrian University and Brexit. He'd had enough of it all, so tuned the car radio to a music station.

They were playing a catchy seasonal song with a 1950s feel called *Happy to be Home this Christmas:*

Happy to be home,
You should never be alone,

Happy to be home this year.

Crump thought back to his childhood in the modest semi in Kent. That was the only place he had ever really felt at home – but it wasn't his home any more, and nor was that town.

He supposed his home was wherever he washed up really, wherever he lay his hat – though he didn't even own a hat.

As the Christmas song sung itself out on the radio, and the streetlights blinked, Crump determined to text Fatima when he got home – to ask her out, for a coffee, a meal, and maybe more.

*

That evening, Crump was in Rob's apartment at the Marina. It was ultra-modern and minimalist, an occasional expensive-looking vase on otherwise empty shelves. There was a magnificent view of the sea and the whole bay through the widescreen penthouse window.

Crump gazed through the dusk at it all. He realised he had never ever in his life been inside an apartment like this, certainly not in The Town. So how did it all seem so familiar?

'Ah yes,' he thought, 'TV Scandi-drama series.' He could almost have been in Denmark. So silly how people – especially developers and interior designers – just copied trends like that. But hey, he didn't want to pee in anybody's sugar sandwich…

"D'you want normal tea or gay tea?"

Crump winced with a smile.

"What's 'gay' tea, Rob? Purlease…"

Rob laughed loudly.

"Only kidding, Crumpet. I keep gay tea in for the girls – y'know, herbal stinky stuff, no idea what's in it…"

"Just… normal… tea… is fine, Rob. Milk no sugar."

Rob clapped his hands – twice – in a manner which reminded Crump of Yul Brynner in *The King and I*.

As if by magic, two pretty Oriental girls appeared. They looked about eighteen or nineteen - certainly no older than twenty. They were identical, and dressed in the precise same pretty silky Oriental dresses too. Rob muttered something to them and they hurried into the open-plan kitchen area.

"That one's Preeda – which means 'joyful' – and she's her twin sister Malee, which means 'flower', in Thai language. Nice innit? Better than Brenda or Tracy or Sharon…"

The girls smiled coyly at Crump, who blushed a bit – he couldn't help it.

"Blinding, aren't they? My beautiful girls…"

"I… I think all names mean something, originally,' said Crump.

"Ah I forgot, Crumpet – you're the English expert!"

"Well, not… an *expert*…"

The Thai sisters arrived with tea and some biscuit-type snacks. Crump tried one. It was all delicious – those savoury Thai flavours swirling like the sea in his mouth.

"Bit of a foodie these days," said Rob, patting the stomach that was squeezing against the buttons of his shirt. "Well, I was already a fattie and drunkie, so… why not get the full matching set, eh?"

He had accepted an invitation from Rob to travel to Cardiff to attend a lecture by Jorvic Andersson, who Crump had vaguely heard of. He was a controversial Canadian academic who had been banned – 'no-platformed' – by most British universities, including Cambrian, and The Town council too, for his views challenging the now-orthodox feminist and 'politically correct' view of the world, and his resolute defence of freedom of speech and the values of Western civilisation.

On the way there, in Rob's smooth, blue BMW, they discussed Cambrian University's unilateral declaration of independence from Brexit Britain.

"I'm no lawyer, Crumpet," said Rob. "My hourly rate's lower for a start, ha-ha!"

Crump chortled at that. He remembered the eye-watering rates he'd had to pay solicitors on the few occasions he had dealt with them in the past.

"But from what I hear, it all revolved around the founding treaty of 1912, which gave the university autonomy, and was signed by no less than King George V —"

"Sailor king."

"Spot-on – who was bit pissed up, some say, and didn't bother to read the treaty in detail before signing it off, on account of badly wanting to get out for a day's bobbing about and gin-swilling on boats."

"Really?" said Crump. "I didn't think he was a drinker. His dad, Edward VII when Prince of Wales, and his son, before he briefly became Edward VIII maybe, but —"

"S'all with the damn piss-dribbling shithead lawyers now anyway – and you know what that means?"

Crump shrugged.

"One – it'll cost a fucking fortune, for whoever's paying, probably the taxpayer, and... Two – it'll go on for months and more likely years... I'm still fighting a property case in Hong Kong from four years ago. Got a lovely girl over there goes by the name of Li Ming – means 'beautiful and bright'. Nice, eh?"

"How many... girls... do you have around the world, Rob?" asked Crump, genuinely curious.

"As many as I want, vicar! No need to be all holier-than-thou, Crumpet – we all do it!"

"I don't – unfortunately," Crump mumbled.

"Ultimately, all sex is a transaction, always. All marriages always have been – the Asians are more honest wiv stuff like that, an' all. So I've got the dosh, property, blah blah – the girls've got, well… you saw…"

Crump had. And he had to admit he envied Rob his life full of beautiful girls, the bottomless pot of money, the expensive properties around the world. He couldn't help it. It was, indeed, enviable.

He wondered momentarily what swapping his life for Rob's for a day, or a week, or a year, as in some crass Hollywood comedy, would be like. Would it be empty and meaningless? Would he yearn for the nobility of honest work and the quest for knowledge? Or would he just have a ball? He had no idea.

But then, Crump had never been happy-go-lucky as Rob had been at school. No, Crump had always been a worrier, often awkward and frustratingly unable to enjoy the moment. Would he be the same if he were lying in bed with two beautifully naked Thai girls desperate to fulfil his every wish and demand and…

Rob was also right in saying he was just doing what feminists advised women to do – he was living the life he wanted, how he wanted, without hurting anyone, as a 'strong, independent man'. The 'equal and opposite' rule applied: if a female human being had been living such a life, then that would be seen as a positive thing and her right, as a strong, independent, empowered woman. So why should it be any different for a man?

After parking the car, they walked towards the theatre where Jorvic Andersson was speaking. They heard the yells and chants of the protest before they saw it.

"Bloody feminazi sisterhood," said Rob, "but what d'you expect. Feministas are so fucking predictable."

As they drew closer, Crump recognised a few faces amongst the two-hundred-or-so protestors. Abi Rainbow, women's officer from Cambrian University was there, with her blue Mohican and piercings, yelling and screaming angrily as per usual.

But with her, and holding the usual banners – on 'Toxic Masculinity', 'Rape Culture', '#TimesUp', '#MeToo' etc – were faces which had remained burned in Crump's brain for a decade: the fanatical man-haters Cecilia and Margaret No-Name from London's Thames Metropolitan University. They hadn't changed a bit, especially the pale, female and stale Cecilia, who still looked like she had bled white. And with Margaret No-Name was a child of around ten, a daughter, with Down's Syndrome who, for some reason, looked oddly familiar.

And there was another child, about the same age, who looked like a boy but was dressed like a girl in a dress, and had blue hair, shaved at the sides – looking like a mini-me Abi Rainbow, but male. Definitely male. Clear to see, even at that age.

Crump hated how people used children to promote their views on demonstrations such as this – he didn't care what the cause was. It was exploitative – it was, in fact, tantamount to child abuse. *Keep the kids out of it!*

Then, as if acting as one organism, the protestors all seemed to turn and look straight at Crump, glaring angrily as they screamed their hateful slogans into his face. Some of them recognised him too – he could see it in their eyes.

Suddenly, something spiralled through the air and splatted on the pavement near his feet. A white and red creamy puddle grew on the ground. A milkshake. There were one or two splashes of on-trend multicoloured milkshake on his shoes and jeans too.

Then another milkshake missile whizzed past Crump's ears – no more than a couple of feet away from his face.

Crump was grateful for the arm that grabbed him and pulled him into the theatre foyer. It was Rob. Crump sighed in relief. He looked at his hands and realised he was shaking.

Through the glass theatre doors, Crump could see Abi Rainbow still staring right at him, rage fizzing and hissing like hate in her misandrist face.

"Y'alright, Crumpet?" asked Rob.

Crump nodded. He breathed, shakily.

"Bloody idiots. But remember, this is an age when *hurty* feelings come above everything else, especially free speech. Sums up our stupid *clownworld* backward feminut times, eh?"

"They say men are in crisis," said Jorvic Andersson from a podium at the centre of the stage. "Well, it is true that in Western civilisation, at least, men – and boys – the 'masculine' – is under constant attack. You only have to look at the media or watch TV, especially the BBC…"

Booing from many in the packed theatre.

"Some of you here will have experienced personally the disadvantage meted out to men in the family courts. To them, men are sperm donors and wallets on legs – no more. What rights do fathers have?"

"None!" shouted several men in the audience.

"And we all know, that children, especially boys, who grow up in families without fathers do worse on every single measure – whether it's failing at school, getting involved in crime via the dad-substitute of the gang, falling prey to the epidemic of depression and drugs, especially opioids, sweeping our countries and communities."

Loud applause around Crump. He could see some fellow audience members in tears – big, strong men, weeping.

"Men lose custody of the kids in 80–90% of break-ups and get full custody in only 14% of divorces. We make up about 85% of homeless people, are 76% of suicides, 70% of murder victims, 97% of war deaths. In your great NHS, specific women's healthcare gets at least *seven times* the funding of men's healthcare. And yet the feminist industry lectures us about *white male privilege!*"

More huge applause. Crump looked around him at the audience. It was predominantly white and male.

"They say women are oppressed by an invisible monster called 'The Patriarchy' which many feminists use as an excuse to blame men for all they mess up in their own lives."

Cheers from the stalls.

"I call this 'The Patriarchy Myth' – and the idea women have been oppressed through all of history is simply a silly, terrible, myth – which is basically a lie, but one which conveniently lets mediocre women demand promotion and leadership opportunities they do not deserve via so-called positive action. Positive for them, yes. Most of them wouldn't stand a hope of getting promotion on merit, eh?"

Laughing all around.

"Most people have been oppressed in history, men included, by the ruling class, which included – and *includes* – women, both directly and indirectly. That ruling class is now the so-called liberal 'political elite' that runs society – the ones who ban and 'no-platform' the likes of me from speaking at universities, because what we say – otherwise known as '*the truth*' – may offend people."

Booing around the auditorium.

"The tyranny of accepted thinking and conformity, the spiral of silence in the head through self-censorship caused by fear: it's everywhere in our sick society – the silent surrender of civilised values. But free speech is never frightened speech. It is high time to stand up to the bullies. The ability to express ourselves freely is fundamental to a free society. If we do not believe in freedom of expression for those we dislike or even hate, then we do not believe in it at all!"

Crump was cheering and clapping now, as was Rob beside him.

"What we know as 'identity politics' is a dangerous game and also a lie. As with gender politics, so with ethnic and religious demands. In a free society, everyone should have the right to criticise religion – all faiths, and lack or faith too, and all political ideologies. In recent years, we've let religious extremism set the terms, and that is wrong."

Loud cheers all around.

"Islamic extremism is on the rise. We have a real problem with radical Islam, and yet, the political elite want to stop us talking about the faith that inspires terrorists – TV reports of the massacres at Manchester and London never even mentioned the word Muslim or Islam or Jihadist. Why? They kept referring to 'terror attacks' by 'attackers'... so I was thinking, what sort of attackers?"

Wry laughs from the audience.

"Maybe they meant... attacking *rabbits*, eh?"

Huge guffaws of laughter.

"Because they never once mentioned that all those attacks on your country, and the ones in France and Germany, were done by Muslims in the name of Islam as part of their *jihad*, their holy war, against infidels who do not share the extreme version of their faith. Feminists might like to note that these people tend to have attitudes to women that date back to the seventh century desert, and they're certainly not very '*woke*' or '*#MeToo*', for sure, and that their prophet had several wives, including one only six years old..."

Huge cheers – the atmosphere was electric and Crump himself felt as though he was buzzing, charged and energised, almost sparking in the dark.

The cheering from every corner of the auditorium which was so ear-splittingly loud Crump thought the roof of the theatre would blast off.

"And, even though this is not my country – that's Canada, eh? Unless you didn't know..."

Warm ripples of laughter.

"It's the same for men and boys throughout the Western World – which *really* hates us now, wants to keep us down, just because of how we were born, via so-called 'positive action' or equality schemes which ignore merit in favour of quotas for women and 'people of colour', all designed with one purpose – to unfairly discriminate against the male in society, especially white men and boys. But..."

Loud applause from an audience whose members recognised themselves.

"... but, do not become resentful at the injustice of the world – work and fight to change it."

Cheers and cheers and cheers.

"Do not avoid fear – embrace it."

More cheers.

"Happiness is a silly, meaningless goal. Remember, life is pain – life is suffering. Deal with it. And don't compare yourself to others, but to the man you were yesterday. That is how to live and grow. Work hard – be kind – see what happens."

More warm applause.

"At some point, you have to decide what kind of man you want to be. So, and I say this from the bottom of my heart, be the man you were meant to be – and forget the rest. Thank you."

Jorvic Andersson stepped back from the podium on the stage. The audience rose as one united organism, clapping and cheering and thanking the man before them. There were tears in many male eyes.

As Crump turned his head, he knew that even cynical old Rob's eyes were moist as he cheered and applauded enthusiastically.

But then Crump could only see him in a joyous blur, because his own eyes were warm with tears too.

*

"I hadn't really heard of him before," said Crump.

He was having lunch on campus with Fatima the following week.

"*Mais oui*," she said. "He is too famous in Canada, eh? He is speaking French real good too…"

"I'm surprised any university there still employs him," said Crump.

He knew from his Canadian friends and previous visits to Ottawa just how 'politically correct' Canada was – even more so than the UK. He had heard of academics there, and in the USA, whose careers had been ruined for daring to challenge the now-orthodox gender-neutral thinking, for example by emphasising innate, biological brain-difference causes of variation in male/female behaviours, abilities and career choices, instead of explaining it all with the 'officially approved' emphasis on stereotypes, social conditioning and lack of role models.

"Oh, by the way, did you hear about what has happened to Johnny Blue?" said Fatima.

Crump shook his head as he chewed his tuna sandwich.

"He is suspended, and now he has left."

"No!" said Crump, genuinely shocked.

"*C'est dommage, ça*… He has been writing on the social media the things which have been going against policies of the university."

"Like what?"

"Oh, you know, he has the opinions on the environment, and the over-population especially, *non*?"

Crump did. He remembered that over-population was a central focus of Johnny Blue's crusade to save the planet, and how disparaging he was of what he called trivial 'green-posing' issues, such as banning plastic straws.

"He is stating online how the people in Africa and Asia are breeding like…"

"Rabbits?" suggested Crump.

"Rats..."

"Oh," mouthed Crump.

"And..."

"And?"

"*Alors*, he has said especially India and China are killing the planet Earth, with pollution and overbreeding... like..."

"Rats?"

"*Ah oui*. And he was talking about sterilisation to save the planet. Some students, they are complaining to the university – and the police..."

"The *police*?"

"Yes, the police were giving him interview under caution. It is *the low*."

"The law!"

"This is what I said – the *low*. But police have been releasing him with no charge, and then Johnny he has told me..."

"Told you... what?"

"*Alors*, he went to university manager and..."

"And?"

"He told them to 'fuck off and die', and then he has resigned."

"Where's Johnny now?" asked Crump, concerned.

"He said he is going abroad, to work for organisations environmental."

"Oh," said Crump, "that's a shame. But maybe for the best, if he's doing something he wants to do. Poor Johnny."

"He ask me to say 'goodbye' to you. *Au revoir*, he has said. He likes you."

Crump stared out of the cafeteria window at the university forecourt, which, for once, was not celebrating a day or week for something or other, and so had no protests or banners – except the usual blue EU flags fluttering forlornly everywhere and, of course, all the posters about missing pets pinned to noticeboards and trees.

The miserably grey wet weather – not, it has to be said, unusual for Wales in late November – meant most of the international media had gone to ground too, back to their four-star hotels with well-stocked mini-bars, no doubt. Crump knew the media – they'd keep feet on the ground here, ready to pounce when any developments happened regarding Cambrian University's unilateral declaration of independence from Brexit.

Crump saw pages from a copy of the crappy *Cambrian Daily News* damp and abandoned on the puddled ground. The front page yelled the headline: PARKING FURY OF MUM OF FOUR. Nothing like breaking news…

It was then that Crump saw Dylan.

"What the…"

"Yeah, I know, it's a bit random, kindathing…"

"But… why?"

Dylan, the mixed-race, dark-featured, curly-haired kid who looked – or so Crump always thought – coolly attractive, if so laid-back he was almost horizontal, had, for reasons best known to himself, got his hair bleached the whitest shade of peroxide blond.

"YOLO," said Dylan.

"You look like that Yazz woman."

"Who?"

"Y'know, that *Only Way Is Up* song… from the late eighties?"

Dylan shrugged and shook his head. Too bloody young to know eighties music, that was his problem! And kids these days had so much choice, they could avoid hearing any music – or, indeed, being exposed to any knowledge at all – that they didn't already know and like. Very different from his generation, with only four TV channels, no internet and only one or two music stations on the radio.

How the hell did he get so sodding old?

Then Crump detected a coy sheepishness in the contours of Dylan's face, the way his almost-smile sat serenely on his lips.

"Ah," said Crump with a knowing grin, "you've got yourself a girlfriend!"

Now it made sense!

"Laters, gotta bounce," said Dylan, and he was off.

'Oh, to be young and free!' thought Crump, though he did wonder where the laid-back always-almost-comatosed kid had got the energy.

*

A couple of days later, Crump was in the Richard Burton Theatre, together with anyone who was anyone at the university, for the annual beano that was the Cambrian University Student Awards.

It had been announced that in the next academic year, it would be renamed the Sir Anthony Hopkins Theatre – probably because the university stood bugger all chance of squeezing any donations out of Richard Burton any more, on account of his being dead. Tony Hopkins, however, despite being over eighty, seemed a much better bet for scribbling a nice fat cheque now and again to a Welsh university theatre which bore his name. This was all unsubstantiated rumour, of course…

The Student Awards had been introduced a few years earlier to, as the glossy brochure stated, *'celebrate the success and achievements of our diverse and vibrant students'* which, when translated from marketing-PR-bullshit-speak, meant: *'we cobbled together these awards so we can promote the university overseas and attract yet more lovely lucrative international students who already make up almost three-quarters of our post-graduate cohort, the Chinese alone representing almost a quarter of those richly diverse, richly vibrant, just plain rich, kerching-ing cash cow foreign student customers!'*

Such collective events were, however, useful for Crump to get to see university staff members and managers especially, and with handy name badges too – thanks to the present craze for offering a choice of which pronouns, from the multi-gender plethora available, people wanted to be known by.

Crump took his seat. He knew there'd be wine and nibbles and a spread afterwards, so was prepared to endure the awards ceremony, if only for that.

The lights on one side of the auditorium kept flickering bright and dim (which could, Crump thought, be a metaphor for his own students) no doubt yet another consequence of a maintenance department which seemed completely unable or unwilling to maintain itself. Such light outages, and other faults with doors, windows, desks, ceilings, floor fittings etc, were now more or less tolerated by staff and students. They all knew nothing would ever get done, even if they complained, which paradoxically meant that the worse the maintenance department's performance, the lower the number of complaints, so the higher they were rated by the university.

It was a bit like police boasting of falling rates of mugging, when street crime was rising, because no-one could be bothered to report it any more and go through all that hassle, because everyone knew nothing would be done, no-one would be caught and any property nicked in the robbery would never be coming back.

If the maintenance department got even worse, their level of complaints may even fall to zero, their perfect score thereby proving how spectacularly successful they were. Similar dubious statistical methods were used at many UK universities to prove the high quality of the education offered too. *Hoorah!*

Crump looked around at the audience. It was all so vibrant and diverse and colourful, with a great many international students – and some of their proud parents –

dressed in bright African robes, traditional Chinese dress, colourful saris and sarongs and headscarves and turbans, and, inevitably, the resolutely puritanically black burqa, largely from the lucrative Saudi contingent.

He could see the ever-smiling Joint Head of the English Studies Department Tanya Snuggs there, her bouffant dress billowing around her like a big pink cloud. Still no sign of alleged Joint Head of Department Karen Crisp who was, no doubt, at yet another conference, on sick leave, away with the fairies, searching for the Holy Grail, abducted by aliens, or whatever. In fact, Crump was starting to doubt whether she existed at all – or whether, perhaps, the university had just made her up in order to keep down Tanya Snuggs' hours and salary as departmental head. But they wouldn't do that, would they? *Would they?*

Shabs was sitting nearby with other English Studies colleagues, including Melanie Spunch and Hilary Squonk, but Crump was glad they were a safe distance away so he wouldn't have to engage in conversation with any of them.

The plus-size Head of School Melissa Jenks was there, squeezed into a seat, as was Head of Politics Kim Vyshinsky, grey-suited and looking like a Bond villain. Head of Peace Studies and Professor of Race Hitler Mazimba was sitting next to Kwasi Wakanda (AKA Keith Cheese), Head of Diversity, who was dressed up like an African warrior, complete with a headdress which resembled the head of a leopard similar to those Crump remembered seeing tribal chiefs wear in old Tarzan films. He looked as though he was about to perform a *Juju* ritual. Kwasi was sitting next to a man dressed up as an Arab Sheikh, in white robes and a head covering tied with a golden braid band. Crump assumed this was the university's Principal Diversity Officer, the unfortunately-innuendo-named Mustafa Fouk. Crump bit his smiling lip at the memory. He then thought of all the diverse, inclusive, tolerant places in the Arab world – or would have done, if any existed.

Looking around the auditorium at all the university staff members there, Crump thought, not for the first time, about the theory of *Nominative Determinism* – basically, the idea that you'll end up in life doing the job suggested by your name. He remembered that he'd had a music teacher at school called Mr Bell, for example.

The Music Department at Cambrian University was run by a Mr Singh, a Ms Sang Sung, with the Performance courses run by Miss Sitzprobe and Composition by a Mr Ozzy Ostinato. Meanwhile, the Food Technology Department heads were Miss Needham, Emily Eatwell and Oobah 'Rum' Baba. Over at Ceramics, where they were well known to be a bit potty, there was Miss Moorcroft, Mx Wedgwood and Mr Ichikawa Chojiro. Ms Dresswell ran Textiles, Ms Singrid Nutall was at Psychology, Mr Ball at Sports Science with Hugh Spume lecturing in surfing studies and Mr Groo was at Botany, with Donna Cakebread in charge of Bake-off Studies. The Head of Architecture went by the improbable name of Alexandra Pallas, Business Studies was headed by Mr Freddie Cash, Economics by a Mr Keynes, Geology by Ms Stone, and Geography by a Miss Mammatus – which Crump knew was the name of a breast-shaped cloud. Probably all a coincidence. Crump wasn't quite sure which department Linda Stinkhorn and Miss Trixie Muff worked for though…

Suddenly, the lights went down – including the flickering ones – and a reminder was given over the PA to turn all mobile phones off. Crump did so.

Then the audience jiggled Jazz Hands as the university's senior management – plus Student Union representatives – took their seats on stage.

For the university: the bearded Vice-Chancellor Angharad Ap Merrick, in a delightful chiffon dress which wafted around him/her; then Mike Mumpsimus, whose medication must have been converting his usual Tourette's outbursts into the merest *cunty* mumble; then Miss Parminder Zugzwang, Head of Strategy, etc. The three Student Union representatives – Olivia Octothorp, Aled Rantallion and Shelley Shunk – followed them onto the stage, together with several assorted professors, including, Crump noticed, Professor Pip Pooman, and a bekilted Donald Dougal Angus Hamish McGinty McDonald McClounie who, bizarrely, was carrying bagpipes.

The Welsh Studies Lecturer twins Gruffyd and Morgan Tewdwr stood one each side of the stage, ready to translate everything said that evening into Welsh. This would, quite literally, double the length of the awards ceremony.

Crump closed his eyes and made a wish not ever to hear even one ear-bending cat-throttling note emit from Donald the English-hating Scot's bagpipes that evening – or, for that matter, ever.

He opened them again to see local musician Max Pop bounce onto the stage, complete with acoustic guitar, and about to burst into song.

The Vice-Chancellor stood up, then called Max over and whispered something in his ear.

"Oh, but can't I play just one song?" pleaded Max, loud enough for the whole audience to hear.

"Maybe later, Max – yes, no, indeed, absolutely..."

Max bowed his head theatrically in disappointment, eliciting a couple of 'Awww' calls of sympathy from his fans in the audience. But, as instructed, he carried on with the job he'd been hired to do – namely, to MC the evening and introduce the entertainment, which he did.

On cue, Boyo Bellylaughs MBE bounded, with something of a wobble, onto the stage.

Jazz Hands everywhere offered their silent applause.

"Sorry for the wait, like, but I's always had a weight problem! Fair play too!" he bellowed. "Aye-aye!"

"Aye-aye!" replied the audience who knew the routine.

Crump almost expected a drum or cymbal to sound, marking the end of a gag – as with Ken Dodd and all the great traditional music hall comedians – but drum came their none, due to the noticeable lack of any band.

"I was on an Oliver Twist diet once. Gruelling, it was, to be honest. What d'ya call a fake noodle? Impasta! *Impasta!!!* Oh, I knows – plenty more where they's come from!"

Crump laughed, sat back and relaxed. He always enjoyed the silly and relentlessly cheerful routines of Boyo Bellylaughs.

"This student, she comes up to me earlier, right, and says, 'I know you from the vegetarian club.' Strange, I thought – I've never met *herbivore*... HERBIVORE – HER BEFORE," Boyo groaned, and singled out an audience member. "Have he got it yet? He have? Just checking..."

Laughs all round.

"Beautiful place this, isn't it, eh? The Richard Burton Theatre. The last time I saw a show in the theatre I was chucked out for bringing my own food. Well, it was ages since I'd had a barbecue! Aye-aye!"

"Aye-aye!"

The audience laughed and a few even clapped – not even strictly-enforced Jazz Hands could stop the knee-jerk laughter caused by a good old joke.

"How many men does it take to change a toilet roll, madam? I don't know – it's never been tried!"

Laughing throughout the audience, especially from the women.

"Working in a coalmine. Is it beneath me? Of course not! Imagine my grandfather seeing me now at a university. My bampi was just a miner, mind. Well, a minor offender... but... So, without further ado – *Have he got it yet, mam?* – it's on with the Student Awards ceremony..."

Award followed award followed award, as Boyo Bellylaughs MBE and Max Pop shared the compering duties. Every announced winner climbed the steps to the stage to collect their gong – well, a piece of see-through Made-in-China plastic on a stand and a mass-produced piece of paper called a certificate – from the Vice-Chancellor, to the cheering silence of Jazz Hands. A glittering prize, indeed.

Awards included: Best Science Student, Best Humanities Student, Best Postgraduate Student, Best Research Student, Most Improved Student, Most *Improved* Improved Student, Best Diversity Champion Student, Best Disabled Student, Best Self-Defined Female Student, Best Cis-Female Student, Best Student Over Thirty Years of Age, Best Student Under Twenty Years of Age, Best Vertically Challenged Student, Best Vegan Student, Best Transgender Student, Best Non-Binary Student, Best Working Class Student, Best Absent Student of the Year – for any student whose illnesses, physical or mental (or made up) facilitated their absence from the groves of academe – and Best Student of the Year with a Criminal Record. It was won by a former mugger called Choko from Tottenham, who casually swaggered onto the stage in low-slung jeans, puffer jacket and headphones, nodding to rap music as he snatched the award from the Vice-Chancellor, who knew how important it was to celebrate such rich and vibrant diversity, even if it never said 'thank you'.

Best Muslim Student of the Year followed, and Best Chinese Student, Best South American Student, Best Russian Student, Best Polish Student, Best EU Student, and various other assorted nationalities, and then, it was time for the final award of the evening.

Crump could hardly wait – to have access to a glass of wine and nibbles in the foyer. He gripped his mobile phone, ready to switch it on again and make a dash for the buffet as soon as the end came. He knew from limp-lettuced, fish-paste-sandwiched experience the perils of being a straggler arriving late at a freebie buffet feast.

"So now," announced Max Pop, "it's time for a very important award, that of African Student of the Year. As a musician, I sometimes feel a bit African myself, when I hears the drums behind me in the band, because that's where rock n roll came from – Africa – partly at least, via Memphis and... Cardiff... and... Dave's Records down the covered market..."

He noticed a glare from senior university management behind him, and some rather impolite hand gestures signalling for him to 'hurry up and get on with it'.

"Right, and so without further ado, I am proud to announce that, this year's African Student of the Year is..."

Max opened the envelope as slowly as he could, extracting the card which bore the winner's name.

"*Really?*" he said to himself. "Are you sure?"

He looked round to see senior management egging him on – they were all keen to get to the buffet too.

"OK, so, this year's African Student of the Year is..."

Hushed expectation from the audience.

"*Boyo Bellylaughs Umbe...*"

"What?" Crump mouthed to himself.

Hushed whispered in the auditorium as Boyo Bellylaughs MBE – or 'Umbe' as it was stated on the winner's card – bounded on stage to accept his award from the Vice-Chancellor. Everyone looked at each other, baffled.

"But he is white!" shouted Mrs Njumbo, a huge – even elegantly elephantine – African woman in a colourful robe and massive hat.

The whispers grew louder and louder and, eventually, grew into jeers and boos.

"It should have been Shaka Nkomo!"

"No, Goodwill Gwangi Ngongo is the best!"

"Kanye Katanga must win!"

"Oh-Be-Joyful Mbuto must be the winner!"

"No – Idi Amin Dada!"

"WHAT?!"

Stunned silence swallowed the noise in the auditorium.

"No, not *him*!" explained a proud dad clad in a colourful robe. "My son, Idi Amin Dada – he is good boy, top of class, Business Studies, yah!"

The hushed crowd let out a communal 'PHEW!', before normal chaos resumed.

Uproar!

Bedlam!

Mayhem!

Before long, some of the audience were brawling with each other, and one man was heard to regret not bringing his machete.

Before long, more students and parents, of many different nationalities, joined in. This was real international co-operation in action!

The Vice-Chancellor appealed for calm – but nobody heard him/her, on account of Donald the fake Scot starting to play his bagpipes.

Max Pop saw his chance. They never allowed him to play his acoustic guitar and sing a song at these things. It just wasn't fair! He always brought it along and offered, and they always said 'no'.

Well, this time he'd show them. And so Max Pop stood centre stage, strummed his guitar, thrust his face into the microphone and started to sing *Let it Be*. Unfortunately, this was not the song being played – badly – on the bagpipes...

Together with most other audience members, Crump joined the crush of people pushing their way out of the auditorium, though whether to escape the violent scrum of a multicultural punch-up or the discordant cacophony assaulting their ears was uncertain.

Once out in the foyer, Crump thought he may as well pile into the buffet and partake of the wine on offer before going home.

He turned on his smartphone as he was surveying the spread.

There were several missed calls showing – all from the hospital.

CHAPTER SIX

Going Under

They say young men don't feel their bones.

But Crump was not young any more.

And, as he sat there, watching his mum's life ebb away, he could feel the aches of every bone in his body, every organ, every nerve. It felt, too, as if he had a rat in his skull, gnawing away at his brain.

His mother had suffered a major stroke, they said. They'd given her medication, of course, as soon as she'd arrived at the hospital from the care home. But she was so very frail, nothing could save her now.

All that was left was for nature to take its course.

Some patients did recover from such strokes, though it was less certain whether the disabled half-life they were left with was worth living. Younger stroke victims fared better, but the older patients were, the worse the probable outcome.

Crump had known people whose elderly parents were left bed-ridden by strokes. Unable to eat or drink, they were fed by a tube or a stomach peg, and could no longer talk or walk or read – or really live in any meaningful way. His own mum had made clear in her wishes that she would not want to be kept alive to live like that. It was a sort of death-in-life, she had once said to him, when talking about a friend who had ended up that way. Real death was far preferable to a living one, she'd argued, and so had prepared a 'living will' in case the same thing happened to her.

Margaret was non-responsive. She lay there with her eyes closed, an oxygen mask on, blind as the night. Her son watched her breathing in and out. He knew there was little chance of recovery, but he just had to stay.

He went to the dayroom and made some calls to the university – he would not be in to teach the next day. It was near the end of term anyway, so at least his absence would be less disruptive than if it had happened at the start.

It seemed his mum had had the stroke early that afternoon. The hospital had tried phoning him then, they said, and left messages on his phone. It was only when the person on whose phone messages had been left called back that they realised their error.

The nurse phoning had been Spanish and, in common with much of Europe, the way British people wrote the number seven was almost the way they wrote the number one on the Continent; their number seven had a horizontal line through its middle, always. So, as Crump's phone number had three number sevens in it, and had probably been written down by a British nurse by hand, the foreign nurse had been calling the wrong number and leaving messages on a stranger's phone. It'd be surely worth the NHS introducing some training on that for any migrant workers?

But it had made no difference. Crump's mum had suffered a major, life-changing stroke, and, despite the clot-busting medication, it was unlikely she would survive.

Crump didn't see any point in going home. He certainly wasn't hungry – the thought of eating anything made him feel sick.

And so, he stayed. All that evening and through the cold winter night, sitting in the individual hospital room with his jacket around him, only leaving for toilet breaks or when the nurses needed to clean his now-incontinent, unconscious mother.

He held his mum's hand – talked to her. He knew that patients can often hear what is happening, despite being unconscious, and that hearing is the last sense to go – so he kept talking, telling his mum how much he loved her, remembering the past, sharing happy memories.

She did not respond in any way – but that did not mean she did not hear.

How small his mum looked – how tiny, like an old wrinkled child wrapped in the sheets and blankets of that hospital bed. She had seemed so big when he was a boy, so huge in character, even though she was barely over five foot tall. Now she seemed so small, as if she were fading away into nothing – which, of course, she was.

Dawn broke. The usual clatter of nurses and breakfast preparation and distribution of meds signalled the start of a new day on the hospital's stroke ward.

There were shared single-sex wards, for patients to recover from their strokes. The most severely ill had single rooms, like Crump's mother.

The stroke ward was on the seventh floor, with a spectacular view over the bay. Occasionally, during the night and day, Crump would stand, walk to the window, gaze blankly at the vast seascape vista, watch the constant lighthouse blinking at him, then retake his place on the chair by the bed.

He would stay. No matter how long it took. Or even if his mother recovered, showed any sign of improvement – though if that happened, what life would she have in future? He remembered his mum talking of a friend of hers who lived a further five years after a severe stroke, in bed, unable to do much. And his mum was well into her eighties. He had to remember that.

Crump had always thought that with all the diseases, deformities and dangers of the world, it was amazing really that anyone lived beyond the age of three and a half. Of course, many didn't, in the past, and in many countries now too. But then, as Johnny Blue had said, the human population was growing at an unsustainable rate which was destroying the Earth and everything that lived on its surface, because of the sheer number of newly hatched human consumers born. No wonder babies cried when they entered the world.

How he wished he could bring his mum back to life – somehow recharge her, like a mobile phone, however absurd that sounded.

But he was helpless. All he could do was watch and wait.

That afternoon, he went back home for a couple of hours, to have a shower, check post, log into his laptop and check emails, and forward lesson plans and information to those covering his classes.

Then it was back to the hospital, and the vigil beside his mum's bed.

The doctors came, told him to prepare himself. They removed the oxygen mask from his mother's face.

Crump stroked his mum's fine white hair, combed it back from her face.

Then it grew dark again, on the last day of November. Dark as midnight by 4pm. The lighthouse blinked the drizzled hours away as he watched. The weather looked as miserable as he felt.

Crump sipped hot tea but just did not want to eat anything. A knowing knot of anxiety tightened in his stomach, and seemed to spread its worry and sadness to every part of his body in his blood, like strength-sapping bacteria no antibiotic could ever kill.

Another cold night in the chair by his mum's bedside. Her breathing was growing gradually slower now.

Crump realised it was now 1st December. He changed the date on his watch.

Early in the morning, as a nurse was rearranging the pillows on her bed, his mother groaned weakly. Soon after, a painkilling morphine injection was administered.

'At least it seems painless,' was the only positive thing Crump could think, as he watched his mother becoming weaker and weaker. It was a grim business.

He snipped off a small lock of his mother's hair using some nail scissors he found in a drawer of a cabinet by the bed, wrapped it securely in some tissues, and placed the memory in his jacket pocket. He didn't know why he had done that. But it just seemed right – natural. No doubt loved ones had been doing the same for millennia.

The early morning ward clatter again. Nurses, chatter, breakfast, doling out the meds. Cups of tea. Always, cups of tea.

Margaret's breathing slowed more. He knew her body was shutting down.

Crump kissed his mum, held her hand, told her how much he loved her, and thanked her for everything.

Then, the breaths came every five seconds, then every ten. And then, with a final exhaling breath so small Crump could barely hear it, and a silent slump of her head, his mother died.

And so it ends.

It was over at last. A good death, maybe, of an old lady at the end of a long life well lived. Sometimes, death is a kindness.

Gently, Crump kissed his mum on her forehead and said goodbye.

Already, the blood was leaving her flesh – he watched her hand turn white in his.

He kissed her hand for a final time, then placed her arm next to her body.

"And in that sleep of death, what dreams may come," he whispered, alone.

Then he went out of the room to inform a nurse.

Presently, another nurse came. Then a doctor who, as Crump waited outside the room, officially recorded his mother's death. He had told the doctor that she had died at precisely 11.35am that morning – Crump had looked at his watch when it happened. Force of habit, he supposed.

Crump stood in the corridor, waiting. He pondered the fact that people went through such things every day of the week – death, birth, injury, accidents, heart attacks, strokes – and often at a much younger age. This was really nothing special, in the great scheme of things. He was really nothing special either, he knew. But this was his mum, and she was special to him, and that was all that mattered, there and then.

He was now an orphan in the world, even if over forty, so hardly an Oliver Twist predicament. And the one big reason for him tolerating being in The Town had now departed too.

Crump had read somewhere that at the moment you exhale your terminal breath, your body becomes the property of the government. So now, the state owned his mother. She didn't – and he, as her heir, didn't either. But then, she wasn't there, not really – just the shell she inhabited for over eighty years. Margaret had left us.

When the doctor had finished his paperwork, Crump re-entered the room. His mother's old wrinkled face was now near-white as the blood had drained away through force of gravity, as a consequence of her body's still, unbeating heart. Her head was leaning back, mouth open, as if gasping for breath. It wasn't a pleasant sight. But then, we must all wither and die.

After a while, a nurse entered with some white flowers in a vase. Lilies or something similar. Crump knew his mother hated those types of flowers – too tropical-looking for her. And anyway, she was no gardener. In fact, she always used to joke that she was the kiss of death to any houseplant, so never bothered with them. Crump smiled at the memory.

He told the nurse he wouldn't stay. And, as he was an only child, there were no siblings to visit either, and no other family really, apart from a few elderly first and second cousins, some of them resident overseas.

Crump decided to go home, make the calls and emails he had to, contact the funeral directors, and then go to bed for his first proper sleep in over two days.

The next fortnight was something of a blur.

Crump organised everything regarding the funeral, let everyone know about his mother's death, and also managed to teach lessons in the last week of term too. He didn't tell his students he had been bereaved – he hated the reaction he knew would follow on from that, one of sympathy mixed with embarrassment.

No, he'd get his teaching out of the way, set assignments for all his students to do over the Christmas holidays, and then have a break himself, after the funeral.

He felt tired. No, weary, more than tired. He badly needed to somehow recharge his batteries.

The funeral was on 18th December at the local crematorium.

Crump would go, do his duty as a son, but he knew the funeral was not for him or even for his mum. She was gone. The funeral was for her many friends, so they could commemorate her life.

And so, he bought a new suit, polished his best black shoes, and endured the funeral which, he thought afterwards, was probably more fun for his mum than for him. It was a relief for it all to be over. For both of them.

Now he could relax, but he wouldn't bother with Christmas this year. He was in no mood to put up the usual artificial tree and decorations, though he had always loved doing that. And anyway, it was only him at home. So why bother cooking a Christmas dinner – with all the trimmings – just for him? It was bad enough that the usual forced seasonal celebrations would be on TV – he would keep that off too. Read some books. Listen to music. Get some work done on the laptop. Sleep.

His mother's ashes were given to him in a cardboard tube, apparently designed to facilitate easy scattering. He'd get that done in January sometime. His mum had specified she wished her ashes to be scattered at one of the most beautiful beaches on Gower, so that is what Crump would do in the New Year. There was no rush, after all. His mum wasn't going anywhere.

He also knew he'd soon have to deal with the council regarding the cost of his mother's care. That would probably mean they'd want to sell the end-of-terrace house where he lived in the Highlands district of The Town, to recoup money they'd spent on the care home. That meant that Crump might soon be homeless. It was yet another worrying thought to add to his growing headache collection.

Maybe that was why he started drinking. Or maybe not. Whichever was true, he just felt like drinking. He did a big supermarket shop to stock up on booze the day before his mum's funeral. As soon as he'd got home after it, he opened his first bottle of wine…

Crump was not sure what day it was, and did not much care either. How many days had he been drinking now? He had no idea. He'd got through most of the wine he'd bought and was now on the beer, and there was whisky and vodka at home too, in case he needed something stronger.

He wasn't stupid enough to drive in that state, so went on another booze shop locally and got a taxi home.

And he kept drinking. And drinking. And drinking.

"I'd rather have a bottle in front of me than a frontal lobotomy," Crump mumbled to his drunken self, more than once.

Then, one afternoon, on a day which the radio told Crump was 22nd December, Crump suddenly felt like company.

So he walked, drunk and unsteady on his feet, down to the centre of The Town where, a carol service would be taking place in Fountain Square – a post-war concrete area which was usually dominated by a huge TV screen, but which could also be used to demonstrations, events or, in this case, a concert.

Crump had always liked Christmas carols, the more traditional, the better. Those tunes had lasted for a reason: they were catchy and meaningful. He was less keen on more modern carols, and detested versions of carols which were updated and modernised. The old carols work. *Leave them be!*

And now it was 22nd December so all things had a right to be Christmas-y. Why did some shops insist on starting the festivities in October or early November these days? That never happened when Crump was a kid. Now Christmas often started full-on in October, and in some stores even in September, certainly for mail order catalogues.

Crump thought, not for the first time, about how things were better when he was a boy. Better for kids then too, and for parents. Back in the days when he had modest, small presents, which his wonderful mum bought throughout the year and especially in the January sales when they were reduced. All except one year, when he was eleven, and got a brand-new bike he'd picked out of a shop showroom himself, which was a combined birthday and Christmas present. It was the only time he got a new bike – he'd had three second-hand ones before that, from the age of six or seven.

These days, rampant consumerism at various times of year, with the constant pressure to buy yet more, then more, and then yet more stuff, never seemed to go away. It was always on, always there. The clang of cash registers and the plastic tap of credit cards at tills real and digital was the miserable soundtrack of our age, and if ever the sound started to get quiet, dire warnings of recession were sounded. And so, it seemed in our wonderful wealthy Western world that we consumers, drugged up like lab-rats on the promise of improvement via acquisition, had to keep buying crap we neither really wanted nor needed in order to prop up the entire edifice of our consumerist society. It all seemed so wrong somehow. Silly, perhaps; pointless, certainly. Couldn't people just enjoy themselves without spending money all the time?

Crump stumbled and staggered down the pedestrianised shopping streets of The Town, past the Christmas market which offered overpriced fare to shoppers too pissed or deluded to care about what they were buying or why.

He stopped at two or three pubs, maybe more. It was days such as these that all-day drinking was invented for, and Crump was taking full advantage. Sure, he hoped none of his students or university colleagues would see him in that state. But even if they did, was this country now so utterly miserabilist that anyone getting a bit tiddly or squiffy two or three days before Christmas Day was somehow committing a crime? Was our culture really now so po-faced and disapproving? Had we become, wallowing around in a politically correct pity-party puddle of moralising, a New Puritan Western version of some judgemental, religious dictatorship? Was it back to the future again?

Crump took his seat in Fountain Square, somewhat unsteadily, it had to be said. It was just a seat on one of the concrete steps of the square – not one of the reserved plastic seats further forward. He felt alright, though terribly tired. Alcohol always had that effect on him – it made him unable to sleep, and the kip he did get didn't seem to make him any less tired at all. But if he felt too finished later, he'd leave and get a taxi home. As it was, he was fine, sitting these on the cold concrete and listening to the Christmas carol muzak being pumped over the PA as a taster of the carol service to come.

Crump looked around, squinting through his spectacles at the couple of hundred people present. The usual families, all bobble-hatted, woolly-scarfed and winter-coated against the December chill, though the temperatures were certainly nowhere near sub-zero. He could see the kids' choir in the wings, standing on the pavement beside the concrete podium, waiting to come on stage. Near them was a man setting up a video camera – it seemed the show would be filmed, but whether for public consumption or the theatre's own 'safety' security reasons, he didn't know. Sadly, there was no real band – Crump used to like the real brass bands you sometimes saw before Christmas, the Salvation Army and others. He scanned the crowd again. The faces and backs-of-heads all became a blur after a while. Crump closed his eyes against the tiredness.

Then the recorded introductory music started and the kids' choir crocodiled onto the concrete stage. The carol service started, with *O Little Town of Bethlehem* which, Crump knew, was based on an old folk song called *The Ploughboy's Dream* (although they usually sang it to a different tune in the USA). He wondered how many people there knew that, or knew that the church had banned carols in the past as they were in local languages such as English – or Welsh – and songs of the people, rather than Latin liturgy. Thus, Christmas carols were sung *outside* the walls of the village church. He also knew *Deck the Halls* – more properly called *Deck the Hall*

– was based on a 16th-century Welsh folk tune. It was somewhat depressing that so many people though songs like that were American in origin, thanks to Hollywood appropriating them.

Suddenly, Crump felt so overwhelmingly weary and dizzy, so short of breath, that he seemed on the point of collapse. He hadn't slept properly since his mum's funeral, and had been drinking steadily for the past three days and nights. He badly needed bed.

He didn't want to interrupt the carol service, but he knew he had to get out of there and go home. He stood up – slowly, steadying himself on his drunken feet – and gradually made his way down the concrete steps towards the side of the stage, and the pedestrianised shopping street, off which he knew there was a taxi rank.

And he was almost there, and the choir was not disturbed, as they launched into a gutsy rendition of *We Three Kinds of Orient Are*, yet another Christmas carol ripped off from a Middle Ages tune.

But as he got to the front, something happened. He felt a shove in his back and he stumbled, having to steady himself by holding the shoulder of someone sitting down watching the choir.

"Oh sorry, sorry," he slurred.

"You ginger wanker!" came a voice behind him. "You mind rapist of the phallocentric patriarchy!"

It was Abi Rainbow, intersectional activist committed to violent peaceful protest, complete with bright rainbow-flag-coloured bobble hat, which concealed her blue Mohican haircut – that was why he had not seen her there earlier. Her angry pierced face sneered at him, even as she pushed into him, almost rubbing her body against his.

And he saw the person he'd leant on in the audience was none other than the fat child he'd seen with Abi Rainbow at the Jorvic Andersson protest in Cardiff. It was her son, who was dressed as a girl, and whose name '*Jazz*' was writ large on a home-or-school-made glittery Christmas-y name tag pinned to his coat. The child wore a rainbow flag bobble hat identical to his mother's – in fact, all their clothes were identical, with the poor boy dressed up in some punky dress. It seemed as though she was trying to create her own gender experiment in the child, her own brain-washed non-binary gender-neutral mini-me to play with. It was, however, a blessing the child's face was not pierced or his body tattooed like his mother's – yet.

The alcohol swirled around Crump's aching brain like hot blood.

He mumbled 'sorry' again, to himself as much as anyone else, then stumbled away as quickly as possible so as not to cause any disturbance. He was sure he would have been able to leave completely quietly, had someone not shoved him from behind. Who had done that? And why?

He staggered to the taxi rank and went home. As soon as he got in, he slumped into an armchair in the living room and passed out. It would, perhaps, be inaccurate to say he fell asleep. More, he sank into a deep drunken stupor. Crump needed to recover from his drinking binge and lack of sleep; even in his exhausted and drunken state, he knew it. He'd probably be ill for the next two or three days, but so what? He didn't want to celebrate anything this year anyway. As far as he was concerned, Christmas was cancelled.

Crump breathed deeply, and sank deep into the armchair, losing consciousness somewhere on the long, tiresome, troubled road to sleep.

And then, it happened.

When, he didn't know.

How long after he'd arrived home, he didn't know either.

But suddenly, there was an enormous noise, thumping bangs and something splintering and crashing in, then loud shouts.

Crump struggled to his feet.

There were three, or maybe four, men in uniforms with him in his living room.

Was this a dream? Were these men in uniforms Nazi stormtroopers like in *An American Werewolf in London*? Was he going mad at long last?

Then, one of the men in uniform was putting some sort of blue plastic bags on his hands.

And another stated, robotically.

"Kevin Crump, you are now under arrest for sexual assault, and for sexual assault of a child under thirteen. You do not have to say anything. But, it may harm your defence if you do not mention when questioned something which you later rely on in court. Anything you do say may be given in evidence."

*

The world was a blur. A weird, nightmarish, nasty blur.

Faces stared at him in dreams.

Dark dreams of people and places both unknown and known.

Various creatures, angry animals, snarling snouts and faces, teeth bared, growling at him. Laughing at him. Cackling in glee.

Then he was back at home – his childhood home, in the garden. A small boy, playing.

He had loved that back garden, enjoyed its scruffiness, its wildlife and the freedom he had at that age. It was evening, and the sun was setting.

His mother would usually have been there, in the kitchen, cooking tea, doing the washing up, or reading her newspaper and listening to talk on the radio.

But she was not there. Of course, she was not there. Because she was dead. And this was just a stupid dream.

Crump woke up in a windowless police cell. He was lying on a cold blue plastic mattress. His clothes were not his own – grey sweatshirt and flannel trousers.

On the bare wall was a painted slogan about drug and alcohol addiction.

In the corner was a stainless-steel toilet, with no seat, and a small metal sink with a tap for water. There was nothing else in the cell. Except him.

Crump stood up, slowly, from the low mattress. He was dizzy and could feel himself wobbling. But he needed water. He could feel himself still drunk, yes, but also parched. He felt sick and ill.

He cupped his hands and sipped as much water as he could drink. Then he steadied himself to have a pee, his first for… he couldn't remember.

How long had he been there? Why was he there? Slowly, like his reflection clearing in a rockpool, memories of the recent past crystallised into focus in his mind.

Now he remembered. The police. Smashing down the front door of his house. He worried suddenly if the front door was still broken and open. Everything he owned was in that house.

Then it all came back to him. Arrival at the police station. Processing. Taking details. Testing. Swabs. Fingerprints. Humiliation. Taking off clothes and putting on new ones – the grey flannel uniform of all suspects.

Vague memories of questions asked. Unclear memories of seeing a doctor, pills taken.

Put in the cell. The hatch in the heavy metal door occasionally clanking as his gaolers checked on him.

'Shit,' thought Crump, sitting down on the plastic mattress. 'What the fuck happened?'

He knew he was now a suspect, remembering what the police officer had said in his living room.

Sexual assault.

Against a woman and a child under thirteen.

He would never sexually assault anyone. He knew that in his bones, in his being. And he definitely had no desire to have a sexual relationship with a child.

Fuck!

FUCK!

It was a nightmare – he couldn't believe this was happening. But it was – it was all horribly and soul-crushingly real.

How in God's name had that happened? He hadn't done anything wrong or assaulted anyone either, sexually or otherwise – he knew that. He had just gone down town to a carol service. Then what?

THINK!

He remembered Mx Abi Rainbow, the blue-haired freak who hated men. Her obese son whom she dressed up as a girl was there too.

Then someone had pushed him from behind. He'd leant on the child's shoulder so as not to fall over.

Then Abi Rainbow had pushed against him.

It was *her*. This was *all her*. He knew it. She had form – had made accusations and destroyed the lives of innocent men before.

Crump repeated a mantra in his mind:

I refuse to be upset by people I neither like nor respect.

Over and over again.

Suddenly, the door clanked open.

"Doctor wants to see you," said a police officer.

Crump stood up, left the cell and shuffled barefoot down the corridor, past the regular cell doors either side. He felt like prisoners he'd seen in war films, arrested by the Nazis, chucked into cells, the key thrown away – until the fateful day came when they were taken out and shot.

But this was not the Third Reich. He would not be taken out and shot. But, if he was charged and convicted for the offences he was accused of, which he had in no way committed, then the effect on his life would be much the same.

A real-life nightmare was coming true. Crump had thought in the past how awful it must be to get accused of something you hadn't done, maybe go to prison for it, when no-one believed you to be innocent.

He really did feel ill now, sick to his stomach.

He was seen by the duty doctor. She said not a word to him when doing various tests, blood pressure etc. Then he was led back to his cell.

Crump rested his head in his hands and scrunched his eyes tight shut. He stayed like that for a minute, maybe even minutes. He hoped that when he opened his eyes again, the nightmare that had swallowed his life like a monster would be no more. That he would be back sitting drunkenly in his usual armchair, waking from a bad booze-invoked dream, ready for a bath, a big fry-up breakfast and a long peaceful sleep.

But when he opened his eyes, the awful world yawned at him.

This was no dream. This was the hell of reality.

The heavy door clanked open again.

It was time to be interviewed.

*

"I'm Detective Inspector Anna Cornetto, and this is Deputy Inspector Linda Likflap, of the sexual offences team of Cambrian Police, and for the benefit of the recording the time is three minutes past eight on the 23rd of December…"

Crump confirmed his name when asked.

Next to him in the coldly lit interview room sat Tony Bones, whose presence was mentioned by DI Anna Cornetto. He was a solicitor provided for free, as for all suspects being interviewed. There was no way any accused or arrested police officer would set foot in an interview room without a solicitor present, so no other suspect should either, Crump knew.

He was in a deeply vulnerable place. His only hope was legal process and the truth of what happened, but he knew that it would be his word versus some very serious accusations indeed – accusations that, in these paranoid and hysterical #MeToo misandrist mob days, were likely to be assumed to be true.

We now had trial by accusation in the Western world – the equally bad, opposite side of a coin, whose other face was the one in much of the developing world, where women were not believed when they said they'd been raped, or publicly shamed and shunned by their communities and families, or told they needed four witnesses to prove it according to religious law – or even incarcerated for just making an allegation against a man. Each system was equally awful and destructive and unfair.

If you're not worried, you don't understand the problem.

They went through the events of the afternoon and evening before.

Crump remembered it all pretty well, considering how much he'd had to drink, though in a circular rather than a linear way. He supposed that was because he was used to consuming rather too much alcohol, and possibly because he had been drinking for three days solid. It was all a bit of a blur at times – but, importantly, it was a blur he could mostly recall.

He remembered going down town, visiting a few pubs – which he named and gave approximate times too – had something to eat in one of them, walked to the choir service, took a seat, closed his eyes. Listened to the beautiful carols begin, then felt overwhelmed by such exhaustion that he knew he had to go home. He stood up, went to leave, got pushed from behind, held out a hand to steady himself – against a seated child – then felt someone push, or rub, against him, and turned to see Abi Rainbow's angry pierced face sneering at him. Then he walked past the side of the stage to the pedestrianised shopping street and on to the taxi rank, where he got a cab home – where he collapsed into an armchair and immediately fell asleep, only to be woken by the police smashing down his door, and...

"The thing is, Kevin," said Deputy Inspector Linda Likflap, with a cynical sneer, "you keep on saying 'I think' I was here, 'I think' I was there, so I'm thinking maybe you were too drunk to remember anything?"

She was the bad cop. Anna Cornetto, who had been all friendly and pally, was the good cop. It was just like he'd seen on TV.

Crump felt ill. The alcohol withdrawal was making him feel sick, despite the tranquilisers given by the doctor. But the police tactic was another reason he was feeling sick and ill. He knew what they were doing, even in his exhausted and traumatised state.

They were trying to claim that he had been too drunk to remember anything and, if he had stated that (which would have been a lie), then the police would have been free to impose their narrative of events onto the evening – one which surely would ensure Crump was charged with sexual assault, against both Abi Rainbow and her son. And then what? Trial? Sentencing? Prison?

FUCK!

"I remember the events of yesterday evening pretty well, considering how drunk I was," groaned Crump, "and I have told you what I did but... I can't remember the precise times – "

"What clothes were you wearing, Kevin?" asked DI Anna Cornetto.

It was an odd question. As a bloke of over forty, Crump rarely knew what clothes he was wearing on any given

239

day. He just put on what was clean and what was there. He put little thought into making any fashion statement – ever.

"Jeans and a T-shirt… and jumper—"

"What colour T-shirt, Kevin?"

"I don't know, maybe black or blue… I've got a lot that colour—"

"And the jumper?"

"It was a cheap Christmas jumper, I bought it last year, in London, no, this year, January sales—"

"And on your feet, Kevin?"

"Shoes," he said, stating the obvious, "errr… trainers—"

"Colour?"

"I don't really know, blue maybe, black, just basic trainers—"

"And socks?"

"Yes, but… probably black or grey or blue or something. I think—"

"So," said Linda Likflap, "you *think* you were wearing those clothes, Kevin?"

"Well… yes… I really don't pay… much attention to clothes… and—"

"Just like you *think* you went to the places you say, and you *think* you did not deliberately touch anybody?"

Crump looked at his solicitor, Tony Bones.

"I think we'll take a break there," he said.

In the break, Crump stated his feelings to his solicitor.

"They're trying to set me up – to make out that because I don't remember precisely where I was at any exact time, or… or… just because I cannot remember the exact clothes I was wearing, therefore I can't remember sexually assaulting anyone? A child? For *fuck's sake*!"

"They have yet to interview the… woman and child—"

"It's all her, I know it, that fucking man-hating monster Abi Rainbow—"

"They didn't call the police, apparently – that was Paul Pizzle, Memorial Theatre Choir Manager, and he was filming the whole thing – I'll ask the police to see that."

"Look, I did not touch anybody deliberately or sexually. I was exhausted – I was just trying to leave… go home… to bed."

"Paul Pizzle claims you were told to leave."

"That's bollocks!" said Crump. "A total bloody lie."

"Doesn't surprise me. I've known Paul Pizzle for years. He's basically a jumped-up security guard who climbed the management pole – he now thinks he's in *The Professionals* circa 1978, or *Starsky and Hutch* – but he's more like *Mr Bean*."

Tony Bones laughed. Crump didn't.

"The man's obsessed. He's always reporting sexual assaults to the police – which may have something to do with the tiny seats in his theatre… Munchkin chairs, I call them!"

The solicitor laughed – again. Crump didn't – again.

"The police like to bully, smash down doors, scare people – men, usually. It's just a technique, a tactic – don't worry. I've seen it so many times…"

'*Seriously?*' thought Crump. 'Is that where we are in the UK now?'

"And these days, all allegations of a sexual nature, especially made by women, or by children, or adults about so-called historic sexual abuse, are automatically believed. Look what Cliff Richard and the rest went through, for years too."

"*The world has gone mad*," muttered Crump.

"Got a bit saner lately though at the CPS – after all the dropped cases and proven liars convicted – so you timed it well!"

"So… how am I doing?" asked Crump, ignoring his solicitor's sanguine stance.

"Fine fine – just keep on doing what you're doing."

"Then what happens? Can I go home?"

"They'll bail you. Later tonight. Twenty-eight days initially, though they can ask for more. All depends on what witnesses say."

And so, Crump's fate was in the hands of members of a mob raised on paedo-hysteria and safety-obsessed in a manner in which those from Generation Common Sense, like his late mother, were not.

What the hell had happened to this country? Was he to be branded a Bogie Man by the mob? Was he the witch to be burned in this McCarthyist, paedo-obsessed witch hunt? Only time would tell.

And how many other poor sods had been convicted of similar crimes using the techniques used by the two officers interviewing him? How many innocent men sat in segregated sex offender prison cells because they'd been convinced in police interviews to say they were too drunk to remember anything, even when they were not?

The interview continued in the same vein. At a certain point, Tony Bones asked to see the still from the video of Crump at the carol service, though he had never denied being there.

DI Anna Cornetto turned the screen to show Crump and his solicitor the image. There he was, looking unsteady and drunk, in the process of leaving – though it did not show the alleged offence. His solicitor said they could get to see that though, if it even existed, before any charges were brought. If anything could prove him innocent, it was that.

Witnesses say what they want to say, see what they want to see, say and see what they think others expect them to say and see. They were about as reliable as a local bus timetable. But the camera never lies.

But what if charges were brought? There'd then be a wait of many months before a trial – and there'd be publicity about it all too, in the local press, quite apart from a ruined career. Even as it was, Crump would have to inform both the university and the Foreign Office about his arrest. It would be an automatic suspension, he knew.

Of course, nothing whatsoever would happen to his accuser if he was released without charge. It never did. Not even for the most blatant of compo-chasing liars, with masses of evidence proving their deliberate lies. That was a scandal, and so deeply wrong that Crump could not even find the words.

The interviewers went on and on about the same thing – the timings, events of the evening, what he was wearing. Crump was not sure how long it all lasted. He was so worn out – and together with the shock and the alcohol withdrawal, he was now feeling very ill indeed.

He turned to Tony Bones after yet another repeated question by Linda Likflap about his memory or drunken lack of it. She *so* wanted him to admit he remembered nothing of the evening because of the drink, which would have been a lie, he knew; she *so* wanted to break him, to set him up. He could smell it on her.

"I think we'll end it there," said his solicitor.

Some more time in the police cell while everything was processed.

Then Crump was led out and bailed, by a rude rugby-player-gone-to-seed police sergeant who treated him like a proven paedophile. All eyes of all officers at the desk were on him, as he stood unsteadily leaning on the counter and signing the paperwork.

Bail conditions were set: no contact with anyone under the age of eighteen. No contact with anyone vulnerable – which, Crump knew, meant all students, so he was, in effect, banned from teaching for the time being. No contact with the woman and child he had allegedly sexually assaulted. No moving from his present address or going abroad.

The police handed back his personal belongings, such as his wallet, money, keys, in a scrunched-up plastic bag. He would not get his clothes back. They were to be sent for DNA testing.

He also discovered his laptop and smartphone had been seized for analysis, so the police had been in his bedroom at home too. He wouldn't get those back either – not for months, or ever, if he was charged. Not for twenty-eight days, if not. Either way, it was all yet another inconvenience to deal with, another worry in his aching skull.

At least it was the Christmas holidays, when nothing much happened. It would have been worse to lose them in the middle of a term. But he needed a computer just to live his life, as most of the population did now. Weird, when you thought about it, how these digital things had enslaved us all. Maybe he'd have to buy another laptop or similar, just to get by, in the meantime.

He was given a lift home by Anna Cornetto and Linda Likflap, in an unmarked car.

On the street outside his home, he saw it – the smashed, splintered front door. Yes, it was locked, but how securely? It would have been pretty easy for anyone to have broken in during the time Crump was at the police station. But it hadn't happened, so at least one disaster had been avoided, though others were catastrophising the world enough at that moment.

Crump went inside and checked the front and back doors were locked. He stripped naked, pulling off the police-issue grey flannelling clothes and forcing them into the kitchen bin – he wanted none of that stink on him at home.

He then climbed the stairs and, feeling sick inside and much older than his forty-plus years, crawled into a ball under the covers of his bed. He pulled them over his aching frame and cried himself to sleep.

The next day was Christmas Eve.

Crump stayed in bed, venturing out only occasionally for calls of nature and to refill the pint glass of water he kept on his bedside table and sipped from continually to get rehydrated.

He slept, on and off, but his sleep was disturbed. He was having the most awful dreams, and flashbacks to the carol service, and the events afterwards. More than once he woke with a start in a cold sweat.

He took painkiller after painkiller, and just lay there, a sheet pulled over his head like a shroud, as if he were a corpse. Maybe that was what he was now really. He might as well be, if the police charged him after their investigation. He had to wait twenty-eight days for that, less holidays. Twenty-eight days of agony. Twenty-eight days of hell.

Crump wondered how many people – meaning men, mostly – killed themselves while waiting on bail to hear if they'd be charged with sexual offences and their lives ruined forever? If women had been vulnerable to such accusations, then the well-funded, well-organised, celebrity-and-politician-supported feminist movement would be there, campaigning for laws to change, for the possibility of false accusations to be emphasised, and no doubt calls to arrest false accusers and dole out the most severe of punishments. As most of the accused were men, however, and most accusers, women, the feminists naturally had the opposite opinion. Some women's groups were even now arguing that no women – ever – should be sent to prison, because 'women have special needs'. Not Myra Hindley, Rosemary West, or the worst of the worst.

And, even if Crump was not charged, he knew most would assume him to be guilty anyway, using the 'no smoke without fire' hypothesis – one which left out the possibility of a smoke machine manufacturing lies. The principle of presumed innocence no longer existed, not with certain accusations. People always thought they were civilised and fair, but most were just members of the baying mob, donning their smocks and waving their pitchforks as they jeered at the poor unfortunate victim branded a witch, just to feel better about themselves. And what better way to prove how righteous and innocent you were than to accuse another? It was the madness of the crowd, and it was everywhere.

Suddenly, the bedroom door smashed open and there, in front of him, were four men, in black uniforms like the SS, brandishing machine guns and knives. Their faces were screaming skulls – literally.

Crump woke up with a gasp, panting for breath.

He looked around.

Nothing.

Just another stupid – horrific – dream.

He got up, put on his dressing gown, and went downstairs to make a cup of tea.

He had got at the foot of the stairs in the hall when he saw dark figures shadowed through the window in the front door.

The thump of a battering ram, and the door splintered and smashed open.

Police officers entered – the same ones as before – but this time with Anna Cornetto and Linda Likflap.

Then the door to the living room opened, and out walked his mother.

"Leave it be," she said softly. "Worse things happen at sea."

And then Crump woke up for real, feeling sick, his skin sticky with cold clammy sweat. He sat up and tried to breathe slowly to calm himself down.

A figure loomed at the end of his bed.

Crump let out a yelp.

"Kev-een – is me, Marek," said a voice. "Everything OK."

The main light came on.

"Wh… what the fuck are you doing here?" panted Crump.

"Happy Christmas!" smiled Marek, holding out a bottle of what looked like vodka. "You like alcohol, yes?"

"No more booze," groaned Crump. "Not for now, anyway."

Later, after he'd had a shower and got dressed in clean clothes, they shared an ice-cold vodka shot and a cup of tea in the living room, while Marek's Polish friend, Bogdan, was banging and sawing away, fixing the door.

Crump told him everything that had happened.

Marek shook his head.

"Is just like Communism. The secret police, y'know, Stasi, they are do thing like this many time —"

"But this is *Britain*," said Crump, realising instantly how ridiculous that sounded.

In the past, and especially when teaching foreign students, Crump had always emphasised – proudly – how the good old 'British bobby' was the best in the world. None of the foreign-Johnny-style water cannon or beating protestors with batons or shooting protestors with guns in Good Old Blighty.

Not any more.

Crump no longer trusted the police. In fact, as he admitted to himself somewhat sadly, he no longer trusted anyone or anything, with very few exceptions.

Marek was one exception. Crump didn't know why precisely, but he just trusted the man – implicitly. Maybe it was his athletic frame, his air of authority and confidence, his genuine smile? Or something else he could not even identify. But Crump needed friends at the moment, so he was pleased to have Marek there.

"How did you get in? The front door was locked and—"

"I can to get in anywhere, Kev-een. When I was in army, special forces, I am learn many thing…"

Crump so wanted to correct Marek's errors in English. But as it was Christmas Eve, and Crump was so exhausted he felt like going to bed for a month, he decided to let it go.

Marek's face took on a sudden serious expression.

"Tell to me Kev-een, you doing this thing?"

"Sexual assault? No way. Not on anyone – woman or child."

Marek looked deep into his eyes, for what seemed like hours, but which was probably just a couple of seconds.

"I am believe you," he nodded. "You not are rapist man. I can to tell. We having many rapist Russian pig in war in Moronia, *yeshush-maria*…"

"Thank you," said Crump.

Bogdan came in and handed Marek some newly delivered letters.

"You got the snail mail!" smiled Marek.

"Put 'em with the others, yeah?" said Crump, nodding to a table upon which sat around the letters of various kinds – junk mail, bank statements, other official-looking ones.

Marek did so.

"They took my laptop, and mobile…"

"Oh I sorry… I can to borrow you laptop."

"I can *lend* you a laptop…" corrected Crump, rubbing his sore eyes.

"You can?"

"No, I mean… well, thanks, a laptop?"

"Yes. You want?"

"Sure. I need one. The police…"

"… are check for child porno, yes?"

Crump thought of his laptop, smartphone and all his clothes undergoing tests in police labs goodness knew where. A shiver crawled up his spine. It was like being violated. Invaded. Raped. For it was a kind of rape he had suffered, he knew. This is how it must have been under Communism or Fascism every single day, and night.

"The laptop's what I need, thanks, Marek," he yawned.

"Is no problem," Marek smiled.

Just then, his cleaner Eva came into the room. Marek said something to her in Polish, then:

"I am text to her. She make you food."

"You do not worry," said Eva. "I do everything…"

"Thanks," said Crump – and he meant it.

*

For the rest of that month, Crump lived a sort of half-life, feeling not quite there most of the time, something not helped by his disturbed sleep patterns.

Rarely could he sleep more than two or three hours without waking up, usually in a cold sweat, usually after vivid flashbacks of black-uniformed figures smashing down his door and, sometimes, starting to drag him away or saying they were going to kill him – sometimes all watched by the gleeful, man-hating face of Abi Rainbow.

The screaming abdabs, the heebie-jeebies, *delirium tremens*, DTs, whatever.

These awful dreams were now his constant companion, though he often dreamed, too, of his mum. Sometimes he would see her and say 'shouldn't you be dead?' or words to that effect. Only then would he realise he was having a dream and wake up. The dreams of his mother were warm and reassuring though. They were not bad like the others.

Crump had been spending a lot of time looking through old family photos, especially of his childhood, with his mother – in the back garden, on various seaside holidays, Christmases, birthdays. He felt so sad looking through them. It was all gone. All just moments, spots in past time, stained on paper. His parents were both dead, and he was now utterly alone. If he died, all these photos would probably be chucked in a skip too, as he had no siblings or other close family, just some cousins he hardly ever saw, and he doubted they'd be interested.

The old school photos made him sad too – all the hope glowing on that unknowing, smiling primary school face. All the other children looked the same, of course – all children did. Even Hitler looked sweet as a little boy.

All that hopefulness and expectation and optimism just *there*, on and in those pre-pubertal faces – snapshots in time captured in the brittle years before sex rammed itself into all their innocent, unready little bodies.

Maybe Crump was happy then. Maybe he wasn't. He didn't know. But he certainly wasn't happy now.

It was the troubling flashbacks that he hated most of all. They happened almost every night, so much so that he sometimes tried to stay awake to avoid falling asleep and experiencing another.

He spent a lot of time on the laptop Marek had lent him. He had to read up on the law, now he found himself on bail for two sexual assaults. How could that happen? Did anyone making any accusation, however ludicrous, automatically get believed by police? Yes, in a word.

The worst example Crump found was a man who had brushed past a woman at a crowded London train station. He was charged with sexual assault, sent to trial then acquitted by a jury within half an hour. Because the CCTV footage quite clearly showed no sexual assault had taken place. The man, carrying a bag in one hand and a newspaper in another, had brushed past a woman – who could not be named 'for legal reasons' and who identified herself as a 'well-known actress' – and yet she claimed to have been both hit and 'penetrated' by him. Those were pure lies, utter fantasy. And yet, the Crown Prosecution Service not only decided to charge him and bring the case to trial, but they also allowed the prosecution to deliberately slow down CCTV footage to make it *appear* that a completely innocent man – who was just going about his business – had lingered near the woman to sexually assault her. The man was the victim, not the woman – yet no charges would ever be brought against her, nor her identity revealed. The accused man, however, had to undergo two years of hell, have his face and name splashed across the media for months, and lose his job and only source of income, before being completely exonerated at his trial. There was something *very* wrong in that.

The man was now crippled by extreme anxiety, and had suffered, in his words, 'mental torture sanctioned by the state'. Crump was suffering the exact same thing. The man also said that no matter how times he told people he was innocent, he could see them thinking 'of course you would say that'. No smoke without fire, they say. Well '*they*' are wrong. There is. Women lie. Children lie, often to please others by parroting what parents say, or because they lack empathy. People lie, shamelessly and often. For sympathy, for attention, for compensation or because they're deluded. It is shameful that anyone making such accusations is automatically believed.

Was this the CPS and police deliberately trying to increase rape and sexual assault convictions – lowering the bar of evidence – to hit targets? Was the fact so many police forces and the CPS now have female bosses a factor? Yes or no, it didn't matter. In today's victimhood-craving culture, accusation proved guilt – if the accuser was a woman, or child, and the accused was a man. It was no different in Salem, or the Pendle, Warboys or Bideford witch trials in 17th-century England, or any witch hunt for that matter, real or metaphorical. Then, as now, the innocent suffer at the suspicious hands of a righteous baying mob.

Round and round and round everything swirled in his head. He went through everything in his mind over and over and over again. Constant 'what if' questions arose, as well as a wish that he'd stayed at home that evening, and not gone down town to drink in pubs and then sit, exhausted, listening to the carol service which he then decided to leave early.

Was he depressed? Yes. Suicidal? Sometimes. Just what was the point?

What if he was charged with those sexual offences? He would be branded a sex offender – a paedophile – for life. And, he knew, if that happened, his life would not be worth living. The fact that he was innocent and had done nothing wrong mattered not a jot.

He went to the GP, a young man in training, and was offered anti-depressants – Crump took them for two days, but felt even more ill, so stopped. Counselling was suggested. The disturbed sleep, the flashbacks, the feeling sick and worthless, the jumping out of his skin whenever he heard a loud noise on the street, the sick terror that gripped his heart whenever he saw a police car. It all pointed to severe anxiety, depression and, most probably, Post-Traumatic Stress Disorder. All part of him now, in his DNA, his blood, his flesh and his bones.

Depression. Melancholy. Ennui. The 'black dog' barking in the very omphalos of his being. Take your pick – they all failed to accurately describe the yawning pit of hopelessness that engulfed those unfortunate enough to be in despair.

Crump thought that any employer, especially a state-funded university, should step in at such moments with help and support, if they cared about their employees. It was a big 'if' that spoke volumes. The only messages he received from them were cold and harsh, informing him of the seriousness of the matter and that he was suspended, and could not now access any university buildings either, including the library, or access the intranet. It was as if they wanted to worry him more; it was, in fact, as if they had already *assumed* he was guilty as accused, just like the rest. Crump resented that. It was, indeed, the *'tyranny of opinion'*, as John Stuart Mill called it, and everyone was every bit as bad as each other. Lone misanthropes were seemingly the most 'woke' people of all…

Grey day followed grey day in January, as the unhappiest of new years began. Crump knew that one day soon he'd get news from his solicitor about what the police intended to do. He felt sick thinking about it, about what could be, about what his future held. All he could do was wait, and live, and breathe…

He was, in a way, living two lives in two different worlds.

One – the one where he efficiently emailed the university, and Sir Clive Silverback at the Foreign Office, to keep them fully informed; the one where he opened all correspondence, including from the council stating his mum's house would have to be sold to raise a sum of over £75,000 to repay her care home costs, thus making Crump homeless; the one where he looked to the future, planned lessons, did research and reading; the one that was, despite his suspension, relatively normal, a world where his problems could be seen clearly, managed and thus coped with.

Then there was the other world, the world of utter darkness, where everything was hopeless, where there was no future, where he felt well and truly doomed, and completely powerless, awaiting his fate like a convict in a cage, listening daily to the dreaded thump of the executioner's axe as others met their destiny. That was a world of constant worry, of mind-twisting, stomach-churning anxiety, a world of no hope or laughter or happiness or light. A world with no future. A world where up to fifteen men a day in the UK kill themselves…

253

And things got worse, not better, as the month dragged on. The shifty looks from neighbours didn't help. Nor did the isolation, despite the ever-helpful Eva coming in to cook and clean for him, and do his washing. Nor did the darkness of the world, inside and out, with the short, gloomy, grey days reflecting and displaying exactly the monochrome numbness of Crump's soul. He was just another victim of a witch hunt, exiled to an island of silence in a spiteful world.

People who used to say 'hello' or 'good morning' to him now just skulked away with a nod avoiding any eye contact – that is what rumour does, and of course the neighbours all knew why his door had been smashed in, and the police at the time made no effort to hide it, or the reason they were doing it either.

Some of his neighbours seemed so provincial-minded it was doubtful they'd ever read a book without pictures, or even with them. Their horizons seemed only to stretch as far as living the dream of a job for life with the council – and some, incredibly, had never even visited London, a mere three hours away by train, or wanted to. Crump had always despised the lack of ambition of these people, their tiny uninterested uninteresting minds, their satisfaction with smallness, their 'settling', and the way they wanted more of the same for their equally uncultured kids. But it'd be a shame if they all now shunned him because they automatically believed him guilty as accused, abiding by the 'hive mind' of assumption and lies.

What difference was there between these people and the smock-wearing vengeful peasants of the past, the same little lynch mob doling out their twisted self-serving version of 'justice' to anyone different, or eccentric, or individual, with the rough music of the mob? How were they any different from the peasant mob on the Universal Horror movies *Frankenstein* and *Bride of Frankenstein*, old 1930s movies Crump had always loved. He was, he now had to admit, the thing they sought to destroy. He was the monster. Kevin Crump. Little old him.

Then there were the usual brawny builder/handyman and van-driver-type neighbours, three vehicles apiece – Crump detested them anyway, for the parking problems they caused, if nothing else, and had never really spoken to them, especially as most seemed solely concerned with making a profit by turning residential streets such as his into student accommodation HMO-holes so they could turn a quick profit.

Ditto for the dog shitters, those selfish chav-wankers who used his street as a toilet for their mutts. There was so much excrement on the pavements some days you'd think the council had instigated a dog shit festival – (maybe Diversity Dog could be the poster boy?).

Crump never ever blamed the dogs. They all had to do their business, as do we. But the dog owners who let their pets shit on pavements, right outside people's houses, when locals lived and children walked – how Crump would love to smear their shithead faces in that dog poo, stuff it into their selfish mouths and force it down their loathsome toady throats. If only…

He had, on occasion, exchanged some small-talk with a few neighbours who now looked right through him – smock-wearing peasants all, no matter if they wore smart blouses and considered themselves tolerant and modern and middle-class. The lesbian nurse over the road blanked him too, as did her neighbour, a woman the same age who copied her shamelessly in dress sense, hairdo, even choice of car make and car colour. Crump remembered such silly 'best fwend' girls from the primary school playground. This was no different. Except that these women were over fifty years of age.

Then there was the local teenage twat shouting abuse and insults up at his bedroom window now and again – Crump couldn't be bothered, and didn't want to, report that or anything else to the police as his trust in them had evaporated entirely.

'He'd learn,' Crump thought – and he may well one day be in the same shoes, which both he and so many innocent, and always-vulnerable, males found themselves forced into these days, with the growing man-bashing #MeToo mob mentality and paedo-hysteria of now, which bore no similarity to reality or any real-world risk, and a never-ending media-stoked victimhood culture of false accusations.

But there were a few decent people. A long-time neighbour of his mum's opposite; the almost-retired direct neighbours next to him; some students, and especially some of the very few local ethnic minorities – they seemed to empathise with the injustice; and an always-elegantly-dressed woman called Jan from up the road whom he'd often seen picking up litter or, incongruously clad in rubber gloves, giving the pavement a good scrub after the binmen (AKA 'refuse management operative persons', even though they were all male) had spilt the usual rubbish from split bags on bin day, leaving the place looking like some Mumbai slum.

Crump's predicament was the same as any innocent falsely accused in the whole of history, from supposed witches, to harmless heretics, baby-eating Jews, and all the victims of twisted thinking, religious or otherwise. He felt a sudden empathy with them all. He knew what they knew, felt how they had felt, suffered like them.

Crump thought back to an amateur production of *The Crucible* that his mum had taken him to at the local Whitworth Theatre when he was twelve or so. He wondered what it would be like to be crushed to death by heavy rocks placed on his chest, as an old man character in that tragic tale, a satire of the McCarthyist witch hunt of alleged Communists when it was written in 1950s America, but which could equally apply to the false allegations of the androphobic, compo-chasing, victimhood-craving vengeful #MeToo mob of now. He felt as if he was halfway there already anyway, unable to breathe, as if underwater, lost in the blur of the world.

Then, one day, he realised he still had his mother's ashes in the cardboard container in her bedroom – a room he had left completely alone since moving into her house.

He knew she wanted them scattered at a beautiful beach on Gower. So that is what he would do.

It was fairly late, just gone three in the afternoon. It'd be getting dark soon. But he still had time. And anyway, so what if he scattered his mum's ashes at dusk? There were no rules. And, on the plus side, at least it wasn't raining now, after the drizzle of the morning.

And so, Crump drove out to the beach, his mother's ashes on the passenger seat beside him.

The sea loomed black in the half-light. The waves were small, the windless day meaning at least the sea was not rough, so scattering the ashes would be easier.

Crump stood on the shore. He looked around. No-one was there with him on the vast expanse of sand. The two cafes and ice-cream shop were all closed for the day, and possibly for the winter. The whole place looked as dead as he felt.

And then, he sensed it – a sort of smooth, soothing certainty entered him and became one with his bloodstream. He could end all the suffering then and there. No more worrying about what will be, about possible charges, which, the more Crump thought about it, and how many lives Abi Rainbow had ruined with her accusations, looked increasingly likely as each weary day dragged by.

It was so easy!

He could – he would – walk into the sea, with his mum's ashes in the cardboard tube. Keep walking out on the sand, into the peaceful water.

And so it ends…

As it has ended so often before for the nameless miseries of numberless mortals.

This beach was one of those locally where American troops had practised for the D-Day landings, he knew. And he also knew 75% of the first wave of British men to land on the Normandy beaches were killed, and no doubt a similar statistic for the Americans, creating a shore of corpses. And yet, if he was honest with himself, he would have swapped places with any of those men – what they would have to face, even if it meant death, was preferable to the mental hell he had suffered these past few weeks. It would save him the bother of ending his life too, if someone could do it for him, just shoot him, pepper his shank with shattered jagged shrapnel as he stood there on the beach, blow him to bits with mortar or mine.

He had endured so much hurt, so much pain. Why should he let that go on? Why shouldn't he take back control of his life, even if it was to end it?

Just what was the point?

It was easy to see why ancient cultures believed the gods were playing with us.

They were.

Crump looked at the cardboard tube containing the ashes of his mum.

"I'm sorry," he mouthed. "I love you."

And, with that, Crump started to walk down the beach, and into the shallow sea. Soon, the icy water was over his ankles and up to his knees.

Before long, he knew, it would be at his waist. Then his chest. Then he wouldn't be able to touch the bottom.

Then his clothes would get waterlogged and drag him down, the current pulling him out to sea, or under it. The freezing cold water would numb him into a painless nothingness.

And then, the end.

The vanishing point.

This was it.

As Crump walked forward into the water, the greatest emotion he felt was relief – relief that, at last, it would all be over.

He pulled open the cardboard tube, and scattered the ashes in the sea around him.

"Goodbye, Mum," he said, his voice breaking, letting the empty carboard tube float away briefly before it was swallowed by the waves.

Even in the near-darkness, Crump could see a grey sheen of ashes coating the surface of the sea, though he knew the heavier remains had sunk to the bottom already. So that is what we were, minus the H^2O. A quintessence of dust, of minerals and metals and broken bone fragments.

Now they mingled with the silt on the seabed, sucked into an eternal salty silence, save for the scratching of crabs and dancing dabs and the secret songs of seals.

He was not afraid of death. We are not scared of it before we are born, so why should we be scared of what happens after we die? Our lives are but a blip between those two points. Some blips are longer, some shorter. Crump's blip of life was, he thought, just right. He'd had enough.

It's over – the hurt and the pain. I'm free!

Just then, he heard a cry. More of a wail really. And in amongst the cries and wails, the word *'Why?'* repeated loudly over and over again.

Crump squinted through the dusk to the edge of the sandy beach, where the limestone rocks rose up to a coastal path.

He could see a silhouetted figure standing on a rock high above the sea below. It was certainly a well-padded figure. And it was a man's voice with a local accent which yelled hysterically to the heavens:

"Why me, Lord? What has I done? Fair play too!"

Boyo Bellylaughs MBE!

Soon, Crump was with him dripping on the rocks.

"I knows you," said Boyo.

"I'm a... I *was* a lecturer at the university—"

"Aye, and I's the Chancellor, till they got rid of me, like," said Boyo, his voice breaking with emotion.

"I've been suspended too," said Crump, "for things – alleged – allegations – accusations. Not true, but—"

"And I's been banned by the council – can't perform anywhere local, like! All them places I played over the years – I's now banned from doing my act anywhere. No-platforming, they calls it. Sounds like something at Birmingham New Street station..."

Crump laughed a little laugh, like a lonely wave lapping at the sand.

"S'not funny, is it?"

"No," said Crump. "It's not. But..."

"But?"

"Why was... why *were*... you sacked again?"

"Oh I sinned – I'm a poor sinner. Oh Lord my God, save me... See, boy, I's being punished coz I been Prideful, and Pride be the worst of the Seven Deadly Sins."

"Is it?" Crump said, then remembered learning that when he read Marlowe's *Dr Faustus* at university.

"Vanity! All is vanity! I was guilty of the sin of Pride! I wanted another award, so when some poor dab makes a mistake and shortlists yours truly for African of the Year, *Boyo Bellylaughs Umbe*, then, well, I says nothing, see, because I wants another gong, another prize, another poor bauble, to insult the grace of God..."

Boyo Bellylaughs wailed at his fate, then broke down sobbing.

Suddenly, Crump had an idea. It flashed into his brain like a flame, lighting up the darkness, enveloping the world in a vibrant, bright, loving light.

"Isn't your God a forgiving God?" he asked.

"So they say, boy, so they say—"

"And isn't anything possible, with your God?"

"Oh I knows it, I does—"

"So," suggested Crump, "why *can't* you be African of the Year?"

Boyo Bellylaughs stopped sobbing as suddenly as if a switch had been thrown.

"Because I's not African," he said in a whisper. "I's not even black."

"Yes, you are," said Crump, straight-faced.

"No, I is not," said Boyo Bellylaughs, holding out his hand and examining the back of it. "I's definitely not even a bit black – not even in the dark, like—"

"Have you ever heard of self-definition?" asked Crump.

Boyo blinked ignorance.

"Well, the principle of self-definition says that you are basically whatever race or ethnicity – or, indeed, gender – you identify with and as. It's a concept used by all authorities, even the police," said Crump.

He could almost hear the cogs in Boyo Bellylaughs brain crunching into gear as he thought it through.

"So, you means, if I says I is black, then I is black?"

"Yep."

"And if I says I is a woman, then I is a woman?"

"Yes, again."

"That's bloody bonkers, that is, mind," said Boyo Bellylaughs. "But I doesn't want to be a woman, like… what with the high heels and make-up and… all the jokes I tells, like."

"Boyo, just think – you can, if you want, become a black comedian. Like a born-again African! And do you seriously think the university or the council would ban a comedian 'of colour'?"

Suddenly, the life returned to Boyo Bellylaughs MBE, as if he'd been plugged into the mains. A broad smile spread across his face.

"You lovely boy, you," he said, giving Crump a big kiss on the cheek. "Good man! That's absolutely phenomenal, that is!"

"Welcome to a brave new world, Boyo Bellylaughs, the best black comedian in South Wales."

Boyo giggled in glee.

"Say it now, say it loud – I'm black and I'm proud!" shouted Crump.

"Oh, I is – I is black and I is proud, so God help me. Tidy, like! Fair play too, boy – you's a bloody genius!"

"Well, I just—"

"Sorry bout all the tamping and tears, like..."

"Oh no, we all get a bit... down and... off-kilter... sometimes... when things go awry... and people get into a kerfuffle... y'know... all discombobulated..."

"Dis-con-*what*?"

"I think it's a newish American word," said Crump.

"They did the trial runs for D-Day, here on this beach, the Yanks did," said Boyo.

"I know," said Crump, shivering now, but warm inside.

"We's not in their shoes, at least, eh, off to get shot at in Normandy? Thank the Lord," said Boyo, looking heaven-ward.

"Thank crikey," said Crump, knowing that the bullets aimed at us these days were not made of metal at all any more, though they were still flying around, whizzing past our ears.

After that, Crump no longer wanted to end it all. It was as if by preventing Boyo from doing the same, he'd saved himself. His life had some purpose, after all. If he didn't know any better, he'd think it was the plot from some classic Hollywood tearjerker movie...

No, Crump would not let them break him. And if he was charged, he would defend himself in a court of law. He had done *absolutely* nothing wrong. He would fight the good fight with all his might – and he would prove his innocence, no matter what.

Crump gave Boyo Bellylaughs MBE a lift to his home in one of the suburbs of The Town.

On the way, the comedian was buzzing with excitement and plans for his new life to come, as the best black comedian in South Wales, and the jokes came thick and fast:

"As my late father said, sorry I'm late. What d'you call someone with no body and no nose? Nobody knows."

"*Boom-boom!*" said Crump.

"I remember playin' Noah in the school play, like, when I was a kid. The memories are flooding back. But seriously, why are mountains funny? Because they're hill areas. HILARIOUS? Geddit? Geddit?"

Crump did, and laughed as he drove, though his wet feet squelched the pedals.

"Life is like a box of chocolates. It doesn't last long if you's a fat bugger like what I is. Time for a diet, mind... gotta look my best on stage... Oh I could kill for a cuppa..."

"Me too," agreed Crump.

"What kind of tea is hard to swallow?" asked Boyo Bellylaughs MBE.

"*Reality?*" Crump said with a smile.

"Oh, you knows it too, buddy," said Boyo with a sad smile. "There we are. The old ones is the best..."

And so Crump drove onwards through the night, along the long length of the bay, back to The Town, and now, at last, ready for anything life could throw at him.

It was nice to be alive.

*

Soon after his evening at the beach with Boyo, it had started raining. Not unusual weather for The Town, it was true, but even for a place used to westerly winds which could bring rain on any day of the year, this was unusual.

It seemed to have been raining solidly for over a week, and was now raining harder than ever.

Some places locally had flooding. No chance of that where Crump lived in the appropriately named Highlands area. Everyone there lived on a hill, with views of both the bay and the rivers of rain flowing down the streets to the sea, some twenty minutes' walk away.

And then Crump got an email. It was from the solicitors.

He could feel his heart skip when he saw that in his inbox. After he'd made a cup of tea, and breathed deeply several times, he clicked it open. He was well aware that the news contained in this email would decide his future and his fate.

Crump leant forward, squinting through his glasses at the tiny text:

> I have been informed by the officer dealing with your matter that you have been Released without Charge and there will be No Further Action taken.
>
> As such, you are not required to attend further bail appointments.

Crump heaved an enormous sigh of relief. NO FURTHER ACTION or 'NFA' meant that he was innocent, that insufficient evidence existed for the accusations made against him and/or that no-one was actually accusing him of sexual assault in the first place. The police would have charged him if they'd thought there was any chance of conviction, for sure – so obviously they didn't. And yes, despite knowing he had done nothing whatsoever wrong, other than the bad manners of being drunk at a carol service, Crump was more relieved than he could say.

But what he felt more than anything else was anger – a raging pulse inside him at all the pain and injustice he had suffered, just because someone had seen fit to make a disgusting allegation against him, for their own sick, vindictive, spiteful, man-hating reasons.

He had come so close – so *very* close – to walking into the sea.

Damn them! *Damn them all!*

He slammed his fist down on his desk, and vowed to himself that this would not be the end of the matter. Now it was his turn to take action against those who had tried to ruin his life.

He listened to the rain pelting down, lashing against the window, bulleting down on someone's corrugated iron garage roof nearby.

He phoned the police who stated he could collect his things the following afternoon from the central station – the same place he'd spent the night in the cells. The same place where the police had tried to set him up, working so hard to, in effect, force him to lie and say he was too drunk to remember anything. Just so they could get another arrest, tick another box, slice off another scalp.

Crump felt a rage welling within him. He was deeply thankful for his education and intelligence, and his stubborn character too, inherited from his mother – without that, who knows what would have happened?

It was a relief that he was going out for the evening. His Polish cleaning lady Eva had invited him to an all-you-can-eat buffet in town. It would be good to get out of the house, clear his head – just enjoy himself, for once. The last five weeks or so of his life had been perhaps the most difficult he had ever lived. He felt bruised and beaten – deeply damaged by it all. Wounded. Maybe permanently. But not fatally, at least.

At the buffet – which was not as vast as those he had been to on trips to Canada, but which still had an adequate array of various dishes – Crump found that he was actually enjoying himself. And that hadn't happened for quite some time.

There were various Polish friends of Eva around the two tables joined together: Zofie, Krzysztof, Maya, Bartek and Bogdan, who had mended Crump's smashed-in door. Crump was the only Brit present, but there were other colleagues and partners of the Polish people. There was Anand from India, Tatiana from Russia, Chukka and Adebayo, students from Africa, Bao from China, and Marjorie, a nurse from the Philippines. And everyone got on perfectly well without the need for any risk assessment, diversity audit, or any recourse to gender and ethnic quotas.

It all reminded of Crump of his past life of a decade ago, teaching at West London College, and his good fun colleague, who used to sometimes invite him round to Sunday lunch with her huge extended Jamaican-British family.

Crump slugged his bottle of beer and thought of Becky. She'd died over five years before from breast cancer aged just thirty-six. He missed her.

"You not worry!" said Eva.

And with that she ordered another round of drinks from the smiling Chinese waiter.

As was usual at such all-you-can-eat buffet places, Crump ate all he could eat – and a plate or two more too!

Well, why not?

By the end of the evening, he was stuffed, and rather drunk, as were a good many people around the table.

When Crump got out his wallet to pay, Eva told him to put it away. It seemed Marek had taken care of it already, and he wasn't even there. The meal was his treat. Crump made a mental note to thank him next time he saw him.

Crump more or less waddled out of the buffet restaurant with the others. Eva's friend Krzysztof was even more drunk than he was, and when they were outside on the pavement, he started singing a Polish folk song and doing what Eva says was a traditional dance.

Well, Crump had always wanted to see some Pole dancing…

CHAPTER SEVEN

Wising Up

Torrential rain ran in rivers down the pot-holed hills of The Town.

It was pelting down – bucketing it – raining cats and dogs – nice weather for ducks. Yep, it was English idiom rain again, in Wales.

Crump drove down to the police station and collected the evidence bags which contained all his clothes, his trainers, his laptop and his smartphone.

It was nice to get them back. But they all seemed soiled somehow, having been pored over, prodded, examined and DNA tested at a location goodness-knows-where by goodness-knows-who.

He'd hang on to the mobile and laptop, of course, but not the clothes. They were old anyway, and none was what could be called expensive designer wear.

The first thing he did when he got home was to take a large pair of scissors out of the drawer, cut up the old jeans, the Christmas jumper, the T-shirt, underwear, socks and to have a go, at least, at making the trainers unwearable. Then he unlocked the back door and braved the rain to stuff the lot in the dustbin.

He knew he could never bin or erase the memory of what had happened or the stain on his soul. He was well aware of that. But that was precisely what he was symbolically trying to do in whatever trivial and pointless way. He had to do it, get rid of those soiled clothes – they were infected by events as potent as any plague virus in his mind. It felt good – cleansing, in a way. Crump hoped they would all be incinerated soon, or end up in landfill. He wished he could do the same with the memories that clung to them – and him – like a sickly smell.

Rushing inside, he locked the back door and brushed the rainwater off his face and glasses.

Later, he was getting his old laptop up and running in his bedroom when he heard a noise. Definitely a dripping noise.

He wandered from his bedroom to the landing, looking at the ceiling for evidence of a leak. No stain or wet patches anywhere.

Then he looked at the door of his mother's old bedroom. He rarely went in there. It was still hers, despite the fact she was no longer alive, despite death emptying the space of its rightful inhabitant, so he hadn't touched it since he'd moved in – he just didn't want to. There was enough room without it, and he'd get round to sorting through her clothes and donating them to charity shops in time.

Slowly, respectfully, Crump opened the door. He bent his neck back and stared up at the ceiling.

"Oh bollocks!" he said to himself, faced with clear evidence of a leak, spreading like a damp cloud in the middle of the Artexed ceiling.

He'd just have to go up to the loft to see what was happening. After finding a plastic bucket in the kitchen and putting on a pair of old trainers, he made his way up the metal loft ladder that hid in a cupboard off the landing. He turned on his torch and opened the hatch.

"What the fuck, Marek!" Crump yelled.
"Is no problem," said Marek, with a casual shrug.

"No *problem*?"

"I call Bogdan – he fix roof."

"There's a fucking gun in my attic!"

"No – there is two gun. One is AK-47, other is Makarov pistol, from Russia."

"One, two – what the fuck does it matter?"

"Yes, it matter – with two gun you can to shoot two person at same time."

Crump shook his head in disbelief.

"But you must to know, Kev-een, killing it not make you a man. Killing only make you killer. I know this."

"I was *on bail*, Marek, for nearly a month. If the police had come round—"

"Police has not come—"

"No, but if they *had*, I could have been sent to prison! Fuck's sake!"

"But you not in bail now?"

"No, but… they're fucking *guns*, Marek. *Guns!*"

"They not are loaded, so you not worry—"

"Oh my god, this is *so* illegal," muttered Crump, worry bubbling in his stomach.

"I sorry, Kev-een. Really."

Marek touched Crump reassuringly on his shoulder. If Crump did that to anyone, he'd probably be facing another arrest for sexual assault.

"But you say I can to put stuffs in your house, no?"

"Guns is not '*stuff*', Marek – it's… it's—"

"Is protection. Moronia is not the safe place – there, have many dangerous person. Life, it is cheap. You not understand."

"Oh, I dunno. You ever been to the Valleys?"

"What is?"

"A joke. Never mind. But anyway, the thing is, this is not Moronia, this is Wales, the UK, and we don't do guns here unless you're a gangster or a drug dealer or… so why did you put two fucking guns in my loft?"

"I need hiding guns, not in my home."

"Why?"

"Because I think peoples they will to steal from me... They breaks on."

"*In*. But why?"

"Moment," said Marek as he answered his ringing mobile and walked into the bathroom from the landing for some privacy.

'Well, at least he hasn't shot me,' thought Crump, 'yet...'

While Marek was taking his call, Crump went onto his laptop – it was an old friend he had missed terribly while it was with the police, whose IT operatives no doubt pawed over it looking for illegal porn, opened all his files, scoured his history and cache. They went back a long way, had spent so much time together. Marek could take back the replacement he'd lent him that afternoon. It just wasn't the same...

Crump noticed that he was now allowed back on the university intranet and email system now his suspension was over. However, the uni HR department had also sent him very matter-of-fact emails to say he would only be allowed to start teaching again after an obligatory meeting with Melissa Jenks.

Apart from that, the usual emails – endless reminders from various departments and diversity champions about the usual box-ticking nonsense. People in administrative offices tended to suffer from *email-itis*, he noticed – a constant compulsion to spew emails out at the world, like some endless spraying wave of unpleasant, digital diarrhoea. He couldn't have been the only one who scanned them all quickly before deleting. It was perhaps both sad and hilarious that those bureaucrats who bombarded staff with emails actually thought the receivers read through them in detail, and perhaps in some weird masochistic way even appreciated the never-ending avalanche of emails addressed to them and usually marked 'URGENT' with a red flag. Delusions came in many forms…

But one email jumped out at him. It was from Johnny Blue, and it was dated Christmas Day, almost a month before.

When Crump opened the email, a sick worm of worry twisted in his gut and he felt the blood drain from his face.

"Is not problem, Kev-een, I take guns now and — "

"Marek, can we go here – now – please?"

Crump pointed to an address written in the email from Johnny Blue. The rest of the email consisted of these words:

> You'll find me here.
> Sorry.
> Johnny

*

They smelt him before they saw him.

When Marek opened the locked door – so easily, and within seconds, with a piece of plastic the size of a credit card – a gust of death smell hit them. Crump covered his mouth and held his nose. It was that sweet, heavy, earthy scent that Crump had only smelt before when he'd stumbled across a dead sheep in the countryside on one of his walks.

He didn't have to see any actual rotting body to know what had happened. But it was still a shock when he did.

Johnny Blue was hanging by the neck from the bannisters. The face was discoloured, and decomposition was well advanced, thanks in part to the warmth of the central heating. All paid for with Direct Debit, no doubt, so no-one would notice when he was gone. That's why he'd emailed Crump. Well, how was Johnny Blue to know Crump had been going through his own personal hell at the time, arrested and down the police station, then recovering at home, with a laptop and smartphone confiscated, and no access to the university email system or intranet?

Maggots dripped from the sockets where Johnny Blue's eyes used to be. The bloated, hungry buzz of flies was the only sound.

Crump said nothing. He just sighed sadly as he stared at the cold corpse of his friend who, supposedly, had gone abroad to join an environmental charity.

Didn't he have any friends who called round? Obviously not. And Crump knew he had no home phone or even mobile – Johnny hated the things – though he was digitally proficient and had a laptop.

In fact, Johnny had helped him when he'd first arrived at the university, and even let him log on with his password before Crump eventually got given his.

Why hadn't Johnny talked to him – anyone – or said anything? That was always the question, and always would be, when people chose to end it all. Nobody knew anything – that was the only conclusion to draw – and never would.

But then, when Crump was in the process of taking a fatal, self-annihilating walk into the sea earlier that month, he could have asked himself the same thing. If he hadn't heard the suicidal cries of Boyo Bellylaughs MBE, then, well…

"I must to go," said Marek. "You must to stay and calling 911."

"It's 999, Marek."

"Is 911 on box-set detective show"

"That's America, we're Britain…"

Marek nodded. "You like Little America, yes?"

"No," said Crump, getting annoyed, "they're more like Little Britain."

"I go," said Marek.

"But… why can't you stay? I don't…"

He handed Crump his smartphone. On it, was a photo – of Marek's face, looking confident and serious in a suit and tie. Underneath was his name 'MAREK SIRKO' and under that, writing in Moronian. Even as a non-speaker, Crump's knowledge of various languages meant he could understand the words which said: 'FOREIGN MINISTER'.

"You're the fucking Foreign Minister of Moronia?"

"No – I *was* fucking Foreign Minister of Democratic Republic of Moronia. Until fucking bastard new Communist Party scum take under – "

"*Over*," said Crump, always keen to correct a phrasal verb error. "Come on, Marek, you gotta be taking the piss – "

"No, I not want piss…"

Why hadn't Crump looked up Marek on the internet before? Come to that, why hadn't he looked up any of his students? For all he knew he was teaching world leaders, dictators, oligarchs, gangsters, war criminals, or members of their families at least. He well knew that anyone teaching at any posh public school or top university definitely *would* be teaching the offspring and extended family of such people. Well, someone has to pay for the upkeep of all those beautiful historic buildings and manicured lawns, not to mention the perks and pensions of the staff.

And who cared where the cash came from, if it was legal? And it was all always legal, even if it was illegal – efficient money laundering saw to that. Indeed, without the proceeds of organised crime and the theft of plutocracies, it was highly likely that top universities and charitable-status private schools would be facing a financial crisis that would close quite a few of their heavy oak doors for good within weeks.

It was all relative anyway, as academics had been

telling us all for years as they promoted relativism as the 'new normal' – that there were many different ways of 'knowing' and that they are all equally valid; that because you can know nothing, you might as well believe in anything; that there was no such thing as right or wrong, good or bad, moral or immoral – or, indeed, amoral – or life and death.

Though as the stench of death hung round him like a sweet dark cloud, Crump could certainly tell the difference.

"I go," said Marek. "I still have the *immunité diplomatique*, we always are say in French language in my country."

"You've got diplomatic immunity? *Seriously?*" said Crump, stunned.

"Is what I say. But dead body here, and I Foreign Minister—"

"Former—"

"Is still problem, Kev-een. I go. You must to making call and report, then take taxi to home."

Crump waited till the sound of Marek's car had faded, then dialled 999. As he did so, he noticed something on the small hall table, under a ceramic bowl with keys in it.

Johnny had left a note.

Crump read it with a sad sigh.

'Oh you stupid, stupid boy, Johnny,' was all he could think as the 999 operator asked which service he required.

THE WORLD POPULATION IS NOW OVER
SEVEN BILLION.
IT IS NOW THAT, LESS ONE.
PEOPLE ARE SUCH POLLUTION.

GOODBYE HUMANITY
AND GOOD RIDDANCE.

I USED TO SEE THE BEAUTY IN THE WORLD, BUT

NOW I SEE ONLY THE TRUTH, AND I HAVE SEEN ALL
THE TRUTH I CAN BEAR.

I'VE HAD ENOUGH.
WHAT'S THE POINT?

JOHNNY BLUE

*

"People simply didn't know what they were voting for!" said Polly Pointy, doyenne of the Labour Party's hereditary elite who lived in a Strawberry Hill mansion worth somewhere north of five million pounds.

"The Leave campaign's lies mean the referendum result was invalid," said Hayley Naylor, Lib Dem MEP, who very much enjoyed her salary of €101,808 a year, plus a generous expense account and free travel.

"It seems *wee-lly* clear to me that the only way to *wee-solve* this *cwi-sis* is to *wee-peat* the *wef-er-wen-dum* with a people's vote," said Sir Michael Haxeltine, sometime failed Tory leadership hopeful with a net worth of over a hundred and fifty million quid.

"We already had a people's vote on 23rd June 2016 and we the leavers won – you losers lost. Deal wiv it! Get Brexit done!" said Dan Crabb, self-made multi-millionaire Brexiteer businessman and the biggest Leave campaign funder.

"No less than 17.4 million people voted to leave the EU – that's more than have voted for anything in British history – ever – and you remainiacs, you remoaners of the political elite, want to overturn that democratic decision just because the working class vote didn't go your way," sneered Steve Fabricant, former TUC official from the unapologetic hard left.

"It's funny, isn't it, that the usual suspects – the out-of-touch metropolitan so-called liberal elite – claim people didn't know what they were voting for when they don't

275

get the result they want? Then they claim, in their epic *whinge-athon*, that all those 17.4 million voters, 52% of us, were all somehow ignorant and racist…" laughed Neville Wellcome, former Tory, sometime City trader and long-time campaigner to leave the EU.

"Well, you *are* a racialist, Neville," sniffed Polly Pointy, who was always keen to show how non-racist she was by employing foreign domestic servants, cleaners and gardeners on minimum wage to look after her London townhouse.

"Not at all. Are all those Labour voters who voted leave racist too?"

Sir Michael Haxeltine's chortle suggested he agreed with that.

"But *why* not have a second, confirmatory referendum – a people's vote?" added Hayley Naylor MEP.

"But why?" retorted Neville Wellcome. "We had a people's vote in June 2016 and incidentally, all the traditional parties said they'd accept the result. The people voted against the Euroshambles! You anti-democracy Remainistas and Euro-rats just want to repeat the referendum till you get the result you want – admit it!"

"Yet more lies from the Brextremists!"

"Oh, we know the old Eurocrat tactic, alright – they did it before with Maastricht ratification in Denmark and the Treaty of Nice in Ireland in 2002. Same old same old!"

"How many d'you want, love? Best of seven?" laughed Dan Crabb.

"Respect the democratic decision of the people," said Steve Fabricant, forgetting momentarily that he was, in fact, a Stalinist and yearned for the day a true Socialist dictatorship ruled this realm.

"Oh, you're just ignorant," said Polly Pointy.

"No, *you* are, pretty Polly," said Dan Crabb.

"*Bigot!*"

"See, Remainers always claim to hate populist policies, then adopt the worst aspects of European populism themselves, always supported by the Remainstream media," sneered Neville Wellcome.

"Now then, let's calm down a bit, can we?" appealed omnipresent BBC presenter Jason Hussain who was chairing the TV debate. "The thing is, is that Brexit will harm the economy, won't it? Neville?"

"The stranglehold of the EU empire is what's harming the economy. Most of their economies are stagnant at best, with no growth, lots of 'em in recession, massive debts their banks can't repay, an unemployment rate at least double or triple Britain's, and all propped up by generous German subsidy – take that charity lifeline away and watch the house of Euro-cards come crashing down."

"We've paid Europe over two hundred billion pounds since 1973," added Steve Fabricant. "The UK pays 17% of the EU's total income."

"Two hundred billion spondoolies!" shouted Dan Crabb. "Lotta wonga, that, mate – they're bleedin' us dry!"

"And another thing, we want our country back. The people have spoken – they want us to have control of our own affairs, so we can do business with the whole world on our terms, not theirs."

"*Bwitain* will be devastated by *Bwexit*," said Sir Michael Haxeltine.

"*Wubbish!*" mocked Dan Crabb.

"Well *weally*, do you know who I am?" harrumphed Sir Michael.

"Why? You forgotten, mate? Town clown!" sneered Dan Crabb, to the delight of his fellow Leavers on the panel. "Destination Brexitland, here we come!"

"What about all the recessions that have happened since 1973 when we joined the Common Market, eh? The jobs lost, the millions of unemployed?" said Steve Fabricant.

"Hear hear!" boomed Neville Wellcome.

"'Ere we go, 'ere we go, 'ere we go," sang Dan Crabb, rhythmically punching the air in the good old *Inger-land* tradition.

"The referendum was just a protest vote, and it *was* all about immigration, as Neville well knows," said Polly Pointy.

"All those disgusting anti-immigrant posters," sneered Hayley Naylor, who seemed on the verge of tears.

"Well, I actually think a well-managed limited immigration system is a good thing," added Neville Wellcome, "but what we don't need is open borders where anyone – and three million people in the last twenty years – can come from any EU state to the UK, and we don't even know for sure how many are here, as we have no identity cards—"

"Like the Nazis?" said Sir Michael Haxeltine.

"Like France, Germany and all other EU states with an ID card system," added Steve Fabricant.

"We're a small island – we're full," boomed Neville Wellcome. "Ever heard of the housing crisis? That's what happens when you have five million migrants in twenty-five years, that's a city the size of Birmingham every year, and it's still going on!"

"Send 'em back – if they're illegals," said Dan Crabb. "One-way tickets back to whichever shithole country they come from. I'll pay."

"Errr, language please, guys," reminded the host, Jason Hussain.

"You see, Jason – yet more racism," said Polly Pointy.

"What about the NHS? Where will the doctors and nurses come from in this Brexit mess?" added Hayley Naylor.

"Maybe we could train British people for British jobs? Now there's a novelty," said Steve Fabricant, perhaps wishing he could play doctors and nurses with Hayley Naylor.

"What utter *wot*," muttered Sir Michael Haxeltine who had seemed about to nod off.

"What a genius idea, Steve," sarked Neville Wellcome. "Funny how nobody ever thought of that, isn't it?"

"It won't be enough, and not in time either. Patients will die…" said Hayley Naylor, her voice breaking.

"It's a big world out there, love," said Dan Crabb, "and besides, loadsa nurses come from all over the place, not just Europe—"

"But… but… I want my future back," sobbed Hayley Naylor, "a future… in a united Europe… of peace…"

"India, Africa, the Far East – we can trade freely with all these places once we are free of Euro-bureaucracy and do business with the whole world – regions with growing economies, unlike most EU countries," explained Neville Wellcome. "Do you know that trade with the EU is just 8% of our GDP?"

"But it's true, isn't it, Neville, that society is angry, and more divided than ever before?" asked Jason Hussein.

"Hate crime soared after the referendum," added Polly Pointy.

"Yes, and some was fake news or exaggerated reporting… and now it's gone down again. These things go up after any major event in history, and it's all stoked by the negative Brexit news-peddlers at the BBC and the *Remainstream* Project Fear media of the metropolitan elite," insisted Neville Wellcome with a winning grin.

"And so, we can all agree then," said host Jason Hussein, "that we're divided as a nation like never before—"

"*W-ight* you are. At least since the *te-wibbly* bloody English Civil War," said Sir Michael Haxeltine.

Nods and 'yeses' all around the round table.

"Well, then at least we're all united in that!" laughed Neville Wellcome.

"Nice one," said Dan Crabb, with a loud Cockney barrow boy laugh. "Bish bash bosh!"

But none of it mattered and no minds would be changed, because the UK had slid into a situation where politicians speak and no-one listens, not really. It was a sort of mental breakdown of the electorate – or, possibly, an awakening. And it had been long underway by the time of the EU referendum too, and not just in Britain either.

It said a great deal about privileged politicians that very few of them, here or abroad, seemed to even notice that anything had changed.

But one thing was sure: it would never ever change back. Not now.

Crump made himself a cup of tea. He was enjoying a night of telly – he hadn't felt much like it in the preceding weeks of trauma. But now he was catching up on news, especially regarding Brexit and the situation at Cambrian University.

Next up was a BBC Wales discussion about the university's unilateral declaration of independence and continued membership of the EU.

It all depended on the validity of that 1912 founding treaty.

The TV programme went into fascinating detail about the intricacies of treaties past and present, the most fascinating of which was about a Welsh pirate called Robert Edwards who, in the early 18th century, was given seventy-seven acres of the largely unsettled area of Manhattan by Queen Anne, for his services in disrupting Spanish sea traffic. The land was now estimated to be worth 650 billion dollars.

Apparently, after the pirate's death, the property went to two brothers who were wardens of a local church on a ninety-nine-year lease, on the understanding it would revert to the heirs of Robert Edwards after that time. But that never happened.

The original document stating as much was now lost, and even if it was found, it would now be invalid, statute-barred due to the passage of time – though that hadn't stopped several claims by Edwards' heirs.

The land was now owned by the Episcopal Church of New York, and it seemed that God had told them, quite categorically, never to give it back.

Such were the tangled matters involved when documents and treaties were disputed, as they always would be – lucre-loving lawyers would see to that.

And such was the position of Cambrian University in its campaign to remain in the European Union and declare independence from Brexit Britain.

It was the last stand of the Remain campaign, their Battle of Worcester in the English Civil War, their Somme or Battle of Amiens in the First World War, their decisive Stalingrad stand in the Second.

It all rested on this – a small scroll of parchment hidden away in the dusty archives and ignored for over a century.

*

And so, the fateful day dutifully came, in early February, when Crump returned to teach on campus, now that it had been officially decided by the Crown Prosecution Service that he was not, in fact, a dangerous rapist sex abuser paedophile pervert.

Crump almost felt like smiling, such was the unending, relentless joy of the occasion.

Things carried on as normal – or, at least, as normal as it could get at the doolally pc mad house that was Cambrian University in an age when the whole of the UK, and indeed much of the world, resembled a huge lunatic asylum, but rather less lucid and sane.

Of course, first he had to get the meeting with Melissa Jenks over with. The criminal justice system had found there was no case to answer and so decided on No Further Action. But universities, much like the Church, or other corporate entities, tended to see themselves above the law, and so had their own disciplinary procedures which they were free to enact on a whim, even if an individual had not been charged with any offence and even if they'd been found not guilty in a court of law. This was, in essence, an assertion of power and status, the flexing of bureaucratic muscle – but it was something that had cost many a man (and it was usually men) their careers and, indeed, health, marriages and futures.

It seemed even that these institutions all cared far more about their reputations than anything else, and were more than willing to chuck innocent victims under the bus, or maybe feed them to the lions, or maybe send them away on a bus driven by blind lions, if that protected their precious reputation and 'good name'. Self-preservation trumped justice and fairness every time.

Crump was sitting in the Head of Faculty's office on the third floor of The Learning Tower. Melissa Jenks seemed to have put on even more weight since the last time he'd seen her, and with her pale face, red lipstick and black hair she looked more like a plus-size china doll than ever.

"We take accusations of sexual assaults very seriously at this university, Kevin," said Melissa Jenks.

"And so do I," said Crump. "I was accused of something I hadn't done and then I was found innocent."

"No, you weren't," insisted Melissa Jenks. "There was insufficient evidence for the CPS to charge you – that is not the same thing as being found 'innocent'."

"So... you're saying if a man is accused of sexual offences, then he must be guilty – that there's no smoke without fire?"

"I am merely stating the obvious. As I said, we take the safety of our students and staff, especially women, very seriously at this university. Do I make myself clear?"

"Well, I'm no threat to anyone, sexually or otherwise."

"Hmmm," said Melissa Jenks, with a little cynical cough of disapproval.

Crump hated her for that. Is that what his life would be now, as a man once accused of a sexual misdemeanour? One smug harrumph after another, shifty sideways looks wherever he went, whispered suspicions as the soundtrack to his new life as a man falsely accused and publicly shamed for it? Had some *no-smoke-without-fire-itis* infected the entire world?

"We have agreed to reinstate you provisionally, which means you will be monitored closely to ensure a safe environment exists for all learners."

"I have done nothing wrong," insisted Crump.

"Nevertheless, we as a university have a duty of care, and we take that…"

"… very seriously indeed," said Crump and Melissa Jenks in unison.

They stared unblinking at each other, like cats on a wall.

"I'm sending you on a course, Kevin," said Melissa Jenks, at last, her multiple chins wobbling with certainty.

'Oh please, not another bloody *diversity doughnuts* course,' thought Crump.

The mere thought of it gave him a cross between the shivers and goosepimples. Maybe he could celebrate the diversity between them?

"Merry Christmas!" said Melissa Jenks.

It was February. Was she even more bonkers than she looked?

Crump stared blankly into his boss's blobby, obese red-spectacled face.

"Merry… Christmas," he replied, baffled. "Or is it *Winterval* these days?"

Maybe this was some new exciting university initiative to celebrate their Christmas after the real one? Like a six-term school year, a two-year degree, or as Crump called it, *mucking things up*.

"No!" snapped Melissa Jenks. "*Mary* Christmas – she's in charge of mindfulness at the health centre, together with Amber Green —"

"Amber Green?" said Crump. "Seriously?"

"We take mindfulness training very seriously at this university. The trainers are excellent. Amber Green is very well read…"

"Of course,' thought Crump, 'red until she turns green again… '

And Mary Christmas to you too!

*

On the campus forecourt were the usual protests about this and that – usually that. Whatever 'that' was. The feminist #MeToo movement, the race campaigners, the various assorted SJW virtue-signalling 'woke' snowflakes – and, as ever, the pro-Remain anti-Brexit protestors. Blue EU flags fluttered their stars in the sky above Cambrian University still, as they had been doing since before the referendum on that rainy day in 2016.

There were the usual **BOLLOCKS TO BREXIT** and **WE HEART EU** banners draped wherever draping was possible. A lone member of the international media was taking photos of the scene.

There seemed more missing pet posters up than ever before too – new ones since Crump was last on campus. Obviously, the police were not interested in attempting to solve this mystery, even if the local cat and dog population was being stolen and sold on, or – and Crump hoped this was not the case – skinned for their pelts. He'd heard about such a trade in China, with cat and dog fur used to line jackets exported back to the UK. He hoped Nelson the cat was still around or back in his loving home with Mrs Trichobezoar.

It was as tricky as Crump had expected that morning in the English Studies Department, with all the sideways glances and suspicious looks. But Crump had mentally prepared himself for it. And anyway, did he even care what these people thought of him? So why then should he care about the opinion of people he neither liked nor respected. As with the other teaching jobs he'd done, at FE colleges and university, he always seemed to like the students he taught a heck of a lot more than a lot of his fellow teachers who could, Crump knew, be the rudest, most stuck-up and pompous people on the planet – not to mention spies reporting 'incorrect' opinions to management as efficiently as any sly Stasi informer.

Tanya Snuggs was as cheerful as ever, all pretty in pink, like the song. She told Crump that, '*to all intensive purposes*', the world was his '*lobster*' again, that she didn't want to '*cast nasturtiums*', and that he had a right to be there and teach – it was his '*provocative*', apparently, *irregardless*. Crump liked her.

"I ain't gonna *bee around the bush,* people, so let's *cut to the cake*! A rolling stone gathers *no moths,*" grinned Tanya that morning through the huge gap in her front teeth. "So let's get a wiggle on!"

Still no sign of her elusive Joint Head of Department Karen Crisp – in Australia, apparently, for a crucial conference.

It was a lovely sunny day, unseasonably warm for February, so Crump sat on a bench outside and perused a found copy of the local paper, the *Cambrian Daily News*.

The earth-shattering headline news that day was all about the 'fury' of a grandmother of five, aged forty-one, whose hair in the photo seemed to be alternate shades of green, blue and purple, complaining about potholes damaging her car and demanding compo from the council. It shared the front page with a man who'd found a Pringle in the shape of Dylan Thomas's face: "*Lucky really, like, coz I could of scoffed it, like. I takes a Pringle out the tube, like, and he's there, Dylan, like I is talking to you now, right there, in front of me, like, but in a Pringle – an' I will say this, like, he have changed my life, mun. He could be worth a fortune if I flogs it – on eBay, like, or… does you want to buy it, boy?*"

The rest of the rag comprised various people feeling 'fury' at parking problems, roadworks, noisy students etc, others experiencing 'joy' because they'd won some prize or award or other, pages of photos from whatever charity fundraising beanie bash people had managed to leech a free lunch off that week, and puff PR pieces from the council and university about what wondrous work they were doing for The Town. There was nothing in the paper – absolutely nothing – about any problems at the university, or the way it was refusing to Brexit, or indeed about the funding crisis that Crump had heard whispers about and which he'd also seen featured in the national educational media. But then, the university was one of the *Cambrian Daily News*'s biggest advertisers, and he who pays the piper…

Then, of course, there was the local veteran author, whose play *Mamgu's Burned Her Welshcakes, Mam* had gone down so well at the local state-subsidised Memorial Theatre, which never said 'no' to any of his allegedly comic plays, no matter how unhilariously bad. And, as per usual, *Cambrian Daily News* regular Paddy Muldoon was in the news – his old dog had a bit part (two seconds precisely) in a background shot of a Bollywood movie shooting locally. '*Would Hollywood come calling?*' asked a local reporter. 'No,' thought Crump. It wouldn't. *Most def.*

"No pizza? I mean, no way! It's *so* random, kindathing – majorly out of order!" said Dylan, sitting beside Crump, and unusually agitated about something.

"Eh?" said Crump, looking up from the newspaper.

"I mean, *no fucking pizza* – it's the fucking *Learning Tower of Pizza*, for fuck's sake. How can there be *no motherfucking pizza*?"

"Language," tutted Crump, sounding like his long-dead dad. "I don't actually think The Learning Tower ever really had the word 'pizza' in its *official* name though?"

"It's just... *so* unfair... ." wailed Dylan, tamping like a truculent toddler.

"Whatever," said Crump, with a wink. "Someone's a grumpy bunny today."

It seemed that it was Cultural Appropriation Awareness Week at the university and, because one student – a revolutionary Mexican Marxist apparently – had complained that South American culture was being 'culturally appropriated' by the use of tomatoes in pizza, it had been taken off the menu. Everyone was complaining, especially the handful of Italians at the university.

Crump just couldn't resist winding Dylan up.

"It's all part of your *'learning journey'*," he said, using a key phrase all lecturers were taught to parrot to leaners. "Happy Cultural Appropriation Awareness Week!"

"Yeah, right," sulked Dylan, pouting like a spoilt child – which is precisely what he and other over-protected over-praised over-coddled Generation Z students were, in a way.

"YOLO," smiled Crump, casually flicking through the paper.

"So random, kindathing, that Johnny Blue hung himself," said Dylan, when he'd manage to un-sulk himself.

"*Hanged*, Dylan. Pictures are hung, people are hanged," said Crump, sounding more like an irritated schoolmaster than he'd intended.

"Does it matter?" said the kid.

"Most def," said Crump.

"Jim Slingsby too. Not hung… hanged… he just died, kindathing. Injuries, the drink, game over. Life sucks."

Crump stood up and peered into the distance to the grass verge opposite the entrance to the university drive. Former maintenance men Dean Guttery and Mr Scumble were sitting there, cans of extra-strength lager in their hands. Crump was sad Jim Slingsby had gone – he supposed getting knocked over by a blind university taxi driver had been the final nail in the coffin for his broken booze-soaked body. It was Abi Rainbow that had accused him of a sexual assault, who had broken his brain, caused all of this. Crump hated her more than he could say.

And, of course, with the all-female maintenance crew there was such a huge backlog of work to do now. Everywhere in the university, toilets and pipes were leaking, lights were dark or flickering, broken handles of doors and windows stayed broken (such as the one damaged when a hopeless student from the ever-sobbing Creative Writing Department had defenestrated herself) so were boarded up or cordoned off.

Though none of that stopped the university celebrating its commitment to gender quotas and an all-female maintenance team in its new glossy prospectus, complete with copious photos of women in blue boiler suits holding spanners and ratchets, together with all the other diverse snaps of BAME students and staff. Crump counted just three photos of white males, or four if you included the bearded ex-man Vice-Chancellor, Angharad Ap Merrick. There were no photos of broken doors and windows though, or lights that didn't work, or leaking toilets…

But there was a grinning photo of Boyo Bellylaughs MBE – the prospectus had been printed before he'd been sacked as Chancellor. All the signs pointed to his being reinstated soon, now that he was causing quite a stir as the best black comedian in South Wales. He'd even been praised in national papers such as *The Guardian* for his 'timely post-modern BAME irony' and celebrated for being so open about being black, even though he was clearly white.

"The truth is like the sun. You can shut it out for a while but it ain't goin' away," said Dylan.

"John Lennon?" asked Crump.

"Elvis," said Dylan. "Mam's a mega fan. Gotta bounce."

"Oh, are you a beach ball?" smiled Crump.

"Gettin' some munchies in town. Laters…"

And then he was gone.

When Crump looked up from his newspaper, he could see why.

Abi Rainbow – or, as Crump liked to think of her now, 'the blue-haired man-hating freak'– was walking across the concourse, together with the boy-dressed-as-a-girl unfortunate enough to have her as a mother.

Crump tensed up as much as Dylan as she approached.

Next to her was the ever-smiling witchy figure of Lesley Snyde. Crump was still not sure what she did. Something in the PR or marketing department. But Dylan was clearly scared of her.

Abi Rainbow had apparently withdrawn her complaint and accusation against Crump after being shown the video footage taken by theatre boss Paul Pizzle at the Christmas carol service. It clearly showed Crump had not deliberately touched either her or her son Jazz. This was after the CPS had made a decision not to charge Crump with anything through lack of evidence, of course.

In fact, the CCTV footage clearly showed Abi Rainbow pushing against Crump, then shoving him at her eleven-year-old son – who always looked so anxious. The police had not arrested her for anything, of course – her claim that *her* perception had been that Crump had sexually assaulted both her and her son was valid, because we now lived in a land where accusation proved truth and perception was evidence. It was enough to make both Henry II and Hywel Dda spin in their ancient graves.

"Rapist!" spat Abi Rainbow under her breath as she walked past Crump, her face a twisted picture of raging hatred. "We don't want abusive men like you in our beautiful cohesive community – this tolerant town!"

Crump slunk off towards The Learning Tower (No Pizza) where he was due to meet his friends and colleagues for lunch. But just seeing Abi Rainbow had made him feel physically sick.

As he reached out his hand to push open the swing door to EATZ, he could see his hand was shaking and felt himself sweaty and short of breath. He didn't go in. Instead, he leant against the wall before the entrance, breathing deeply until he had calmed down.

These anxiety attacks were all part of the PTSD, he knew. He hated it, the way it had affected him. Hated the fact that he just couldn't get it all out of his head, the memory of the hell he had gone through – hated the flashbacks. And maybe the worst thing is he had no idea when these panic attacks would hit him, when the stress and fear would grip his body, paralyse his brain, make the world a weight pressing down on him, squeezing in on him, like those moving walls in old movies, coming ever closer to crush him to death.

"Kevin, you are OK?" asked Fatima, when he finally sat down at their usual table.

Crump had never been good at hiding the worry which was now, he knew, smeared on his face with the sweat.

"Yeah, fine," he lied. "Just a bit tired, tonnes to do, y'know…"

"I was so sorry to hear about Johnny," said Esther Isaacs. "Unbelievable."

"So sad," said Fatima.

"Sadly, not rare though, male suicide," said Crump.

"Just terrible, but he was having a point about over-population – I mean, what are all these people being born going to *do*?"

"Bloody computers will put everyone out of work," added Esther Isaacs.

"Poor sod," said Andy Stone, who'd just arrived, pushed by his loyal carer, Casper. "I'm gonna miss the miserable bastard."

"Is it true he left over three hundred grand?" asked Khalid.

"*Fuck!*" blurted out Pete Parzival. "I mean… OMG."

"Left it all to environmental charities," Crump nodded.

"But he lived like a pauper, yeah?" said Pete.

"And no funeral?" said Esther Isaacs.

"It was his choice – all of it," said Crump. "He didn't want any fuss, he said."

"Oh, I forgot, you found him."

"That must've been hard," said Khalid.

"Still, life goes on," sighed Esther.

"It does," said Crump – because it did, no matter what.

"He liked you, Kevin," said Fatima. "Maybe he had the problems *emotionable*?"

'Don't we all,' thought Crump, but said nothing.

"How've you been, mate?" asked Andy Stone.

All eyes were on Crump. They all knew about his arrest and consequent temporary suspension from the university.

"Oh, y'know. Keep calm and carry on. You know me."

"S'like what we used to say in Camp Bastion," grinned Andy, "what doesn't kill you makes you *stranger*, eh?"

"There's always a light at the end of the tunnel," said Esther, cheerily.

"Though it could be a train coming, logically speaking," said Khalid with wink.

"Oh, I'm an optimist," lied Crump. "I'm always absolutely 100% positive things are going to get worse—"

"Before they get better?" asked Esther.

"Perhaps."

Always think of the worst to avoid too much disappointment in life.

Crump was so enormously glad – and touched – that his friends were treating him just the same. If they thought he was some sort of sexual predator and abuser and child molester, then they were hiding it well.

"Never complain, never explain – thass what the Queen says, innit?" said Andy Stone, smiling at Casper and touching his hand.

"Off with their heads!" screeched Esther with a wave of her hand.

"Thanks, Alice," smiled Crump, remembering the Queen of Hearts in *Alice in Wonderland*, and thinking how that surreal fantasy made more sense than his life had in the last couple of months.

Just then, two young men joined them at the table.

"Everyone, this is Oli—"

"Oliver—"

"And he's with Stan… Nah, not really, this is Jay," said Andy Stone, motioning towards a young black guy who had no arms.

Crump looked at Oliver – the left half of his face was one big scar and looked as if it had been boiled – like *The Phantom of the Opera*, or victims of acid attacks. His eyes were white – and obviously blind. They reminded Crump of the marble-hard eyeballs of the whole baked fish you got in restaurants abroad. When he sat down, Crump could also see he had a false left leg and arm too.

He wondered why Jay didn't have false arms.

Everyone greeted each other.

Pam Fadge from EATZ carried over their trays of food and placed them on the table.

"There you go, lads," she said with a smile. "You'll enjoy that, so you will."

Andy Stone saw Crump staring at his veteran friends.

"These pretty boys are gold dust – stars – best mates in the world," said Andy.

"He always says that when he wants us to get a round in," said Oliver with a smile curved on his deformed face.

"Yeah the only reason he didn't lose his arms too is coz they was in his pocket chained to his wallet," laughed Jay.

"They've got what I call 'the Afghanistan look', like me – very similar to the Iraq look, but an older model…"

Looking at the devastated bodies of the two young men, Crump felt so ashamed of himself. What did he have to complain about in his life? Yes, he'd been through hell. Yes, it all still deeply affected him. But, despite the scars dug deep into his brain, nothing he had endured compared remotely to the damage done to the two men in front of him, who'd suffered the storm of war and paid the price. And Andy Stone himself, of course, with fresh air where his legs used to be.

"Just as well I never wanted to play the piano," said Jay, with a grin. "I was never that good wiv me hands."

"That's why you never got us a pint from the bar then, eh?" laughed Andy Stone.

"Well, you was always legless anyway," guffawed Jay.

"I *see* what you mean," grinned Oliver, staring into space with his blind white eyes, "but then I'm not just a pretty face!"

Crump could tell everyone else was a bit shocked at their black humour, but the three ex-servicemen clearly loved joshing each other and making light of their disabilities.

'Well,' thought Crump, 'how else could they cope?' How on earth would he cope, if that happened to him? He honestly didn't think he would. But then, the three damaged lads before him probably thought the same thing too, before the bombs blasted the flesh from their bones and sucked the sight from their eyes.

"*Kuffar!*" shouted a voice from the queue at the EATZ counter. The extremist Jihadist activists from the Muslim Society were back.

"Fuck's sake, not those idiots again," groaned Khalid.

"OMG," said Pete Parzival.

"Bugger it," said Esther Isaacs. "Can't the university *do* something?"

Fatima laughed to herself, then looked down at the table. The three Jihadi students were yelling things in a language Crump could not understand, probably Arabic, or Urdu.

Then the three Islamists noticed the three ex-servicemen. They stood at some distance, laughing and calling names, mimicking the limping gait of injured soldiers. One mocked Jay by holding his arms behind his back. Another pretended to be blind, wandering around and bumping into things.

"Where's a suicide bomber when you need one?" said Esther. "Sorry."

"It's OK," said Andy Stone. "I was finking the exact same fing."

"Me an' all," said Jay. "If me and you could, we'd give 'em such a pasting."

"Snap," said Oliver.

"Oh, there's lovely," said Khalid. "Islamofascists abusing Jews, Muslims *and* ex-servicemen."

"Well, at least they're committed," said Crump, with a wry smile.

"They should bloody well be committed," said Esther Isaacs, "or preferably interned on some rocky, lifeless island somewhere – let them fight it out amongst themselves!"

Just then, Pam Fadge, all five foot nothing of her, appeared from behind the counter and starting yelling at the three extremists.

She didn't raise a hand or touch them. And yet, simply by the use of her sharp Irish rapier tongue, the three Islamo-hooligans looked so brow-beaten and cowed that they left the cafeteria.

"Sorry about that, lads, so I am. You gets eejits the whole world over," said Pam Fadge, before going back into the kitchens.

"We could of done with her back at Camp Bastion," said Andy Stone. "She would of scared the living shit out of the Taliban."

*

After his teaching that day – more Chinese students barely able to speak a word of English, more native British students who all expected top marks merely for attending class – Crump walked wearily home.

He had to, on account of his old rusting car making some sort of screeching, clanking, dying sound when he'd started it that morning. He'd dropped it at Mike the Mechanic's garage in Highlands before getting a taxi to work.

But it was a dry day, so he didn't mind the half-hour walk home. No need to waste cash on a cab. And no way would he ever take the bus again in The Town. Crump was, he thought, of average height – for a man – at around six foot. But he found the seats on the local buses were so small he could not sit on them and put his legs in the space in front of him – so he had to engage in what feminists sneeringly called 'man-spreading'. And with the present hysteria for accusing men of sexual assault, he wasn't going to risk it. It seemed public transport was institutionally misandrist – all designed for those who are about five foot five or six – so not most men then, but perfect for most women.

Oh, how he guffawed and bent double with laughter when he heard some professional feminist on the radio plugging her new book, all about how 'The Patriarchy' had designed everything in the world for men, not women. Maybe if that victimhood-craving feminist were six feet tall, and she tried to go on public transport or sit in a Munchkin-sized theatre seat, she'd realise how wrong she was. But, even if she was tall and accidentally touched someone next to her, it was doubtful she'd ever get accused for sexual assault or arrested – that hell was seemingly the sole preserve of men.

There was also the PTSD issue. The last time Crump had been on a crowded bus, he'd got so breathless and sweaty in an anxiety attack, with the world spinning around his head and all eyes on the bus staring at him, that he'd asked the driver to let him off at the next stop.

Anyway, at least the park was beautiful – all dancing daffodils and colourful crocuses.

Crump said hello to Sandra the pig who, he was sure, recognised him and who, it seemed, could sense, or smell, his approach. Her fat, round, piggy face was always there, staring up at him with an unchanging expression of smug porcine condescension, every time he peered into her compound. How could a pig recognise him? Or hate him? How could a pig be his enemy? It was absurd. But it was what it was.

No sign of Nelson though – Crump hoped he was OK, and somehow knew he would be. He was that kind of cat.

There was no time to dawdle, however. Crump had to get home, shower and change. Because he had invited Fatima to dinner that evening, at a Chinese restaurant he liked.

His stomach was butterfly-fluttering. He hadn't been on a date for, well, how long? Not since he'd dated his girlfriend, who he'd then gone on to live with – so, what, three years ago? More. No wonder he was all tense expectant fear, twitchy as a needy teenager.

"The *low* is powerless to help you, not powerless to punish you," said Fatima, crunching into a spring roll.

"The law – and the police – should be defending people like you who get bullied and abused by other Muslims," said Crump as she chewed and swallowed.

"They are not doing this, not in UK, not in France, not in all EU."

"It's like the coppers – the police – are on the side of the extremists, especially if those nutjobs belong to a minority faith and an ethnic minority," said Crump, through a mouthful of prawn toast.

"*Oui, c'est ça,*" said Fatima. "I know many members in France of *Ni Putes Ni Soumises* – they always are having the trouble with *les flics*. And in Netherlands, when Islamist threaten people who campaign against the extremists, police are blaming them for speaking – they are never blaming the Muslims who are making the death threats."

"Yep – look at Pim Fortuyn and Theo Van Gogh, murdered in cold blood on the streets, because they dared speak out about extremist Islam – and they were definitely not right-wing extremists either."

"It's the *Islamofascists* who are from the right!" said Fatima as the mains arrived. "But our media and politicians are never daring to criticise those Muslims —"

"No British TV channel or newspaper showed the Mohammed cartoons."

"This is disgusting!"

"Yeah, I know – they invite on Jihadists to promote radical Islam, yet do not dare show a satirical cartoon –

just because it's lampooning Islam. They would, if the satire were aimed at atheists or Christians or —"

"*Mais non*, I mean, this is disgusting," said Fatima, pointing at one of the dishes on the table.

"I think that one's... spicy pig's intestine... oh, sorry, I didn't think... no pork and all that —"

"It is OK – I did not taste."

"Try some ox tripe in sauce, sautéed ox omasum... that's the third stomach of a cow..." said Crump, stupidly, "... sorry... maybe some pak choi... chicken... or prawns, the fleas of the sea, my dad used to call 'em!"

"It's OK – I have the *stomach* for it – I like the tripe," Fatima joked, helping herself to some omasum.

She sipped from her glass of wine, then noticed Crump's puzzled expression.

"The Prophet himself was drinking wine – so Muslims can drink alcohol too."

"Well, the word 'alcohol' is from the Arabic."

"But I am never eating the pork —"

Stupid stupid stupid! Why didn't Crump think when ordering? Maybe because Fatima, with no headscarf, long beautiful hair, make-up on her face, and sipping from a glass of wine, did not fit the devoutly strict, spartan, austere, abstemious stereotype of Muslims promoted constantly by the media and by conservative, literalist mosques and imams too.

There were, of course, plenty of modern, liberal-minded Muslims out there in the world – and yet, their voice was usually silenced by the yells of the hellfire and damnation puritanical radical Jihadists. Why?

"Kevin, it is OK – I can eat most foods. I like *Chinoise*."

"Me too," said Crump, with a shy smile.

"So, do you get compensation from police for —"

"No," said Crump, and he continued in a whisper to avoid any problems with other diners. "They told me that if the police are just doing their duty, acting on an accusation of sexual assault, especially against… y'know… a child… then they can smash down your door, confiscate whatever digital… things… they want… No apology, no compensation whatsoever for damage done to property, let alone health. It's fucking outrageous. Pardon my French…"

Fatima tutted and muttered something gallic and angry under her breath.

"But at least now the police cannot keep people on bail for years, as used to happen," continued Crump. "Some poor buggers were stuck in limbo like that for two years or more, after some fantasist claimed they had abused kids in the distant past—"

"Ah *oui*," said Fatima, tucking in to her chicken with ginger and pepper prawns.

"I suppose I'm lucky I wasn't tasered," said Crump. "Plenty are – and the police say a taser is not a weapon if it's in their hands, but a resource. A resource! It's nuts out there. It'd be a weapon if you or me had one, that's for sure."

"*Mais oui, c'est ça.*"

"But remember," Crump said with a wry smile, "the police are not there to create disorder – they're there to *preserve disorder*."

"Most def," said Fatima, then added, "as students say now, yes?"

"Yep, the kids say that alright. OMG, YOLO, FOMO, LMAO – sometimes it's like talking to a car number plate!"

Crump wished Fatima could say she was his BAE (*Before Anyone Else*).

"You are very funny!" Fatima laughed.

Crump loved the way she flicked her hair when she laughed. It was beautiful. Even if she did have a dribble of sweet and sour sauce trickling down her kissable chin.

"The *low* it is fascinating, *non*?"

Crump nodded, but did he really want to talk about the law, the police, the criminal justice system and the nightmare he'd been through with Fatima who, he realised, was a woman he was falling in love with.

"Can we… errr… talk about something else, maybe?" said Kevin, holding up his glass.

Fatima raised her glass with his and nodded.

"To us!" said Crump.

"*Salut!*" said Fatima.

"Cheers!"

After the meal, Crump kissed Fatima – on the cheek.

She had insisted on footing half of the bill in the restaurant too, despite Crump's insistence on paying. It seemed she never let any man pay for her – on principle.

Never before, in his entire life, had a woman refused his offer to pay, not since he'd started buying drinks for girls as a teenager. He had to admit he admired Fatima for that, but was simultaneously annoyed. Did her refusal mean something? Anything? Or was he just 'overthinking'?

He'd asked Fatima is she wanted to come back to his – for a coffee. She had declined. He'd forced a casual smile which made his face ache as much as his heart.

"*Alors, moi je suis très fatiguée,*" said Fatima through a somewhat theatrical yawn. "Sorry… so tired… I am sure you understand, Kevin."

"Course," lied Crump, mock yawning, "I'm so tired too…"

He watched Fatima's taxi pull away into the sad night.

Nearby, some charity workers were distributing food to a group of homeless people, some as young as his students. He noticed some were from a group connected to the Welsh Nationalist Party, and others from a local Christian charity and hostel.

'Now that,' thought Crump, 'is what political parties should be doing' – not the bigoted race-hating victimhood-craving nationalism he'd seen from Donald the fake Scot and the angry swivel-eyed Welsh nationalists on campus. Same for religions too really.

Just think what could be achieved if all the energy and effort of the Remain and Leave campaigns, and all their angry epigones, were focused on things in society which needed fixing. Just think how Britain could be changed for the better.

As he left, some paramedics arrived to care for an injured homeless man – what great work they did too, and paid a fraction of the salaries of the faceless hospital bureaucrat bosses and the meddlesome management consultants who stalk the wards of hospitals like vampires, sucking the places, and their funding, dry.

But what preoccupied Crump's thoughts as he walked back through the warm February evening was 'would he and Fatima happen?' He had no idea.

As he huffed and puffed up the hill to home, the corner of his eye saw a shape run across the empty road, and sit on the pavement a few feet away from him.

It was Nelson the cat, who always seemed to see everything.

Crump smiled sadly at him – and he was sure the feline smiled back.

*

"Rob, why do you insist on calling me Crumpet?"

"Well, that's your name, innit? Like, you call me Rob, not Robert, like what my old mum and dad does. You was always Crumpet at school."

"When we was... *were...* teenagers, yeah. We're over forty now!"

"Young at heart though, eh?"

"Not really, no."

Age was just a number, true, but it also represented the road to relentless decay which led, ultimately, to the final destination called death. Crump was well aware that he was probably over halfway through his life, maybe even more than that. And what, really, had he achieved? He couldn't think of much, and certainly nothing he was really proud of. The thought was depressing.

Crump was in Rob's impressive apartment at the marina. They'd just eaten Sunday lunch Thai-style at one of the more pricey restaurants there – the sort of place where Crump could smell the lingering scent of expense accounts.

Rob had been late for lunch because of a protest. Or, as he put it:

"All them fucknuggets, wankspangles and shitgibbons blocking the roads. Total twunts and cunticles! Those Remaineroids are a real pain in the arse!"

Despite being neutral on Brexit and respecting everyone's opinion, Crump couldn't help but laugh at that.

Rob's Thai twins, Preeda and Malee, were back home in Bangkok, where Rob said he was due to fly the following week, on business – he didn't know for how long.

"That's why I invited you round now, Crumpet, to get all the *malarkey* sorted before I fly off into the sunset to the land of smiles. Ever been to Thailand?"

Crump shook his head.

"*Luverly* place, it is. *Blinding!* You should come over. I'm sure we could get you set up with some gainful employment, and a pretty girl or two."

Rob paused, then leant forward and whispered.

"Boy if you want, Crumpet... or even a lady boy. Some of 'em are simply *stunning*, and I mean... most blokes couldn't care less as long as they're getting their willy tickled..."

"No, Rob, stop... stop," said Crump, raising the palm of his hand in a 'halt' sign. "Wait, what 'malarkey' exactly?"

"Oh, didn't I mention it before?"

Crump gave his head an ignorant little shake.

"I bought your house. Well, your mum's house. In the process, like. Via the council."

"Wha...?"

"Well, not bought it exactly. Yet. But they want you to sell it, yeah? Then they can take their share – half the value – to pay for your mum's care, bless her soul."

Rob was right. They did.

"Well, I've... had a word... and agreed to buy it, pay off the bastard shithead council, then everyone's happy. Because you, Crumpet, are a mate. And I, Rob Tyler, always look after me mates. You can still live there, s'long as you want... s'all sorted."

"But Rob," said Crump, "I can't pay you... that sort of money. The council want over £75,000. I haven't—"

"Don't you worry 'bout wonga, Crumpet," boomed Rob. "I'm fucking loaded. Stinking rich. So, I buy your house – your mum's house, may she rest in peace – and you stays living there, as long as you want, like, and pays me back when you can – and if you can't, so what? I'm happy, whatever."

Crump couldn't help it. All the stress of the previous weeks and months seemed to well like a spring within him, as he remembered all the worries he'd had about soon being homeless, all the sleepless nights. Before he knew it, he had his head in his hands as he sat on the sofa, crying his eyes out.

Rob put am arm around him.

"It's OK, mate," said Rob. "I know... I know... Thing is, it's only money. Yeah, it's great to make it, to have it—"

"Money has its place," sniffed Crump, wiping the tears from his eyes.

"Oh it does, Crumpet, it does. So you make loadsamoney, you live, you die – you ain't done nuffink really, nuffink good—"

"Such as?"

"I dunno, err, helping people, making the world a better place, like what you wanna do. Like... a nun..."

Rob and Crump frowned in unison.

"You want to be a *nun*, Rob?" smiled Crump.

"Eh, we'll have *nun* of that! Geddit? *Nun* of *that*! Ha-ha! Keep on smiling, Crumpet. Keep on keeping on. Good to have you back!"

For the rest of that Sunday afternoon, they drank beers in the swish apartment, just talking. Crump told Rob everything about getting arrested, the false accusations, the lot. It seemed Rob already knew, somehow, despite there being no publicity, though Crump was thankful for that.

"Ah the plods are such knuckle-dragging fucking bone-heads. Had me own run-ins with the woodentops, I can tell yer. Never charged once though."

He told Rob all about the university, the intolerance and political correctness, the no-platforming, the insane policies, the banned books – how Crump had to fight so hard against it, and how he wanted to change it all.

"Thing is," said Rob, "if you have a go, people will always have a go. Same when *yours truly* started a business—"

"They're no friends of business at the university," said Crump.

"Tell me about it! Best left to their book learning - most of 'em couldn't organise a piss-up in the proverbial, and most university managers wouldn't know an economic opportunity if it slapped 'em on their big fat hairy arses."

Crump didn't disagree.

"I was once working on a development with a uni down south – most of the managers were utterly clueless, didn't seem to be living in the real world, know the price of a pint of milk, that sort of thing. Probably why they all love the EU, eh? Endless meetings about meetings, and then nothing decided or done at the end of the day."

"Sounds about right," said Crump, swigging from his bottle of beer.

He told Rob about the anti-Brexit protests at the university, and the international media – he already knew all about the attempt to remain in the EU, all the legal wrangling over the 1912 founding treaty.

"The biggest strength of any organisation is also its biggest weakness. For universities, that's the fact they ain't got a clue what they're doing business-wise but assume they do – like the wankspangle Welsh government an' all – and also their total reliance on increasing student numbers and foreign ones, and creating new campuses outside of Blighty, especially in the Far East now. It'll all go tits up, course – but they just can't see it. They're just rearranging deckchairs on the Titanic. Glug glug!"

Crump didn't doubt Rob's business acumen.

"Y'know, I remember, one day when I was walking back home from school, through dog shit park – remember that? *White* dog shit? Mad."

Crump did.

"Well, there was these two dogs, OK – one big, one small. And they was stuck together – I mean, the big dog had its cock stuck in the little dog's fanny, or maybe arsehole – I didn't ask—"

"Rob, please—"

"Alright alright, and anyway, they was limping around, like some weird alien eight-legged dog sex monster… It was *such a laugh!*"

"Not for the dogs, obviously! I think their… penises… swell up, after, y'know, they… to prevent another dog from… gaining access… impregnating the female."

"We had a dog when I was a kid too. Right slag, she was – let anything do her, prob'ly some boys at school if I'd let 'em, s'long as she got some Bob Martin's treats later."

Crump shook his head and tried not to laugh, but he couldn't help himself.

"Then again, some boys at our school prob'ly would've fucked a puddle of mud, given half a chance. Still would, some of 'em, I'm sure… Ha-ha!"

Crump giggled with Rob. He didn't disagree. And he was glad his car was out of action, as he wouldn't want to be driving home this pissed either.

"How on earth did we get onto talking about boy-dog-mud-puddle sex from talking about the EU and Brexit?" slurred Crump, with a drunken slump of his head.

Rob laughed and took another swig from his bottle of beer – though he was one of those people who never really seemed to get drunk, no matter how much booze they put away.

"The way I see it is this. In every marriage, there's a *fucker* and a *fuckee*. Same as with any personal or business relationship. And, it seems to me that in our relationship with Europe, the EU was always the *fucker* and the UK was always the *fuckee*. All that happened in the 2016 referendum was that the British people got tired of being *fucked*, so voted to leave. And that's all there is to it, innit?"

It was, quite possibly, the best analysis of Brexit that Crump had ever heard.

*

"Happy Burqa Day!" said Crump.

"Whatever," said Dylan, nursing an obvious hangover.

It was over a week since Crump had got drunk with Rob, so he was clear-headed and clear-sighted enough to see his buddy's post-binge suffering.

"I've got some paracetamol in my bag if you want one," said Crump.

"Nah, s'OK," groaned Dylan, slouching on the bench on the uni forecourt and covering his face with his hands.

It was a dry day and not cold, though overcast and dark, so Crump had eaten his lunchtime sandwich *al fresco*.

"YOLO," said Crump, with a wry smile.

Dylan said nothing as he hid his hungover eyes from the daylight.

Crump sat and watched the truly ludicrous spectacle of Burqa Day, because on that day all women (or, more precisely, those who identified as female) were encouraged to wear burqas – or *burkas* or *niqabs* (a small face veil) or *chadors* (the full Monty whole body burqa), if one wants to be nit-picking – to express solidarity with Muslim women all over the world.

And so, he watched as the black blobs of both students and staff glided around in their burqas, a bit like nuns – but with added value.

His view on burqas hadn't changed in the decade since he'd endured a teaching job at London's Thames Metropolitan University, complete with its Department of Islamic Studies and its hidden hordes of Muslim women dressed in that uncompromising face-concealing garb.

It seemed so extreme and, importantly, impractical. How could communication take place when people were wearing what were, in effect, masks, he wondered? How could one converse with a piece of fabric, he thought, and how could anyone communicate with someone whose eyes squinted through a little postbox-like slit at the world? How on earth do you speak to a mask, Crump pondered? There was no expression, no feelings, no humanity, in his opinion, anyway. Crump knew that linguistic research showed around three-quarters of our understanding of speech came from visual cues too.

It was truly bizarre – and, indeed, shocking – that British schools, colleges and universities allowed not only students, but teachers, to wear these communication-hindering masks, as did courts and even airports. Burqas, like all other masks, were an enormous barrier to effective communication, not to mention a security risk, Crump thought. These veils were not liberating at all – they were walls, keeping us out and them in, in Crump's opinion. Surely, he pondered, Britain's social fabric and security both now and in the future mattered more than custom and choice?

Even more weirdly, the women's lobby and most feminist groups actually defended and supported the wearing of burqas, as they always supported a woman's right to choose to wear whatever she liked. Some even declared wearing a burqa was 'empowering'. Crump couldn't understand that logic.

It was ironic, too, as no male student or staff member was expected to wear anything different on Burqa Day – something Crump was enormously grateful for. It was bad enough not knowing who was who amongst the women in his department – what with them all looking exactly the same when sporting identikit black burqas. It made communication slow and confusing, though there was no mistaking the bubbly Tanya Snuggs as she bounced into the team room. Not even a puritanically black full-body covering could disguise her ebullience – her bubbly voice *sounded* the same shade of shocking pink she usually wore, even when her entire face and body were blanketed in a dowdy shroud of anonymous and miserabilist black.

And, of course, the issue was also that if you allowed Muslim women to wear such garb to work and in their everyday lives, and simultaneously didn't allow those who were *not* Muslim or female to do the same or wear concealing garments and items which come from their culture – such as Halloween masks, crash helmets, balaclavas or snoods – then you were not only a hypocrite, but also guilty of promoting both sex and, possibly race – or, at least, cultural – discrimination. No test case had ever been brought before a court or tribunal, sadly. It would certainly be interesting from a legal point of view.

The forest of EU flags on campus fluttered in the fresh February breeze.

Dylan yawned.

"I'm so majorly broke," he said, suddenly.

"End of the month – you get paid soon, don't you?"

"Yeah yeah, most def. I just can't stop spending the scrilla, kindathing. My bad. But s'just so random," he groaned.

"Well, I don't want to lecture, but… couldn't you do a budget, or stash some cash in a savings account now and then?" advised Crump.

"Thanks dad," yawned Dylan. "Whatever…"

Crump smiled. He liked the kid, despite his undeniable dopiness.

"S'like, some people've gotten *so* much money –"

"Yes, Dylan, they're what is known as *rich* people," snarked Crump, "and the past tense of 'get' is actually 'got' and not the Americanism 'gotten', which was the original British English form in the 17th century, and which our cousins over the pond never grew out of, but I'm sure you –"

"S'like the management here – they're so loaded, man. No wonder they love the EU and shit, what with all the fucking funding they get – they been creaming their share off the top for years kindathing, making a stash. Why can't –"

"*What?*" said Crump, sitting up. "What did you just say? Dylan?"

"Errr…" said Dylan, waking up.

He opened his eyes and sat up too. It was as though he'd been talking to himself and had only just realised there was someone else in the room.

"Nothing… I'm just tired, right?"

"No, Dylan, you said the management here were creaming money off the top of EU funding."

Silence.

"Oh, I don't know what I'm talking about, kinda thing… errr… you know me, I'm just confused… tired… Got so wasted last night. Need coffee. Gotta bounce."

And then, Dylan was gone.

As if by magic, Fatima then appeared by Crump's side.

"Are you alright, Kevin?" she said.

Crump was pleased, but not at all surprised, to see that she wasn't wearing a burqa or even a headscarf – unlike most female staff and students that day.

"Yeah, yeah, fine," said Crump, still processing what Dylan had just told him, however inadvertently. "It's just… nothing…"

Fatima sat on the bench beside him.

"And may I say how gorgeous you look in your invisible burqa," smiled Crump, and Fatima smiled back too.

"You are crazy in this country. Your political correctness, it is the fascism of now —"

"Ah but at least it's fascism with manners," added Crump with a sardonic smile. "We British are very polite."

"It is tolerance of things we must not tolerate! In France, the *low* bans this burqa in schools and in the university. It is a one-woman prison! But you crazy English —"

"Errr… British… or Welsh…"

"You do whatever the worst Muslim men in all the world tell you to do, the imam scholar from Islamic States. So you are making all the women to dress like this…"

Just then, there was an enormous crashing sound – in fact, several metallic crashes and bangs in quick succession, together with a squealing of brakes.

They both stood up and looked towards the road, down by the bay, where the main entrance to the university campus was located.

"Bloody hell," gasped Crump.

"Mon *dieu*," said Fatima, under her breath.

There had obviously been a crash – and maybe more than that. It sounded like a pile-up involving several vehicles.

A slow black plume of smoke was, by now, snaking into the sky.

Soon, Crump and Fatima, together with other staff and students, were running downhill towards the entrance to the university drive and the main coast road. It was an instinctive response – Crump doubted they could be of much help. But what else could they do?

Some people were calling emergency services – and already, they could hear the ambulance sirens, probably because a hospital was nearby.

As the crowd moved as one downhill towards the scene of the pile-up, Crump noticed the three Theology Department lecturers running past them, jostling for position.

"They say it's a dead child!" said Ridley Crick, Christian.

"I will be there first!" said Muslim scholar and university imam, Saladin Malik. "Guide all their souls to paradise!"

"Must… celebrate… their… lives!" panted Androo Spoon, Humanist.

"Christians will return home… to the Lord!" said Ridley Crick, and then, quietly, when he thought no-one was listening: "Oh, I do hope it's a dead child!"

"We are all born Muslim," said Saladin Malik, neck-and-neck with Ridley Crook as they overtook an exhausted and over-fed Androo Spoon who had stopped to catch his secular breath. It was never like this in The Woodcraft Folk…

Crump watched them run to the scene of devastation and carnage.

At least ten vehicles had been involved in the pile-up, and some had been so crushed they resembled crumpled balls of waste paper. At least three were on fire, spewing rancid black smoke, which smelt of oil and burning plastic, into the air. Indicator lights and other things bleeped somewhere. There was an occasional, quiet, human groaning or wailing sound, perhaps from those trapped in the wreckage. Oddly, there were no screams.

Crump could see former university maintenance men Dean Guttery and Mr Scumble, who spent their days drinking on the grass verge directly opposite the university entrance, checking the wreckage for signs of life, as the emergency services got to work, with yet more arriving all the time. Saladin Malik was kneeling down next to a crushed vehicle, reciting words in Arabic.

Crump knew it could have been him – he drove along that road most days of the week, in his old rusting Ford which he'd been glad to get back from the garage the week before, after some minor repairs. It could have been his corpse bleeding out, trapped in the twisted sinews of metal, having to be cut out of the wreckage by firefighters. It could have been him burning to a cinder with his seat belt still strapped safely around his torso and an airbag bursting in his melting face.

He also wondered if the pile-up had been caused, at least partially, by the restricted vision of a driver – or drivers – wearing burqas. Or perhaps blind university taxi drivers, listening to tinkling bells…

Crump realised they could be of no real help, as did Fatima, so they made their way back up the hill to the main university concourse. They didn't want to get in the way of emergency services. Others were told to stay back too, due to the risk of fire and explosions.

As they ambled back in sad silence, Ridley Crick rushed past them with Androo Spoon.

"Typical!" Ridley spat the word angrily through his clenched Christian teeth. "It's *always* a damn dead Muslim."

"Well, they do have more children on average," said a disappointed-sounding Androo Spoon.

Crump was glad when he could no longer hear their conversation.

After a last look down the hill at the chaos and carnage, Crump turned to go into the English Studies Department.

And there, sat on a wall, and watching it all, was the ginger figure of Nelson the cat, whose big yellow eyes stared unblinking, as his ears twitched keenly at all the noise and nonsense of the naked-ape-addled world.

CHAPTER EIGHT

Burning Up

It was 1ˢᵗ March, St David's Day – or, in Welsh, *Dydd Gŵyl Dewi Sant* – the national day of Wales, on the day the 6ᵗʰ -century bishop of Mynyw (now the tiny westerly Welsh cathedral city of St David's) was martyred.

And so, that Saturday evening in the Richard Burton Theatre, a local male voice choir sang the Welsh National Anthem, *Hen Wlad Fy Nhadau, Land of My Fathers.*

Crump didn't understand a word. But then, nor did many others in the audience, or the nation, as only 11% of people in Wales spoke the language fluently, though 23% understood some Cymraeg, a few words here and there.

The Welsh dragon flags were waved in the auditorium, as were a great many blue, starry EU flags – all highly ironic seeing as a clear majority in Wales, and in The Town, voted for Brexit. No clapping happened though, as per usual – just Jazz Hands – in case any autistic people were triggered by applause.

Very ironic really as a group in the audience – who, apparently, were all on the autistic spectrum or had Asperger's – had been laughing and shouting throughout the entire St David's Day concert of songs and readings. When an old lady had complained about the disturbance, it was she who had been escorted out of the auditorium by the ushers, for being so intolerant of the neuro-diversity of the special people present.

Mike Mumpsimus, Dean and Quality Control Director, was there, together with his Tourette's, blurting out 'Fuck', 'Wank', 'Cunt' at regular intervals, which was particularly noticeable during the readings and dances.

Cambrian University's Vice-Chancellor, the bearded Miss Angharad Ap Merrick was there at the front, next to the Head of Strategy Ms Parminder Zugswang, and a selection of *'the crachach'* – the often-Welsh-speaking wealthy cultural elite upper class of Wales who run most institutions in the Principality.

Most there were wearing a daffodil, real in most cases, or artificial. A small minority wore leeks, one or two miniature leeks, or plastic ones or badges. Some people were even in national costume – though they were mainly the local schoolgirls who'd given a dance performance earlier in the concert. One or two people wore kilts, supposedly a symbol of unity with Celtic brothers in Scotland, but actually invented by the English Georgians two centuries ago. 'So much of the nationalistic stuff people thought was ancient was so utterly fake and fabricated,' thought Crump, as he looked around the audience. Same for all countries, nations and tribes, of course. Nationalism was always in the head, not in the blood.

And, of course, everyone was wearing their gender pronoun badges, just in case anyone mistook them for a chair, or perhaps to aid them if they wanted to hook up and get a room after the gig.

Crump felt the *'Cwtch of Cymru'* of the St David's Day concert, and he liked it. It was enjoyable, as far as it went, and he was glad he had attended.

How typical of the nationalists to spoil it.

"Yer nae Celt, Englishman," came a voice after the concert was over. "Yer wee reactionary beastie!"

"Talking to me?" said Crump to the bekilted fat man who was standing beside him, complete with sporran, tartan cap and a set of bagpipes.

"Och aye," said the fake Scot, "that I am, laddie. I cannae lie! Or else I'm not Donald Dougal Angus Hamish McGinty McDonald McClounie!"

"*Cymru am byth!*" shouted Gruffyd and Morgan Tewdwr in unison – which meant 'Wales forever'.

Much cheering from the three spotty nationalistic sidekicks Huw Pugh, Richard Pritchard and Hywel Harlech. No doubt these three foot-soldiers were some of the nationalist 'cybernats' – some Welsh, but mostly Scots nationalist activists – who continually trolled, attacked and abused anyone online who dared oppose 'independence' (or actually reliance on EU subsidy and rule) or expressed support for the successful political union known as the UK. JK Rowling had been trolled for stating as much, as had thousands of others whose only 'crime' was to express an opinion which a majority of Scottish and Welsh people agreed with. Social media was crawling with these aggressive bigots, an ugly abusive mob whose self-appointed nationalist members lived under the delusion that they were 'progressive' and 'liberal' when they were anything but. Their instincts and methods were pure playground bully and racist, yet no nationalistic political party had taken action against them or even criticised their behaviour, suggesting that these *cybernats* were actually part of their jingoistic English-hating campaign teams and their trolling methods had party approval.

Most of the noise always comes from the shallow end of the swimming pool.

Crump yawned, theatrically.

"The Celtic colonies of the English empire will soon be free!" said one of the three Welsh nationalists in the Welshiest accent ever.

"We'll drive the English oppressor into the sea!"

"Freedom from the English government in... that London!"

"Aye, lads, and we cannae do worse than think on the great achievements of that proud and true-born Welshman and Prime Minister, David Lloyd George," said Donald, wistfully.

The three young nationalists jumped up and down whooping and squealing, like a trio of deranged beardless Bee Gees.

"... who was born in England – Manchester, I think," added Crump.

Much frantic conversing and whispering amongst the nationalists.

"Aye," said Donald eventually, "due to oppression by the perfidious English making Wales so impoverished that his parents had to leave to find work in the enemy's land, just like our fellow exiled Celtic kinsmen from Scotland and Ireland."

More cheers from the racist English-haters present. The spotty youths there started to sing a tuneless, mangled version of *Danny Boy*.

Crump rolled his eyes and thought of his mum – it was one of her favourite tunes, and always tear-jerking when sung properly.

"The lyrics of that song you're now singing were written by an upper-class English solicitor in Bath, I think you'll find,' said Crump, before taking his leave of all tartan Nazis, racists and bigot nationalists present who, as per usual when he called them out, looked rather lost and insecure as they frantically conferred about whether the English-accented man before them was actually right.

Crump was grateful he left before the sturdy, solid, manly frame of Bethan McBurnie, well-known manly Scots historian and author of academic tomes of such overwhelming tedium that she was invited to be guest lecturer at numerous universities worldwide, came over to join her fellow nationalists.

It was a truth universally acknowledged by anyone who had attempted to read books by academics that the vast majority simply could not write well. But then many could not teach well either, as, unlike school teachers, they did not have to train to do it – they just did degrees, undergraduate, postgraduate, maybe a PhD, then they were let loose on the educational world to bore and confuse the next generation of uninterested, spotty, smartphone-fixated, social-media-weaned students.

Many could lecture – which, in essence, meant waffling away to oneself with... occasional pregnant pauses and... gaze focused into that vast middle distance... meaningfully... between the rows of a lecture theatre – all of which gave the (probably) bearded lecturer's face the look of an alleged intellectual – or possibly a cat having a crap. Crump had played the game himself.

But he knew, having taught at FE colleges and classes of teenagers overseas, that lecturing was not teaching, which was another game entirely. Lecturing was more like talking to yourself without the risk of being taken away by the men in white coats. And, if you did it long enough and badly enough, they gave you a secure, well-paid job for life and a big fat index-linked pension too.

Crump knew he was tolerant – if he was honest with himself, he knew he didn't harbour within him any conscious prejudice about anyone, no matter how absurd he thought things like 'self-definition' for choosing a race and colour and gender for yourself were. 'Live and let live' was his instinct, and he hated bullying and unfair discrimination when he saw it.

And that was his issue – or one of them – with many nationalists. They were just bullies, plain and simple, who wanted to intimidate people into granting them their demands, despite a lack of popular support. Surely, their time and effort would have been better spent ensuring Wales was not fourth of four in UK nations for education, healthcare and business success? Maybe their energies and that of many others would be better focused on addressing that scandalous state of affairs.

Crump also hated the dishonesty of nationalists – the sheer fabrication and fraud of it all. For decades, the nationalistic myth had persisted – that the Welsh were pure-blooded Celts and the English, supposedly the coloniser (though most people centuries ago were poor and oppressed, no matter where their kings came from), were pure-blooded Anglo-Saxons, all descended from invasions of Britain by Germanic hordes in the 5th and 6th centuries, who slaughtered or forced out the true British Celts from England to Wales, Scotland and Cornwall.

But now DNA testing (yet another Great British – in fact, English – invention, from the mid-1980s) had shown the truth. Namely, that three quarters of English people could trace an unbroken line of genetic descent via their parental genes to settlers who arrived long before farming, 6,000 or more years ago. Long-term Scandinavian trade and migration contributed the other quarter, and the land now called Scotland had more Nordic immigration than that. The supposed 'Anglo-Saxon invasion' only contributed a tiny fraction of the English gene pool, as did later migrations, of Vikings and Normans, for example, which were often much exaggerated, often by those wishing to promote more mass immigration now.

The peoples now known as the Celts originated in the area now called Spain, and arrived via sea routes thousands of years ago, though Celtic languages came in later still. The entire idea that the Romans found a uniformly Celtic population in the British Isles was a lie and had survived, as so many lies do, especially about national identity, because enough people liked the lie to repeat it enough to make it a truth – a myth masquerading as a fact.

Added to which, there had been such massive immigration into Wales from England during the 19th century, when the Welsh had been the first people in history to work more in industry than on the land, so the vast majority of people in Wales have English ancestry, whether they liked it or not.

And oh, how Crump hated the victim pose of the Welsh nationalists! They even blamed the English when the Welsh were racist. All the fault of what they now called the 'English' – not 'British' – Empire. No doubt they blamed the potholes on Welsh roads on the English too, and the rain, and puddles, traffic jams, the price of beer, and indigestion, and piles. It was the creation of an enemy to bolster tribal loyalty, and you could see the same thing when the angrier feminists blamed men for everything (even for when women did bad things, because it was men who created the patriarchy so everything was their fault, apparently) or, these days, when Remain campaigners blame everything that was bad on Brexit, somehow forgetting the several recessions the UK suffered when a member of the EU, including the crash of 2008, or the massive unemployment and other economic woes of many European Union member states today.

Crump didn't enjoy the Victim Olympics, and never had, so was glad when he left that evening.

He was also glad he hadn't bothered going to the 'Diverse Welsh Voices' art exhibition on at the university to mark St David's Day – and not just because it would feature the work of what Rob always called 'subsidy monkeys', those government-funded persons who often got taxpayer-funded grants thanks to their contacts, or perhaps by emphasising their nationalistic 'diversity' credentials, which happened a lot with self-consciously Welsh authors, especially those who wrote in *Cymraeg*.

It was no good. Try as he might, Crump just didn't like modern art, or the non-figurative stuff that was known as 'conceptual art' anyway. He'd been to Tate Modern and the Saatchi Gallery in London, as well as Modern Art exhibitions in various cities around Europe. But it was no good – no matter how hard he tried, he found it all so... '*trying*'.

One thought always struck Crump as he stared at whatever monstrosity of conceptual art stood before him, whether an unmade bed, a pickled shark, deformed child mannequins, piles of sand or rice or wood or rusting lumps of metal, and that thought was always, every time: '*I could do that! I couldn't paint a Monet or a Renoir or a Rembrandt or a Leonardo, but even I could cobble together this crap.*' And any art that had to be explained to be understood had somehow lost the plot too.

These were the reasons why Crump did not bother to enjoy entering a room full of Welsh dragons made of various substances, from hay to straw to stone to metal to plastic to glass to poo – yes, human and animal poo – that a Welsh artist (who'd arrived a decade ago from Austria, possibly to avail herself of Welsh Arts Council grants) had created. So, too, did Crump miss the piss sculptures of Lorna Lapetus, the Cornish-born Scots-Irish-Welsh artist who had been pouring pee collected from volunteers into glass vases and receptacles of various shapes for two decades now – this time, a huge Welsh dragon see-through vase, which glowed all yellowy-urine-y in the gallery skylights.

He also avoided experiencing the award-winning menstrual flower paintings of Finella Furnstein, and her special huge canvas of the Welsh flag done entirely in dried menstrual blood. On display was also Furnstein's famous artwork 'INVISIBLE' – a blank canvas she had stared at every day for three years and which was on loan from a New York gallery which had purchased it for three million dollars five years before. And the university gallery had even managed to acquire and display some of the artist's famous 'INVISIBLE SCULPTURES' which consisted of nothing but air, because there was – literally – nothing to them. This, however, did not stop art critics praising them to the skies or, indeed, art galleries worldwide purchasing them – though more than one vanished in transit, and another was stolen to order by notorious art thieves. In the INVISIBLE SCULPTURE space, a silent song cycle, also written by Finella Furnstein herself, was playing on a perpetual loop of complete and utter silence, creating 'a sonic tapestry of the contemporary in a diverse space'. As one admiring critic gushed: "The theme of silence haunts the piece and in particular the way silence can be enriching and fertile." No-one could really agree what key it was in though…

No wonder then that the sculptures and music had won so many awards and prizes, and guaranteed the artist a substantial state-funded Welsh government grant for the next three years.

Well, when it's a choice between fixing potholed roads, the school system or the Welsh NHS, versus funding a highly talented artists who could truly put Wales on the map, albeit ever-so silently and invisibly, and in such comically creative ways, then it's all a no-brainer really, isn't it?

Well, isn't it?

*

Crump drove home listening to local news on the radio. It was confirmed that four people had died in the pile-up outside the university, and others were still in hospital.

Yet, there was no mention whatsoever on the news that people wearing burqas, or, indeed, blind drivers of university vehicles may have been a contributing factor.

It was all just portrayed as a random accident. Crump knew that was highly unlikely. Yet any 'diverse' factors were being utterly ignored in all news reports, in the same way they always failed to mention that terrorists who slaughtered innocent men, women and children in cold blood in Manchester, London, Paris etc were in fact Jihadi Muslims killing in the name of Islam, something their cries of *'Allahu Akbar!'* (literally, 'God is greater') more than hinted at. The BBC and other news services in Britain preferred to ignore that Islamo-elephant in the room, thanks to the odious truth-munching virus called 'political correctness' and 'diversity worship' enforcing 'fake news' on us all – a version of the news that didn't offend our precious and diverse sensibilities and told us to think 'correctly'. It was just all so wrong and dishonest. The entire media seemed to be admiring the emperor's clothes endlessly. Just where would it all end?

Crump wondered if any research had been done at any university comparing road safety of drivers wearing masks or burqas, or being blind, as compared to a control group of those not afflicted by either hindrance. He doubted it. Asking questions that were considered non-pc could lose you your job at many a university these days.

But how could asking questions – any questions, on any topic, no matter how controversial – *ever* be wrong? Yet this anti-education ethos was now embedded in the education system in the UK, which took its lead from the US, like one of those disgusting botfly larva that burrow deep into the flesh of animals and humans, which could only be removed by cutting off their air supply with grease and teasing them out with tweezers. Removing the infestation from education would be a much harder and more disgusting job, for sure.

Was the entire education system – which was meant to inspire debate and deep thought, to encourage the asking of better questions – really so shot to shit it acted against those things? And, if so, could it really call itself an education system at all? When what it was *not* doing was educating anyone, but indoctrinating its victims according to whichever bigoted one-note orthodoxy was 'on trend' this week? How exactly did that differ from brainwashing by the Nazis, Communists or any self-serving dictatorship or religion?

"Oh, you *total fuckers!*" said Crump to himself, arriving home to find – yet again – all parking spaces on the street where he lived taken by the work vehicles of his handyman builder neighbours.

He could count at least five white transit vans. But there was nothing he could do – he didn't own a semi with a drive, but parked on the street outside his end-of-terrace. He'd rather have students as neighbours any day, despite all the local whingeing about them in other streets nearby. So long as they weren't *too* noisy, that is.

Crump's bad mood was getting worse with his swelling headache. Happily, it was Saturday and he was well stocked up with bottles of beer and wine and ready meals to get him through the weekend.

He sat down with a plate of curry and rice, swigged from a cold Italian beer with a sigh, and reached for the remote.

Was it just him or had TV turned to total shite in recent years?

For a start, you couldn't escape Brexit, not even on a Saturday night. Crump flicked around the channels, where a predictable selection of guests snapped and yelled at each other using the same arguments they'd been using since the 2016 referendum. Had anyone changed their mind at all? Not by this evidence, they hadn't.

"*Will, lits* not ac*ci*pt *Brixit – niver yis to Brixit,*" said some screechy female non-entity of a political panel show guest whose vowels branded her as a New Zealander.

"*Will, git* off my *tilivision thin,*" mimicked Crump, switching over.

Brexiteers were called Fascists. Remainers were called traitors. And those who disagreed were called 'the enemy'. It was a ceaseless civil war, and it was getting worse.

Why were people always so damn angry nowadays? Crump thought back twenty, thirty years, to what TV, the media and society were like then. He was sure he remembered watching political TV shows where people could disagree, yes, but not with the vile vitriol of now. Was social media to blame? Or just plain selfishness? People's assured belief that their feelings mattered more than anything in the known universe and so anything they disagreed with, or which 'offended' their precious sensibilities, needed to be shouted down, condemned, banned and the holder of those views abused, shamed, damaged, savaged, sacked and worse. All political sides were as bad as each other, as were both sides of the Brexit debate. And, in the end, no-one won.

He skimmed through the multi-channel dross, all reality TV, dancing shows, being-nice baking shows in our new twee age of safe quaintness, jeopardy-faking drivel for the masses, glorified talent contents, and all presented by identikit autocuties of various genders and skin tones, all with whiter-than-white bleached teeth, all desperate to scrawl a televisual scratch on the surface of the Earth to claim the fame they felt they'd always deserved – *because they're worth it* – until he reached…

Boyo Bellylaughs MBE, who was on a national chat show. Since coming out as a black comedian, he'd really made it, throughout the whole UK, not just Wales as before – though, thankfully, the slick gimmick of self-definition did not require blacking up.

"See, I was thinking of 'avin a sex change, like – but I couldn't pull it off."

Laughs. Gurning, smug, overpaid BBC chat show host smirks right on postmodern irony cue.

"A mate of mine's a Rastafarian, like, and he asked me to do his hair. I's dreading it. Aye-aye!"

Laughs and groans of an audience relieved that the joke wasn't racist.

"A penguin walks into a pub and asks the barman: 'Has you seen my brother?' and the barman asks: 'What does he look like?'"

Wild applause and laughter.

"Welsh joke now, right. Two sheep in a field. First one says 'baa', second one says 'moo'. So the first sheep says to the second, 'What d'you mean "moo"?' And the second one says, 'I's learning a foreign language!' Aye aye!"

Crump turned the idiot box off. He wasn't in the mood for Boyo Bellylaughs.

Nor was he in the mood for dire warnings of 'nudity, sexual scenes, violence and offensive language from the start' before some war film given by some quasi-Victorian-fit-of-the-vapours continuity announcer nanny. Was such a trigger warning necessary at 9pm on a Saturday night? It was as though the entire world was some enormous creche where we were all always infantilised with continual catastrophising by those whose primary concern was avoiding litigation of any kind.

And he was definitely not in the mood to watch adverts by new universities, all glossy PR puff pieces by former polys attempting to market trendy courses to gullible kids who don't know any better, and don't give a thought to how much money and time they might go on to waste by following some mediocre media or business studies or fashion course which would not, in general, lead to the glamourous well-paid careers these institutions were promising potential students. At best, it was deception; at worst, fraud. Either way, it was hard to stomach when you knew the truth.

But then, that's where a massively expanded racket of a consumer-led higher education system gets you when an arbitrary target of '50% of young people must go to university' is set by politicians keen to attract the parental vote: graduates in pointless courses nobody wants to employ, and yet a dire shortage of those in fields the economy is crying out for – medicine, nursing, engineering – or those well-trained in skills – such as plumbers, electricians, carpenters, factory workers, or catering and hotel staff, most of whom seemed foreign these days. There was no good reason for that. It was testament to the incompetence, failed policies and short-sightedness of those in charge who preferred to rely on mass immigration to promote low wages and a benefit culture that suited their electoral needs.

Crump turned on a pop music radio station instead, something that played oldies, songs with real tunes, not the rantingly rappy, crappy, infantile three-note bleep-filled EDM beats of today. After quaffing a few more beers, he opened up his laptop and went online.

First, he checked his emails and found, as per usual, several from various departments and admin at the university who seemed to believe all staff were 'always on' and available to read and answer their tedious insignificant unimportant emails (always marked URGENT) at any time of the day or night and on any day of the year. Crump scanned through them without opening them or reading them – he'd do that on Monday, when he was 'at work', though he may well get told off again for not keeping on top of things over the weekend.

There was also a message from the library. It was a list of banned books, and those on the 'trigger list', which were hidden away like top-shelf dirty magazines from schoolboys, back in the day.

'Better late than never,' Crump thought – it was now a full five months after his request.

Crump downloaded the list, which was twenty-three pages long. He would read it in detail later, when he wasn't so sozzled. But he couldn't resist skimming it.

It was really incredible which books the university had banned completely, or sent to the sin bin in the 'trigger' section which students and staff had to complete an application to access, so dangerous were the tomes within. *The Great Gatsby*, for a start – Crump had done that for A-level English, back before the world went totally woke pc loonytoon mental mad. The list showed it was banned on grounds of racism against African-Americans, sexism and violence against women. Most Joseph Conrad too, *Heart of Darkness* and the always-banned *'N-word' of the Narcissus*. Even Roald Dahl. Graham Greene, as well as the much-maligned, Nobel-prize-winning, scribe of Empire Rudyard Kipling, of course. Classics such as the 'racist' *Robinson Crusoe*, as well as Mark Twain, some Dickens and even a few Shakespeare plays, such as *Othello*. Was there even a single Shakespeare play which would *not* be called sexist or violent in modern terms? But, to be fair to the bard, he plagiarised all his stories.

Almost all banned or 'trigger-literature-warning' books were by white men, Crump noticed. Someone somewhere had decided they could somehow be harmful – on grounds of racism, sexism, transphobia, misogyny, violence, anything at all – if read by 'vulnerable' people, which 'they' tended to define as just about anyone who wasn't a white man over the age of twenty-five. The justification for banning such books was all based on some theoretical oppression-matrix cobbled together in some sociology department back in the 1960s which had somehow become the accepted and orthodox new normal of now.

But who were *'they'*? Were they elected? Accountable to anyone? Or were they just, as Crump decided, some self-appointed, anonymous, paternalistic/maternalistic, righteous woke moral guardian elite who saw themselves as superior to everybody else and whose rightful duty it was to protect lesser mortals from themselves? The high priests of the Church of 'Political Correctness' maybe, where diversity was worshipped with a devotion that would be envied by devout zealots of even the most fanatical faith?

Then Crump made a mistake. He didn't usually go on social media – it all was a seething sewer where much unpleasantness happened, much abuse was hurled, and nothing whatsoever achieved by joining the digital cesspit. He knew it was a stalking ground for the sanctimonious, the smug and the self-righteous, who loved leaping to conclusions and seeking offence, usually on behalf of others they neither knew nor resembled, whether they were defending men, women, transgender people, Muslims, Christians, goths, blacks, whites, browns, all POC (people of colour), or any special interest group or identify they could think of.

But he just couldn't resist a look…

And, as he got drunker and drunker, the arguments on Twitter and Facebook became more intense and abusive – with mad man-hating feminists, and racist abusive Welsh and Scottish nationalists – until, eventually, he snapped. Someone mentioned Johnny Blue – said he was an idiot and deserved to be dead.

Welcome to the wonderful world of internet connectivity, run by firms who care so much about those they enslave that they do their very best to avoid paying any tax in the UK at all – a disgrace all facilitated by the EU and its legal, tax-dodgers' heaven of a haven called Luxembourg, where Corporation Tax is only paid on profits made from sales in that tiny enclave of a 'Grand Duchy' where literally millions of companies are registered in a handful of offices.

The next morning, Crump woke up lying the wrong way on his bed, and still in his clothes. His head felt as if it had been through a mangle and his mouth was parched and tasted of sick, stale beer and curry.

Still, it wasn't the first hangover he'd endured in life, so knew it would ease eventually, especially after a Full Monty fry-up. But he had no eggs, no bread and no bacon in the house, and no milk either, so there was only one thing for it – a traipse to the shops to get the required emergency supplies. He certainly wasn't going to drive feeling as wobbly and dizzy as he did, so, after a few spoonfuls of reinvigorating cold curry and rice, he put on his mac and started out on his heroic walk, despite the drizzle.

As he approached the parade of shops, he noticed a young woman sitting in the passenger seat of a parked car. She seemed to stare and smile at him as he walked in her direction on the damp pavement. Did he know her? Maybe a student? It was hard to tell, especially as his eyes were as blurry as his brain that Sunday morning, even with his glasses on.

And so, as he got to the car he peered inside, just as a man was getting in the driver's seat. As Crump leant forward for a closer look, an angry male face glared up at him from inside the car.

Crump realised he didn't know either person in the car. Were they boyfriend and girlfriend, father and daughter? Crump didn't care. But as he walked past the back of the car to cross the road, it started to reverse – and just missed his legs. Crump looked back when he was on the opposite side of the road by the newsagents.

The man opened the car door and shouted: "FUCKIN PERV!" at him.

Crump went into the shop and waited by the newspapers, facing the door, just in case the nutjob man came in wanting to attack him or take him on. He had no idea what he'd do if the man had a knife or another weapon – something getting more and more common throughout the UK.

'What the *fuck* was all that about?' thought Crump, walking back up the hill with his shopping.

Jealous boyfriend? Overprotective dad? But the girl looked at least late teenage. And did she deliberately look at Crump and smile for a reaction? What they used to call a 'prick-teaser' at school? One thing was certain – whenever men fought each other, there was more often than not women or money involved.

Crump had been attending mindfulness sessions with Mary Christmas and Amber Green, which, to his surprise, did alleviate his anxiety a bit. His flashbacks and nightmares were certainly reducing in frequency, though whether that was due to the mindfulness or the passage of time, he wasn't sure. But he couldn't help but get angry at the hysteria in society about 'strange men' – of which, he had just been a hapless, innocent victim.

He was certain most other countries (except, perhaps, those of north America) were not so hysterical, didn't molly-coddle children and young people like caged toddlers, didn't assume any man walking down a street was a pervert. He was, he realised, liking his country less and less these days. How did it all get like this? How did parents get so paranoid? How did everyone get so angry and easily offended? Where had it all gone so wrong?

Back home, and well fed after a massive English breakfast fry-up, Crump opened his laptop and went online.

When he looked at Twitter, he could hardly believe what he saw: 87,000 impressions. He usually averaged 3–500 a day.

He scrolled through the tweets and abuse – from all the #cybernats and other nationalists; from the feminist man-haters; from those who had gleefully gloated at the death of Johnny Blue and maliciously mocked his suicide and any opinion he had ever held. He had, in short, been the victim of a toxic Twitter storm, that had spread like a bacterial infection in his digital body, even as he was sleeping it off. And it was just as bad on Facebook. He was called 'gammon', a 'boomer' and, worst of all, a 'Daily Mail reader'.

Crump felt sick. He immediately changed all settings to make his social media accounts private and locked. But the damage was done. Some of the viler and nastier trolls had copied in other trolls as well as his uni – Crump, perhaps rather stupidly, had stated on his Twitter tag that he was a lecturer at Cambrian University.

Just imagine a world where social media did not exist. For a start, plenty of celebrities and media types would still have their jobs, because, in our po-faced, censorious, 'cancel culture', New Puritan Age, anyone who dares to make a joke others deem 'offensive' or 'inappropriate', or states an opinion not seen as being within acceptable 'politically correct' parameters, can see a career crash in an instant.

These people, and Crump himself, were victims of that awful herd instinct group-think encouraged by social media, that vile hive-mind which feeds off itself like a swirling swarm of stinging hornets, or a growing shoal of cannibalistic cyber-sharks, soon moving on, together as one entity, one organism, to attack their next called-out victim. The hectoring press and media, all amoral in abundance, then run with the bile-dripping baton, happy to crash careers and smash lives to pieces under an avalanche of public scorn and abuse. Add to that the rampant hypersensitivity in modern Britain, where pretty much anything online can be, and is, called out by the self-appointed moral guardians for being racist, sexist, or generally unacceptable, and you have the sort of perfect storm that will kill, destroy and flatten all resistance in its path. And there was nothing whatsoever moral about that.

Moreover, a sort of 'competitive intolerance' cry-bullying had developed, perhaps encouraged by the pandering of the 'politically correct' to Islam. So now those of all religions and other identity groups, such as those for gender and sexuality, and, in fact, all special interest groups, like vegans, goths, and possibly even Liberal Democrats, demanded immunity from criticism which, if it was ever made, was immediately labelled 'hate crime' by a 'speech-criminal' and complained about to social media companies, authorities and even the police, when in fact it was just stating an opinion and valid criticism. Universities were keen to kowtow to every diverse identity in their student body, and thus was intellectual debate utterly extinguished via no-platforming and censorship any dictator of old would have been proud of.

The larger the crowd, the lower the individual intelligence of every member of that crowd. That was a maxim proven beyond doubt by the mob mentality of social media. And it was making society more hateful, abusive and divisive, as every digital day clicked and flickered by.

Crump dozed through that Sunday afternoon, sipping sweet milky tea and half-watching old episodes of *Poirot* on ITV3.

Then, at around 4pm, there was a knock on the door. It was the police. PC Christopher Cockwomble again, and a very young and dim-looking lad in uniform who was introduced as PC Pood.

"You called her an 'utter cunt'," said PC Cockwomble, reading from his notepad. "Now, why would you say that?"

"Yeah, that's like the worst word ever, like," added the intellectual giant, highly educated linguist, gormless teenage trainee plod standing beside the old-timer.

"Would you say that to somebody sitting next to you on the bus?"

"Errr… I don't take the bus… and I… wasn't on one," said Crump, his hangover throbbing painfully through his aching brain.

He was sitting in his kitchen with the two members of the pc gestapo looming over him. He'd let them in when they'd asked, scared that if he hadn't, they might have arrested him on the spot.

Now, at this point, Crump could have educated the linguistically ignorant plods before him on the etymology of the word 'cunt' – on how it was an ancient word in English, used by the 14th-century author Chaucer no less, and indeed Shakespeare on many occasions, most notably in a whole scene of *Henry V* when the teenage princess is having a French lesson and plays on the c-word with reference to the similar-sounding word 'count', both for numbers and for a member of the nobility.

He could have explained that 'cunt' was a really wonderful word, which came from the 13th-century Germanic and was related to older Middle German and Norse. It was a rare swearword in these sweary days in that still had the power to shock. Every other one had lost that, especially the trite, omnipresent, international parvenu word 'fuck', a 17th-century addition to English, so not Anglo-Saxon at all – it apparently came from the name of a Dutch family when Britain was at war with that wealthy trading nation. It was, quite possibly, the best-known word in English throughout the world.

But really, what was the point? The two coppers in his kitchen would probably just arrest him for some nonsense, waste his time for hours, maybe lock him up for the night, then release him without charge and all just because he'd shown, as if it needed to be shown, how uneducated in the English language police officers were.

"But... I didn't know..." Crump added, "that... it was... Abi Rainbow... I didn't see her name or photo on her Twitter account—"

"It's not down to her to protect herself from you harassing her," said the baby-faced thicko plod-kid, "causing her alarm and distress."

"But there were... loads of people... trolling me, posting abuse, saying such bad things about... y'know... Johnny... Blue... who—"

"Yes, we know," said PC Cockwomble, blankly, "but everyone has the right to express an opinion."

"Oh, except me?"

The two police officers glared at him.

"You harassed an innocent woman – she didn't harass anyone. And you never used her chosen gender pronoun. That's a hate crime, that is. I been on a course."

'What bollocks!' thought Crump. 'She's been harassing me for months, other men for years probably, and her false accusations have destroyed lives.'

"I just reacted... I didn't do anything wrong!" snapped Crump.

"It's for us to decide that, Mr Crump," said PC Cockwomble, with a hard ploddy stare. "Section 127 of the Communicativity Act 2003 made 'grossly offensive' online speech a crime. I could arrest you now. But instead, I'm issuing a PIN—"

"A what?"

"Police Information Notice. You need to sign it and return it to me at the station."

Crump let them out. He felt like disinfecting the house – he was sick of the pigs piling in, for the most trivial of reasons. Yet again, the mad man-hater Abi Rainbow was trying to hurt him and spoil his life, as she'd done for so many others. What on earth was wrong with her?

Apparently, a full 40% of police time was now spent monitoring online and social media messages, which meant a great deal of taxpayers' money went on it too, and for what? Meanwhile, muggers and thieves, gang-members wielding knives and guns, and common or garden terrorist obsessives, skipped happily down the lanes of this lax and liberal land utterly unhindered by the forces of law and order, who were too busy responding to silly complaints made to them by even sillier women playing the victim about how they were 'upset', 'alarmed' and 'distressed' by what other people said to them on social media. All even more ironic when you realise research has shown it is men who get trolled and abused online far more than women, but just seem able to deal with it better, without wasting police time.

Anyone trolled should do what Crump had done, namely setting all his social media accounts to locked and private. He wished he'd done that earlier too and, were it not for one or two contacts overseas he knew via Facebook and Twitter, he'd leave them both in an instant, and good riddance. He no longer saw anything healthy or useful in them or any other exploitative social media company who, despite claims of bringing the world together, seemed to have the opposite effect, causing and exacerbating division. And instead of being free, they actually cost many people dear, because every single piece of information anyone put on social media was data-mined by those companies and sold on: you are the product, whether you know it or not.

Crump decided to go back online after the police had left and was so glad he did, because his old friend and colleague Raj, who now lived in India, had got back to him at long last after his message the week before. They were soon on a video call on *WhatsApp*:

"Long time no hearing, you scoundrel," said Raj, smiling as always.

"It is, Raj – you're looking well," said Crump, knowing that he himself didn't.

"This is because I am living in Jaipur in great Indian state of Rajasthan and working in bloody good job in IT with decent salary and quite wonderful future prospects, not living on cold, rainy island called UK in terrible university job… like you, right?"

"Well, *'the beggars cannot be the choosers'*, as you used to say."

"It's all a business and all a game, isn't it?"

"It is," sighed Crump, "and how is your wife, and family, Raj?"

"Quite wonderful," smiled Raj, "I am liking the family life exceedingly."

He held a photo of his wife and two young children to the webcam.

"They all look very beautiful," said Crump and meaning it, though feeling suddenly cold and alone.

"Actually, old friend," said Raj, "you are looking quite ill—"

"Thanks," said Crump, with a weak smile, wishing they'd *Skyped* instead and not used video call. "Well, y'know… heavy Saturday night… I'll be better by tomorrow."

"Do you remember Athena?" asked Raj.

"Of course," said Crump, the bitter-sweet memories aching his brain – they hadn't been in touch for ages, though sent occasional emails, postcards, Christmas cards etc.

"She now is teaching in university in Athens – and also she is helping the refugees, which is jolly good show."

"Yes, she was always… helpful," said Crump. "They've had some economic problems in Greece, but—"

"The life it is going on, isn't it?"

"It is. Listen, Raji…"

"Yes, Crumpie?"

"I was wondering, could you do me a teeny-weeny favour?"

*

And so, March marched past, the days falling by like rain on the hustling, bustling campus of Cambrian University.

But the world was in bloom. In the flowerbeds of the campus, daffodils and other pretty spring flowers

337

bloomed – though no white ones, as they had been banned for being potentially racist and risking causing offence, especially to certain lucrative international students.

And everywhere the blue EU banners fluttered, often damp and soggy in the spring showers. Occasional media people lingered, in case of any breaking news about Cambrian University's declaration of loyalty to the EU, but most had retreated, if not to their native lands, then at least to their expenses-paid hotel rooms and well-stocked minibars.

Crump signed the PIN the police had given him and posted him off, after phoning his solicitor to ask what the hell it was and if it was safe to sign. According to Tony Bones, it was pretty meaningless, all a pointless box-ticking exercise like most police work these days, because the record of the officers visiting his house, and why, was on the system anyway. But it was still injustice. Crump had done absolutely nothing wrong in responding to the vile abuse aimed at both him and the late Johnny Blue.

According to Tony Bones, it would not have been in the interests of justice to arrest or charge Crump with anything for tweeting what he had, and any magistrate would have slammed down the time-wasting pc police for bringing such a case.

And so, the term trundled on, plodding towards the Easter vacation, before which students would be set various assignments, and during which some teachers could earn extra cash from revision classes.

A meeting was scheduled in the English Studies department. Crump sat in the crowded team room with both teachers he knew and ones he had never even seen before, awaiting the pink presence of Tanya Snuggs. The water pipes within the walls were clanking away for some reason, and one of the lights in the team room flickered on and off – but these things were so common now on campus that Crump barely noticed them, rather like people living under an airport flight path or by a railway track stop hearing the roar of planes and trains.

He picked up a copy of the ever-tedious, trivia-riddled local paper the *Cambrian Daily News* that was lying on a table. The front page was preoccupied with parents' 'fury' at 'disgusting obscene graffiti' at a local children's playground, which Crump knew almost certainly had been done by kids themselves. The page was shared by a preview of a feature inside featuring local character Paddy Muldoon, whose dog – star of dogfood ads and extra in local TV series and Bollywood films – had just died. Crump turned the page to skim the stories inside the rag – yet more 'fury' at noisy disruptive students, potholes, rubbish collections, endless roadworks, parking problems. Some 'joy' by those who had won prizes locally, one a Welsh author who'd got an award for her book of suicidal poems; another, a student who'd not had a day off college. The usual crimes and court cases; the ever-more-common puff pieces and feminine features on fashion etc. And of course, the ongoing campaign by the veteran Highlands author – famous for his hit 1995 play *Bampi! He Done It Again, Mam!* which sold out the Memorial Theatre for three weeks straight – for more public toilets. There was nothing whatsoever about the pile-up any more – people obviously didn't want sad, negative news stories – or anything about the university and what was widely rumoured to be upcoming redundancies.

"Hiya!" announced the ever-ebullient pompom of pink Tanya Snuggs as she bounced into the team room. "Sorry for being so *illusive*, people – nothing's really been the same since the 2016 European *reformation*, has it?"

'No,' thought Crump, 'no, it hasn't."

Joint Head of Department, the ever-elusive Karen Crisp, was apparently still on study leave. Maybe she was studying 'perceptions of absence'?

339

"Man dem well vexed, d'ya get me, bruv?" said Shabs, shaking his dreadlocks.

"Maybe people should worry more about the possible redundancy crisis," said Crump, only to get hard stares from Hilary Squonk and Melanie Spunch, even though it was an open secret that job losses were on the way.

"Crisis? What crisis?" said Tanya Snuggs, happily, through the gap in her front teeth. "I have no idea what you're *eluding* to, Kevin."

Then she frowned and listened.

"What's all that banging?" she said.

"Pipes," someone said.

"Maybe a ghost?" smiled Crump – yes, a ghost of the dead, long-forgotten dreams of what your life could actually be...

"Maybe we need to *exercise* it then?" said Tanya Snuggs.

'Would *pilates* do it?' thought Crump, but said nothing.

"Now, I know you all have a passion for learning and do your *upmost* best every single day to inspire our students..."

'A passion for learning? Well, it all depends what *"learnification"* you're talking about...'

Crump had a passion for Fatima, for sure. But whether he had a passion for learning was debatable. He had perhaps learnt too much in his life, seen too much, like the *Ancient Mariner* with a dead albatross at his feet, doomed to wander alone through a cold and uncaring world. Or perhaps he was just hungry...

"*A point in case* is that we all have to make *110% sure* that our teaching *passes mustard* – we have to be *mellifluous* about attention to detail, really *hone* in on it, to make sure we get everything *200%* correct, or else after the Easter break, we may well find ourselves *playing ketchup* to *pass mustard*... Are you alright, Kevin?"

"Yes, fine," groaned Crump, wearily lifting his head from where it had buried itself in his hands after hearing the English language disembowelled inside his ears.

"You used to be so... *lucky go happy*..."

"Just tired," he sighed, rubbing his eyes and thinking of the time he mentioned a production of *Don Quixote* he had once seen, which Tanya Snuggs had thought was called '*Donkey Oaty*', and then proceeded to ask if it was anything to do with *Donkey* in *Shrek*, coz she thought that was, like, '*SO funny*' that she'd watched it over a dozen times on video – or nine, to be precise, she said...

"But I would be interested in extra revision classes over Easter, if they're in the offing."

They were, and Crump signed up. He could do with the extra cash, for one thing.

Then Tanya told Crump that Melissa Jenks wanted to see him – now. It came as no surprise.

"We take our reputation very seriously at this university," said Melissa Jenks, as she sat squeezed into in her swivel chair.

"As do I," parroted Crump, "but I was the one who was attacked online – I was trolled and I just responded."

"After the... issues... you had before with Abi Rainbow... you then have to call her... those abusive things on Twitter. Why, Kevin? Why?"

"First, I didn't know it was her, and second, did you see what she said about Johnny Blue?"

Melissa Jenks nodded sadly. Crump got the distinct feeling that she disliked Mx Rainbow as much as he did.

Maybe Melissa wasn't the termagant she had, at first, appeared to be.

"He was a good friend," said Crump, "worth a thousand of *that*... of... *certain* people."

Silence.

"I've made my Twitter and Facebook private now, so it won't happen again. I'm actually thinking of closing all my social media accounts... I just can't be bothered with it any more."

"I sympathise with your... predicament... and I do not want to justify any online 'judgement culture'..."

Crump knew this was a phrase used by 'fat activists' like Melissa to condemn anyone who condemned or judged obese people with 'fat shaming' and the like, via a *normalised thin aesthetic and the promotion of fear, shame and anxiety, making fat people objects of disgust, less human and equal than those our culture decides are thin and beautiful* – or so it said on the framed statement on the Head of School's office wall.

"... but, as I said, we take damage to our reputation very seriously at this university, so I am duty-bound to issue a written warning. Online abuse or 'trolling' is a serious matter and will not be tolerated. Do I make myself clear?"

"Yes," sighed Crump, knowing this would all get back to Sir Clive Silverback at the Foreign Office too now. It was déjà-vu all over again...

"By the way, how are the mindfulness sessions with Mary Christmas and Amber Green going, Kevin?" asked Melissa Jenks, gently.

"Oh, they're very... mindful," said Crump.

"Good. Be mindful..."

Crump walked to the park to clear his head.

He sat on a bench and practised the mindfulness techniques he'd learnt – the focusing on his breathing, and nothing else, for five minutes. Hard at first, but he'd learnt how to get there eventually. It wasn't so different from what his mum always used to tell him before any stressful event or day at school – to take three deep breaths. *'Life's all in the breathing really'*. Crump smiled to himself at the memory.

Sandra the pig was still there in her compound when Crump wandered by, staring up at him with that round brown face of such unutterable smugness. She was just like one of those people you meet sometimes who you instinctively dislike. There was no logical reason – it was just some aura, some feeling, some sort of scentless smell about them that made you detest their presence. Of course, Crump had good reason to have a problem with the porker – she had bitten his hand and drawn blood. But why did *she* dislike *him* so much? He had no idea, but made a mental note to buy some bacon at the supermarket on the way home to have for his tea – or maybe breakfast tomorrow.

Then, the strangest thing – a big black dog ran right past him.

Diversity Dog!

Crump hadn't seen him for ages!

But this dog was not chasing anything. It was, in fact, being chased – by Nelson the cat. A world turned upside down, indeed…

The animals ran off towards the university campus. A poochy-moggy game? Or a fight to the death? Who knew? But it seemed to go against the laws of nature and what was expected.

But then, when you thought about it, so much else did too – but that did not make it separate to nature, or unnatural. Quite the reverse, it made it a significant part of nature, an exception not to be ignored.

And things were as they were in higher education because people had decided that things would be like that, people who had lived many centuries ago. Universities had, after all, been created in the Middle Ages to train the aristocracy and the priesthood. They were now arguably contemporary monasteries, which cost British taxpayers £20 billion a year, just so half the nation's youngsters – and usually the richer half – could please their proud parents by spending three years out of the labour force, not generally being trained in the skills our nation desperately needs, but pondering perhaps why they're getting into forty grand of student debt doing a grade-inflated course at a university, maybe one of questionable reputation, via a three-year structure of lectures, essays and exams barely changed in a century.

The question was always: *'What are universities for?'* Crump certainly couldn't answer that one any more. Were they a scholarly retreat for modern monks? A national investment for the sake of our future economic success? Or maybe just a finishing school for the rich and middle class and those who aspired to be classed in that bracket?

Was the modern education system simply a skeuomorph of what came before, in the days when educational institutions existed, at least in large part, as an intellectual, noble, improving endeavour, a quest for knowledge enabled and facilitated by freedom of thought and speech, achieved despite the opposition of the Church or the State or the Academy itself? Was it now just a cheap Made-in-China counterfeit copy of all that? Maybe that was just a metaphor for the modern age – so at least it was 'relevant', something which would no doubt get it full marks in a teaching observation assessment these days.

Crump's old soak of a colleague Dr Sandy Buttery at London's Thames Met always used to say *'it's all a business and all a game'*, and maybe he was right – though maybe the same could be said of life itself.

It was perhaps all a bit like national spending on defence. You suspected half was wasted. But you could never tell which half.

And so, the mindfulness was over. Crump was thinking again – thinking his own thoughts too, thinking for himself. It was a good job he was down the park and not on campus, or some sort of alarm may well have gone off.

"Fancy seeing you 'ere," came a voice. "You cottaging or what?"

It was Andy Stone, in his wheelchair, being pushed along by his Zimbabwean carer.

"Oh just... taking a break... after meetings, y'know," said Crump, nodding a 'hello' to Casper.

"Thass what they all say!"

Crump had always liked Andy and Casper – there was a warmth between them that was often lacking in couples, especially the married variety.

"Seein' as we're here, like," continued Andy, looking Casper in the eye as he held his hand, "You can be the first to know. We're engaged."

Andy held out his hand with a silvery ring on the fourth finger and Casper did the same.

"Oh, wow – congratulations!" said Crump, shaking the men's hands, and leaning forward to kiss Andy when he gestured, then the same on Casper's cheek.

"Good job I didn't lose me arms in Afghanistan, eh," laughed Andy Stone, "or I'd be fucked tryin' to wear it!"

"Not engaged to be married, however," said Casper.

Crump frowned in confusion.

"Nah, see, Casper here's been married before —"

"In my culture – my tribe – I was very young – in my family, they —"

"They always marry off a young 'un after they've boiled a missionary in the pot," laughed Andy.

"No," said Casper, smiling and shaking his head vigorously, "in Africa we prefer them fried, with lots of oil and special cannibal spices!"

"So anyway, it's just a 'blessing', sometime in the summer, on the pier. Proper priest an' everyfink. Wanna come?" asked Andy as Casper nodded approval.

"I wouldn't miss it for the world," said Crump, delighted at the invite. "Fancy a celebratory drink... down the pub?"

"Course," nodded Andy Stone. "You're paying, ta."

"Praise the Lord," said Casper, with a wink.

April 1st, the international, inclusive and diverse day of fools, arrived with the bright spring sunshine, leaving the shivery showers of March behind.

The blue EU flags and banners fluttered in the stubborn British breeze, together with banners stating **BOLLOCKS TO BREXIT** as well as more racially aware ones with slogans such as: **STAY WOKE, #BLACKLIVESMATTER, END WHITE MALE PRIVILEGE** and **REPARATIONS NOW!**

The campus was in the middle of its earnest and worthy commemoration of 'Slavery Awareness Week', raising awareness for the plight of slaves of the present and the past, all of whom seemed to be black in posters and displays. Crump pondered the fact that every human civilisation had practised slavery since time immemorial, and, indeed, the Barbary pirates of north Africa had stolen an estimated one million white slaves from the European and, especially, British Isles coastline until the late 18th century. Historically, slavery was colourblind.

But anyway, everyone's awareness had been raised to such an extent that it was probably the stiffest, most erect, most vertical and proud raised awareness than ever there had been on that campus or any other. *If they weren't careful, they'd have someone's eye out…*

Students and staff – though only those identifying as 'white' or 'Caucasian' – had been encouraged to wear chains when attending university that week. Not real clinking clanging 'Marley's Ghost' chains, of course – though some people did walk around campus with real lightweight metal chains round their necks – but symbolic ones, like monochrome Christmas paper chains coloured white, grey and black.

Crump was having none of it. He'd never owned a slave, traded slaves, or even profited from slavery via his family – unlike, he knew, a lot of the rich African and Arab students and staff at the university, who, not being of white European stock, were not expected to wear chains because the present 'fake news' history taught, learned and accepted by all was that only white Europeans had ever enslaved anyone.

Still, at least the university was making the effort to emphasise the scourge of modern-day slavery – often, Crump noted, perpetrated by East European gangmasters or Irish travellers, though out of respect for our diverse communities, that was never mentioned.

Several plays, new and old, were being staged at the theatre to mark 'Slavery Awareness Week'. A new production of *'Young Winston'*, bizarrely starring a black actor as Churchill, all in the name of 'colourblind casting'. In other 'repurposed' theatrical productions, the casting was always deeply and accurately diverse though. Following the 'Stay in Your Lane' campaign, only disabled actors now played disabled roles, gay actors, gay roles, and so on. It was a lovely theory, albeit slightly spoiled when an actress with cancer playing a woman dying of cancer died halfway through a play's run.

Crump couldn't help thinking that maybe actors could try actually *acting* maybe? As in, pretending to be someone they're not? But that was obviously just ridiculous – not to mention racist, sexist, homophobic, disablist etcetera etcetera etcetera…

It was also now usual for trigger warnings to be given at theatre productions regarding content audiences may find 'upsetting'. So, warnings about 'racial slurs and reference to drugs' or 'some violence and sexual references which some may find offensive', were standard. But these days, the advisory warnings were spoilers too, such as: 'In the first half of the play, a man beats up a migrant worker' and 'In the second half, a man repeatedly places a hand on a woman's knee, causing her discomfort.' Never before had Crump been so pleased *not* to be a man of the theatre or a particular fan of the stage, no matter how 'woke' and 'diverse', 'relevant' and 'immersive' it was. The phrase 'ladies and gentlemen' had gone too as it excluded those who don't identify as either.

He was more a TV drama man, but increasingly less so these pc days. Most BBC drama seemed just a box-ticking exercise in social engineering, diversity and inclusion, with the main aim being attempted indoctrination, and not just telling a good story. The clunky way these proselytising dramas crowbarred social issues into drama, as well as now orthodox pc opinions, and were fast and loose with their rewriting of history too, was laughable. Worrying, when kids watching would think them all a true reflection of historical fact.

Crump used to love *Dr Who* as a boy – not any more, not with all that preachy, 'wokie' nonsense occurring. US drama seemed so infinitely better, and the box set stuff didn't seem to follow the same 'diversity-worship' quota plan as the *BB-She* which now had a target of 50% main characters in TV drama being female and 20% BAME. Crump wondered how they'd make any war dramas ever again really. It was all too silly for words, but very easy to turn off the pc polemical diversity dross, which he and millions of others did. So much TV was seemingly just emo-porn to get the older female viewer ratings anyway. The 'Beeb' seemed, in a way, to be committing a sort of slow, 'woke', *hara-kiri*. Probably be gone within a decade. BBC RIP.

"A whole bunch of people here today, kindathing," said Dylan, sitting down besides Crump in the April sunshine and slurping on his multicoloured milkshake like a toddler.

"Dylan, bananas and grapes come in bunches. People come in crowds, or groups—"

"OK, boomer! Whatever. Not too shabby anyway."

"I suppose you heard about my social media storm, on Twitter and Facebook?"

"Facebook's for old people, s'all just majorly FOMO—"

"Fear of Missing Out, you mean?" said Crump.

Dylan smiled and lifted his sunglasses.

"Not bad, Grandad. You learnin'…"

Crump was thinking of some witty, cutting remark to hurl back, when Dylan suddenly sat up.

"Oh, d'you hear 'bout Donald?"

"Fake Scot Donald?"

"Yeah, well, I heard a rumour kindathing but… now it's confirmed. He was adopted at birth. His real name's Marmaduke—"

"*No!*"

"And his real dad's… *English*—"

"*Seriously?*" smiled Crump, thinking of the abuse he'd received from that mad Scots nationalist.

"And more than that, right, coz his real dad's Sir Tarquin Salt, Tory MP, and descendent of none other than King Edward the First—"

"The 'Hammer of the Scots' who defeated William Wallace? Bloody hell!"

"Whatever… So anyway, Donald's now '*missing, presumed fed*' like my auntie's cat."

Crump laughed loudly – an unusual occurrence at any of Dylan's so-called jokes. It was indeed hard to imagine Donald doing without several haggis-based meals a day.

"Well, I hope he's OK," said Crump, half-heartedly.

Just then, the tartan-clad, kilt-wearing, bagpipe-bearing figure of Donald – AKA Marmaduke Salt, Englishman – stumbled past them, wild-eyed and mumbling to himself, something that sounded like:

"It cannae be true, och, *laddie, it cannae be!*"

He wandered off babbling into the bushes behind The Learning Tower and disappeared – again.

Suddenly, a trumpet sounded. Crump and Dylan were sitting on a bench some way off, with a panoramic view of the podium where the 'restitution' ceremony was to take place.

For it had been decided that all relics and artefacts owned by Cambrian University were to be returned to the peoples they were bought or looted or half-inched from by the English (AKA the British) back in the day. First up, was a tribe from a South Sea Island in Polynesia, somewhere off the coast of New Zealand.

Suddenly, a group of a dozen or so semi-naked men in grass skirts and with bones through their noses and ears appeared and started their 'Haka' dance, much in the manner of the All Blacks rugby team. The Haka was a fierce display of a tribe's unity, strength and pride, a loud call-and-response chant accompanied by violent moves, foot-stamping, body slapping and tongue protrusions.

Facing the tribesmen on the podium were the university's senior management – the Vice-Chancellor Angharad Ap Merrick, Mike Mumpsimus and Parminder Zugzwang – but also three representatives of the Sir Arthur Evans Department of Archaeology and Anthropology – Professor Mary Hare, Dr Elgin Tooky and Dr Byron Spolasco, who, it had to be said, looked rather scared of the South Sea warriors noisily gurning gruesome faces at them. What made it worse, perhaps, was that – whether willingly or not – the management team all wore metal chains around their necks as a mark of respect for 'Slavery Awareness Week'.

The international media there were loving it, with TV crews from a great many countries and, as per usual, the omnipresent Jason Hussein, BBC presenter of, well, everything. Of course, this sort of ceremony never happened in nations and places who were slaving centuries before the Brits: Spain, Portugal, the Arab world or the Far East – or, indeed, Africa itself.

"Did the British Empire ever trade any slaves in Polynesia?" wondered Crump out loud.

Dylan shrugged.

"They know how to drink majorly though. Bought me an alcopop, kindathing. Saw 'em all down town last night on the piss."

"What, in their grass skirts and bones through their noses?"

"Nah, they told me they just wear that for the tourists, like. All in jeans and T-shirts usually. Talk like Aussies too. Only use native lingo, like, for their chanting ceremonies."

'Like most people in Wales only speaking Welsh to sing the national anthem then,' thought Crump.

"They was all moanin' about the food with their host families – what they all really wanted to eat was wild pig, kindathing…"

"Hard to come by in South Wales, wild pigs."

"Most def."

The Vice-Chancellor stepped forward as the Haka growled into an angry, tongue-poking silent tableau finale.

"Yes, no, indeed, absolutely," said the bearded Angharad Ap Merrick in his/her deeply masculine voice. "We here today are ashamed of the English empire…"

"British," tutted Crump under his breath, as he noticed the usual Welsh nationalists grinning in glee at that.

"… who raped and pillaged and stole your culture, your history, your artefacts and even, disgracefully, your shrunken heads… well, not *your* shrunken heads, obviously… because your heads are healthy and… exotic… native heads… and very beautifully… diverse… heads far… more so than the ugly white English colonial heads of those who enslaved you —"

The Welsh nationalists erupted into applause again.

"… but the shrunken heads of your ancestors, or… of the people they killed with the clubs, spears, weapons

351

of various woods, which we also stole... and their holy bones, which we had no right to take, no, yes, indeed, absolutely—"

Ripples of applause. No Jazz Hands today...

Then the three Student Union representatives, Olivia Octothorp, Aled Rantallion and Shelley Shunk, crawled forward onto the stage on their knees, dressed in rags and loin cloths (borrowed from the theatre prop department) and wearing real rattling and clanking chains, all whilst whipping themselves on their bare backs with what looked like replica *cat o' nine tails* whips.

"So please forgive us, like, yeah..." they wailed in disunion as they beat themselves like mediaeval monks. Real tears rolled down their snowflaky-white privileged 21st century Western cheeks too, as they begged: "Forgive us the sin of slavery! Coz, it was, like, really bad and stuff, yeah?"

Crump winced at the infernal 'Upspeak', all learned from Antipodean daytime TV soap operas.

He could see some of the South Sea Islanders smirking – as if they realised how absurd this all was. Their ancestors had never been taken as slaves. In fact, they'd enslaved – as well as butchered and head-shrunk – a fair number of men, women and children from enemy tribes for centuries. It said in their oral histories that their 18th and 19th century ancestors had been delighted to flog their old artefacts and shrunken heads to the 'idiot long pig white men' in return for guns, technology and modernity, instead of the mumbo-jumbo of the 'old ways'.

They also looked rather hungover – as if they could all use a beer, and quick. Despite it being only midday, Crump felt the same. Maybe his inner slave needed the aid of alcohol to overcome the memory trauma; or perhaps his inner slave-trader needed it to overcome his guilt. Either was fine, so long as the beer appeared...

Then, after the self-flagellation of the Gen Z Student Union wokeling snowflakes, the academics from the Sir Arthur Evans Archaeology Department stepped forward and, with a low grovelling bow of apology, handed over several wooden and cardboard boxes to the South Sea Islanders, as well as some larger, longer items wrapped in sacking.

Slowly, the natives opened the boxes and bags, and took out various wooden clubs, shields, axes, spears and other Polynesian weapons which Crump knew from TV antique shows could be worth an absolute packet. They lifted out some old bones in plastic bags, and held tiny shrunken heads up too. Looking skywards, the South Sea warriors then chanted something that sounded like prayers or incantations, but for all Crump or anyone else there knew could have been a menu from their local wild pig restaurant.

And then it was over, and everyone applauded, and the TV people interviewed the South Sea tribesmen – who, as Dylan rightly said, had thick Antipodean accents, rather like Crocodile Dundee. Keen to leave for a beer, no doubt, the natives then vamooshed. So the media's attention turned to the university management and Student Union reps, who clearly adored the celebrity of being interviewed.

Crump saw one foreign news team clock him and start walking in his direction, but he made his escape before they reached him, heading off with Dylan in the vague direction of a local pub. He had enough problems, without suffering an unwanted fifteen minutes of fame on TV.

*

That evening, Crump sat at his laptop at home talking via a private online connection to Raj in India.

"But this is… *incredible*," he said.

"Well, I am believing it," said Raj, "and not too bloody surprising either, isn't it?"

"I mean… they're all at it!"

"Indeed – and jolly good we can be exposing this."

"But… how can we do that? I mean, will you, Raj?"

"Not bloody likely – I have family, wife, children. No, you are needing to save all informations on memory key, then send them from anonymous computer to all contacts at university, all media, newspapers, some such sort of thing…"

Crump remembered that he still had Johnny Blue's university log-in details.

"Will that be a hundred per cent anonymous?" he asked.

"Nothing is hundred per cent, Kevin, except death. But the beggars cannot be the choosers."

"True," said Crump. "I… I think I can do it – I have someone else's email address to use."

"I am sure this will all be quite wonderful, and jolly good show indeed when bloody fireworks are going off."

Crump uploaded all the files to a memory key, put it in his jacket pocket, then poured himself a much-needed glass of wine and went out into the dark of the back yard.

It was a warm night, for early April in South Wales at least, and the weather melded with the alcohol in his blood to leave him perfectly at peace.

The all-seeing eye of the lighthouse by the pier winked at him from its lonely rock in the distance, and he knew what he had to do.

He sniffed the evening air. The smell of smoke. Roasting meat. Pork and crackling maybe?

He could see the orange glow from fires in the local park, with smoke and glowing embers floating up into the night sky.

Maybe someone was having a barbecue? Or it could be yet another council-sponsored festival. There were so many these days – what with Eid, Diwali, and the multifarious multi-faith multi-sexual omni-inclusive celebrations of, well, just about everything – it was impossible to keep up.

Crump hoped that the people having a barbecue down the park were having a good time.

Raj was right. The incendiary information he had stored on that memory key, he would ping off the next day to, well, everyone who mattered. And that would certainly cause fireworks, and a conflagration of such intensity it'd make the barbecue fires look like, well, fires at a barbecue...

Crump raised his glass in the general direction of the park revellers and the winking lighthouse.

"Cheers, Johnny Blue," he said, finishing his wine before going inside to order a take-away.

Crump was feeling a sudden hunger for pork spareribs...

*

The next day, Dylan told him all about the South Sea Islanders.

"They went like well berserk, kindathing. Flogged all their ancestors' gear to a local antiques place, then on the piss downtown big time, then..."

"Then?" squinted Crump.

"They all ended up down the park, and killed the pig—"

"Sandra?"

Dylan nodded.

"Cut her up, cooked her on fires... Boom!"

"Well, they did ask for roast wild pig..." said Crump.

"Police left 'em to it, they were like, whatever, respect cultural diversity, so—"

"So that was the fiery glow I saw last night—"

"It was well sick."

"YOLO," said Crump, with a satisfied smile.

Later, Crump found time between lessons to slip off and find a lonely computer in a room behind the library. He logged on as Johnny Blue.

Then, quickly, he uploaded all files from the memory key – all the excel spreadsheets, all communications, all real evidence of wrongdoing – and emailed it off to a list of university managers, plus local and national politicians and media.

This wasn't a 'schlonk' – that moment when you accidentally click a button that has suddenly shifted position, so you go to a page you don't want to go to, delete something you wanted to keep, or, worst of all, ping an email to all in your list: the cause of many a disciplinary hearing and suspension or sacking from work. No, this was clear and purposeful action which would, Crump knew, speak truth to power, and bring those in control down.

Crump logged out of the computer. Then he left the room and walked back through the library to peruse the journal section.

As far as he knew, the only person to see him was the librarian he'd spoken to months before about the banned books list – Arwen Redmore. And what could she prove? Just that he'd been in the library, which was hardly unusual. They had nothing on him.

As far as the world was concerned, a former university staff member called Johnny Blue, dead since Christmas, had sent them mind-blowing information – and there was no way anyone could cover it up, not now Crump had sent it all to so many journalists and media sources.

Even the local paper would have to react to this, instead of its usual focus on local nobodies moaning and whingeing about, well, everything that didn't matter.

This mattered, and Crump knew it. It was explosive – digital dynamite.

And the world would never be the same again.

Not at Cambrian University anyway.

The mood in the Moronian class later that day was tense, to say the least. It was Crump's last lesson of the day, and for that reason, he always made such 'fag-end of the day' lessons a bit more relaxed, sometimes using music – the reason why he'd brought in a CD player.

"We have party, yes, Kev-een?" said Marek, with a broad smile.

"Maybe later," said Crump.

"No problem!"

And then Marek said something in a language Crump didn't understand across the class, and the student called Vladimir stood up and started angrily shaking his fist.

Other students joined in, and soon Crump had to raise his voice to get everyone to sit down and be quiet. He had no idea what was going on and why everybody was so tense and on edge.

"You know, in Communist time, when Russian pig in charge, we used to be telling a joke," said Marek. "Doctor, I do not feel well? *Who does?* say doctor!"

The class fell about laughing – all except Vladimir and Zoltan, the ethnic Russians. Angry words were exchanged between the multi-ethnic Moronian students.

"You want know traditional Russian recipe?" asked Marek. "It always begin the same: *First, you must to steal six eggs...*"

More laughs from most of the class and angry shouts from the ethnic Russians.

"You must to visit in Sgrot, best city in all world," smiled Oksana.

"Well—"

"Yes, you come," said Svetlana.

"Come to Moronia – you are welcome to it," grinned Taras.

Then more angry yells and shouts – Vladimir and Marek had squared up to each other and were reaching into their jacket pockets. For guns? Surely not. This sort of thing just did not happen here.

But then, Crump had seen Marek's two guns. Should he have contacted the police? Then what would have happened? He'd have been arrested, that's what!

"Right!" yelled Crump at the top of his voice, banging his fist on the desk. "Sit down and shut up!"

The class all stared at him, but they did what he said. They sat down and they shut up and they all looked at the front of the class at their teacher, just like obedient infants. Of course, Crump knew of the teacher training trend which said 'never ever shout', 'always praise', and that was how to control a disruptive class. But he would dearly love to parachute some of the 'expert' educationalists who wrote such theoretical bollocks and tosh into any difficult class in any college or school anywhere in the UK. They'd soon wipe the scales from their ignorant eyes with the tears, when they were actually up against it in the real world.

But these were professionals he was teaching, politicians and educated adults from Moronia, not inner-city kids.

"I'm *very* disappointed… in your behaviour," Crump said, quietly, almost in a whisper.

Then he paused for silence and for effect – as teachers and lecturers do, to get attention. Sometimes it worked; sometimes it didn't. But it did now.

"You are all – all of you – Moronians, yes?"

Mumbled yeses from the class, even from those like Vladimir with crossed arms and scowls on their faces.

"You are all one people, one nation, yes?"

More mumbles.

"So you should be working *with* each other, not fighting *against* each other."

"Yes!" said Tomek Glusky.

"You – we – should all be showing each other respect and consideration… and, yes, love – "

"The *loaf*?" asked Zoltan.

"Yes, the love," said Crump. "Love for your fellow man – and woman. Love for your country but not hatred of others, 'the other', anyone different from you in any way. Love for what *could* be, for what is *possible*, not past feuds and hatreds. To help create, together, a perfect union. And yes, if you try to work together, to co-operate, you can do it – you *can all* do it, no matter what ethnicity or tribe you are from or what language you speak or where your ancestors came from."

"Yes, we *can*," said Marek.

Other class members echoed his words:

"YES, WE *CAN*!"

"To believe there can be better days ahead, that what unites us all is stronger than that which divides us, to know that we are one people, together, in love. Because love is enough, and love will find a way. All you need is love."

At this precise point, Crump pressed the start button on the CD player he'd cued up earlier and *All You Need Is Love* by The Beatles echoed loudly around the room.

Gradually, one by one, the students stood up, and when the chorus came, joined hands singing and chanting 'All You Need Is Love' over and over again.

It was a joy to see – even though Crump knew in his heart that it was a load of old cobblers, as, he was sure, did Marek and the others. Love is great, yes – but you also need a roof over your head, food on the table and, if possible, a well-paying job that didn't treat you like shit either.

But at least Crump had somehow managed to prevent a war breaking out amongst the Moronians, though he was not really sure why it was happening in the first place.

No doubt Marek would give him all the juicy details later. It probably involved money. Most wars do.

Suddenly, Dylan burst through the classroom door without knocking, out of breath from running.

Crump turned off the CD player.

"Yes, what is it?" he snapped, annoyed at the interruption.

"The Learning Tower..." panted Dylan, "of... no pizza... It's..."

"It's what?"

"It's *ON FIRE!*"

Outside, the stench of acrid smoke hung heavy in the air as the flames took hold in The Learning Tower.

Crump had herded his Moronian students out quickly, pointed them to the park, a safe distance from the campus.

But many stayed, wanting to help.

Marek, as Crump knew he would, took charge of the situation. The emergency services were yet to arrive, and the fire had spread so quickly. This was perhaps because most sprinklers seemed not to be working, or because the material used for cladding on the tower was making it go up like a Roman candle. Thick black plasticky smoke billowed out of some of the open or broken windows on the higher floors and from the roof as flames licked around them.

Dan Guttery and Mr Scumble were there, checking in case anyone was still inside the building.

Lucky that it was late in the day so most students had gone home, and most staff too, by the looks of it – unless they'd all just done a runner?

The British students there were helping too, under the guidance of Marek and Crump, who ordered them to: "Just leave the *fucking* books!" when one student wanted to try and carry some of them out to save them.

They've banned all the best ones anyway...

Soon, the heat from the flames was so intense that they all had to move away from the tower, and keep a safe distance too in case of debris falling from any of the fourteen storeys.

It was then that Crump saw a figure standing on the roof – which looked, though he couldn't be sure, like Lesley Snyde. She, too, was on fire – like a human candle or flare, standing still as the flames rose around her, on her, within her. And then she was gone – like the Devil.

Crump was sure he then saw something in the window of the seventh floor. It looked like a big black animal with bared teeth.

Diversity Dog?

He saw it leap up and grab in its jaws the throat of a man who looked from that distance very much like Professor Pip Pooman, dragging him down to his doom.

Or maybe not. It was hard to know what you were seeing in the choking smoke and the orange redness of the flames – they seemed to create colours and images you were not really sure were there at all, like seeing shapes and faces in the clouds. But whatever the professor got up to in his secret laboratory, Crump knew instinctively it was no bad thing it was all being incinerated.

By then, everyone had backed well away from the burning building, to avoid breathing too much of the foul-tasting, black acrid smoke into their lungs.

At this point, the emergency services arrived – but you could only just hear their sirens wailing through the awful roar of the fire, which was now a raging inferno. They had got there fairly quickly – but the fire was quicker, engulfing the entire tower in flames within what seemed like seconds, and certainly no more than a couple of minutes.

The heat was so intense, even many metres away.

And the noise...

The noise was like demons screaming from the gates of hell itself.

Nobody and nothing would survive this now, not if they were still in there.

Everyone just stared in silence at the sight of a tower block which, moments before, had looked as it always had, on a normal everyday early evening at Cambrian University, but which now resembled a scene from *The Towering Inferno*.

It had all happened so quickly.

There were no words.

Or, rather, the only ones Crump could think of were from one of the library's banned books, *Heart of Darkness*.

"The horror!" he muttered to himself watching the fire light up the night, as the flames devoured the tower before him.

THE HORROR!

CHAPTER NINE

Moving On

The next day, the whole world was in shock.

Fire crews had fought the fire through the night, but there was no real hope of getting anyone out after the flames took hold.

The worry now was more that The Learning Tower would collapse, possibly onto the main university building and others surrounding it. But it didn't. There it stood, a big black tombstone looming above the campus.

It was like the aftermath of a bombing in a war, with people wandering around aimlessly and lost, with blank neutral faces and middle-distance stares into nothingness. It was the same vacant look you saw on the zombie faces of refugees on TV news reports.

And everywhere in the air, that dreadful smell – an acrid, chemical stench that clung to your clothes and seemed to seep into your skin, slithering under it until it rested within the flesh. You could taste it on your tongue. The bitter sweetness. *Was that death?*

The world's media was there of course, lapping up the tragedy. BBC star reporter Jason Hussein was there too filing a report to camera, hamming up the tragic looks while all the time inwardly gleeful to be there on the ground for the biggest news story for ages. Others were just as bad. The international crews were who *in situ* already for the story of the university's unilateral declaration of independence from the UK and loyalty to the EU, now focused on a bigger, better, '*death-ier*' story.

Already, there was a #LoveTheLearningTower hashtag on Twitter, and countless thousands had changed their Facebook pages to images of it. The power of FOMO included the *Fear of Missing Out* in sharing the pain of a tragedy like this, even if you lived on the other side of the world.

Crump remembered the evening before, how suddenly it had all happened, how it all seemed like a dream. Unreal. But all too real too.

Those there had worked so hard to save people from the burning building, and to check no-one else was inside. They had done all they could to save everyone. Some people were dead – they all knew that, though not precisely how many, or who exactly had been trapped in the building. Names were being checked, students and staff called, texted and emailed. Everyone was asked to confirm they were safe. Now they'd all just have to wait and see who did, and didn't, reply.

It was over to the firefighters and investigators now. They'd search the blackened shell of the building when it was deemed safe and bring out the bodies.

Crump thought he had seen Lesley Snyde burning on the roof and Professor Pip Pooman, possibly, in the jaws of Diversity Dog. But now he couldn't even be sure of that, and was questioning his own memory. False memory was a common thing – the way people would swear they saw a red car if witnessing a crime, only for it to be later shown to be blue; the way people 'remembered' abuse that never happened, especially if already prone to psychological pain. The part of the brain responsible for memory and imagination were located in the same area, it seemed, hence the whole issue. You really couldn't trust your memories, after all. They were all created in your brain, as was everything you saw and heard. All fact was fiction.

There had been such bravery the night before. Dean Guttery and Mr Scumble, together with some local homeless people – including the ginger-haired guy Crump always saw in Highlands – had been there, entered the burning building, and done what they could.

Marek had been a great leader – organising everything, giving orders with a tone of authority no-one could ignore or disobey. His very expert presence inspired such confidence – in Crump, too, who did whatever he asked, as did all the other Moronians there present, even Vladimir.

Most impressive of all, for Crump, was the way the millennial 'snowflake' students had responded to the fire. These kids – for that is what they were – suffered separation anxiety if away from their mobile phone comfort blankets for minutes, overcome by *No-Mo-Phobia*. They had learned to demand safe spaces where they could never be offended, upset or hurt by any opinion they disagreed with, supported no-platforming of anyone with a non-pc view or any opinion their righteous woke moral guardians deemed 'offensive'. They had books banned from the perusal of their unready eyes just in case the events, scenes, characters portrayed therein were sexist, racist, nasty, angry, upsetting, or if events of violence such as war were shown.

However, when faced with a real disaster as large as The Learning Tower fire, they could, when allowed to, step up to the plate. They could and would excel, take risks, show great bravery and strength of character, if freed from their mental baby harnesses and allowed to operate freely as capable individuals – especially when directed and guided by someone like Marek.

And so Crump had watched while all the Olivers and Harrys, all the Olivias and Emilys of Generation

Snowflake helped other human beings escape a rather real-world offensive and dangerous triggering maelstrom of an inferno which had nearly cost them their lives. It was impressive and good to see – if anything on that night could be called 'good'.

It showed than if you want to help the young, you do not do everything for them, hold their hands to cross the road beyond infant years, wrap them up so safely and snugly they can hardly breathe in their bubble. No, you should teach them how to cross the road alone and let them learn how to deal with the risks and difficulties of life themselves too. Free them from that stifling, sterile life of 'safe spaces' and over-protection by well-meaning but very wrong and misguided catastrophising adults and paranoid parents, who keep them cooped up like battery hens in digital prison bedrooms, suckled by suffocating screens and stunted into always-worried runts, babied into a toddler-brained adulthood because they have not been allowed to grow up as nature intended. If shown how to do stuff for themselves, and guided by others, they *could* do it. These special snowflakes of Generation Blub, they *really could* do it. *So let them!*

Crump had seen the Student Union rep Aled Rantallion help out too, and some of his own EFL class students such as Mads, Heiner, Chang, Koen, Jordi, Julie, Birgitte, Giulia, Bjorn, even Jesus and others – they had obviously been present on campus for a lesson with another teacher. Ahmed and Rashid had shown up later to help out, no doubt after their shifts at the takeaway. Crump was proud of them all.

But what he had not seen was many staff members. Had they all already gone home for the day? Or had they simply scarpered? He had no idea.

It was all very quiet – too quiet. And then Crump worked out why. For the first time ever on that campus there had been no sobbing and crying coming from the

Creative Writing Department – ironic, seeing as there now there really *was* something to sob and cry about, rather than the typically lyrical lines of obscure literary fiction hardly anyone will ever read or care about.

Crump watched the firefighters work, from behind the safety barrier. He knew there was nothing more he could do here – and he had been here all night long, had watched the sun rise on the wreckage of the night as dawn broke bruised on the horizon of the bay.

The TV crews were interviewing people. Marek was nowhere to be seen, and nor were most Moronians, but plenty there were happy to say what they had seen and done. Not Crump.

As soon as the TV people approached him with that eager whore-y media stare, camera and microphone beelining towards him, he knew it was time to go. The media could feed on the flesh of the dead and wallow happily in the tragedy without his input. Anyway, he needed to sleep, if only for a couple of hours.

His car was there in the carpark, but he felt like walking home, so made his way towards the park.

It was then that he saw the skip – and what was in it.

Crump entered the park somewhat warily. He knew the South Sea Islanders were there – the fires on which they'd roasted various parts of Sandra the pig were still smouldering. But he couldn't see anyone about anywhere.

He knew from Dylan that they 'liked a drink' and so maybe they'd all been on the piss down town and gone home to their host families after their feast?

Suddenly, a South Sea tribesman in full warrior regalia, complete with grass skirt, a bone through his nose and brandishing a very lethal-looking wooden club, jumped from a tree and landed on the ground in front of Crump. He contorted his face into an image of eye-glaring anger and stuck his tongue out in full 'Haka' style.

Crump turned around, ready to leave the park. The decision to visit it may not have been one of the best he'd made in his life.

Right then, another warrior dropped from a tree and blocked his exit and with a very sharp-looking spear in his hands.

The dark worm of worry in Crump's stomach tightened, that knot of anxiety so well-known to him from his childhood, his constant loyal companion in life.

"Errr… good morning," he said, cheerfully and stupidly, first to one bloodthirsty barbarian cannibal, then the other. "I was out for a walk and… errr… I found these…"

The South Sea warriors looked at each other, then moved closer to Crump as he held up the bag.

Then they burst out laughing.

"G'day mate. Don't look so worried – we's only *gammin* with you. This here's Winston and I'm Clem. Fancy a cold one?"

Soon, Crump was sitting on the grass watching the smouldering bonfire and feasting on delicious crackling-coated roast pork (which used to be a bit the vicious psycho pig called Sandra), all whilst sipping on a 'tinnie' which was, indeed, cold, thanks to an ingenious South Sea Islander beer storage net that they'd lowered into the pond in the middle of the park.

The tribesmen in grass skirts with bones through their noses were soon back in jeans and T-shirts, and the weapons were all put away too.

Crump took the shrunken heads and bones out of the bag – everything he'd found in the skip.

"Coming back like a bad penny, mate. Fair dinkum!"

Crump blinked at the genuine Antipodean 'upspeak'.

"So, you don't want… your ancestors' bones and… shrunken heads and—"

"Nah, mate – even if they is our fathers' fathers – more likely, our ancestors were *stoked* to do 'em in."

"Heaps of warring tribes back in them days where we comes from," said a tribesman.

"Skull this, mate," said another, handing Crump his third beer of the morning.

"Listen, no-one ever asked us if we wanted any old bones. They just assumed we did, and sent an invite, all expenses paid, so…"

"A holiday's a holiday, *fair dinkum*."

"But don't get us wrong, fella. We're no *bludgers* – we work."

"It's hard *yakka* dancing for them fat camera-dangler tourists, mate."

"Bloody grass skirts and bones in noses and tongue-poking. But that's what they want—"

"So that's what the buggers get!"

"We flogged most o' the clubs and stuff to dealers—"

"Big money!"

"Only kept some for sentimental reasons, like."

"Spent the *beans* in the *Bottle-O*, got us well *stoked*."

"But no bugger wanted the shrunky heads and bones."

"Human remains can be… problematic, legally speaking," said Crump, remembering a local man who, bizarrely, found a 2,000-year-old arm of an Egyptian mummy on a Welsh beach and ended up spending hours being questioned by police.

"Well, we don't want 'em, mate."

"*Strewth*! No way are we putting them on the *barbie*!"

"So… what should I do with them all?" asked Crump. The South Sea Islanders looked at each other and shrugged.

"Maybe put 'em back where you found 'em, mate?"

"What – chuck 'em back in the skip?"

"They's all *carked it*, years ago. Makes no difference to them. Or us."

"Or give 'em to a museum some place?"

"But we don't want 'em back, no way."

Crump told them all about the fire in The Learning Tower.

"Fuck me dead, mate," said Clem. "We been on the coldies all day. Must've snored through it all."

"*Strewth*, you gotta be *knocked-up*!"

"*Fair dinkum*, I'd *crack the shits* if my place turned into a *fire stick*."

"Get that coldie down yer neck, mate."

"Fair play," said Crump, quaffing his fifth beer of the morning. Something told him it wouldn't be the last.

As Crump chewed on the delicious Sandra-sourced crackling, he could see, sleeping in the long grass by the trees, the well-fed comatose form of Nelson the cat, who'd been gorging on roast pork all night long...

*

And then, more questions started to be asked.

Especially who, if anybody, who was responsible for the fire?

There were various theories. That it was Muslim terrorists, an Israeli Mossad plot to make Muslims look bad, Welsh nationalists, Scottish nationalists, Irish nationalists, English nationalists, Socialist workers, Socialist shirkers, Tories, Fascists, Neo-fascists, Crypto-fascists, Liberal Democrats, Illiberal UnDemocrats, ISIS, Al-Qaeda, the IRA, the CIA, the BNP, the BBC, the *BB-She*, HMRC, the TUC, the RAC, the Luftwaffe, the Leftwaffe, the populist right, the non-populist right, Red Nazis, Blue Nazis, nasty Nazis, Nazi nasties, the Mafia, the Taffia, Russians, Prussians, Brextremists, Sextremists, Remainiacs, Brainiacs, perverts, converts, reverts, right-wing racists, left-wing racists, rapists, papists, racist rapist papists, atheists, agnostics, Europhiles, paedophiles, pyromaniacs, kleptomaniacs, dipsomaniacs, transmaniacs, #MeToo, #YouToo, #BooHoo, transsexuals, pansexuals, non-binaries, bi-nobodies, bi-somebodies, intersex activists, intersectionality activists, otherwise-inactive activists, dyslexics, dyspepsics, TERFers, surfers, flat-earthers, virgin-birthers, animal rights activists, anti-vivisectionists, pro-vivisectionists, yobs, slobs, multifarious mobs, heathens, vegans, Moonies, loonies, red bandits from the boonies – twitching guilt-seeking fingers were pointing frantically in all directions.

A few suggested arson by students, or possibly university management, after what was being exposed in the media now, all thanks to Crump and Raj blowing the whistle. One or two even mentioned Donald McClounie the fake Scot, who was one of the missing. And some posited that floating embers from the South Sea Islander bonfire barbies in the park could have started it.

Certainly, the run-down state of The Learning Tower, its dodgy electrics and the fact many of its sprinklers were not functioning contributed to the fire spreading, and maybe even started it. The diversity-quota all-female maintenance team was arguably a factor. The flames of the inferno were certainly very diverse and inclusive in destroying everything and everyone equally. So, on fire service advice, the man-excluding maintenance team was immediately disbanded, replaced by one headed by Dean Guttery and Mr Scumble, back in their old jobs, who were free to select their crew on merit, even if that meant it was all-male.

The cladding on the outside of the building was being cited by many as a reason the fire spread so quickly and turned The Learning Tower into a fireball, a Roman candle lighting up the night with its awful glow. Apparently, there had been concerns about cladding made from ACM (Aluminium Composite Material) before, in many places around the world, and for years.

The building's architect, Otto Zatkin, could not be located for comment. He was thought to be employed somewhere in the Arab world or China, as he had designed scores of skyscrapers there in recent years.

It was pointed out in the media and by the university that The Learning Tower had won armfuls of awards when it had first opened. But then so had every single relentlessly grey and miserable concrete council estate tower block in Britain – though it was perhaps telling that the architects who designed these monoliths never ever actually lived in them.

An inquiry was announced, headed by highly respected top lawyer Lord Twombly and Crispin Willeard QC. Its conclusions wouldn't be known for at least a year, possibly two or more.

As somebody on TV stated:

"If they knew, they were complicit. If they didn't know, they were incompetent."

'They' was everyone in charge: the university management, those responsible for maintenance and fire prevention, those who appointed them, maybe the council and central government too. Though, no doubt, a frantic game of 'pass the fizzing cartoon bomb of responsibility' would now ensue, with every member of management trying to simultaneously pass the buck and cover their own back. It was ever thus.

With a sense of timing that must have been honed over years to be as crass and callous as possible, three hundred redundancies were announced that day in the press. It was the last thing the Cambrian University management team did before their suspension.

When the proverbial really hit the fan, as the files Crump had emailed the media using Johnny Blue's account were opened and read, all members of senior management were suspended and, at long last, lost their slippery grip on power. And it was all, always,

372

about power – which attracts the worst and corrupts the best too. Vice-Chancellor Angharad Ap Merrick, Mike Mumpsimus and Parminder Zugzwang were escorted off campus by security. Rumours swirled about possible arrests.

The information Crump had sent the media revealed that senior management all had their 'fingers in the till'. Never so obviously as that, of course, but skimming off funds was standard, both government money, student fees and European funding: no wonder they were all such ardent Remainers!

There was a gaping black hole in the university's finances – even bigger than the one affecting every single UK university, none of which will in future be able to afford to pay the pensions they have promised to their often-long-lived retired staff, and who will eventually all need to be bailed out by the taxpayer (the government are keeping that one quiet!).

No, the black hole in Cambrian University was deeper and wider than that. It was a bottomless pit of unfathomable Quatermass proportions, hidden for years, via complex creative accounting, all exposed in the information Raj had hacked into and sent to Crump.

Then there were the adventures abroad. In common with many UK institutions, Cambrian University had not only relied on cash cow foreign students but had started partnerships with institutions overseas, especially in the Far East, opening branches of their brand thousands of miles away, many so weakly monitored that they were, in effect, selling degrees to paying students who hardly, if ever, attended class or submitted assignments. Cambrian University had one such college which was run by a former K-pop star, and both had been creaming many hundreds of thousands of pounds in fees from it, yet it was now shown to be nothing more than a shell company. It was Degrees R Us, and then some. And they were all at it.

Melissa Jenks and Kim Vyshinsky were named acting joint Vice-Chancellors, though Crump did always wonder whether some jobs were suitable for job shares. There can only be one person driving the bus, after all. But as each would continue in their previous roles too, and this was only a temporary acting joint position towards the end of the academic year, it *could* work…

And then the dead and missing were named. Crump watched the body bags being carried out of The Learning Tower. He was eternally grateful that he was not able to see the charred body parts and distorted corpses within.

The confirmed deceased included Lesley Snyde. Dylan had said 'she's a disease' and he was right. The information sent by Raj showed that she, indeed, was a thief and a liar, the puppet master, with spies everywhere, and people reporting back to her. She was the real black widow at the centre of the web, and when he saw the emails, Crump knew it was she who had been behind Abi Rainbow's vile accusations against him and others. Crump, for one, would not mourn Lesley Snyde, a vile, vindictive, spiteful witch who, were she not dead, would surely be in a prison cell right now. She was predatory and malign, a psychopathic entity void of compassion, and the sole architect of her own wrecked morality. People like that were like evil bacteria blooming on the surface of the Earth, a virus that made things die. The world was better off without the likes of her.

Professor Pip Pooman, medic and Manager of Managing Fairness Fairly, was also confirmed dead, as was IT Manager Dr Tomos Splodge. The bodies of Colin and Karl Kunti from The New York Diner were found with Pooman, though investigations as to precisely why were not yet complete. Crump heard gossip about a great many animal corpses found in his lab on the seventh floor too.

It seemed Allah chose not to save Saladin Malik, Islamic Studies lecturer and imam, and the logically scientific randomness of the cosmos did not throw its dice in Humanist Androo Spoon's favour either. Evangelical Christian and BBC *Thinking Today* broadcaster Ridley Crick was lucky – he was off on one of his missions to Africa, and thus avoided the bright light welcoming heavenly void the others were lucky enough to enter.

Donald McClounie was still missing, as was Pete Parzival, whom no-one had seen for ages. Memories of Johnny Blue worried Crump. Would they find Pete rotting at the end of a rope too? Or washed up cold and broken by the waves crashing on the rocks of some lonely, beautiful beach?

So, seven confirmed dead, two missing. No students, thank goodness.

It was all in the national and world media, and even the crappy local *Cambrian Daily News* had taken a holiday from reporting stories of potholes, bin collections, noisy seagulls, noisier students, public toilets, local 'characters' with dogs, tales of disgustingly popular dogging in seaside car parks (with full directions given), and the many silly trivialities of provincial existence, and instead focused on some real news for once: the tragic events at Cambrian University – the memories of lives lost, the tales of bravery, the stories of horror, the tears and the anger, the surprise and joy of survival.

And it had also broken its silence regarding criticism of the university, a policy stuck to for years because of the amount of advertising placed. Now it was open season – because the *Cambrian Daily News* had been anonymously sent, as had all national media outlets, the full files from Crump, which exposed in intricate and jaw-dropping detail the massive corruption that had been going on at the university for years.

And then, quite suddenly, Cambrian University issued a press release which stated, in a single sentence, that it was no longer pursuing its claim of unilateral independence from the UK and continued membership of the EU – for reasons of cost, they claimed.

The starry blue EU flags fluttered forlornly in the warm April Brexit-y breeze at the news.

It was over.

*

The next day, Crump saw Dylan for the first time since the fire.

"I *know*," he said.

"Know what, kindathing?"

"Dylan, I *know*. Everything. What you've been doing all year – spying on me."

"You're joking me."

"No, I am not 'joking' you."

"Oh."

"Oh."

"So?"

"So *why*, Dylan? Why spy on me? Report back to Lesley Snyde – you hated her!"

Dylan shrugged like a truculent toddler in a sulk.

"Just doing my job, kindathing."

"Oh, so your job is snitching for a living, is it? Betraying people, spying on them like a common… spy?"

Crump looked at the kid standing in front of him staring at his shoes like a naughty schoolboy caught with a cheat sheet in an exam.

"I trusted you, Dylan. Really, I did."

"So… she made me do it…"

Crump mocked him:

"*She made me do it – boo hoo hoo…* How old are you?"

"Twenty-one."

Crump looked hard at the boy-man before him.

"Why didn't you tell me?"

"If I would've told you, you would've gone off on one though, innit?"

"If I *had* told you..."

"Told me what?"

"No, I'm not telling you anything – I'm just pointing out the correct usage of the third conditional, as in 'if I *had* told you, you *would've* gone off on one'."

"That's what I thought too, innit, kindathing."

Crump squinted at Dylan's young, open, mixed-race face which was as blank as his muddled mind. He remembered how scared the kid had been of Lesley Snyde, and then the lightbulb moment came.

"She had something on you, didn't she? Lesley Snyde, I mean."

"She's a disease," said Dylan with a shudder.

"What was it?"

Dylan said nothing.

"She's dead now anyway," said Crump.

"Most def," said Dylan.

"Good riddance, eh?" said Crump with a nod.

Dylan smiled. He clearly wasn't going to reveal what Snyde had on him, and Crump wasn't going to press him. What did it matter now anyway? It was probably something drug-related, knowing Dylan's appetite for weed. It couldn't be anything sexual – most of the time Dylan seemed too unenergetic and apathetic to even have sex with himself, let alone anyone else.

"Is this what you want – in your life?" asked Crump.

Dylan shrugged.

"Whatever. It's a job – I'm happy here, kindathing."

"Seriously? You're young – what about your hopes and dreams? Your ambitions. I mean... what do you *want* out of life?"

Again with the shrug. It was Crump who should be

shrugging – his dreams had been utterly crushed, his hopes dashed, his ambitions thwarted. But this kid had his whole life ahead of him.

"I mean, the world's your... oyster..." said Crump, just avoiding saying 'lobster' like Tanya Snuggs. "I mean, what reasons do you have to stay here?"

"I got less reasons to change – I get good money here."

"*Fewer* reasons, Dylan. Not less."

"Does it matter?"

"Yes, it matters. *Most def.* It's the English language. Example: there are *fewer* expensive restaurants over there, because most are *less* expensive than the restaurants over here."

"What restaurants? Over where, kindathing?"

"There are no restaurants! I was giving an example of when to use the words *less* and *fewer* correctly, and—"

"Chillax, man. You're obsessed."

"Of course I'm obsessed – I'm an English teacher!"

*

In the English Studies Department, they informed Crump that Donald McClounie had been found – stark naked and wandering wild-eyed around a beach singing *Flower of Scotland* to the seagulls.

"Man dem say he was, like, *pleasuring himself* wiv a bagpipe," said Shabs,

"The bag or the pipe?"

"Both."

Crump winced.

"Dat is well nasty, dat ain't normal, d'ya get me, bruv..."

Apparently, he'd been taken away to a mental ward, which no doubt would have pleased the police immensely – a new diversity target they had was to section more white men to thereby lower the high percentage of black males who got sectioned.

One way they were achieving this was by loitering outside community centres on pensioner days, and sectioning any old boy they saw leaving who was mumbling to himself.

It was, indeed, *madness gone politically correct...*

Crump's thoughts turned to Pete Parzival who was still missing. Due to the intense heat of the fire, it was perfectly possible that his remains would never be found, if he had been unfortunate enough to perish in the blaze.

Or he could have been somewhere else entirely. He could already be dead if he'd walked into the sea – he'd been missing for ages, after all. Crump tried not to think of it, to instead cling on to the sliver of hope that he was alive and well, and just not in contact for a good reason – though Crump struggled to think of one.

Tanya Snuggs was taking a staff meeting. She looked worried – not her usual 'lucky go happy' self, bouncing around all-smiles-ebullience and fluffy pinkness. As per usual, Karen Crisp was not present, off at some conference in Canada this month, they said.

"So, I'm here all Easter holidays – can't stand flying – had terrible *flatulence* once coming back from the *Costa Bravo*. Never again. But I don't want to go off on a *tandem*. Kevin, you're doing Easter revision classes?"

"I'm always here – you know me."

"To all *intensive purposes*, classes are the same but of course they won't take place in The Learning Tower, on account of it *combustulating* in a *tornado* of *flamification* — "

"I heard we have other classrooms?" asked Crump.

"*A point in case*, yes – fortunately, the council and some local businesses, and the Memorial Theatre too, have stepped up to the *slate* and made available some local space locations to be *requivisioned* for *eduficatory* purposes."

Someone asked about resources, now that the library and the computer room in The Learning Tower had been incinerated.

"As you all know, there's resources online and we can contact everyone by email – so use the *interweb*, people."

"I'll tell students everything's online," said Crump.

"It won't be easy, but I don't have to remind everyone how important these assignments are, and the exam revision, Kevin. It's *imperatative* that we get it right, that we don't become *escaped goats*, and that the department *passes mustard*."

All staff members nodded solemnly. The events of recent days were an ordeal for everyone, but for once people were all pulling together, avoiding any sniping and focusing on what needed to be done.

"For those of you off on your hols, enjoy yourselves! For we *work houses* who remain for the Easter staycation, all I can say is…"

"*Get a wiggle on! Yay!*" chanted Tanya and all staff members present in tuneless unison.

"*Yay!*"

*

That weekend the weather was glorious. Sunshine shimmered on the mirror pond of the bay, and the sky was a big cloudless cerulean blue.

As it was only April, it wasn't too hot either. Perfect weather, then, for a long walk on Gower. Crump had been meaning to get more exercise. He never seemed to have the time – or make time, at least.

But now, as he walked by the sandy bay where he'd scattered his mother's ashes, and saved the 'on-the-rocks' Boyo Bellylaughs that night – he felt, if not perfectly at peace, then at least not in crisis, and confident of survival.

Yes, it had all been stressful. It still was. There were revision classes to teach over Easter, and with students who would not, he knew, be coping stoically with The Learning Tower fire, or the corruption scandal at the university, or the end of their anti-Brexit dream. Crump was thankful he didn't have to field all the calls from parents worried about their offspring's safety – apparently, too, more than a few foreign students would not be flying back to the UK after the Easter break.

Cambrian University was shown to be corrupt, and to have been awarding degrees at overseas branches students there did not work for or deserve. So now, quite possibly, its brand was toxic and a name change would be called for. This wasn't really fair, because Cambrian University was not, in general, a poorly performing educational establishment – though of course it indulged in all the grade inflationary jiggery-pokery tricks all other universities used, and rarely failed any foreign students, for fear of losing that lucrative customer base. But whoever said (university) life was fair?

One 'trick' often used by universities – and schools, come to that – was to try and make courses as coursework-based as possible. That was much preferred to the old exam-based approach, because with coursework, teachers and tutors could pre-mark assignments over and over again, to boost student grades. Exams were more of a wild card over which educational staff had much less control. When the UK government introduced GCSEs in the late–1980s, the Department of Education ensured that schools could choose 'up to 80%' of the English GCSE syllabus to be coursework-based. Schools didn't have to go up to 80% – they could do 60%, 40% or 20%. There was, apparently, not a single school in England and Wales that did not opt to take the full 80% coursework option.

Crump had always thought the difference between assessment by exams or coursework to be a bit like that between execution by hanging, or something more long and drawn out. Would you prefer a quick snap of the neck at the end of a rope – or the weeks, months and years of misery, rotting in a dungeon somewhere, your brain breaking and tortured, waiting for an end you know you can never avoid anyway?

The view was beautiful that day as Crump walked the coastal path. The azure ocean seemed endless as it disappeared into thin mist in the distance.

As various wild birds chirped and darted amongst the gorse, Crump breathed in the fresh saltiness of the sea – it tasted alive on his tongue. The world seemed utterly at peace, a scene of easy harmony.

Just then, he stopped. On the path in front of him was a snake. Small – about a foot long – and still as stone. It looked newly made and perfect, basking there in the sun, as if carved of green marble.

Crump knew that spring was the time when the young of many species emerged into the world, like mewling kittens, or newly fledged seagulls, all downy and brown.

He stood a while admiring the young snake, its fresh skin camouflaged well against the grey gravel and concrete of the path – it was no wonder some people accidentally trod on these baby snakes every year, and felt the adders' fangs sink into their ankles. Their own fault really – the snakes had been here way longer than we had. They were just snakes being snakes – it was in their nature to shyly hide from possible threats, but if you got too close when they were sleeping in the sun, you may well taste the ancient toxins in your bloodstream too.

Just then, the young snake seemed to wake up quickly, and beautifully slithered quickly back into the bushes. Perhaps it had seen this strange two-legged ape standing nearby, or smelt him. It was not wrong to be scared of people, for sure.

Crump smiled to himself in pleasure at seeing this creature. It was rare to see an adder, though he knew they were there, basking in the grass, hiding inside the silent landscape, lying in wait for passing prey.

He continued on his walk, enjoying watching the bobbing heads of a couple of seals in the sea from the coastal path. They occasionally ducked under the surface out of sight, no doubt keen to catch a hapless crab emerging from the crags and crevasses of the underwater rocks below. It was low tide, but the sea never retreated completely from these rocks – only from the wide sandy beaches at strung intervals along the coastal path, where a scattering of people walked and played, some of them bobbing in the surf like seals too. Come high tide, the surfers would be out, he knew. They always were, even on Christmas Day.

Then, some way up ahead, blurred in the heat, Crump saw three black birds. Crows, squawking noisily at each other. It looked as if they were fighting over something. They were too far away for him to see what.

Then one crow took off holding what Crump saw was a wriggling thing in its beak. A baby snake! It had to be.

The two other crows followed behind the one holding the snake, squawking loudly as they flew upwards over the craggy hill.

'Red in tooth and claw,' thought Crump, wondering at that snake's bad luck that day and the good luck of the one he'd seen basking on the sunny path. It was all 'random', as Dylan always said. For them and for us.

You just never knew when it would be your day to be faced with the final sharp hungry beak of your very own black crow.

Crump drove home feeling much better for his walk. Spending time outdoors did seem to have a calming effect on him, far more than the mindfulness classes he had attended. Maybe they should put nature and wildlife on prescription...

Driving home, Crump picked up a takeaway. He couldn't be bothered to cook, and the next week he had been summoned to a meeting in Cardiff with Sir Clive

Silverback from the Foreign Office, so he wanted to spend some time ensuring he was on top of everything and could talk confidently about his time at Cambrian University. Crump had no clear idea of why Sir Clive wanted a meeting in person. Maybe it was to praise him for his work, for his efforts during the devastating fire, for doing revision classes willingly and without complaint. Or maybe it was to offer him another role at the Foreign Office? He had no idea.

In the Highlands, Crump popped to see Kevin in the stationers to buy some supplies, and the chemist for some more dispersible aspirin. He always tried to use local shops – the newsagents/post office, Mike the MOT mechanic, Chris the keycutter, the charity shops, the bakers, the supermarkets, and the takeaways too. It seemed a shame that high rates were forcing so many small shops out of business, even as internet companies who don't even pay tax in the UK undercut them constantly. There was something very wrong about that.

On his way home, he could see that The New York Diner was now boarded up and closed down – though the same ginger-haired homeless man sat outside it on the pavement, hand hopefully outstretched for spare change from charitable strangers.

*

"Wonderful Wales, land of poets and song – I'm loving it!" said Sir Clive Silverback with a Senior Civil Service smile.

Crump was sitting with him in a rented office space inside a converted synagogue in the suburbs of Cardiff. He still had no idea why he'd been called to a meeting.

"Dame Shirley Bassey —"

"She lives in Monaco now."

"Sir Tom Jones, Sir Anthony Hopkins —"

"They live in America, sir."

"Oh, right. Well... Max Boyce. *Oggy-oggy-oggy, oi-oi-oi,* yes? That big leek eh? Hilarious!"

Sir Clive's smiling eyes wandered around the rounded whitewashed walls of the former synagogue office.

"Not many Jews left around here now obviously," he said "but then they always did like sticking together – all gone to London or Manchester probably, or back home to Israel."

Crump said nothing.

"So, Kevin, how are you coping with university life – after the famous fire?"

"Oh, y'know, it's been difficult... challenging... for everyone, students and staff – I'm doing revision classes over Easter—"

"Happy Easter, by the way," smiled Sir Clive.

Crump looked back, blankly.

"So, Kevin, Kevin, Kevin," said Sir Clive, leafing through a file. "You seem to be a very able, educated and hard-working individual... but..."

But?

"... but a fellow with a few flaws."

"One man's flaw..." said Crump, thinking, "... is another man's ceiling?"

He smiled. Sir Clive didn't. Instead, he shot Crump a steely glare over the desk.

"Hmmm... well..." he said, turning a page of a document, "you've certainly got yourself noticed."

"Is that... a *good* thing?" said Crump.

Maybe Sir Clive and the Foreign Office had been informed of his bravery the night of the fire, or the extra mile he went teaching his students?

"So... no, Kevin, it's not a good thing, going forward..."

"Going... forward?"

"Yes, no, yes..."

"Yes?"

"No… yes, no…"

"So…?"

"So, the thing is, Kevin, we all have to play the game… going…"

"… forward?"

"Yes."

Sir Clive was one who always 'played the game' – born into privilege, good school, climbed the career ladder, talked the talk, walked the walk, ticked the boxes, covered his own back, followed the leader, passed the parcel, claimed to be 'passionate' about working as a team and empowering others, a selfless pose which was in reality nothing but a thin and brittle layer of veneer hiding the obsessively selfish and ruthless career ambition beneath. Crump had seen it all before. This was the hallmark of most university senior managers too.

"So, considering the context and… events…"

"Events? Context?" queried Crump.

"Yes, no, well, we cannot ignore complaints of racism and sexism… transphobia… abuse on social media… bringing your employer into disrepute… and the *arrest*! I mean—"

"I was never charged. It was a false accusation. Malicious. Vindictive. Wrong."

"You were arrested, Kevin, for sexual assault of a woman and a child under thirteen. A *child*, Kevin—"

"—a *child* I did *not* sexually assault! I was innocent. I *am* innocent. Until proven guilty. Isn't that the law? Justice? *Habeas Corpus* and all that?"

"So…"

"So, I was set up – I was pushed into that kid… by… a twisted piece of…"

"We at the Foreign Office—"

"I was the victim in this! Still am!"

"—cannot be expected to continue payments to Cambrian University for—"

"What payments?" said Crump, confused.

Sir Clive leant back on his chair and sighed.

"You don't *seriously* expect the university to have offered to employ you without incentive, do you? Not after you were 'rationalised' from the Civil Service, and what with your previous record at Thames Met, the accusations of racism and… all the other… complications —"

"You mean you *paid* the university… to give me the job in the first place?"

Crump had seen payments listed in the spreadsheets hacked by Raj, but he assumed they were to fund the Moronian politics class, to promote Foreign Office interests via higher education – not this.

"Your face didn't fit, Kevin," said Sir Clive. "So… we generously eased its way in, if you see what I mean, with the lubrication of filthy lucre, so to speak."

"Is it because I'm male… and white?" asked Kevin.

"No no no, yes. You know how it is. We've all been working very hard to promote inclusion at the Foreign Office and in higher education as part of our heartfelt commitment to our core values, on our diversity journey, going forward —"

Then, at that moment, the world seemed to crystallise bright in Crump's eyes.

"Are you sacking me?" he said.

Silence.

"I mean, 'rationalising' me, if you want to call it that."

"No, Kevin. We're *liberating* you."

"*Liberating* me?"

"Yes," slimed Sir Clive with a smile. "It's a no-brainer, it really is. As you know, we have been paying your salary since you joined Cambrian University."

"So?"

"So, we are now freeing you from that obligation, Kevin," said Sir Clive.

"What obligation?"

"The obligation to keep drawing a salary from us, when you no longer actually work for us."

"Because you 'rationalised' me and sent me to work at a university in Wales!"

"We're all on a learning journey, Kevin, as part of our exciting new mission."

"So, you're 'chucking me under the bus'?"

"No no no," chuckled Sir Clive, "yes – we sometimes have to 'punch a puppy', Kevin—"

"I'm… a puppy now?"

"—although I'd prefer to focus on the positive, and not be so *negative* all the time."

"You're sacking me? How is that *not* negative?"

Silence.

Smiles.

From Sir Clive, anyway.

"Beautiful country, isn't it? Just beautiful. I'm loving it! How *is* your mother, by the way, Kevin?"

"Dead."

"Ah…"

"Who'll be paying my salary from now on then?"

"The university, of course. Provided you apply for a position there and your application is successful."

"They've just announced three hundred redundancies, and there's rumours of more to come."

"Oh, I know, terrible isn't it?" tutted Sir Clive.

"But I don't want to apply for a position I already hold. I've been employed by the Foreign Office for over seven years – I was a loyal employee, before I was…"

"Rationalised."

"… so how can you sack me?"

"We're not *sacking* you, Kevin – we're facilitating exciting new change, *empowering* you to embrace wonderful new future opportunities."

"But you won't be paying me any actual money any more?"

"So, under your contract of work, which you signed some years ago, together with the Official Secrets Act, may I remind you," said Sir Clive, leafing through another document like a lawyer, "you will see that if your actions or behaviour bring the Civil Service into disrepute or fail to abide by our diversity and inclusion policy, then—"

"So you're sacking me, just like that?"

Sir Clive smiled, then his face hardened.

"We are generously offering a modestly generous goodwill payment, to help you… find your feet, going forward."

Sir Clive closed the file and stood up.

"Thank you for coming today, Kevin," he said.

Sir Clive Silverback held out a hand which Crump instinctively shook, but instantly wished he hadn't, even as the sweat from the palms of his hands was mingling with his superior's in that final fateful shake.

"So," grinned Sir Clive, "I can see it's all good, going forward. You're so lucky living in Wales – such a beautiful little place, isn't it? I'm *loving* it!"

Oh yes, Sir Clive, I'm loving it!

Sir Clive, you complete and utter upper-class over-privileged self-righteous hypocritical mealy-mouthed two-faced total and utter fucking tosser shithead cunt!

Oh yes, I'm loving it.

I'm loving being made to feel like a useless piece of dirt for working my guts out in a long hours, low wage, no expectations culture, serving someone whose family have been in charge of everyone else and owned their souls, not to mention most of the fucking country, since ten sixty fucking six.

I'm loving the way the richest 20% in Britain earn over ten times more than the poorest 20%, the richest 10% has more than 100 times the wealth of the poorest 10%, and how the top 1% owns more than the bottom 55% of the population put together, and nobody ever thinks that is strange or wrong, or that anything should change.

I'm loving the bragging swagger of self-defence from the privileged, the princelings and princesses of all races and faiths, who blindly believe in their own brilliance from birth, whose surreal sense of entitlement means they never dare confront the possibility of their own mediocrity, as they slip seamlessly from one useful job opportunity to the next, thanks to family connections, and then smugly indulge in that constant, emoting, paternalistic concern about the environment or the developing world or 'poor people', so common amongst the stinking rich, who then ask us to pity them all and reward them with a gong in the New Year's Honours for their selfless, well-advertised, world-changing, ego-feeding fabulous charity works.

I'm loving the way 10% of British people own second homes, but 40% own no property at all and stand zero chance of ever being able to afford to buy any, seeing as they can barely pay their rising rent each month, to rapacious landlords whose wealth grows like the property-price-boosting immigration figure, and the obedient misery of their tenants, year on year, and politicians are all glad that the price of property has gone up forty times since the early 1970s but wages have only gone up by a factor of ten, because that keeps the consumer economy going when the home-owners feel rich from spiralling property prices, finger the wads of dosh in their humid little hands, and spend spend spend on the high street, even if it's on the internet, and the real high street is a boarded-up has-been ghost town where they never set foot amongst the losers, the homeless and the druggies, preferring instead to make their purchases online, and buy yet more Made-in-China plastic on-trend tat that they don't need or even want in a desperate attempt to make their meaningless lives look and feel happy and successful.

I'm loving zero hours contracts and the gig economy, flexible working and no job security or pension or holiday and sick pay, with people working longer and longer hours for less and less, hoping that one day, somehow, they'll get to be like the masters they serve and deliver takeaways to, or have smiley call centre conversations with, but knowing in their dull thudding hearts that they never ever will, because social mobility is *so* last century.

I'm loving how so many prefer to lose themselves and smother their pain in a fog of booze and drugs, both illicit and prescribed, including all the opioid boys and girls who seek solace in the legal oblivion of Xanax and codeine and fentanyl and anything to blot out the reality of it all because even a slow drugged-up journey to an early death is better than a long life endured in this cruel, shitty, unjust, fucked-up world and the residual sticky horror of it all.

I'm loving the seething digital sewer of social media of Facebook, Twitter, Snapchat, Instagram and whatever tax-dodging data-mining shyster shithead influencers are making profit off our personal information today, where memes, selfies, clickbait, revenge porn, sexting, slut-shaming, cat-fishing trolls, trojans, ransomware scammers, and live-streaming suicide are the epic fails of a generation, where finding an instant little sexual fantasy online is far more alluring and satisfying than the messy and complicated reality, where people get rewarded for hating more, hating better, and posting views more polarised, more extreme, than anyone else, grooming or being groomed, losing their minds for the sake of a smiley emoticon, where posting a photo of what you had for dinner is what you hope will get you more likes or pokes or follows from strangers you pretend are friends in a life so lonely and isolated you might as well be living on a desert island in the middle of an empty dead sea or in the dusty dark at the bottom of an old, closed coal mine where your grandfathers used to work.

I'm loving the endlessly emoting, gloating gormlessness of TV, the emotional diarrhoea that passes for entertainment, the self-obsessed non-entity celebrities bravely wallowing in a precious pity party puddle they pissed out earlier, playing the victim for all they're worth as they share the pain of their journey and bang on endlessly about how fucking strong they supposedly are to survive their alleged hell of a useless life lived through the fake prism of falsity and fame, the left-behinds – the feral kids and feckless parents and *chavtastic Jeremy-Kyle-icles* – all dangling hapless on a televisual gibbet for the dreadful delectation and entertainment of a smug supercilious middle-class mob, the teeth-and-tits autocuties who gurn at camera and complain about sexism in the media industry when they owe their entire careers to their pretty fuckable looks, as all show formats trawl the depths of exploitation for tears and hugs, in a world which worships feelings and despises intellect, where knowledge is what the adverts tell you as they try and sell you whatever digital gimmick some dollar-a-day slumdog slave in Asia worked themselves to into an early communal grave-pit for, and people actually believe these green-cloaking corporate companies care about society or people or the environment or equality or anything despite their one sole over-riding reason to exist being to squeeze as much profit out of idiots like you as they can.

I'm loving CCTV which watches everything everywhere all the time, predictive policing and creepy face recognition systems where an algorithm can get you arrested as a suspect if your face fits the criminal profile the computer pukes up, which is more often than not male, and/or black, despite 80% of people flagged up being entirely innocent and face recognition technology 95% inefficient, police raids with no consequence – for them – and lives ruined by casual accusation, smart TVs and 'virtual assistants' which allow law enforcement authorities as well as corporate data miners to listen in to what we say in our homes, security services to access our emails, and webcams to watch us 24/7 even when our laptops are off, just like the worst cybercriminal spamming scammers, and worst of all, the complete and utter obsequious fuckwits in the majority of the population who justify surveillance the Stasi would be proud of by robotically parroting the lie-bound logic of the enslaved everywhere: 'if you've got nothing to hide, you've got nothing to fear'. *Yeah, right.*

I'm loving the lies spoken as truth, the social media parasites who claim to be 'building communities' by 'promoting respect', but are instead pushing addiction to filth and misery, to violence, hatred, anger and bullying, as human life is reduced to nothing more than data to be taken, stored and sold like your broken soul in a new, improved slave trade, personalised to your every perverted need and want.

I'm loving the cretinisation of culture, the determined dumbing down, the endless celebration of degradation, the aiming low, the fucking up, the getting out of your head in this land of anger via a digital drug because there is nothing else worth getting up for, because you prefer the virtual world to the one you can really see, feel, hear, touch, taste, because your main hobby is hating anyone who holds an opinion you don't, where you can meet up online with the smock-wearing baying mob, which thinks so much like you it *is* you and has *become* you, and then all wave your digital pitchforks at your next victim, just because they're there and not like you, not like the right-thinking virtue-signalling finger-jabbing self-loathing woke keyboard warriors wanking their brains out in a toxic culture where nobody can trust or believe anything at all any more.

I'm loving it. LOL. YOLO. FOMO. AMA. NSFW. ROTFLMAO.

OMG. FFS. WTF.
Oh yes fucking YES!
I'M LOVING IT!

*

Crump took his old rattling Ford up to 100mph on the motorway driving back to The Town. She was a tough old girl, he knew, and unlike people, she'd never willingly let him down.

And if there weren't sparks spitting off the speeding steel of the bodywork or chassis, then it certainly felt as though they were coming off his own knackered, worn-out, betrayed, raging brain and body. He was so angry, so engulfed in the betraying flames of fury, so... so... *so...*

"Get out of my way!" he said, the next morning, to PC Christopher Cockwomble who was blocking his path to the English Studies Department, all because Crump could not show a valid university ID card.

He was nursing a hangover that was pounding in his head like a piston, despite all the painkillers.

The evening before, he had drunk bottle of wine after bottle of wine, as he watched the sun dissolve into the sea like an aspirin. He had sat in his back garden, silent and seething, as darkness fell. The lighthouse seemed to be laughing at him, with its blinking wink – or was it urging him onwards and upwards? But its magic hadn't worked for Crump – he was on the rocks and he knew it. No amount of mindfulness was ever going to mend this thing. Not this time. Not ever.

"Get out of my fucking way NOW!" yelled Crump at PC Cockwomble – who knew full well who he was, as the police had been harassing enough lately, so the demand for an ID card was just snide and petty.

WPC Jade Tugswell, who was also there, rolled her eyes at PC Cockwomble, flicking her hair and head to one side. At this, the annoying copper shuffled aside to let Crump pass. At least *she* could tell he was serious and not to be messed with that morning.

Crump would never forgive the police for what they'd put him through and he'd never trust them again. He certainly wasn't going to take any shit that morning, as he tried to collect his teaching files from his *own* English Studies Department at his *own* university, even though it was not strictly his employer, and he wouldn't be there much longer. He had a job to do and he would do it.

There was not a single example in history of police willingly giving up power, but plenty of them demanding more. These days, what with all the tasers, facial recognition technology and predictive policing, constant surveillance by CCTV and of whatever anyone says online, the British police were really overstepping the mark. They always wanted more powers, and more, and more – to boost their arrest stats and targets, and, Crump supposed, just because they liked more powers and saw absolutely no problem with becoming a sort of 'Poundland gestapo'.

Crump entered the building. He was late. He also was aware he smelt like a saloon bar, having slept in his clothes on the sofa the night before. He'd made the effort to brush his teeth and spray on some sickly sweet deodorant, most of which seemed to have found a home in his mouth, if the bitter flowery taste was anything to go by. But his tongue tasted of dried sick anyway, so even that cancer-chemical smell was an improvement.

He wasn't going to miss a revision class, throw a sickie. After all, he hadn't missed a day at the university that academic year, other than when he'd been suspended for the false allegations of sexual assault made against him – the ones which, together with warnings for racism (not true) and 'abuse' on social media, were why he had now been sacked, effective at the end of the summer term, when his FO-paid salary would cease altogether.

Or could it be that the Civil Service merely wanted to disassociate itself from the festering scandal at Cambrian University which included the corruption, the theft of funds and, of course, the fire in The Learning Tower, which was news worldwide and which was bringing shame on the UK, not only focusing on the lax regulations at universities but across the whole country. Shit sticks, even if it's not your shit.

Crump and many others had acted bravely that night and saved lives. But what did that matter, when mere association with a disaster could bring your precious bureaucracy into disrepute and embarrass senior managers? These people always cover themselves, protect their own backs, and were perfectly willing to sacrifice any available innocent to further that ambition. These unjust self-serving people would drop you like a hot brick for the most fickle and trivial of reasons and throw you to the lions – though they wouldn't throw the brick at the lions. No, they'd ask an underling to do that then sack him for misconduct. That's the way it worked. And it stank. Worse, even, than his sickly deodorant.

"Right," said Crump to his EFL class, which had assembled on the pavement outside the Memorial Theatre where some lessons were taking place now that The Learning Tower was no more – though it still stood, a blackened shell, looming over the campus like an enormous gravestone.

He led his students through the swing doors into the foyer and reported to the desk.

The sour-faced woman behind it eyed him suspiciously over her spectacles, then said…

"One moment, please,"

… and went off into the back office.

The EFL students were helping themselves to leaflets about all the shows coming up – all the tedious tribute acts and fourth rate musicals, the unfunny stand-up comedians and the near-pervy ladies-night male stripper shows. There was literally nothing there that would interest Crump. It was all lowest-common-denominator stuff, like Saturday night TV, but much more expensive and uncomfortable, especially with the Munchkin-sized seats at that particular venue.

The ugly usherette returned, but this time on Crump's side of the counter.

"I must ask you to leave now," she snapped.

"But... I have a lesson... there's a room booked."

"Not for you, Mr Crump. Following... events... you are banned from this theatre."

"But... why?"

"Our risk assessment has identified you as a danger to children."

"What?" snapped Crump, his head throbbing. "*No, I am not!*"

"Yes, you are. You were arrested for sexual assault of a child under thirteen at the Christmas choir service, weren't you?"

His students had been listening in and were now whispering amongst themselves, flashing their teacher shifty looks.

"A malicious accusation was made against me – I was never charged – I was released – *No Further Action.*"

"That's as may be, but we have a responsibility to the public and a duty of care."

"Listen, these are my students. The university trusts me to teach them – alone. None is under eighteen or... thirteen... anyway, not that that would make any difference, but—"

"Leave please. Leave now," said the usherette, and now a knuckle-dragging security guard was there too, together with a rather girly and camp male usher, glaring at him.

Crump could see the sneaky face of the theatre manager Paul Pizzle appear at the window of the back office. This was all down to him, he knew. Maybe his arrest at Christmas had been too – it was he who'd submitted the video of Crump stumbling out of the audience to police, after all. Maybe he was in it with Abi Rainbow and Lesley Snyde?

Crump wished the whole damn place would burn down, burst into flames like The Learning Tower, and take Paul Pizzle, the ugly usherette and the rest with it.

He led his class to a local town centre café which was also participating in the scheme to offer the university teaching space. He could feel the little whispers of his students tickling his neck as he led his class to the new location. They'd never trust him again, he knew. That was how rumour worked – and people knew it too. Nothing had to be true. In a way, it was better if it wasn't when the gossips got to work.

"Fuck it!" Crump stated to his EFL class when they had settled in the basement classroom of the café.

The room smelt of old eggs, stale bacon and disinfectant. Crump felt sick, but swallowed it down, and breathed the noisome egg-smell through his mouth so as not to taste it.

He noticed that some students had peeled away and were not there – off to do shopping maybe, or abandoning a teacher they now knew had been arrested for sexual assault so was, in their eyes at least, deeply suspect and forever tainted. Who knew? Who cared? It was their loss.

He liked the ones who remained just because they were there. These were his loyal students, the ones who mattered, the ones he cared about. The others could fuck *right off*. His head throbbed through the dull fug of the painkillers.

"Teacher, you OK?" asked Ahmed, the takeaway guy.

"Too much drinking yes," laughed Rashid.

"No, too much life," replied Crump.

There they were: Bjorn, Mads, Birgitte, Chang, Julie, Fanny, Jesus, Massimo, Jordi, Koen, Heiner and a few others. His students. And he would teach them. Dammit!

"*Fuck!*" yelled Crump, making some students jump. "'Fuck' is wonderful word in English. So fucking versatile and expressive, with such utterly fucking varied grammatical nuances. It can be used to describe a fuck load of emotions and states of being, though it has lost some power in recent fucking years due to over-fucking-use by fuckers on the fucking telly."

Crump looked at his class. All international student eyes were wide awake, and more than a few mouths were hanging open.

"So, it can be a noun as in…"

Silence.

"… as in, 'what the fuck is that?'"

"What the fuck is that?" chanted the class.

"Good."

"Fucking good!" grinned Ahmed.

"Too fucking right!"

"Adjective?" asked Heiner.

"Abso-fucking-lutely! As in, 'it's a fucking beauty!'"

"It's a fucking beauty!" chanted the class.

"Or a verb, as in, 'the football match was fucked by the weather', transitive form, or the intransitive form: 'He totally fucked it up!'"

"He totally fucked it up!" chanted the class.

"Yes, I fucking did," said Crump.

"*Yes, I fucking did!*"

A hand went up.

"But this it is phrasal verb, no?" asked Jesus.

"By golly, I do believe he's got it! To fuck up, to fuck off, are indeed phrasal verbs."

Crump repeated the lesson with the Moronians later that day, almost word for word, which was a traditional trick for all hungover teachers.

"What the fuck?!"

"What the fuck?!"

"Fuck it blind!"

"Fuck it blind!"

"Go fuck yourself sideways!"

"Go fuck yourself sideways!"

"Who gives a fuck anyway?"

"Who gives a fuck anyway?"

"I'll be fucked if I do!"

"I'll be fucked if I do!"

"Good."

"Fucking good!"

"For fuck's sake fucking stop. I'm totally fucked…"

"I'm totally fucked…"

"Totally fucking knackered."

"Totally fucking knackered."

"How the fuck are you?"

"How the fuck are you?"

"OK, I think we'll end it there for today. Now, why don't you all fuck off."

"Fuck off!"

Marek came up to Crump after the lesson.

"Kev-een, you is OK?"

"Oh tickety-boo hunky-dory couldn't be better—"

"I think no."

"Sorry, Marek, just… tired… and other stuff…"

"Oh, I sorry. You is angry, Kev-een, yes? This is reason why you…"

Marek mimed drinking from a glass.

"Well, why the fuck not, eh, Marek? Getting pissed's the only real pleasure I've got these days."

Marek nodded his handsome head, but his large intelligent eyes looked sad. He clicked a number on his smartphone and held it to his ear.

"Kev-een, you do not worry, OK? It is no problem."

*

It was only when Crump got home that day that he realised who Marek had been calling.

"You not worry," said Eva. "I am good cooker, I making Polish kitchen for you – you liking the *soap* of chickens?"

"What? Oh, chicken *soup*? Medicine, they say. Yes, I love it – thanks Eva."

"I will can to make special *reseep*..."

"Oh, recipe, yes?"

"Is what I say."

Crump had smelt the soupy smell as soon as he'd opened his front door – something which had made him ponder yet again an eternal mystery of the universe: why does soup smell so bad but taste so good, when coffee smells so good but often tastes absolutely terrible?

"I am make special *reseep*, from *Zyd*... Juden?"

"Jews."

"I – *Ewa* – from Polish city Łodz who having many many Jew, and many factory for clothes, yes?"

"Oh, mills? Textiles, cotton, maybe like Manchester in the UK?"

"Yes, like this. Jew all dead when German come, War World Two."

"All of them?"

"Err... Some are live after..."

"Survived."

"Survive, yes. Then some *Zyd* coming from USSR, then go Israel after."

"Can't really blame them, I suppose..."

"Before war and Nazi, Jew was 30% population my city, over two hundred thousand persons. Now 300 only."

"Terrible. Just terrible."

Eva shrugged a 'yes'.

"But they give to us delicious *soap* of chickens, yes," she smiled, making a sign of the cross on her chest and kissing her fingers while lifting her eyes to heaven, before returning to her work in the kitchen.

"Chicken soup," called Crump after her, but it was no good – his Polish *cooker* was making *soap* of chickens and that was final.

Later, after Eva had left, Marek called round.

"She very good woman," he said.

"Eva makes very good chicken *soap*... I mean, soup."

"And you are not *chicken spring*, yes?"

Crump thought for a moment.

"Oh, *spring chicken*."

"Is what I say."

"No, I'm certainly not a spring chicken – over forty and all that, well on the way to being a fully paid-up old git. Practically one foot in the grave. Almost two."

Marek smiled his handsome confident smile at Crump.

"Kev-een, you are survivor, like *star of sea*..."

"What?" said Crump, brow furrowed in thought. "Oh, you mean a *starfish*?"

"Yes, *starfish*."

"Do you... errr... get many starfish in Moronia, Marek?" said Crump, trying to work out where the conversation was going.

"Kev-een. We are not have sea. But when starfish has leg cut off, it grow back?"

"I... presume so... but I don't really think it works for people –"

"Yes, it work. You get damage and hurt, they is cut you here and here and here..." said Marek, miming out the swiping stabs of a sword-wielding maniac. "In head, in heart, in balls, yes?"

Crump nodded. It was an effective metaphor for what he had been through.

"But you not dead, you survivor. You grow back."

Crump looked into the depth of Marek's certain eyes.

"You know, Kev-een, every life it come with death sentence. But not yet, yes?"

"Yes," said Crump, remembering all the pain, the hurt, the betrayal. He felt a lump in his throat, and was sure his eyes were moistening.

"Life it is not easy, it is not *cake piece*. It never come on plate. Life it must to be always the fight, it always the pain. You must to work hardly to make success. But you will to survive, yes? Like my country."

Crump nodded sadly.

"Kev-een, it is OK. Pressure, it make diamonds, yes? You are good man. Intelligent man. Strong man..."

Marek mimicked a strong man pose at this point and squeezed his own bulging biceps in his T-shirt.

"So you must to live your life. You must to grab the life by balls, yes? It is there, the life. You must to take it. Like when you fuck good woman!"

"Well... errr —"

"Kev-een, I want show you something."

Marek reached down into the bag he'd brought into the house and took out something wrapped in a towel. He slowly unwrapped it.

"Tell to me, Kev-een, what this is?"

Crump leaned forward to look.

"*Fucking hell!*" he gasped. "It's a *fucking gold bar!*"

"Yes. One only..." said Marek, handing it to Crump for a closer look. It was so heavy, he needed both hands to hold it.

"Is... is that what I think it is?" whispered Crump, peering closely at the mark stamped into its middle.

"Swastika? Yes, this is gold of fucking Nazi bastard... but we find in lake in Moronia. This bar twelve kilo, worth half million dollar."

"Fuck me," mouthed Crump, starring into the rich, buttery gold – it was like staring into the sun itself, such was the depth of colour.

"We find *ten thousand* gold bar in train who crash in lake. Half we are give to Jew and family in Israel and whole world. Half we are keep. Is fair, no?"

Crump nodded. It was.

"So... this is what you were arguing about in class the other day?"

Marek grinned a wide smile at Crump.

"This one thing, yes, but not only – "

"Marek," said Crump, handing him back the gold bar. "I hope you don't want to store any Nazi gold here like the fucking guns."

"This not necessary," laughed Marek.

Then a thought struck Crump.

"Wait here a moment, Marek," he said.

Crump returned with the South Sea Islander bags of bones and shrunken heads he had hidden in the loft – he couldn't face chucking them all back in the skip where he'd found them.

"Yes, we take!" grinned a delighted-looking Marek, holding up a shrunken head by the hair. "Wow! Is like Munchkins, yes? *Wizard in Oz*."

Crump momentarily thought of the theory he'd heard that *The Wizard of Oz* was actually a satire on the failure of the gold standard of the 1930s, with 'Oz' standing for 'oz' = ounces of gold.

"Well, thank you, Marek. You know there are regulations about... human remains... even old ones like these. If I dumped them or even gave them to a UK museum, I could be arrested – "

"Again?" tutted Marek, with a wonderful warm wink of an eye.

"Yes, again," groaned Crump.

"You do not worry. I take in diplomat bag to Moronia,

404

put in National Museum in capital city. No-one will to know where they from or who is giving."

"Thanks," said Crump, handing him the bag of bones and shrunken heads. And he meant it.

"Kev-een, why you stay here, in this town?"

Crump exhaled a large breath and shrugged.

"You should to live in best city of all world, Sgrot, in Democratic Republic of Moronia. There you can to start from scratches, yes? You will to be success, make money, having respect. Here, you will always be fail, always be loser? Tell to me truth, Kev-een."

"Well, yes, things haven't been exactly perfect, but I don't know about—"

"You must to change your life, you must to really living your life, yes? No-one else will to make this for you. You only. I can to help you, Kev-een. I can to—"

Just then, Crump's mobile rang.

It was the hospital calling – about Fatima.

CHAPTER TEN

Getting Out

Crump could see Fatima lying in a hospital bed through the internal ward window.

But he did not enter the room where she lay. Instead, he just stood and stared, loitering in the corridor. Why? Because he could hardly believe what he was seeing.

Dylan was there, sitting by her bed. He leant over and kissed Fatima. Then he kissed her again. Then once more, a long prolonged snog this time, with loving arms awkwardly around each other.

Then Dylan walked out of the ward, looking longingly back to Fatima as he left. He bumped into Crump, who was now going in.

"My bad," said Dylan instinctively, before looking up and realising who he'd run into.

"Most def," said Crump in a low whisper.

Dylan said nothing. The two just stared at each other, each shocked and wary, unsure how to react. And then, wordlessly, and stepping aside to walk around Crump, Dylan left.

'Dylan, you complete and utter little shit,' thought Crump.

Crump felt angry, yes – but more than that, stupid. How had he not twigged that Dylan and Fatima had been... *at it?*

But why would he? Fatima was an intelligent and sophisticated lady. And Dylan was, well, just Dylan. You wouldn't expect *her*… and *him*…

And anyway, she was a Muslim, albeit a liberal-minded modern French 21st-century model, and they weren't really supposed to… well… put it about a bit, were they?

Crump rubbed his sore eyes in confusion but made the effort to smile as he said hello to Fatima. Despite everything, he really didn't want to worry her. Her health came first, not his issue with Dylan. And he knew he still loved her, no matter what.

She had a cut above her eye that had been treated, and one side of her face was red and swollen, though blue bruises were blackening under the skin.

"They attack me, on the street nearby to my apartment, hitting me, kicking me, the Islamist Fascist."

"Did you see who they were? Was it the same ones as at uni?"

"They are wearing masks, you know, bandana over their faces, so I just see their eyes… so angry… I thought they would —"

"So what… happened?"

"My neighbour he is coming outside and they run away. They are shouting in Arabic, calling me whore and *kaffir*… telling me to wear hijab… niqab… burqa."

"But you feel OK, yes?"

"*Oui*… it is… the shock. They are doing tests, just in case."

"And the police?"

Fatima laughed cynically.

"*Bof, les flics* – the cops… police. *Putain!* They tell me '*wear your headscarf*' – they say I was provoking the attackers of me."

"Seriously?"

"Is the same in all West countries – Muslim women must cover up or else, it is your fault for not being modest.

Like French artists also who draw Mohammed cartoons. Police are blaming them when Jihadi Fascist are killing them!"

Crump didn't know what to say. Instead, he sat in silence by the bed, holding Fatima's hand. Then he said it:

"I saw... Dylan," he said, immediately regretting his selfishness, and about to apologise: "I mean, I—"

"I am sorry, Kevin," said Fatima, through a weak smile.

"It's OK, really... I... don't want to *'pee in your sugar sandwich'*."

"*Qua?*"

"Oh, it's nothing, just a..."

Fatima squinted in confusion. This was neither the time nor the place to explain Danish idioms, so he dropped it. But then he couldn't help himself continuing with his line of questioning:

"But... with Dylan. I mean, *Dylan*! He's so..."

"He is very pretty boy."

"Well he's pretty something, I'll give you that."

"*Moi, je...* I like him. So soft skin the colour of honey, so slim with hard muscles, so much energy in the bed and—"

"OK, OK... I get the idea," said Crump, curling up inside like a salted slug.

"Sorry," said Fatima.

"No, it's OK. I hope you're very happy together... in love... maybe get married in future, and—"

"*Mais non*, it is just the sex," said Fatima, so matter-of-fact it shocked Crump.

When he had recovered, he asked:

"Well couldn't you have *just the sex* with me?

Fatima laughed.

She had a lovely laugh.

And smiled.

Crump had always adored her smile.

"Oh no, you are very silly."

"Why?" said Crump, trying not to whine. "I mean, why not?"

Fatima was about to say something, then paused.

"Go on – I won't be offended," he lied.

Pause.

Breathe.

And so, we begin...

"*Alors*, well, you are old."

"*Merci beaucoup.*"

"And, you are not pretty – "

"OK. Not on the outside, granted, but – "

"And *alors...* well... you are ginger."

"So's Prince Harry. Ed Sheeran too!"

"For us Muslims and also French persons, red hair is looking *très horrible*, very horrible... *ughhh!*"

"Thanks... yes... I get the idea."

"I mean really so *so* ugly, like *troll, comme un homme déformé*, deformed most horribly, *comme un monstre très hideux*, a monster too hideous, *tu sais*, like *Fantôme* in the opera, *non?*"

"Well, nobody's perfect..." said Crump.

'Probably got concussion,' he thought – Fatima really had been saying some very strange and odd things lately, after all.

Then she smiled, beautifully.

"I pull ever so gently the leg, *non?*"

Crump smiled back, weakly.

The nurse arrived with a porter ready to take Fatima off for more tests or scans or X-rays...

But Crump felt as though he had just been blasted with a very high dose of something much worse than radiation...

*

"So, if I could just say thank you to everyone who took the revision classes over the Easter vacation, and welcome to the new term. Yay!"

"Yay!"

Tanya Snuggs was back to her old ebullient self, all wide gap-toothed smile and pink-tastic bouncy dress, though she did still look tired. But then, so did Crump – and he felt TOTT – *tired all the time* – too.

Karen Crisp was away on sick leave, apparently, so Tanya was, as ever, carrying the full burden of managing the department.

"First of all, I have to say how well everyone coped after the fire… it was all so totally *disbelievable*… especially in the *twennieth centurine* – or even *twenny* or thirty years ago in the nineteenth… but the *gover-ment* and *enviromental* health inquiry is ongoing so I'm not gonna get *melon-dramatic* or be a *fear-mongrel* or look for *escaped goats*."

'Just as well,' thought Crump, 'Wales may be full of fucking sheep, but not many goats escape to them there hills…'

"And just to say I know we all wish Ben Chu, a second-year student, well. As some of you may know, he was attacked last week on the street."

"Disgusting!" said someone.

"And he wasn't even Jewish," said another.

Crump thought. Was Ben Chu, a Hong Kong Chinese heritage student, attacked by the same Islamo-thugs responsible to the attack on Fatima? Did they attack Ben Chu because they thought he was a 'Chu' = a 'Jew'? If so, they were not only disgusting Islamofascists, they were the thickest thugs in history.

"*By in large*, it's a *doggy-dog-world* out there, so be careful, guys."

"We will," said someone, as Crump groaned inwardly at the mutty mutilation of the English language.

"So now we have to make sure everything is *moderficated* properly, so we're all *ringing* off the same hymn sheet, with no *complicatory* crossed *spires*, so we make absolutely sure everything *passes mustard*. Yes, Melanie."

"And, marking...?"

"We must give the benefit of the doubt, for all essays and dissertations, especially for our international students. No fails here – ever. Just *deferred success.*"

'Ah, *deferred success*,' thought Crump.

It was a term he had first heard at Thames Met in London a decade ago, and it still amazed with its rather slippery, yet admirable, syntax. Estate agents used '*deceptively large*' to mean 'small' – well, this was just the education professional's equivalent. For 'fail'.

Universities were now full of the sort of brash, self-loving, bean-counting, statistics-bending types who would otherwise have been suited to selling second-hand cars.

"*To all intensive purposes*, no-one fails, so everyone's a winner, yay!" continued Tanya Snuggs. "Any *not-so-good* papers, bring to me please. Students must be *opportunificated* to resubmit."

"And exams?" asked Hilary Squonk.

"Revision classes arranged, I think, Kevin?"

"Errr, yes, I'm doing them – and Shabs?"

"Yo, man."

"I mean, the marking..."

"All marking up, as before, Hilary, as far as I can *abba-stain...*"

'What?' thought Crump. 'Abba stain? With Björn, Benny, Agnetha and Anni-Frid doing the dirty with Swedish bodily fluids between the sheets to *Dancing Queen*?'

"Oh, *ascertain!*" said Crump, without realising he was talking out loud.

"Is there something you wish to *interjaculate*, Kevin?"

Crump shook his head meekly and studied his shoes.

"Right, so, marking will be *moduficated* and *standardisation-ated*, as usual."

'Ah the magic of modulation,' Crump thought with a smile – how a department's entire marks could all be lifted by 10% or more to boost them and make sure everyone crossed the finish line to grade-inflated good degree glory.

The theory was that marking up, rather than down, was fair, as was lowering the bar to ensure more hard-working students got degrees, and mostly 2.1s or 1st too – which now comprised 70%+ of all degree awards, in stark contrast to results twenty or thirty years before when most got 2.2s. The thinking was that such positive marking would motivate students, ensure they were not disadvantaged in the workplace, against both native and foreign competition for jobs, and that graduates would go on to golden, well-paying careers in future, all thanks to their top grades and degrees from a university which could then perhaps expect, in time, a contribution from its successful, well-off alumni.

However beautiful the theory, however, it's always a good idea to look at the results.

The incessant grade inflation of recent decades, together with the fact that half the population now go on to higher education had, in effect, massively devalued all degrees, past and present. Employers who had long experience of semi-literate graduate application forms now routinely set their own tests and exams for applicants because they just did not trust the grades and skills stated on paper qualifications any more.

So what if there was a chronic and desperate shortage of those trained in vocational trades such as plumbing, electrics, carpentry, or engineering, nursing, the hospitality trade, which all had a glut of job vacancies that couldn't be filled? So long as universities got paid millions to churn out yet more graduates, many of them woefully unacademic, in the arts/humanities/media/ social sciences, then all was well with the world, even if most ended up working in Tesco's at best, or unemployed. Such was the game played at UK universities these days.

And, literally, no-one could fail. The magic of modulation was merely a final trick to ensure all had prizes. As well as that, there was pre-marking by tutors, again and again, if necessary, pointing out to students exactly where they should improve their essays and how, to get those high grades. And then there was the marking up, so much giving of the benefit of the doubt that there was probably a shortage of it by now.

It was, Crump had to admit, all teaching to the test and all – absolutely all – about getting the grades. Not really about thinking better, learning how to ask better questions, challenging convention and orthodox views (such a dangerous attitude could get you sacked these days for being at odds with university diversity and inclusion policies!) or thinking for oneself.

It was all about weighing the pig to try and make it heavier, just as in so many UK schools, where children were over-examined and over-tested and teachers were grade-obsessed to the detriment of, well, everything else, including a good education, because that was, these days, the very definition of their job.

It all begged the question:

'What is education for?'

Surely everyone involved with it in any way should at least attempt an answer to that question? Was it to train cannon fodder up for the battlefield of the workplace? Was it to provide exam-factories, churning out cheap paper with the right rubber stamps, which will make everyone – students, parents, money-grubbing universities – ever so proud? Was it just a scheme to keep kids off the streets, save parents' sanity and give teachers something to do on a salary? Or was education a noble endeavour, drenched in culture and the quest for knowledge, as it encouraged individuals to think for themselves and to ask better questions? Who knew? But, in these pig-weighing days, it was seldom the latter option, it seems.

Whatever the truth, all involved in education should know this: half of what we know as fact will one day be proved false. The question is – which half?

Which half? Snout or wiggly tail?

It was certainly true that 'weighing the pig' had become far more important than checking it was still breathing or whether it had choked to death on its own shame and disillusion. And it was *all* about weighing the pig these days.

"Oink oink oink," Crump mumbled to himself as he collected his huge batch of submitted dissertations to mark. It was going to be a long, short summer term, and Crump's last at Cambrian University, unless he applied to be taken on and was accepted. He knew he had more chance of catching swine flu, frankly.

If you're not worried, you don't understand the problem.

*

"Pan-fried sea-bass?" said Rob. "As opposed to what? Land-bass fried on the fucking ceiling of a burning building, or maybe on the bonnet of a shit-hot supercar belonging to some spoilt brat boy-racer rag-head Arab prince whizzing round Knightsbridge?"

Crump had to admit Rob had a point – the pretentious drivel of swish restaurant menus, all drizzled this, and foam that, and home-made organic the other, had always been a niggle. Just as well he couldn't afford to eat in them then, really.

"I… I'll pay you back for the house, Rob – when I get sorted, get another job, a mortgage, and—"

"Worry worry worry – just like when we was in school.

414

Ain't you never gonna change, Crumpet?"

"Prob'ly not," sighed Crump.

Rob now owned the end-of-terrace house where Crump lived. Everything had been processed by the council and, after many months, he'd received a cheque for what was left after his mum's care home fees were deducted – a nice five-figure sum which would see him through, but the house had gone now. He trusted Rob, and it was very generous of him to help an old schoolmate out, even though they had certainly not been bosom buddies back in the day – but Crump felt uncomfortable living in a house now owned by Rob, even rent-free. It was yet more insecurity in his life, and for that most basic thing: a home. In that, he had a lot in common with a huge swathe of the British population, he knew – just as he knew so many others owned two or more homes. He was on the wrong side of the line – the one that divided the prosperous baby boomer home-owning winners, and the forever-renting penniless losers.

"Fake it till you make it, mate! Be yourself, Crumpet. Enjoy life! Do what you wanna do, 100%. And fuck the rest."

"I was thinking of... maybe... applying to the university for a job, despite all the redundancies – though the problem is teaching's a deeply conservative profession, and I'm an outsider, and with... 'form'... so to speak... so..."

"I thought teachers was all loonie lefties?" said Rob, finishing his pre-dinner pint.

"I mean conservative with a small 'c', not Tories – they don't like change – they love procedure – and as for having any criminal history, even if just arrests, or warnings for racism or sexism—"

"Listen, mate. If you try to be all things to everybody, you end up being nothing to nobody, you hear?"

"Yes, but—"

"And you're a white bloke in a system that hates 'em. Fuck diversity – that's what I say – I ain't havin' none of it. Merit is all. I don't care if the people I pay are male, female, inbetweenies, black, white, blue or fucking green with pink stripes – all that matters is if they can do the fucking job. End of."

Crump finished his pint.

"Not the way they think these days, Rob, what with targets and quotas and—"

"FUCK DIVERSITY. It's all a fucking lie, aimed at doing one thing – culling better white men to overpromote fourth-rate women and ethnics. Just look around you – the council, the government, the police, the Brexit-bashing BBC who got over three billion of our hard-earned dosh every year, every fucking state-run tax-gobbler and now corporate business an' all, they're all keen to tick the fucking boxes, to parachute in the box-tickers, leapfrog 'em over the better candidates, the ones who achieved on merit, the ones who know what the fuck they're doing and know how to do their jobs – and people wonder why the world is so right royally fucking fucked up."

"Well… I'm sure they try to choose the best candidates – it's just common sense—"

"Common sense ain't very common no more, though, is it? And that's what those subsidy monkey cunts who run our universities are like. Seats of learning, my arse! More like Barnum and Bailey circuses where the clowns and freaks, all them flake students, actually pay tens of thousands of pounds to look fucking ridiculous and leave with fuck-all of any real value, just a piece of pissing paper saying they turned up at boring lectures for three years which put 'em fifty grand in debt!"

"Maybe… a *little* harsh, Rob," said Crump, though he had to admit to himself that, after what he'd seen going at in higher education, he couldn't completely disagree.

416

As the food arrived and more pints too, Crump thought back to his school days. True, most of the boys at his single-sex grammar school had been white, though some had one or more foreign parents. According to the present diversity ethos, all those white male manikins were exactly the same in absolutely every respect, like identical Caucasian clones, and all enjoyed such white male privilege in life that they'd never have to work hard to achieve anything as it would all fall magically into their laps, just above their irredeemably male balls.

The truth, however, was that his fellow schoolboys were all so different – led such different lives, in different homes, with different parents, some richer, some poorer, some country mice and some city rats growing up in south-east London council flats. They were, in essence, as different as all other individuals. And yet the diversity and equality 'industry' lumped the lot together in a white male blob, which could then be neatly hated as 'the enemy' and kept down – though, of course, the really privileged white males (and female and brown and black kids too) would thrive, no matter what. This, apparently, was *real equality in action*!

Such diversity-inspired discrimination happened routinely in all institutions and organisations in the UK now, probably topped by the *BB-She*, whose cull of white males lately was much admired, especially by those who had taken their jobs. Diversity worship was almost the new state religion, and woe betide you if you dared challenge or question it – that way led to a heretic's dead end, a cancel culture virtual burning at the stake, with no career or income, and a life in perpetual professional exile.

"S'all a no-brainer, Crumpet."

"What is?"

"You gotta come work for me – out in Thailand. You'd love it—"

"Oh, I don't know, I—"

417

"Just started a new company selling land mines that look like prayer mats. *Prophets* are going through the roof. Eh? Ha-ha!"

Crump knew what would have happened if he'd made that joke, or much milder ones, at university. Some woke snitch of a spy would've reported him, probably a so-called friend too, and he'd be on a suspension again or get yet another written warning as a minimum.

It could be said that Crump had always had a lot of 'alternative friends' – or 'enemies', as some called them. The problem was, so many seemed friendly at first. Then they let you down, stabbed you in the back, betrayed you – like Dylan, and so many others. He didn't trust anything or anyone any more. How could he, after everything?

The food felt and tasted undercooked – though Crump remembered from his rare visits to posh restaurants in the past, that this was how those willing to pay a hundred quid for lunch liked it. That and massive white square plates – or, worse, pieces of slate or slices of wood on which some teeny-weeny meal was served, though thankfully the place they were in used proper crockery, at least.

"Food OK, Crumpet?"

"Delicious," he lied – another ten minutes in the oven would've cooked it properly.

"Bit of a chubster, meself. I loves me grub!"

Rob's ample belly strained against his shirt buttons as if to confirm it.

"D'you know, what some muppet Remoaner said to me th'other day – that Brexit was a shambles – a *Brexit shitstorm*, he called it."

"A complete *catawampus* —"

"You what?"

"Oh, it's just one of my favourite rarely used archaic words in English – American origin, I think. It means something that has gone badly awry. Nothing to do with cats—"

"You book-learners, eh?" tutted Rob. "By the way, Crumpet – is it *referendums* or *referenda*? Fucked if I know, innit?"

"Well, *referendum* is a neuter case word in Latin, and the plural of those usually end with an 'a' – "

"*Referenda* then?"

"But, in Latin, there was no plural form of *referendum* – the word '*referenda*' simply did not exist in Ancient Rome – they used *referendum* for both singular and plural..."

"Hmm..."

"And, of course, in English in everyday usage, we add an 's' to form a standard plural, even with words from the Latin, as in '*stadium*', '*stadiums*', though some people do say '*stadia*' – it's all a stylistic issue, really. I'd say only keep the Latin or Greek forms for technical, scientific, biological terms – for everyday words, use English plural forms."

"So..."

"There are no rules, basically. Like Brexit, I suppose. I'd say the plural is *referendums* or even *referendum*. But others could argue *referenda* was right."

"Well, fuck me," said Rob, "you really are an academic expert, ain't'cha?"

"I just... know my stuff, I suppose. Like you in business."

Rob sighed deeply, puffed his cheeks out, then continued:

"Anyhoo, so..."

"So... what did you say?" asked Crump, forcing himself to swallow what felt like a half-cooked piece of semi-raw boiled potato. Organic, of course.

"Well, I said that it may be a Brexit shitstorm, but at least it's *our* Brexit shitstorm, eh? Cheers ears!"

"It certainly is," said Crump.

They clinked pint glasses and drank, for Brexit and anything else that was going really. These days Crump needed no excuse to get drunk.

It was all just another mad bonkers day in barmy Brexit-land.

"All this crap about 'Brexit wounds' and a 'national nervous breakdown' and all that – them tantrums are like the Brexit-hating Remainiac version of mad cow disease, and believe me, cor blimey, I've known a few mad cows in my time, me old *cowson* Crumpet!"

It had been years since Crump had heard that old Cockney insult. But then the English spoken in London was now not Cockney, certainly not in the mostly Bangladeshi East End, not now that all the real, or perhaps imagined, *Cock-er-neys* had moved out to Essex or southern Spain, seeking asylum from the latest unwelcome wave of mass immigration and the consequent, imposed multicultural diversity.

No, the new sociolect was MLE – 'Multicultural London English' – or, as some commentators called it, 'speaking black', or '*Jafaican*'. Language changes as regularly as the rain in Britain, and always will. *Innit?*

"S'like, most people in all them shithole countries in the world want to come here – and I feel sorry for the poor bastards, I really do. But they can't all come here, can they? Too many come here already and brung a loada shit wiv 'em an all."

"Rob, we're in a Thai restaurant – the owner, chef and waiters here all came from somewhere else."

"I know I know, and I'm a fucking foreigner where I spend half the year an' all – you gotta come over to Thailand, land of smiles, Crumpet – just to visit, eh?"

Crump nodded and smiled as 'yes'. He wasn't sure if he wanted to work for Rob or live in the Far East – though, if nothing else turned up…

But the thought of a free holiday somewhere exotic at some unspecified point in the future sounded good, and even better too now he was on his fourth pint. The world always looked better through the beer window.

"Just look at London now, our overcrowded cities. Young couples got no chance of setting up home, what with house prices, which go up and up the more people rock up here."

"It's a big problem," said Crump.

"One of many, and that's why people voted in their droves to let the Euro-fuckers go down with their own sinking ship. '*The EU contains within it the seeds of its own downfall*' – that's what those in the know are saying, financiers and that. And what did that Gorby once say? That our leaders were recreating the Soviet Union in Western Europe?"

"I don't think we have any gulags yet though—"

"You wait, Crumpet, when the Krauts stop their charity subsidy to the EU and its toy money Euro, it'll drop as quick as a slag's knickers, and then they'll all be going down Titanic-fashion – and we Brits ain't gonna send no fucking lifeboats either, not the way they treated us. Glug glug glug. Ha-ha!"

"People were... are very angry, it's true," said Crump.

"A land of anger – a disunited kingdom? Bollocks. You ever been to Greece? They're practically eating their children now they're so fucking poor, and half young people in Europe are on the dole and skint."

"We have more in common than that which divides us," said Crump, lifting his pint.

"Oh yeah," grinned Rob, raising his own glass, "the tiny stupid differences between us ain't nothing compared to the great big stupid similarities, eh? Cheers!"

"Cheers!" said Crump, and they drank.

"Maybe they'll get in the Old Girl to sort it out..."

Crump's alcohol-addled brain frowned his face in spacy confusion.

"The Queen, Crumpet. Her Maj. Brenda."

"Oh, yes, of course."

"Yeah, she'd knock a few fucking heads together, get 'em to take their fingers outa their expense-account arses, eh? Kraut blood, see – always been good at that sort of malarkey, the Germans. Could all be Millwall really, when you fink about it. Cheers!"

Crump had to admit that history did seem rather to prove that point rather than rebut it, however crude the stereotype. But then, all stereotypes *were* based on truth, often a partial truth and/or an outdated one – like the gin-swilling racist stereotypes of bowler-hatted Brits in Bollywood films – but still emanating from reality, no matter how much the usual pc suspects argued they had come from nowhere, or had maybe been created out of pure spite by evil racist/sexist people in a room somewhere.

And he also had to admit that, what with the present Brexit mess and an angry divided land to reign over, he really wouldn't have blamed the Old Lady – AKA Her Majesty, Queen Elizabeth II, 'The Old Girl' – for lining up the G&Ts on her priceless Chippendale desk at the palace and staying permanently pickled, so as to facilitate a more painless reading of the Brexit headlines in the newspapers and make it unscathed through yet another right royal day.

Like most people, Crump was now sick of hearing about 'Brexit' and all the endless, parroted, repeated, angry arguments for and against, swirling around in their firm certain circles, which never got anywhere or led to anyone ever changing their mind or learning anything new, or even listening to other people's opinions as they endlessly yelled their own dearly held beliefs. Nobody ever listened to anyone else any more – not really.

The UK was more or less evenly split along Remain/ Leave lines regarding *EU-know-what*, just as it had been in the 2016 referendum – the idea that anyone much had changed their minds was sheer fantasy. You could repeat a referendum a thousand and one times, and each result would be roughly the same, split down the middle, varying by a couple of percentage points at most. So about half the voters would be unhappy, no matter what. It was not a recipe for success or for creating a united country at ease with itself.

And Crump knew he'd abstain again, by spoiling his ballot, because no other option made any sense – not to him anyway.

Britain was divided, more so perhaps at any time since the 17th-century. But then, so seemingly was everywhere else – the USA, and every European nation too. Maybe it was just the times we were living in.

And maybe Britain, as well as its constituent nations, had always been split, albeit under the polite veneer of post-war politics, and it just needed the referendum result to make us realise that?

But life went on, no matter what, no matter what anyone thought, or how angrily or loudly anyone shouted. Sound and fury signifying nothing, indeed. And it did always rather seem that most of the noise came from the shallow end of the swimming pool...

Thus it was that Crump made a promise to himself that drunken day, if only for the sake of his sanity and peace of mind, never to use 'the B word' again and to turn off any TV or radio or internet broadcast in which the dreaded word *Br***t* was ever mentioned. The rotting of politics could go on without him.

He'd had enough.

And the funny thing was, he felt better already.

*

Crump sat in the sun on the campus, a safe, cordoned-off distance from The Learning Tower which was now wrapped up in a giant sheet, behind which various white-suited forensic and crime scene specialists were investigating the possible causes of the fire.

He'd just invigilated an exam and had another that afternoon. It was, quite possibly, the easiest yet more boring task a teacher ever had to do. Keeping busy doing nothing was hard – very hard – especially with a hangover when all you could think about was how soft and warm it would be to be still lying in bed. It was a real struggle to keep his eyes open.

The world media was still there, in spits and spots, though the blue starry European flags were fewer than before, now the university had dropped its claim to independence and its historic claim for continued EU membership. Britain would be transitioning with Brexit, and taking the defeated rebel Euro-enclave of Cambrian University with it, like it or not.

"Tidy!" said Dean Guttery to a workman as he emerged from the main university building with Mr Scumble. It was good to see those guys back in the jobs they were born to do, and Crump had noticed how things actually seemed to work in university buildings now – lights, doors, plumbing.

In complete contrast was the forlorn figure of Mx Abi Rainbow. Crump could see her standing there, some way off, sitting on a wall sipping a coffee, looking worried and anxious, and more than anything else, deflated. He hadn't seen her around for weeks, though that had suited him just fine.

How she had changed – her whole look, her demeanour, her very being. Her angry eyes no longer burned with rage but were subdued with worry, making eye contact with the ground only, avoiding the gaze of passers-by. If the maintenance managers seemed more 'full' and fleshed-out after being reinstated to their former roles, then Abi Rainbow looked *less* somehow, deflated and small, as if she'd shrunk since he'd last had the misfortune to see her. She was not at all scary-looking any longer, though the weird piercings still studded her face, which was still topped by a ridiculous blue Mohican haircut, though even that was wilting limp now. She just looked pathetic – like a drowned parrot.

Crump supposed that was what happened to puppets when their string-pulling masters were no more. Her strings had been cut and she was flailing around lost, no wind in her sails, if that was not mixing too many metaphors. She had merely been a pawn of the nasty, spiteful, vindictive twisted Lesley Snyde anyway.

Suddenly, the peace was disturbed by the sharp piercing sound of female shrieking:

"Abigail! Abigail, really! Come here at *once*, you silly girl!"

Crump watched as a woman of mature years appeared, dressed in twinset and no doubt imitation pearls, with a knee-length skirt, looking like a refugee from the 1950s. Her hairdo was pure young-Mrs-Thatcher, though she lacked a hat.

"What on earth have you done to your hair?" she snapped, walking up to what was obviously her daughter and looking her up and down in disgust. "And your clothes, and earrings on your face, and tattoos. You look like something out of the circus!"

Abigail stood in her punk-ish garb, her limp lacklustre blue Mohican wilting on her worried head, her head hanging down in defeat. How utterly pathetic she looked. Crump almost felt sorry for her. Almost – but not quite. This man-hating, vindictive, spiteful liar had almost ruined his life with her malicious accusations, even if the truly evil Lesley Snyde had been the one in ultimate control. He wished her all the worst.

"You silly girl, Abigail. Dressed up like some tuppenny hussy, while your poor father breathes his last on his death bed."

Abi Rainbow looked up – a lost little girl, not at all the angry, scary man-hating force so many had feared. She glimpsed Crump observing her from where he sat some distance away on a bench. His cold stare was blank and unblinking. Abi's face was dazed, as it gazed at an innocent man she'd accused of sexual assault of both her and her child – if the boy, who she dressed as a girl, even was her child. Crump now suspected it was her female partner's son anyway, not Abigail's at all – which was a blessing for the father, at least, even if he did come from (or into) a test tube.

Then, wordlessly, Abigail's mum grabbed her daughter's hand and, as if she was a naughty little madam petulantly pouting in her party dress, yanked her away and marched her towards the car park. Abi looked back – at the campus, at Crump, at all the staring students, and at Dylan who had now appeared. She would never be back. They all knew that.

We are all the authors of our own stories in this little blip of existence called life.

This was hers.

Crump looked up at Dylan. It was days since he'd seen him last – at the hospital – and Fatima was now back at her flat, recovering and resting up.

"Sit down, if you want," said Crump.

The kid sat beside him on the bench. He looked nervous.

"It's OK, Dylan, I don't mind about... well, I do... but... I'm not angry or... well, I am... but... what I mean is... that... I'm not going to... hit you, or anything."

It was a stupid thing to say. A quick, young, lithe kid like Dylan could probably kick Crump's arse in a couple of moves, even in his usual semi-comatose stoned state.

"Cool," said Dylan. "Dope."

"What?"

"It means... sick... like, bad... kindathing."

"Wicked," said Crump, sounding like an 80s music video.

Dylan gave him a pitying look, like a favourite nephew at a sad 1980s uncle who'd just given him a Betamax video recorder for Christmas.

"My bad," said Dylan, "for everything, like – Fatima —"

"Yes, well," said Crump, "to be honest, I'm surprised you had the energy for… whatever."

"Whatever," shrugged Dylan, opening a packet of crisps.

The kid seemed to subsist on an almost exclusive diet of fast food, snacks, pizza, chocolate bars and the empty calories of carbonated drinks. Crump felt a sort of wonder at the fact he was still alive. That he had, according to Fatima, a rock-hard athletic body that could keep at it like a rabbit for hours on end, would have made Crump sick with envy if he'd been young enough to care, or, more accurately, thought he stood any chance whatsoever of achieving the same manly boyish standard. That he didn't, liberated him from such green-eyed monstrous thoughts – to some extent, anyway. But he *so* envied Dylan, just being with Fatima.

"I bet you were the kind of kid at school who got the most Christmas cards from the girls, and maybe some boys," said Crump.

Dylan smirked and smiled, sheepishly.

"I know, you see, because I was always the kid in the corner planning to burn down the world —"

"Random, kindathing."

"Most def," sighed Crump.

"Oh, that theatre guy got arrested for being a paedo, I heard," said Dylan.

"What – Paul Pizzle – from the Memorial Theatre? In charge of the children's choir?"

Dylan nodded knowingly.

"The perv was secretly filming the kids in the toilets and stuff. Lost his job now."

"What a shame," said Crump, a snide smile curved onto his face.

"Not really – he's a paedo."

"No, Dylan, I was being ironic."

Silence.

"Which means I meant the opposite of what I said."

"But why?" said Dylan. "What's the point of that, kindathing?"

"No idea," said Crump with a sigh, taking a clump of crisps from Dylan's offered bag and crunching them into corny mush in his mouth. It was nice not to talk sometimes, and just to chew, munch and swallow...

"So, what you gonna do now, like?" said Dylan after a while.

"Job-wise?"

Dylan shrugged a nod.

"Oh, I've... got a plan..."

"Everyone's got a plan until they get punched in the mouth."

"Muhammad Ali?" asked Crump.

"Mike Tyson," said Dylan.

And they sat in silence for a few moments contemplating the truth of Iron Mike's words of wisdom.

"I could apply for something here," Crump said at last, "but... well... hundreds of redundancies happening at Cambrian Uni now, so... or... I could apply to other colleges... unis... companies... Or maybe go abroad... I taught English in foreign climes a few years ago... so..."

"So, you haven't got a clue, have you, kindathing?"

"Nope," sighed Crump. "Totally clueless – that's me."

"Most def," said Dylan, with a wry spacy smile.

"I could sell my body, I suppose," said Crump, a glint in his eye. "What d'ya think I'd get?"

Dylan thought a bit, then said:

"Dunno. 20p?"

"Well, that's almost half a bag of crisps anyway, I suppose... so I wouldn't starve... if I sold it twice..."

They laughed together.

"Too dangerous being a dodgy prostitute though..." said Crump.

"Don't worry, kindathing. Only popular people ever get murdered, and you're not popular."

"YOLO," laughed Crump.

"Most def," said Dylan, with a grin.

*

The summer term plodded on, as they do – with marking and exams and early summer sunshine mingling with the mid-May rain.

Some lessons, too, with those wanting revision still or the political classes, such as the Moronians. Crump thought he'd teach them all the difference between what British people say and what they actually mean.

"So, 'We'll see' means..."

"'No!'" chanted the class.

"And 'with the greatest respect' means... yes, Oksana."

"'I do not respect you at all and I think you are idiot'."

"Good! And 'I hear what you say' means... yes, Zoltan."

"'I disagree with your absurd opinion and do not want to discuss further'."

"Excellent!"

"And 'that is not bad' mean..." said Taras.

"It mean 'that is good'," said Svetlana.

The class almost cheered. No-one had ever told them any of this before, how what Brits say and mean are often polar opposites.

"And 'that is an interesting proposal' means?" asked Crump.

"'You are insane!'" grinned Tomek.

"Oh yes," said Crump, "and 'I'm fine' means..."

"'I am want to die'," suggested the ever-saturnine Vladimir.

"'But I am enduring the misery of existence for yet another day'," smiled Crump, "or, at least, that is one option."

"Perfect!" laughed Marek, and the whole class gave Crump a round of applause.

Later, in the lunch break, Crump was able to peruse the local *Cambrian Daily News* which was, as per usual, crammed with world-shattering news about bin collections, potholes, and complaints about parking, noisy students and the council.

But it did have an update on what was happening at the university – on the police inquiry and the inspectorate now investigating how The Learning Tower fire started and spread so devastatingly quickly.

Crump also learnt from it that Boyo Bellylaughs MBE was to present that year's much-vaunted but arguably rather racist and divisive MOBO awards, now that he was the premier black comedian in Britain.

There was a report on the shocking case of Paul Pizzle and the Memorial Theatre children's choir too...

And a feature on Welsh nationalists who were expanding their initiative to help local homeless people and distribute food to them. They were the real lovers of their country, Crump knew – the Welsh that Wales can be proud of. Not the thuggish bigoted nationalists who think spitting insults and abuse at anyone with an English accent made them strong and proud.

Then, on an inside page, there was an obituary – of *BBC Thinking Today* broadcaster and Christian academic Ridley Crick. He had been in Africa when the fire at the university had happened, which might have been considered a lucky escape, were it not for his insistence on baptising some devout natives in the local crocodile-infested river.

It was unclear whether the locals had, for reasons even less clear, omitted to inform him of the reptilian risks involved in going anywhere near the water, or whether Ridley Crick's faith meant he thought the Lord would protect him.

Either way, God moved in mysterious ways, apparently. Though the only thing that was moving now was the flesh and bone that used to be Ridley Crick which was making its way through the digestive tract of three large crocodiles, together with the remains of a native 'saved' by his baptism.

'The BBC's loss is nature's gain,' thought Crump as he turned the page.

*

"Oh, I'm so glad!" said Crump.

He was with Esther Isaacs and Khalid in a local vegetarian café, in between exam invigilation duties.

"But why didn't he contact anyone before?"

"Silly bugger got himself addicted – to opioids – big issue now, in the US especially – over ten million silly buggers there hooked on them."

"All legal," added Khalid, "both prescriptions and dodgy suppliers online too – fentanyl, oxycodone, the lot."

Pete Parzival had emailed Esther to let her know he was now in Nepal and, after going through withdrawal and getting clean, had become a Buddhist monk.

Esther showed Crump her smartphone screen and photos of Pete complete with shaved head and purple robes. As he was half Hong Kong Chinese, Crump had to admit he looked the part, despite the stereotyping involved. He couldn't imagine himself as a Buddhist monk in Nepal really – he didn't think they had all that many gingers out there.

Crump read his email:

I had to get out. Just leave, go, kick the pills. So I came to Tibet. Here, I have learnt the concept of balance, of knowing there are very few things in this world and

431

this life that are absolutely certain. To know we are all flawed individuals, to know we have a higher purpose, that we have to respect all life and all lives, including our own OMG.

That life is short, and we must strive to be enlightened. We should always be open to discussion and learning. And learn to listen to others, to the earth, to ourselves.

I have had time to think.

About the beautiful things and the terrible things. The things that matter and the things that don't. The things that will die with us and the things that will live on.

OMG life is so short.

Happy here in Tibet.

Be kind. Peace.

Pete P

'So that's his journey,' thought Crump, 'his way to travel with the troublesome turning of the Earth.'

"Well, at least he's happy," he said, smiling warmly at the photos of Pete Parzival in Nepal.

"And you?" asked Esther.

"I just play it by ear – see what happens…"

"Life isn't about finding yourself. Life is about creating yourself," said Khalid.

"George Bernard Shaw, I think?" asked Crump.

"I thought it was *Game of Thrones*. Sounds good anyway, even to my logical legal ears – and I'm from Yorkshire. Nowt gets past me, lad."

"Well, I don't count my chickens," said Crump. "I've had far too many struggle out of their eggs only to gasp their last before they even get to their feet."

Not for the first time in his life, Crump wished he'd been born a quarter of a century or more before he had. Oh, to be a baby boomer with a mortgage paid off on a house worth fifty times what you'd paid for it in the

1970s, a big fat gold-plated pension for your thirty plus years of well-travelled retirement from a well-paid job you did in a time of low or even no unemployment, not to mention no student debts to pay off when you got that degree in the days when most people didn't have them, and a happy hippy assurance that life would continually get better, in all ways, always and forever.

"Oh I forgot to say!" said Esther with a grin. "I've been selected."

"Selected? For... what?"

"Well, not execution – though seeing the way certain left-wing academic anti-Semitic elements in this country are going, that could well be a future possibility."

"Oh, come on," said Khalid. "I've told you before. First they'll put Muslims like me against the wall. Then it's your turn."

They all laughed darkly over their vegetarian pasties and salads.

"You are now talking to a Prospective Parliamentary Candidate for the Conservative Party."

"Safe Labour seat," sniffed Khalid. "She's no chance of winning."

"Congratulations!" grinned Crump. "I told you you'd be Prime Minister one day."

"Don't be daft. I'm far too much the independent gobby loudmouth for that, and far too honest. But, after losing in a couple of Labour safe seats, they may well offer me something winnable, and then, who knows? Maybe Minister of Truth one day? I've got the chutzpah for it!"

Crump was glad. We badly need more spiky individualists in politics – the contrarians, the iconoclasts, the free thinkers, the rebels, those prepared to be honest and say what they think and really believe, those who have done proper jobs at some point in their lives – and not yet more obedient Oxbridge-educated drones and robots, fresh from researcher jobs with MPs or cushy well-connected careers in the law, PR and marketing.

"Well invite us all to the House of Commons when you get there."

"Certainly! What d'you think this Jew is, tight or something?"

"Nah, that's me. I'm from Yorkshire," said Khalid.

"Course, the people might blow the place sky-high Guy-Fawkes-style before I ever get there, and to be honest, I wouldn't blame them one bit!"

And how they laughed...

"Oh, I forgot to tell you – that disgusting greasy spoon you went to –"

"The New York Diner? It's closed – the owners died in the fire."

"Old news," said Esther. "Bloody incredible really, what was going on."

"What... *was* going on?" asked Crump.

And then they told him. An investigation had revealed that Professor Pip Pooman had been running a lab on the seventh floor of The Learning Tower where he indulged his passion for vivisection – and of locally stolen pets, hence the many missing cat and dog posters up on campus.

If that wasn't bad enough, the repulsive couple Colin and Karl Kunti had, for some considerable time, been collecting the corpses of the aforementioned unfortunate animals from Professor Pooman's secret lab, after he'd tortured them to death and needed to dispose of them, then taking them away and grinding them down into the sausages served at The New York Diner.

Those people were monsters!

How Crump would have liked to get revenge on all the animal-torturers, to slit Pip Pooman's vile vivisectionist torso open from scrotum to throat, to spill the puddle of his bloody guts into the nearest gutter sewer. But there was no need, because now he and his corpse-collecting customers were nothing but carbon and ash. Crump hoped all the animals he killed would be clawing and gnawing at his groaning soul for all eternity. *Good riddance!*

"Now you know why I never go to those places," said Khalid. "You never know what goes into making two things in life – the law and sausages. The former is my profession, so I always try and avoid the latter."

But Crump had already left the vegetarian café and was outside retching and puking up his meat-free lunch which, no matter how hard he tried, tasted disgustingly of deceased greasy cat-and-dog sausage.

*

"So… I hope you haven't brought me any more Nazi gold bars," said Crump, letting Marek in.

"No, before I bring only one, to get testing in UK, yes?" Marek laughed. "Kev-een, how your friend?"

"Oh, she's fine – a bit bruised, y'know, shaken."

"Police catch attacker?"

"What d'you think?"

"UK must to stop these peoples," tutted Marek, shaking his head. "They are like the Fascist or Communist, no?"

Crump nodded. It was truly appalling that his own country seemed to tolerate Fascist thugs – so long as they had a brown face and a minority faith, he thought. That was not equality in any way, shape or form. That was special treatment based on race and religion, in his opinion, and a dereliction of duty by the police and others too. It was wilful blindness that hurt us all – Muslims especially.

"You have the glass, yes?"

Crump found a couple of wine glasses in the sideboard.

Marek took a bottle out of his bag. Champagne. A very expensive looking bottle.

"Moronia is *rich!*" grinned Marek as he popped the cork. They clinked glasses and drank.

Crump had never been a big champagne (or sparkling wine) drinker, but he had to admit the way the bubbles went up your nose and tickled your eyeballs was not unpleasant. It made him want to smile. Maybe that was the intention.

"Well you've certainly got lots of gold," said Crump.

"Is just pennies," scoffed Marek, with his wide confident smile.

Crump spluttered a laugh through the bubbles.

"It's gold bars worth millions... billions... or..."

"Rare. Earth."

"What?"

"We find *rare earth metals.* In ground, in Moronia rock."

Marek pointed downwards towards the centre of the Earth.

"Metal called name like dysprosium, neodymium, other. You see TV screen?"

Crump looked at the flat plasma screen perched on a stand at the corner of his living room.

"They must to use rare earth metal for make this, and laptop, cell phone, solar panel, battery for car, hard drive on computer."

Crump wondered why he'd never heard of these 'rare earths' before. Probably because he was happily ignorant about mining metals and the manufacture of computer screens and hard drives.

"China supply 95% rare earth metals now. In future time, Moronia making 20% for supply of all world, maybe 25%. You know how much money this make on open market? Many *many* billion, trillion, dollar."

"Wow!" said Crump. "They're bound to let you in the EU now."

Marek laughed loudly and refilled their glasses.

"Oh no, Moronia not want joining EU."

"But you said before—"

"Yes, but before Moronia was poor small country, so we want money from EU, like other place in East Europe. Now we rich!"

Marek grinned and laughed.

"Why we join EU so we can to give much money to them and they give to poor country? We keep our money. We are like the Brexit now!"

"Oh god, no," groaned Crump – the B-word made him wince, almost in pain.

"UK is pay EU more money than get back – this big reason UK leave, yes?"

"Well, I suppose so. But Moronia wasn't ever an EU member… so not the same really."

But Marek was not listening – he was fumbling in his bag. He pulled out a notebook, opened it, took out a pen and scribbled something down.

"I can to help you, Kev-een. And I will to help you. So, you not have job now, yes?"

"Well, my contract ends at the end of term and then… who knows? The world is my… *lobster*… apparently…"

"So you come work for me, Marek Sirko, at new International University of Moronia, in beautiful great capital city Sgrot. This your salary. You look."

Crump opened the piece of paper Marek had torn off and handed him.

"Fifty thousand dollars? About thirty grand, so more than I'm on now, and thanks, but—"

"Kev-een, you are the blind man? Read number on paper please."

Crump had misread the figure.

It was not fifty thousand dollars.

It was…

"*Five… hundred… thousand?*" spluttered Crump.

Marek shrugged and smiled.

"Half a million dollars? But that's... three hundred thousand quid, three fifty —"

"In International University of Moronia, you will to be big boss – how you say, *Vice-Chancellor*?"

Crump didn't know what to say. The presently suspended VC of Cambrian University had been on a massive salary, but not as much as Marek was offering him now.

"Marek, this is... thanks... but... this is insane... unreal..."

"Like the life, yes?"

"But... aren't there other candidates, an interview process... anyway, I have no experience of being a Vice-Chancellor... or a boss... of anything..."

Crump cringed as he thought back to his perpetually unspectacular and unsatisfying, low-achieving, mundane middle management career which may, he knew, have had something to do with his lack of self-confidence and general inability to boast or 'big himself up'. But that was just the way he had been brought up. He hated it when people were so full of themselves, as so many overly confident and staggeringly average kids were these days, through a regime of constant over-praise since birth, which had given them an iron certainty in their own special genius.

But Crump had always felt he was supposed to be something more than that, to do something better – more meaningful, more satisfying, just *more*. More than the mediocrity and misery and muddling-through he'd known for perhaps far too long. But then maybe everyone thinks and feels like that sometimes? *Don't they?*

"Your Winston Churchill was great man – he fuck up Hitler, fuck him hard up arse, yes?"

"Well... yes... though I think they phrase it a bit differently in the history books —"

"And Churchill, he have experience to be Prime Minister before he doing job?"

438

"Well, no, but… I think he'd been home secretary and done some other senior—"

"Kev-een, why you are always make the excuses? You are sound like loser, like boring person. I not want boring loser person for top job at Moronia Sgrot university – I am want you."

Crump felt himself blush. He had to ask the question: "But… Marek… *Why?*"

"Because I likes you, Kev-een," smiled Marek, refilling their glasses with top-notch champagne. "You are the honest man, intelligent, independent, talented, very educated, cultured, intellectual man—"

"Thanks, Dad," smiled Crump.

"This is very good, very funny, British sense of humour, yes?"

Marek erupted in a loud laugh.

"So you come, yes, to do big job in Democratic Republic of Moronia? Is so beautiful in summer, so nice lake and forest and hill."

"Sounds like a *Mills and Boon*."

Marek frowned.

"I not know this whisky. Is good one?"

"No, yes, *Mills and Boon* is a… great whisky, yeah. Hard to find though. Can be a tad… too sweet."

"Hmmm," said Marek, finishing his glass of champagne. "Kev-een, if you not are like my country, if it is not your teacup, then you can to leave back to UK after one year, no problem – and you can to keep money."

"Well, I—"

"Half million dollar, plus the free flight and big apartment in best area in Sgrot. Then you can to buy house of your mum, yes? Two house. Three."

It was true, and the salary was insane, as was the job offer with perks and the rest. But something was worrying Crump – something he had to bring up. Marek must have smelt his thoughts.

"I know you are worry," he nodded. "You think Moronia is small stupid East Europe country, we are everybody corrupt, mafia, oligarch—"

"Oh no, I just—"

"Kev-een, tell to me truth."

Marek's wide and kind eyes looked deep into Crump's perpetually worried-looking ones.

"Well, yes, it is a worry... it's just... how I am."

"Worry worry, yes? But Kev-een, what is the corruption? Is corrupt to make much money? Is corrupt for Moronia to spend money on best university in world?"

"Oh no, but... I'm just... British—"

"Kev-een, I tell to you joke we are tell when fucking Russian Communist pig ruling my country. There are two policeman. The first, he say to second, so what you are think of government? The second, he says, I think same as you. So then first policeman, he say, then it my duty to arrest you. You see?"

Marek grinned.

Crump smiled wryly at the dark, stoical Soviet-era humour.

"Your UK university, is not corrupt? All student are pass and get good grades, especially if they from foreign country and pay much money, yes? All the dumb-downing and students who cheating. Nobody fail. But all is legal and 'political correct' also, yes? And people who do this thing, they get good salary and life for this, yes?"

Crump said nothing. But the look on his face spoke volumes. He knew that the worst of what had happened in the UK university system in recent decades – what was happening now – was an absolute scandal, but one people were willing to tolerate, so long as they received more funding from ever more students, especially the lucrative cash cow international ones, and yet more expansion of higher education for reasons no-one could really justify. So long as their safe, solid, tenured salaries were rising and their index-linked pensions guaranteed, as they span around on the magic money-making merry-go-round. So long as students got the degrees they had paid handsomely for. So long as everyone got a prize.

"Some managers at the university have been arrested..." Crump said, in a quiet voice, which immediately made him think of his suffering at the hands of the corrupt Cambrian police.

"They are steal from funding, yes? From EU money? They *idiota*! But most not get punish – they will to get off *Scottish-free*, yes?"

Crump nodded. It was true, and not only for those responsible for higher education either. It seemed those at the top of government and councils, who squandered and wasted taxpayers' money, got off 'Scottish-free' too, as did shysters who lied and stole as they pilfered from PLCs and corporate companies, as did those in charge of the banks and the City who on a regular basis seemed to bring down the world economy, only to be bailed out with public money, so they could recover and start the whole lunatic lucrative cycle again, all while on fat salaries, obscene bonuses and golden goodbye pensions.

If you're not worried, you don't understand the problem.

The world was an unjust, unfair, shitty place to be, especially if you were at the bottom of the ladder or a couple of wobbly rungs up, which is the highest Crump had ever climbed, and which was the highest most people climbed too.

"You are work for Foreign Office since many years, yes?"

"Yep, before they 'rationalised' me and sent me into exile at the Cambrian University gulag... and now, I'll soon be 'liberated', and have no job or income at all."

"Then what you are have to lose, Kev-een?" said Marek, standing up and holding Crump on each shoulder with his big, confident hands.

"You are good man. You are strong man. You are winner. I give to you big break. You take, yes? You make good life. You make big money. You come in Moronia, be Vice-Chancellor, on salary five hundred thousand dollar for one year, yes? Yes? Kev-een? Yes?"

Crump stared into the smiling certainty of Marek's life-affirming eyes.

"Yes," he said, at last. "*Yes, I will.*"

Marek kissed him on both cheeks and hugged him like a loving father. And before he knew what was happening, he felt tears well in his eyes.

We all need someone to believe in us sometimes – to give us the benefit of the doubt – to chuck us our lucky break in life, and maybe occasionally a lifebelt.

So it was time to give Marek, and Moronia, the benefit of the doubt too.

Crump knew he had so many regrets, so many things he would have done differently. He wished he could have thought differently too, and had no regrets, like the song, but that just wouldn't have been him, and so that wouldn't have been true. His regrets were legion, and haunted him like demons.

It was as though Crump had been living in the wrong world all his life. It was time to find the right one.

To really breathe – to really live a full life with meaning, achievement and purpose. To love and be loved, for who he was. To choose to see the beauty in the world and not just the ugly truth. Despite everything.

"Moronia here I come," said Crump, thinking of things.

*

Now that the exams were over, and all coursework handed in, the academics at Cambrian University were in full-on marking mode. The inconvenience of having

442

actual students to teach no longer existed – at least for a while.

Summer terms were always like this, just as autumn terms always heralded the arrival of hordes of fresh-faced bright-eyed students, all wriggling and giggling like worms newly emerged from the Earth onto a new unfamiliar landscape, and one crawling with all sorts of gods and monsters.

'They'll soon learn,' Crump always thought, about the futility of it all, when the failures and disappointments of life and the misery of existence turned them into adults bound for the heady heights of middle management jobs they hated. Just like so many who work in education, then.

Tanya Snuggs looked her usual self, all bouncy and pink and gap-toothed grin – but then again, she didn't. As she came into the department meeting that day, Crump could almost smell the stress dripping off her like week-old sweat.

"Yay!" she said, somewhat exasperated. "It's marking time!"

"Yay!" replied everyone, even Crump, well aware that after his marking duties he'd be gone from this place, this country, everything – perhaps, for good.

There was the usual Tanya pep talk about marking up, never failing foreign students, referring any dissertations which seemed plagiarised or exams which were unutterably bad, to her immediately.

"There is no such thing as failure, people," she said, trying to smile and exude cheerfulness, "just…"

"Deferred success," chanted all staff.

"Yay!" Tanya yawned. "Oh, I'm so tired. Not getting much sleep lately, what with my *Arcadian* rhythms playing up."

Then she mentioned something else.

"If any parents of students… or anyone in their *expendable* family, calls you or even comes onto campus personally in person, then come to me immediately."

"Have there been any problems?" asked Hilary Squonk.

All staff of that department and others were used to being contacted by phone and email by concerned pushy snowplough parents keen to boost the grades of their little darlings. After all, they always pointed out, they're not paying all those fees to fail, are they? Usually, they wanted 1st class or 2.1 grades – and usually their kids got them too. But personal visits were something else entirely.

"The parents sometimes come in and see me here," said Tanya.

"Was that angry woman I passed coming in today one of them?" asked Crump.

Tanya Snuggs smiled a weak, nervous smile.

"We have to *empathicise* with parents – after all, the bank of mum and dad pays our salaries, innit?"

"Yay!" said Crump, sardonic and alone.

"Man dem so vexed, d'ya get me?" said Shabs.

"Getting properly *qualificated* is so important these days," said Tanya Snuggs, gasping slightly, Crump noticed, "the world's their little ones' *lobster*, y'know, and then there's the Chinese – they're almost a *quarterfile* of our postgraduate student cohort, so cannot fail, as the government said —"

"The *government*? They said that?" queried Crump.

"Senior management, higher *educification* department."

"Da boss man," said Shabs, sucking the air through his teeth.

"Parents must *not* be allowed on campus," snapped Melanie Spunch, "not without an appointment – otherwise it's harassment."

It was a rare occurrence, but for once, Crump agreed.

"We must make sure we *pass mustard*," continued an exhausted-looking Tanya Snuggs, "because we are servants to paying customers in a *consumerile* society, so we must... *fust... sum... no... tam... fass... ust... ween... jat... noz... sup... mun... taks...*"

The English lecturers present all looked round at each other, baffled that their Head of Department now seemed to be speaking Klingon.

But Crump had already called 999 on his mobile.

"Ambulance," he said on the phone, when asked.

He knew what a *Transient Ischaemic Attack* – TIA – looked, and sounded, like, as he had seen it before when staying with his mum one Christmas. He hadn't called an ambulance then, just helped his mum to bed and then they went to the GP the next morning who said it was a mini-stroke or TIA, and if it happened again he should call 999 immediately.

He rode with Tanya Snuggs in the back of the ambulance. He would stay with her at the hospital too, no matter how long all the tests and whatever took. Marking and coursework, and especially piss-taking pushy pillock parents, could wait.

Later – four hours later, to be precise – the doctors came by to see Tanya Snuggs who, by that time, was talking almost normally, with just a smidgeon of Klingon lingering in her language. Crump waited outside and came back in when they had all left.

"Mini-stroke," said Tanya, looking sad and drab in her hospital bed in a standard-issue hospital gown, somehow diminished by being stripped of her usual perfect pinkitude.

"I know," said Crump. "My mum had a… TIA… in fact, several—"

"Got high blood pressure. They put me on *medification*."

"Lots of people take pills for that, Tanya."

"But I'm young… ish… *bash… nant… tan… sorrah…* sorry…"

"S'OK," said Crump, holding her hand.

"Thanks for calling the ambulance, Kevin, y'know," said Tanya when she'd recovered.

Crump was angry – not at Tanya, who he'd always liked despite her mind-boggling mangling of the English language. No, he was angry at the university for putting so much pressure on her, all the time. Surely that had been a factor in her having a stroke?

Crump decided that now was the time to tell her.

"Tanya," he said.

"Yes, Kevin," she said. "Is there something you wish to *interjaculate*?"

"Karen Crisp does not exist."

Tanya Snuggs looked at him, blinked, widened her eyes and laughed, almost cackled, at the absurdity of his suggestion.

"Kevin – don't be so silly! I'm not *star-craving* mad! Karen Crisp is Joint Head of Department, with me."

"I know, but... she doesn't exist. I've checked and checked again. I have a friend, in India, an IT whizz, y'know, and the evidence is there. There is no Karen Crisp. Never was."

"But... but... I've talked to her... *conversificated*... on a *regulatory* basis—"

"Have you? Have you really? Have you ever met her? In person? Think, Tanya, think."

Tanya blinked to think, trying to wring some sense out of the nonsense Kevin was talking. Then she smiled, frowned, smiled again, then blinked, frowned a final confused frown, and closed her eyes with a weary sigh.

"But... the emails—"

"Sent from and to Lesley Snyde and her minions..."

"What, those little yellow things? They's funny, they is—"

"No, no, the word 'minion' existed before the cartoon movie."

It was Kevin Crump's turn to frown and close his eyes.

"Some of the things you say, Kevin! Such *pigments* of your imagination. I really don't know where you get your *fantastificated* ideas from!"

446

A good education, perhaps?

"Karen does *not* exist, Tanya. Think about it. She's never here – ever. And the university gets to pay you *less* for being *Joint* Head of Department, despite your being the sole head and doing all the damn work."

Tanya stared at Kevin, unsmiling. She looked somehow smaller than usual too.

"You do *all* the work, for *less* money, which is exactly what they wanted."

Crump also knew that someone like Tanya Snuggs, gullibly susceptible to group-think and concerned about her future career, would never complain or even question anything, ever. That was how these people always got away with it – the bullying, the exploitation, the lies.

Silence. Slow silence. Thinking time.

It now all made sense to Tanya Snuggs, but somehow it didn't at all – a bit like life really.

"So," said Tanya in a small, quiet voice. "It's all about the money?"

"To them, yes. Now, always and forever."

"But... but..." said Tanya, "it's..."

It's what? Mad? Crazy? Bonkers? Incredible? Corrupt? Welcome to the wonderful world of higher education.

"... it's... all gone to hell in a *handbag*... it's such... total... moral *twerpitude*..."

Crump nodded. He had, indeed, seen many twerps and a great deal of total *twerpitude* at UK universities, so Tanya Snuggs' mad tangled language had got it right there, at least.

And so they talked, and talked, and talked, there in the hospital ward.

A 'safe career' was all Tanya Snuggs had wanted, she said, and her university position had made her own mum, an immigrant and a cleaner and a school dinner lady, so proud. But what was there to be proud of now?

Craving that safe career was like crawling into an octopus pot. You try and seek shelter and security in an insecure and turbulent world. Then, before you even realise it, you're trapped – willingly – in your warm storm-free home, until yanked out by your captor into the shitty bleak reality of it all. It was just an illusion – a delusion – but people really believed in it. Just as they believed in 'get-rich-quick' pyramid schemes...

"I was thinking of a career change. I seen these adverts in magazines and in emails – you can *gainer* thousands every month, for part-time hours, have a big house and new car like in the photos, if you get enough *contactification and referrials* and sell enough—"

"Probably best to stick to teaching, Tanya – maybe somewhere else? There's a lot of higher ed jobs out there, for someone like you – hard-working, dedicated, popular, great team leader..."

Masterful mangler of the English language...

"Oh, I'm so tired," yawned Tanya Snuggs.

"Welcome to my world," mumbled Kevin.

But Tanya was already snoozing, fast asleep.

After more tests, she was discharged.

Crump had been up at the hospital for over eight hours, but he didn't resent it.

He took Tanya home in a taxi, made sure she got into her flat OK, said he'd phone and check on her in the morning.

"And Kevin," said Tanya Snuggs, as Crump was about to leave, "if I could just add a *caviar*..."

Crump nodded as Tanya took his hand.

"Thank you..."

"Oh it's nothing, I mean—"

"Thank you, Kevin," said Tanya Snuggs, and she kissed him on the cheek and smiled, somewhat sadly.

As Crump left, he could see that there were tears in her eyes.

*

June began with a heatwave. It was what Crump always called a 'Welsh Summer' – which came often in April or May and made up for the rainy days of August.

It was the day of Andy Stone and Casper's wedding.

Well, not 'wedding' exactly, as the latter was already married. But a blessing, at least, so 'as good as' – as Andy had said.

Even in the early morning, the welcome yellow sun yawned warm in the big blue sky, and the green mirror of the sea lapped its little waves against the shingle of the shore.

They were gathering on the pier, where the 'wedding' was to take place. Crump could always see it in the distance from his house on the hill, as well as the lighthouse which was situated on a rocky outcrop beyond it. Off, now, of course, in daytime – and automated these days at night.

Technology had made lighthouse keepers redundant and so many others too. How many more jobs and careers would go in the 21st due to digital fixes and robots? And what exactly would all the many people on the over-populated planet actually *do*?

Would it be as in Ancient Rome, with bread and circuses for the people, and a free state income, and evermore extreme reality TV in our *visuate* age to take away the pain by inflicting it on others? But then, it was ever thus – from the time the Stone Age makers of flint axes and arrowheads chucked away their tools and knowledge in the face of incoming Bronze Age new technology. Luddites will always lose. Always. History showed that. Adapt – and survive. Don't adapt – and perish. It was ever thus – and still was, for Crump, for Andy Stone and Casper, for everyone.

Whatever gets you through the night - it's alright.

It's alright.

Such were the thoughts humming through Crump's brain that Saturday morning as he stood on the pier, watching The Town in the distance through the early morning mist – like *Brigadoon*, but with more litter, street people, pollution, charity shops and takeaways.

He'd got a cab to the pier. No way was he driving his old banger there – partly to avoid the parking fees, if he couldn't find a free space somewhere in a side street, but mostly because he intended, as he knew Andy Stone and his ex-army mates would, to get absolutely hammered by the end of the day. He'd even written his address down on a little piece of paper to hand to a taxi driver later, because he knew he may well be too blind drunk by then to even form a sentence. *Fail to prepare – prepare to fail.* Crump smiled inside like a very good teacher indeed.

Fatima was there, with Dylan.

Crump said, "Hi."

Dylan said, "Hi."

They all say, "Hi."

Hi!

Esther Isaacs too, with Khalid. Crump lingered with them, all in their finery. He had done his best, but wasn't really a suit man, except at funerals. A shirt and tie and jacket was fine though, and Andy Stone had told him to dress casual. The thought of renting some posh poncey wedding suit sent shivers down his spine.

Marek was back in Moronia. He was hotly tipped, according to reports Crump read online, for high office again, maybe even President. A twinge of guilt tickled Crump's conscience – he really should have spent more time perfecting the Moronians' standard of English to more proficient levels. Any errors – of tense, syntax, word order, prepositions – he heard in any future TV interviews with Marek would be his fault.

At least, that was his typical thought process. *It was all his fault.* Everything. Always. But he knew, in his rational brain, that it really wasn't. None of it. Ever. And, after all, he had been 'tasked' with teaching the Moronians about British political culture, not language alone. That was his excuse anyway, and he was sticking to it!

There were, of course, some academics present at the 'wedding'. But most guests there that day were, well, 'normal' – though some had a few bits missing.

Crump had met Andy's friends from Afghanistan before – two of them anyway. Jay, with no arms, and Oliver, white-eyed blind and with a half-melted face, plus a couple of false limbs for luck.

But now there were maybe ten more. Not all disabled, it's true – at least physically. But three in wheelchairs, at least four more with prosthetic limbs, and lots of scarred, eyeless, young male faces.

And then it started.

Casper standing beside Andy Stone in his wheelchair. Behind them, the backdrop of the beautiful balmy bay. Before them, a cheerful-looking, youngish female priest or vicar – or whatever they were called (Crump wasn't sure) – in a dog collar and with a rainbow-flag scarf-like things (whatever that was called – he didn't know that either). Crump wasn't very good at religious vocabulary…

"Will you be to each other a companion in joy and a comfort in times of trouble, and will you give each other opportunity for love to deepen?"

"We will," said the couple in unison, joining hands.

"With God's help," added Casper in a quiet, devout voice.

Then the vicar turned to each partner in turn:

"Will you, Andy, give yourself to Casper, share your love and life, your wholeness and your brokenness, your success and your failure?"

"Yeah, I will."

And then the same to Casper:

"I will."

"Now let us pray that Andy and Casper may be sustained by God's love."

Some guests bowed their heads in prayer. Others, Crump included, just looked and listened.

"Spirit of God, you teach us that love is the fulfilment of the Law, help Andy and Casper to persevere in love, to grow in mutual understanding, and to deepen their trust in each other; that in wisdom, patience and courage, their life together may be a source of happiness for all; and the blessing of God, Almighty, Creator, Redeemer and Sustainer be upon you and all those you love, today and always. Amen."

"Amen," said Andy and Casper and the guests, including Crump.

And then a ripple of applause and big grins all round.

"Can we snog now?" asked Andy Stone, to gathered laughter.

The delighted female priest nodded God's approval.

The guests clapped as the couple kissed.

Crump wasn't one for religion, or weddings, or soppy slushy snogfests, come to that. But he had to admit, it was all truly beautiful. There was no bad here. Nothing bad. It was all good and right and as it should be.

"I love you," said Casper to Andy, who whispered the same in reply.

"Right then," bellowed Andy Stone from his wheelchair, which swung round to face the crowd. "Let's all get fucking legless pissed – and that's an order!"

And so, they all did.

And it was bloody good too. Amen.

He drank a toast to the happy couple, of course, but Crump also drank to himself – to his new life, his rebirth, his parthenogenesis. To his happiness, at last.

Crump couldn't remember how he got home that night. But he did. Maybe because he knew his mum's house in the Highlands so well that he could practically *'smell to bed'*.

Sure, he'd have a monster hangover the next morning, but he just didn't care. *'For every joy there is a price to be paid,'* thought Crump, harking back to a phrase first used by the Ancient Egyptians – and they didn't do too badly really, all things considered. Except in Michael Jackson videos, that is.

The more the evening wore on, the more of a blur it all became, with a sunset as red as sex on the horizon and the music booming like a heartbeat, alive and raw.

He remembered the songs: *When a Man Loves a Woman* – banned by the university for being sexist, homophobic, transphobic and goodness know what else. *Let It Be Me* by Nina Simone – which Crump had always loved. Then, later, as the action moved with the booze to the function room, *Groove Is in the Heart* and, of course, *Dancing Queen*. Crump remembered in flashes of shattered memories that he actually danced to that – so he must have been totally shitfaced wasted, because he really wasn't a dancer.

And above it all, and flashing through the delightful night, the lighthouse by the pier, blinking and winking and illuminating a dark uncertain world, showing in its stuttering spotlight the way to a new and better day.

*

Last day at school. That's what it felt like anyway – Crump's final day at Cambrian University, on a windy, cloudy day in the second week of June.

The blackened shell of The Learning Tower was still shrouded from view, as they continued with the investigation, which would no doubt take months or, most probably, years. A few bored-looking police mooched around too, and a few members of the international media. Hardly any students, who'd all sodded off by now – at least the undergraduates. The postgrads were still around, and academic staff of course, though fewer than usual as there was no library to work in any more, on account of it being cremated in the fire.

Nothing for Crump to do any more. All papers and coursework done and dusted – and approved, or revised, by 'the powers that be'. Via the magic of modulation, no student had failed that year, with almost 20% getting 1st class degrees and up to 60% 2.1s. No international students failed either, or even got low marks, even if they could barely speak English.

So now, all those potential and very lucrative students in China and elsewhere would be able to see, when comparing universities online, that Cambrian University was an institution where their fellow nationals all got great marks and never ever failed. Any university that dared to fail anyone or give them low marks would soon see their foreign student applications plummet. It was all basically a race to the bottom, which created a race to the top! A perfect circle indeed. Hoorah!

It's all a business and all a game, as Crump's late colleague Sandy had always said – and boy, was he right. With bells on.

Crump was glad to be getting out. But he was not running away – he was making a strategic retreat from a country which had lost its marbles, and one in which the odds seemed stacked against the likes of him, certainly in his chosen (or endured) career.

And it wasn't just Brexit either. No, Britain was now a place where faces like his just didn't fit, a place where no-one had the guts to speak out to defend the freedom to speak out, for fear of the consequences, where universities banned books and films and plays and songs and words deemed 'offensive' and 'upsetting' as standard, and where nobody seemed to have the first fucking clue what was going on. It was time to get out.

His own country had reneged on 'The Deal' – the one he had been promised, and so many others too. All that 'work hard, do well at school, and you'll be rewarded with a decent job, a house you can own, and a fair chance at happiness' shtick. All total mendacious bollocks.

All those wide-eyed blue-skied boyish years of wonder and expectation. All that childish hope that the world, at least in this country, would be fair and decent and honest and true – which were perhaps just the Utopian delusions of youth, shared by ignorant children everywhere. That is, until sex rams itself into their brittle little bodies, and the conveyor belts to careers kick in, with school, exams, bars to reach, targets to hit, hurdles to jump, rules to obey, until that day when every man eventually accepts the reality of life that he perhaps knew all along: that the mundane mediocrity of his miserable existence is only a moderately preferable alternative to self-murder – if only just.

Some kind of innocence had been lost, Crump knew.

But was that a bad thing?

Perhaps he was he just growing up?

How did I get so fucking old?

And Crump realised, with the sort of revelation usually reserved for the devout or deranged, that he was not actually alone in feeling as he did. Everyone was lost, carried like driftwood on the currents and winds of life, all looking to reach some sort of home, some sort of destination and end point, and peace at last.

Life is hard. Life is suffering. Deal with it.

Crump packed a cardboard box with the things he kept at the English Studies Department – which wasn't much, on account of him having no desk to call his own.

The whole place seemed alien to him now, almost like a foreign land. Weirdly, Moronia, a country he had never even visited, seemed at that precise moment in time more his home than here. How weird was that?

Was he deluded? Probably.

But then, he had no close family in his homeland any more, so what was for him here, in this place, in The Town? He loved the beaches and the coastal scenery, but what else was there keeping him here? Nothing. Nothing at all.

The best revenge is massive success – and whoever said that was right. Crump intended to succeed in life, and in doing so, he would show all those who had hurt him how wrong they had been. Quietly, without fuss, and certainly with no fisticuffs – but with certainty, dignity and self-respect.

It was time to fix the holes in his broken soul.

At some point, you have to decide what kind of man you want to be.

Crump had, at last, decided.

And there was no going back.

As he struggled backwards out of the swing doors of the main university building, carrying the cardboard box which contained his academic life in its entirety, and buffeted by a blustering summer wind, something caught the corner of his eye.

A ginger and white cat, sitting on the grass verge at the edge of the campus.

Then Mrs Trichobezoar appeared. Nelson the cat ran up to her and rubbed himself happily against her legs, miaowing 'hello'.

"Oh Nelson, you are such naughty boy! Where you have been? You not say, eh? Yes, I know…"

Nelson said nothing, which was probably for the best. Instead, he clambered into the loving arms of his mistress, who gave him a great big furry hug. He, in return, gave her a great big perfect purr.

As Mrs Trichobezoar turned to leave, Nelson peered over her shoulder at Crump. He seemed to be smiling.

But cats can't smile, can they?

Well, can they?

No wonder Hemingway referred to cats as 'purr factories' and 'love sponges'. Then there was the 10th-century Welsh king, Hywel the Good, who put such a value on mouser cats and kittens, that anyone killing one would face the heaviest of penalties. It seems cats living in Wales had not forgotten this. They totally had it sussed.

The all-seeing, all-knowing Nelson the cat would indeed be worshipped back home with Mrs Trichobezoar, and spoilt rotten, for sure. Not for the first time in his life, Crump decided that if reincarnation existed, and if he was ever coming back, he'd choose to come back as a cat in a loving home.

Then, suddenly, a dog appeared, barking a 'hello' to the world and wagging his waggly tail.

Diversity Dog was alive!

He hadn't perished in The Learning Tower fire, after all!

Crump smiled to himself as he watched the big black dog bounce along on his paws behind Nelson and his mistress, following them happily home, tail a-wag.

After putting his box of belongings into the boot, Crump started his old rust-bucket banger of a car – it revved to life on the third attempt. He was going to scrap it, but when he mentioned that to Dylan, the kid said he'd like to have it. So it would be his, Crump said, on condition that he got it all legal in his name, MOTed and insured, and that he didn't kill himself in it, if at all possible.

He'd miss Dylan, however irritating he was at times, and Fatima, and the others. But he wasn't flying to the moon. He could always still visit and they could come to Moronia too. And then there was always the internet – there was no hiding place anywhere in the world these days what with that digital spy forever breathing down your neck.

As he headed home, Crump turned on the radio.

(Just Like) Starting Over was playing.

'How appropriate,' he thought, remembering the autumn day the year before when he had arrived in The Town with the rain. It seemed so long ago, but it also felt just like yesterday too, strangely.

But what was time anyway? Perhaps it was just an illusion and a delusion, like everything else?

So we plod on, coracles bobbing on the current, spun around ceaselessly into the dizziness of our future past.

Life goes on. Always.

For Crump, life was good.
Life *is* good. Despite everything.

It's your life.
So live it.

That's the point.